WEST 47th

WEST 47th

GERALD A. BROWNE

WARNER BOOKS

A Time Warner Company

Warner Books, Inc., 1271 Avenue of the Americas, New York, NY 10020

A Time Warner Company

Printed in the United States of America
First Warner Books printing: June 1996
10 9 8 7 6 5 4 3 2 1

LC: 96-60357
ISBN: 0-446-51662-7

Book design by Giorgetta Bell McRee

For those who have 20/20
but are, unfortunately, blind

Acknowledgments

The author wishes to express his gratitude to those who in one way or another helped generate this story. Such as Dr. Stephen M. Cohen, Dr. Jay Friedman, Dr. Robert Hambrick, Pam Bernstein, Joanna Tomkins, R. J. and Jill Wagner, Patricia and Robert Jesse Lovejoy, David the Wit and Jason the Clip, Robin Cumming, Norman Weisberg, Mark and Coleen McDowell and my dear cousin Joy Burkett.

Also, a special thanks to the swifts, fences, have-arounds and others of the underside who allowed me to know *the street* as it truly is.

WEST 47th

Chapter 1

To look at him no straight person would think Charlie Gusano was anything more than a doorman.

He had the part down pat: the automatic off-and-on smile, the eagerness to serve, the anticipation and gratitude for tips. The whole convincing package.

Gusano, or Charlie Eyes as he was called by certain guys around who really knew him, had been at the game for twelve years. For seven he'd worked the curb of an upscale restaurant on 53rd Street. The place folded because the people who really owned it, those in the back, as they say, took too much out of it. Otherwise, Charlie would have still been there. For his purpose it was a prime spot.

Since then Charlie hadn't worked anywhere steady. That was his choice. Usually he'd do only a few nights here or there. Sometimes he didn't mind filling in for a couple of weeks or even a month. It depended on the place. It had to be upscale, a place that catered to the well-offs.

Apparently, Charlie was just being practical. People who had plenty could, without second thought or later discomfort, slip a ten or twenty into a palm merely for having a door opened or an umbrella held overhead.

But that wasn't it.

Charlie Eyes.

The sobriquet was appropriate and well-earned. At any reasonable distance Charlie had the ability to tell the precious from the fake. It was like he had natural, built-in loupes. For instance, say a well-to-do finger provided him with a glimpse of a ten-carat diamond ring. He didn't require a closer or even another look to know it was authentic. On the other hand, when even the finest grade, perfectly faceted, cubic-zirconium ten-carater flashed at him he saw it right off as the make-believe it was.

He wasn't infallible, of course, but right more often than not. About eight out of every ten times, on average, which was considered remarkable and appreciated by all concerned.

On that particular July Saturday night, Charlie, properly uniformed, capped and gloved, was tending to the comings and goings at the entrance of a way-overpriced restaurant on East 50th. It was his third consecutive night there. He'd worked the place in the past and it had never failed him. It wouldn't now. Already he had two sure things memorized. As good a night as he was having, in that regard, it didn't, however, make up for the rain.

At six, when he'd come in, there'd been a thunderstorm in progress and, since then, two more heavy downpours. A lot of rumbling and crackling above the city. During the letups the raindrops beaded like gems on the roofs and hoods of cars. The gutters were brooks.

Charlie's shoes were ruined. They were a pair of his newest best. Lightweight, thin-soled, Italian made. Three-hundred-dollar shoes. He'd bought four pair at the swag price of fifty a pair, but these were the only blacks. They'd never be the same.

Fucking weather, Charlie complained in the back of his throat. He flexed his toes and felt the squish of his socks. By two when he got off his feet would be drowned-looking, shriveled. He'd hate them.

He glanced up at the space between the high-rise office buildings. The purgatorial glow of Manhattan. More clouds were roiling, ganging up, getting ready to let go. The city was washed but it didn't smell fresh. It smelled steamy, Charlie thought, like the Upper West Side cleaners where he usually waited while his suits and uniforms were being pressed.

His legs were hurting, the calves, the left one more. An ache and every once in a while a sharp spasm. They'd gone varicose from too much standing over the years. The doorman's ailment, the doctor called it. His advice was to move around more, and that was what Charlie was doing, pacing six or seven steps back and forth beneath the restaurant's canopy.

When the Lincoln arrived. A that year's white Lincoln stretched to the limit. It pulled up to the curb with insolent precision. At once the driver was out, scurrying around. He got to the handle of the rear door a reach before Charlie.

Charlie made the driver. A bully Hispanic in a gray, hard-finished suit that was tight on him. The piece underneath behind his right hip was obvious. It had become the thing for well-offs to hire ex-cons, formidable-looking guys such as this, to drive and be around. The meaner they looked the better, and, having done major time in some hard joint like Dannemora being the best kind of reference, it did wonders to ease paranoia.

The limo door was open.

Charlie was right there with the umbrella so the passengers wouldn't have to suffer a drop. He looked in and saw they were two. A man and a woman. The man was speaking on the car's cellular phone. A serious, important man having a serious, important conversation. He had dark, tight hair and a dark, neatly clipped mustache and beard. Arabic looking. The woman was seated on the far side, most of her out of Charlie's view.

Finally the man got out. He was slender, a head taller than Charlie. He proceeded across the wide sidewalk and on into the restaurant, leaving the woman to follow along.

She emerged from the limo with her head lowered, watching where she stepped. As she raised her head, her earrings came into sight. Diamonds, pear shapes and rounds of fine quality, arranged around oval-cut rubies. To the eyes of Charlie Eyes the rubies were fine Burma quality and would scale around four carats each. The woman straightened up. Charlie saw nine more such rubies and the numerous diamonds of her necklace.

Important jewelry, Charlie knew. No doubt among her best, and that was just it. This attractive Arab woman contending with her late forties with as much artifice as plenty of money allowed would have more goods just as good where these came from.

During his ten o'clock break Charlie went to the pay phone on the corner of Park. He dialed Ralph Lentini's New Rochelle number.

Ralph picked up on the second ring. Instead of a hello from him a grunt like some kind of disturbed animal. No goombah talk. As soon as Ralph heard it was Charlie Eyes, he asked: "What you got?"

"Three."

"Okay, let's have them."

"You still owe me for the last two."

"Fuck I do."

"Last week I gave you two."

"When last week?"

"Thursday I think it was."

"I was in Miami last Thursday."

"Then it was Wednesday."

"That could be," Ralph admitted, "but what I know for certain is the last two were shit. My crew came up empty."

"I heard different," Charlie bluffed.

"Anyway," Ralph bluffed back, "I paid you already."

"Like shit."

"I marked you paid. I'm looking at it right now, paid."

"You haven't been around all week, Ralphie. When you coming around?"

Ralph let the question hang.

Charlie was used to Ralph's routine. It was nearly the same every time. "Look, Ralphie, I'm standing out here in the fucking rain."

"So give me the three."

"Then you'll owe me for five."

A reluctant yeah from Ralph.

"Say it to me."

"Five."

"When will you be around?"

"Sometime during the week."

That was too vague to suit Charlie, however he told himself Ralph would eventually make good. Besides, at the moment Charlie didn't have anyone better to give his information to. Had he still been on good terms with Sal Crosetti he would have used him to make Ralph move. Okay, Ralphie, he would have said, I'm sure Sal will show me more respect. However, it was that sort of playing one against the other that had soured his arrangement with Sal.

From memory Charlie recited to Ralph the license plate numbers and letters of the three, including that of the white stretch, which happened to be a New Jersey. He ran them together and went too fast for Ralph and had to repeat them.

"Which would you say could be the bigger score?" Ralph asked.

"In my opinion?"

"No, in your ass." Ralph figured when he asked something it was asked.

"The Jersey," Charlie told him.

"What color is the Jersey?"

"Heavy red."

"No white?"

"A lot of white," Charlie replied. He could practically hear the churning of Ralph's greed.

"Sure they're not fugazis?" Fakes.

"Don't insult me."

No apology from Ralph, nor any thanks. This was business and he was laying out. He grunted goodbye and hung up.

Ralph had jotted down the information Charlie sold him on one of the telephone notepads he'd brought home from the Miami Hilton. He'd only stayed there two nights but that was more than enough time for him to load up on soap, shampoo, lotion, stationery, ballpoints and even some needle and thread mending kits. Also a couple of towels of better quality than he'd ever buy.

Ralph never stayed at a hotel that he didn't take such advantage. Whenever he came upon a maid's supply cart in a hallway he helped himself. Once at the Excelsior in Rome he'd gotten away with a solid brass hand shower, bracket and all.

As one of the more established and prospering fences in the metropolitan area, Ralph should have been above such pettiness. However it was in him, like a phobia. Just about any liftable or drivable thing that came before his eyes was automatically rated by him according to how easy it would be to steal.

What's more Ralph was cheap. Having to pay caused him psychological anguish, a sort of mental heartburn. Only rarely did he pay full civilian price for something and then only after he'd called around to find out if someone might be offering it at swag.

At the moment Ralph was seated at his kitchen table wearing nothing, not even his watch. The vinyl-covered seat of the kitchen chair was sticky to the cheeks of his bare ass. Charlie Eyes was also sticking him, Ralph thought, as he gave venal attention to the three plate numbers he'd just bought for two hundred each. Not long ago, Charlie's price per number had been a hundred. For doing nothing two hundred was taking advantage. Only way to deal with a guy who took advantage like that was to fuck him over. Next week when he straightened out with Charlie he'd give him only a hundred each and let him beef.

Ralph reached across the kitchen table and turned off the eight-inch Sony color television, reducing the ninth inning of a close Yankee at Cleveland game to a white dot. He hadn't been watching it anyway, even before Charlie's call. Rather, he'd been contemplating the open refrigerator across the way. It was something he often did. Sat there deliberating that vertical rectangle and its illuminated contents as though it was a rendered still-life.

Whenever his ex-wife, Carmella, had found him at it, she'd call him a *spuce* (crazy) and slam the refrigerator door shut. He'd just grin his most intolerant grin, say fuck with a long f and claim he was only trying to decide what not to eat.

Ralph was constantly unfaithful to his diet as well as to Carmella. She was gone but that thirty pounds too many were still with him.

He got a stub of a pepperoni stick from the meat bin, closed the refrigerator and went up the back stairs.

Ralph's house was a nine-room, two-and-a-half-story Tudor situated in a residential area off upper North Avenue. Like most of the homes around there the twenties and thirties had been its better days. Ralph had lived in it nine years. During that time the side lawns had been mowed five times and the hedges trimmed twice. Upkeep, according to Ralph, was declogging a toilet with a plunger and throwing de-icer granules on the driveway a few times each winter.

It wasn't a house one could move about freely in, cluttered as it was with so much swag. A nine years' accumulation of things Ralph's crew of swifts had come in with. Jewelry was always their objective; however when a home didn't yield any jewelry, rather than waste the risk, they stole something. More often than not, even when they did score jewelry on their way out they'd throw something else into a pillowcase, some object they'd spotted and thought might possibly be of value.

"Why you bringing me this shit," Ralph would complain. "You go out for goods, you come back with shit."

He would indulge them, peel off an additional fifty or two for the lamp or vase or little bronze statue that he had neither use nor room for. It didn't matter that among these *extras*, as he called them, shoved beneath a sofa along with some swag scuba gear and a couple of swag VCRs, were two pair of Empire ormolu four-light *bras de lumière* worth at least twenty thousand. Or that the glass figurine of a girl gathering dust along with a crowd of bric-a-brac on the top surface of a stack of swag television sets was signed by Argy-Rousseau and worth twenty-five thousand. Or that those two blue vases in the legion of vases and lamps on the steps of the stairway were exceptional blue ground Meissen circa 1740 worth thirty thousand each.

It didn't matter because such things were beyond Ralph's appreciation and knowledge. All he knew and cared about was they weren't jewelry. Even if he had known that the Chinese-looking thing lost and lonely in a corner of the upstairs hallway was a gilt-bronze figure of an extremely rare eleven-headed Kuan-Yin, where would he sell it?

For some reason the swifts stole a lot of clocks. They were all around the house, upstairs and down. About fifty of them, at least fifty. On the fireplace mantel in Ralph's bedroom were six. An English brass carriage clock that had run out of time and four Seth Thomases with misleading antique faces. The other was truly old. It was mounted in Sevres porcelain and Louis XV ormolu. Ralph had seen a clock exactly like it, or perhaps this very clock, in a 1990 Sotheby auction sales catalogue. Its estimated auction price was twenty-five thousand.

No one Ralph could think of, not even one of his wealthy swag-addicted private clients, would give him twenty-five for it. Or even five.

"*Shit. Ralph, it's only a clock.*"

"*Worth twenty-five large. Look.*" He'd show the auction catalogue.

"*Probably isn't even running.*"

"*It's been running for me. Besides I can have it fixed.*"

"*Pass.*"

And he couldn't risk taking it to Sotheby's or Christie's hoping to have it auctioned. Their experts would most likely recognize it right off and never believe one of his highly original or ordinary lies.

So, there it sat in all its inconvertible spite, taunting him. Fucking clock, Ralph often said aloud at it. Someday it would get him so pissed he'd take it out somewhere and throw it in some dumpster.

Now he got dressed. No underwear. Sixty percent polyester slacks, the day-before-yesterday's shirt, Reeboks without socks and his Rolex Presidential. After patting his sparse hair into place he put to pocket a thousand in hundreds along with the slip of notepaper bearing the three plate numbers he'd gotten from Charlie.

Went out.

An unimpressive gray guy in a four-year-old Pontiac, that was Ralph.

He took North Avenue to where it offered exit 18 of the Hutchinson River Parkway. Two miles north on the Hutch he caught sight of the New York State Police patrol car. It was parked on the wide, inclined grassy shoulder with its lights off.

Ralph pulled off and stopped about twenty feet in front of the patrol car. He took a good look at it. The rain on its windshield prevented him from making out who was in it, whether or not it was Stempke. If it wasn't Stempke he'd simply ask some directions.

The rack on the patrol car came on, began rotating and strobing. Ralph walked back towards it. The grass of the shoulder had been recently mowed. Its slant was slippery beneath Ralph's Reeboks. He nearly went to a knee. The fresh-cut grass was fragrant in the damp, night air. Ralph took no notice of it. He had no side that appreciated such things.

The wet window of the patrol car descended into the door to reveal Officer Stempke. He was close to forty, had a round face with a nearly lipless slash of mouth and not enough space between his eyes. He held Ralph with his look for a long moment before doing a slight smile. "What say?" he greeted.

"I got three," Ralph told him. He read them off so Stempke could jot them down. Ralph thought Stempke would read them back to check that he had them right, but he didn't, he went right at entering them in the patrol car's computer.

Ralph turned away. He wasn't interested in how it was being done, just wanted it done. Headlights of passing cars caught him and let him go. Tires made ripping sounds on the parkway's wet surface. Ralph started thinking about elsewhere. The midtown bust-out bar he spent a lot of his late-night time at. Not tonight. Tonight was business. Tonight would have a big score in it.

He pictured the swag that would be piled up on his kitchen table. Imagined his first sight of it. Spectacular goods. The guys on West 47 would beg just to get a look. It would take him the better part of a morning to count the thousands they would pay. (He didn't trust their counting machines. Besides, those machines took some of the pleasure out of it.)

Stempke was done. "Got a pen?" he asked.

"No."

"You never have a pen. Get yourself some pens." Stempke handed his pen to Ralph. An ordinary sixty-cent ballpoint. He was wearing gloves, was always careful that his touch never shared anything with Ralph's. Except for the money. "Keep it," he told Ralph and in practically the same breath rapidly read aloud from his notes the names and addresses of the registered owners he'd gotten from accessing the Department of Motor Vehicles information terminal.

Ralph got only most of them. He asked Stempke to repeat them so he could fill in, and not until he was sure he had them right did he go into his pocket for Stempke's juice. He counted off six hundreds. "By now I ought to be eligible for a complimentary," Ralph remarked lightheartedly but with a degree of serious suggestion.

"Against my principles," Stempke told him.

Ralph drove home. He sat in his usual kitchen chair and phoned the Brooklyn number. He knew it so well that his finger almost performed it involuntarily.

A female voice answered, not one he recognized.

"Who's this?" he asked.

"Who's this wants to know who's this?"

She didn't sound black, Ralph thought. He disliked the idea of the swifts in his crew fucking around with white women. Not even street whites or pros. He didn't like the way he'd overheard the swifts talking about doing white women. He'd never said anything to them about it but that was how he felt.

"Floyd there?" he asked.

"Maybe."

"Put Floyd on."

"You haven't told me who's this."

"Fuck you, put Floyd on."

Next thing Ralph heard was dial tone. He redialed. This time Floyd picked up.

"Who's the cunt?" Ralph asked, irked.

"Nobody," Floyd told him.

"She hung up on me."

"Man, what do you give a shit?"

"You let a nobody cunt answer your phone on a Saturday night."

"She was just closest to it."

"Dumb thing," Ralph grumbled. He took a couple of deep, calming breaths. "Who you got there?"

"Tracy and me and her."

"Where's Ronnie?"

"He cut out."

"When'll he be back?"

"I don't know, man. From the way the brother went he's gone."

"It's Saturday night. His head must be up his ass. Did he take the car?"

"We don't want to work tonight," Floyd said, as though that was all he had to say.

"Oh?" It wasn't an unusual problem. "What you got to do that's more important?" Ralph asked patiently.

"Nothing. Just hang out."

Ralph handled it by going right through it. "Who can you get to drive?" The absent Ronnie was usually the driver.

Floyd didn't reply.

Ralph let the silence continue. It was now a matter of whichever spoke the next word. Finally, Floyd said: "I suppose I could get Dexter. He may be around."

"I know Dexter?"

"He worked a couple of times."

"When was that?"

"Two years ago."

"I don't remember any Dexter. What's he been doing since?"

"Time."

"Who else can you get?"

Floyd took a moment. "Corky maybe. He'll want a guarantee."

"How much?"

"Five."

"Corky's a fucking cowboy. Anyway, last time he worked he held out."

"What did he hold out?"

"Two nice blues, a four carat and a six. The next afternoon the cocksucker was moving around Forty-seventh with them. He ended up taking shit."

"How you know that?"

"I know Forty-seventh, Forty-seventh knows me." Something Ralph said to influence certain situations. He enjoyed the cryptic quality of it. He believed the pause in their conversation was those words sinking in.

"We don't want to work tonight," Floyd said.

Back to that. Ralph told him: "Just don't work Corky."

"Not unless I have to, okay?"

"Yeah."

"If I have to you'll come up with his guarantee?"

"Fuck no."

"I ain't taking it out of my end."

"Floyd, your end will be so big you won't even feel it."

Chapter 2

Later that same night the white stretch Lincoln was headed for home on Interstate 78. Doing an easy eighty-five and sometimes ninety. The driver kept to the left lane, bullied any car that got in the way by coming up too close behind and blinking the brights.

Sherman, which was what the people in the back had chosen to call him, enjoyed driving. It was one of the things he'd missed when he was inside. He'd done seven of a five to ten and it wasn't until he was out and behind a steering wheel that he realized what a longing he'd had for it. Now, after two years of doing plenty of it, he still didn't feel he'd gotten even.

These people in the back. He glanced in the rearview mirror. As usual the glass partition was up. The man always insisted that it be up. As though that permitted him to be breathing a better kind of air. Also, as usual, the man was way over on the right, the woman way over on the left. A lot of seat between them and no talk. Sherman wondered why they hadn't wanted to call him by his real name. What was wrong with Donnell? It sounded as good as Sherman. It couldn't have been that they knew when he'd been born in San Juan his mother had intended that his birth certificate read Donald but she hadn't known how to spell it.

These people knew practically nothing about him. During long waits at the airport or anywhere, with one or the other waiting with him, it seemed there should have been some personal exchange. But nothing, not even once. To pass that kind of time he usually read some magazine, while they, if they looked his way at all, were satisfied with the back of his size twenty-two neck.

Didn't matter. The same disinterest right back at them. About all he knew about them was what he'd surmised from overhearing. They had money, they were Iranian, they'd been in this country since the early eighties. Their last name was Kalali. Mr. Abbas and Mrs. Roudabeth. Kal and Rhoda to some.

They paid him seven-fifty a week off the books. No benefits, no medical coverage or Social Security credit or anything like that. It was made clear that he wasn't to expect any meals; however, the housekeeper slipped him a sandwich now and then.

For the seven-fifty he was to drive wherever they wanted whenever they wanted. And to get between them and any trouble. Up to now, he'd had to use only his heft a couple of times to discourage overly aggressive panhandlers.

Sherman had given thought to what he might do if someone made a serious move on them, tried to kidnap or hold them up. There was no question in his mind about how he'd react. Not for a second would he put himself on the line.

Not for these assholes.

The white stretch passed a sign that said Millburn. It told Sherman he had eighteen miles to go to his third-hand Honda Civic and the beginning of his day off. He had a place reserved on one of the fishing boats out of Elizabeth Port, scheduled to leave the pier at five-thirty. By the time he got to his apartment in Irvington and got his gear together it would be three. He'd stay up.

"Sherman."

Mr. Kalali on the intercom.

What you want dickhead? Sherman thought. What came out was "Yes, sir?"

"Lower the air conditioning. Mrs. Kalali is cold."

Actually Mrs. Kalali hadn't said a word since the restaurant. It was Mr. Kalali who'd been uncomfortable with the temperature. To admit that, he believed, would be to disclose a weakness in his endurance. No matter how minor and commonplace such admissions might be, they were like demerits. They added up to the man.

Mrs. Kalali did a derisive little scoff. She knew all too well how his male mind worked. She turned to the side window so none of him would be in her sight.

Still, he was in her mind, steadfast there like some tenacious decal that would require scraping off.

Him, Abbas, him and his insolent complacence. Now slouched and stretched out, his bony rump on the edge of the seat, ankles and arms crossed. Tie unknotted, shirt unbuttoned three down exposing a veritable tuft of black chest hair. To think she'd once admired his hair, each crop of it. His beard especially, the virility it had represented.

Could she ever have been so emotionally bound to him? That didn't say much for her, she thought, not unless he'd changed greatly for the worse and she didn't believe he had.

He had always been the man over there beyond reach. His breaths were bellowing this limited space, reeking it. Because of the courses of crab and lamb and garlic and chocolate and the espresso, wine and brandy he'd consumed. As well as the tuberose-based eau de toilette with which he'd doused himself, splashed his armpits. He kept a flacon of it in a compartment of the limousine.

To think.

To think of the years she'd followed along behind his dinner conversations, an accomplice to his opinions and desires. It was as though all that while she'd been in a spell, cast by his patriarchal presence. She'd been lucky to get a feeling in edgewise.

He'd always taken her passion for granted, had never considered it part of his responsibility. He assumed she was so libidinal that it took very little for her to peak and finish. Was that not so with all women? Didn't they need to be kept in check from their erotic nature? If he ever gave thought to the reason she often got up directly afterwards and went into her private dressing room, ever suspected it was for the purpose of some self-administered frictions, he attributed it to her female greediness for another orgasm.

He'd been a spigot and she nothing more than his receptacle. For all those years. More emphatically so for the last three, although he hadn't demanded sex from her as frequently. Once a month on average. That was about the length of time it took for his need to humiliate and fester. When he skipped a month she presumed he'd taken it out on another woman.

He would have her sit on the floor in a corner, trapped-like, or on the toilet commode. No need for her to undress. He would stand fully clothed before her and require that she take his cock out, grope in eagerly and find it as though compulsed. He'd have her include the softness of it with her mouth and remain perfectly still while it hardened. Then, grasping her hair with both hands, he would hold her head in place. Her head an object, a receptacle, that he'd jam himself into thrust after thrust.

She was tempted to bite into it, through it. Each time she vowed she would next time. He must have sensed that, for he hadn't demanded it of her for the past several months.

Last Christmas season was when Roudabeth's self-worth stopped draining. She remembered the exact day, in fact, the very instant when it started being replenished.

She was gift-shopping in the city, had gone into Saks to buy Kal some evening socks. The young male clerk who waited on her showed her the best, black silk. He inserted his hand into one of a pair to have her see the fine weave. To that point he'd been nothing more than a helpful, informing voice. Her attention went from the sock with his nice hand in it up to his face, and for a long moment, a moment communicative because of its length, she remained eyes to eyes with him.

Young, fair-haired man who had lived at least two decades less than she. Clean-shaven young man with a straight, narrow nose and healthy, even teeth within what appeared to be a gentle mouth. Not a pretty young man but nearly. What must he think of her staring? she thought.

She found out later when he got off work for an hour.

His name was Roger Addison.

Next he told her, or perhaps not next but what had registered with early indelible impact, was how stunning he thought she was. How lovely, how aristocratic were her hands. How mellifluent her voice. That was the very word he used, mellifluent.

She believed him. She was empty, famished for such beliefs. She adored his fairness, his hair and complexion such a contrast to that which she'd been accustomed. His name sounded well-off, but he wasn't. He'd completed four semesters at Columbia, would go back when he'd saved up.

They usually met at his apartment, an everything room that fronted on Second Avenue above a fruit and vegetable market. Every so often she'd treat their lovemaking to an afternoon in a high room of the Plaza: vintage wine and delicious nibbles.

Now in the limousine being transported through the damp New Jersey night, she recalled the most recent afternoon she'd spent with Roger, certain joys of it: him kissing her thighs so lightly, his blue-green eyes glancing up to verify her pleasure.

On the opposite side of the limousine husband Kal stirred, as though disturbed by her thoughts. He now had his tasseled loafers off. He re-crossed his ankles. Eyes closed to remain within his self, he lowered his chin to his chest and rotated his head tensely to cause a little unctuous, realigning snap.

He had one of his many strings of prayer beads in hand, these of sapphire. Roudabeth watched his fingers work the beads and wondered if he was supplicating or hoping to pay off delinquent dues. He'd never catch up, she thought, and returned her attention to outside. They had reached and taken the Martinsville turn-off. Then came Liberty Corner and Far Hills and the familiar winding way where large homes self-consciously hid behind high walls or tall impenetrable hedges.

A swing to the right.

A short distance to the steel gate.

The gate responded obediently, slid aside so the stretch could continue up the paved drive. The appropriate door of the four-car garage was equally obedient, completed its opening by the time the limousine got to it. Sherman drove in and cut the engine.

Mrs. Kalali was quickly out and bound for the house via the connecting breezeway.

Mr. Kalali waited for Sherman to open the limousine door for him. He stepped out with his shoes in hand. For the last mile or so he'd tried to put them on but his feet were swollen.

He had Sherman hold the shoes while he took out his billfold. It wasn't fat because it contained only brand-new hundreds. The bills stuck together. Mr. Kalali wet his thumb and first finger and counted twice.

Eight of the hundreds onto the flat of Sherman's palm. Mr. Kalali expected fifty change. Sherman didn't have it. Mr. Kalali reclaimed one of his virgin hundreds and said he'd owe Sherman the fifty until next payday.

Sherman wanted to say no way fucker. Instead he nodded and ducked beneath the grinding descent of the garage door, hurried to his car and was gone.

Mrs. Kalali, meanwhile, had entered the house and turned off the security system. She found a note from the live-in housekeeper on the kitchen counter. A lie about a family emergency and a promise to return Monday morning.

By then, Mr. Kalali, carrying his shoes with his billfold in one, was in the breezeway headed for the kitchen door that had been left open for him.

Floyd timed his move perfectly, stepped out of the darkness to be directly behind Mr. Kalali. Did so with such stealth that Mr. Kalali wasn't aware until he felt the pistol jab his spine.

Mr. Kalali started, bowed his back and turned enough to see Floyd's black face.

"Keep going," Floyd told him.

Mr. Kalali felt legless. It seemed he levitated into the kitchen.

Mrs. Kalali saw Floyd and his weapon and realized what was occurring. She stiffened. Her breath caught, and when she released it, an apprehensive female sound came from her. As though it was called for. She studied Floyd for a moment, then decided it would be best that she look away.

The others came in.

Tracy and the white girl.

They were also armed. The white girl had a Mach 10 machine pistol. It looked too heavy for her.

Floyd hadn't been able to reach out for Corky or anyone else who'd ever worked, and rather than phone Ralph to say it wasn't going to come off because they were shorthanded, it struck him that maybe the girl could drive, just drive. She was all for it at first, but when Floyd explained the work to her, she didn't want to. Not just drive. She wouldn't go along at all unless she could play a more important part.

The girl, whose most recent one name was Peaches, went back and forth about that with Floyd, but, finally, Floyd gave in and it was settled that the driving would be done by Dexter, who didn't care one way or the other. It was also agreed that having Peaches along was something they'd keep from Ralph.

On the drive they'd played a couple of Toni Braxtons, smoked some boo and Peaches had gotten some laughs out of them with stories about four years ago when she was a titless fourteen in Phoenix passing for a flat-chested twenty. Between stories she sucked on Floyd's second finger after alternately guiding it into a pint bottle of Southern Comfort and herself.

They'd had no problem finding the Far Hills area or the Kalali house or which wall belonged to the rear of it. Dexter had left them off and would return to the spot frequently to see if they were there to be picked up.

The wall had been easy, not very high and no barbed wire, spikes or anything, and the rear grounds couldn't have been more accommodating: unlighted, wooded, overgrown with brush and landscaped with mature shrubs from the wall to two-thirds of the way to the house.

Now they were in the kitchen, the thieves and the Kalalis, weapons and edginess. Mr. Kalali was still carrying his shoes. Peaches noticed the wallet protruding from the one. She plucked the wallet out and was delighted with the nice new hundreds it contained. About twenty. She had on lightweight latex rubber gloves, as did Floyd and Tracy. There'd be no fingerprints.

"Who's here in the house?" Floyd asked.

Mrs. Kalali volunteered a bit eagerly that there wasn't anyone else. Floyd made sure, went from room to room. Throughout, the interior was white and sheer, minimally furnished. There was a lot of mirror, chrome and glass. All the floors were bird's-eye maple, fine-sanded slick and bleached pale. There were ten rooms in all, generous spaces with high ceilings. Off a wide entry hall was the living room and opposite that the library. One entire long wall there was bookcases with a sliding chrome ladder to help reach the volumes on the higher shelves. Every book was jacketed in identical white paper, its title and author noted in small lettering at the base of its spine.

The library also served as a music room. A piano, a Steinway baby grand, stood isolated in the deepest corner. Its black, curved form was a dominant contradiction.

Floyd didn't like the house. It lacked comfort and there wasn't a sign of joy anywhere. He thought if this was where he had to live he'd hang out elsewhere, hardly ever come home. Shit, he'd been in cozier bus stations.

He assembled everyone in the library.

Mr. Kalali plopped down onto the white leather couch.

Floyd told him to get up.

"Why?"

"I want you standing."

Mr. Kalali's legs still weren't with him. "I'd prefer to sit," he defied. But there were the guns. He felt his torso sort of float up off the couch.

Mrs. Kalali noticed how blanched her husband appeared. Anger normally caused his complexion to flush, so this, no doubt, was fear. She enjoyed telling him in Farsi to have courage.

"No talking in Hebrew!" Floyd snapped. It sounded like Hebrew to him, had that sometimes guttural, sometimes phlegmy, back-of-the-throat quality to it.

Mrs. Kalali apologized.

Floyd had to merely indicate her ruby and diamond necklace.

She turned to allow him to get at its intricate clasp. He had trouble with it. She undid it for him.

Floyd examined the necklace briefly. His expression didn't change, no appreciation or approval. The necklace disappeared into one of the zippered pockets of his black, parachute fabric windbreaker. Mrs. Kalali, without being told, also removed her earrings.

Peaches had her eye on those. She stepped between Floyd and Mrs. Kalali, with her hand out and her fingers beckoning *give*.

Mrs. Kalali looked to Floyd.

He didn't object. He was amused by what an aggressive swift this little white girl was turning out to be. Like she'd been at it for years.

Mrs. Kalali gave the earrings to Peaches, who went with them to a nearby mirrored panel. Peaches held the Mach 10 pistol clamped between her thighs while she put the earrings on. She turned her head left and right, shook her head vigorously causing the earrings to articulate and throw red and white scintillations.

Floyd expected Peaches would remove the earrings and hand them over to him. Surely she would know they belonged in his pocket. However, Peaches kept them on, as though they were now hers. Floyd decided for the time being he wouldn't say anything about it.

"Now," Floyd said to the Kalalis, "your other jewelry?"

Mrs. Kalali looked away.

"This ain't all."

Nothing from Mr. Kalali.

"The stuff you got hidden someplace."

"We have a safety deposit box at the bank," Mr. Kalali said.

Floyd did a dubious face, looked away impatiently.

"You think we'd be foolish enough to keep such valuables here?"

"Fuck yes."

"You might as well take what you have and leave."

"We're the best at going through houses and finding what's supposed to be in some fucking bank." Floyd flicked his head in the direction of Tracy, who was standing off to the side holding a shotgun at the ready. "Right, brother?"

Tracy nodded and did a sneer.

"If I were you . . ." Floyd told Mr. Kalali, "I'd take a good look at that badass nigger." Tracy intensified his badass nigger attitude.

"Mess with him he'll smoke you. He don't put up with any white shit."

Mr. Kalali assessed Tracy: a young thick-built black with oily tendrils of hair hanging down and a fuzzy patch like a collection of black lint between his chin and prominent lower lip. He did, indeed, appear menacing but possibly that was only a purposeful demeanor he'd developed, something he'd practiced and perfected in front of a mirror.

This other black, the one apparently in charge, anyway, doing all the talking, might be even more of a pretender, Mr. Kalali thought. A cynical, dangerous, experienced black thief was the impression he was striving to make, and, admitted, he was convincing. However, it might very well be the only reality was the color of his skin. As for the girl, she was out of place. A juvenile, a skinny little show-off acting tough. That she was there validated his observations regarding the two others, Mr. Kalali thought.

He complimented himself for such insight. It had, he believed, always been one of his outstanding abilities.

The compliment acted like a restorative to his legs. He drew himself up, elevated his chin and told Floyd unequivocally: "You'll get nothing more from us."

Floyd blinked thoughtfully. "That's a motherfucking shame," he said with sardonic sympathy. He went to a niche that was built into the side wall. It had glass shelves and was lighted. Each shelf held artifacts of antique pottery and glass, evidently a collection.

He took up a small, lopsided, creamy-colored goblet. He nonchalantly tossed it into the air. It smashed to pieces on the hard floor.

Mr. Kalali grimaced.

Floyd had no idea that the goblet was a precious Persian piece that had miraculously survived six thousand years without a chip.

He enjoyed Mr. Kalali's reaction, so, next, he destroyed a pale blue faceted glass bowl that had been created in the holy city of Qom in the first century.

Mr. Kalali placed his hands over his eyes. If he'd had another pair they would have covered his ears.

Mrs. Kalali seemed somewhat amused.

Floyd swept shelves bare. He hurled tiny, two-thousand-year-old, museum-quality Sasanian bottles and urns at the far wall. Mr. Kalali had to duck.

He pleaded with Floyd to stop.

"Give it up."

Mr. Kalali still refused.

"Okay, let me tell you how this is going down. Two ways it can go. One, you give up where you got jewelry, we take it and go. Nobody gets hurt. The other way we have to look for it. It'll take time and trouble but, sure as shit, we'll find what you say ain't there. For putting us through the time and trouble . . . we kill you."

Mr. Kalali looked to his wife. He shook his head ever so slightly and hoped that she understood the message in his eyes, instructing her not to reveal anything. He wasn't going to melt down, especially not in front of her. For some reason she didn't appear to be the least bit frightened.

"What's it going to be?" Floyd asked.

"It's as I told you . . ."

"In the bank."

"In the bank."

"It's here in the house," Mrs. Kalali contradicted. "I'll show you."

Mr. Kalali spat at her.

She ignored him. She led Floyd and Peaches from the library and down a wide hall to the master bedroom area. In the adjacent dressing room she slid out one of the deep drawers of her vanity. It had a false bottom. She opened it for them.

The shallow compartment contained two sapphire rings, a crossover diamond ring, a tanzanite pendant, a tourmaline bracelet, a diamond tennis bracelet, several gold chains, a pair of one-carat diamond studs, and a pair of pavé diamond ear clips. Nothing major but all of good quality.

"My everyday things," Mrs. Kalali explained, as Floyd transferred them from the compartment to his jacket pockets.

Peaches, meanwhile, was into the top drawer of Mr. Kalali's dresser. Confiscating cuff links and evening studs, and a ring set with a five-carat honey-colored cat's-eye chrysoberyl. The perfect, sharp, straight cat's-eye, what gemologists call chatoyancy, fascinated Peaches. She wished the ring wasn't so large. It was even too big for her thumb. Perhaps, she thought, she could wear it on her big toe, go bopping barefoot down some street with the cat's-eye winking at everyone. In that drawer she also found some gold wristwatches. It was like shoplifting without having to be sneaky.

They followed Mrs. Kalali into the bedroom. She kicked aside an antique silk Isfahan prayer rug. At first Floyd thought what he was seeing was just bare floor, but then, Mrs. Kalali pressed a certain place on the nearby baseboard and a small section of the floor sprung up. Lifting that aside disclosed a compartment. Protruding from the bottom of the compartment was the face of a safe. Floyd would never have found it. A highly rated safe. What's more, it was inset in the concrete foundation.

The sight of it evoked a little glee from Peaches. "You can get into that, can't you baby?" she said to Floyd.

As good and experienced a swift as Floyd was he'd never done safes. He knew swifts who did, had met a few who'd offered to impart the basics and finer points, but he just hadn't had the ambition.

So, understandably, he was grateful when Mrs. Kalali reached down in and performed the combination.

The guns and the badass nigger talk had gotten to her, Floyd thought. No other reason for her to be so cooperative.

The safe was open.

Its contents there for the taking.

First thing out, because it happened to be there on top of everything else, was a red Cartier ring box containing a six-carat cushion-cut diamond of superb quality.

Mrs. Kalali provided a blue Fendi valise for them to carry the jewelry away in.

They returned to the library.

Mr. Kalali was on the couch, groaning and holding his right foot up. His black silk sock was soaked red, dripping blood.

"I told the pussy motherfucker to stay where he was," Tracy said.

"I'm badly cut," Mr. Kalali said. In stocking feet he'd stepped on some shards of his antique Persian glass. Some of the same were now crunching noisily beneath the thick soles of Peaches' boots, aggressive black leather boots with shiny steel toeplates. She went so directly to Mr. Kalali that for a moment he thought she had taken pity and intended to administer to his foot.

She stopped in front of him.

She extended the Mach 10 pistol to within inches of his face.

His eyes fixed on the little opening of its muzzle. The miniature tunnel from which his death could come. He didn't dare move his head, just raised his eyes.

There was her blonde, frizzy hair, the slight upturn of her nose between the childish rounds of her cheeks, the inexperience of her mouth, lips slicked like they were coated with baby drool.

Having taken such close stock of her, Mr. Kalali believed he had determined her innocence. Never mind the gun, disregard it, he told himself. Children play. She was merely playing. Her innocence was definitely in his favor.

Peaches was sure she had this guy scared shitless. It was payback for all those times since she was thirteen, even before, when older guys had made her afraid. She didn't intend to pull the trigger. It was like her finger was on its own.

A five-round burst.

The last two rounds went wild. The first three tore off much of Mr. Kalali's head.

Mrs. Kalali screamed. Her composure left her, as did her compliance. She made a dash for the security alarm pad in the entry hall, for the panic button that would summon help.

Floyd had to shoot her.

Chapter 3

The flow from La Guardia was coagulated.

An eighteen-wheeler, like some behemoth suddenly intent on suicide, had swerved across the median, ended the lives of five and now lay there on the Grand Central Parkway with its exposed underside looking rigored.

Mitchell Laughton was the passenger in a much abused fleet taxi sixty-four lengths back from the collisions. In fatalistic measure, death had missed him by, at most, half a minute.

The taxi meter was ticking away voraciously. Each time it went *gu-luckit* to register a greater amount Mitch was made to think how this was another of those wastes of life time. A more equitable arrangement could have been created, he thought. For instance, when forced to wait like this, why shouldn't a person be allowed to call time-out or perhaps even receive a credit on the other end?

He'd certainly done more than a fair share of unfair waiting this day. The flight to Boston had been delayed a half hour because of air traffic; then his eleven o'clock appointment with Grayson at Fidelity Eastern Insurance had to be pushed ahead to one because Grayson was having a root canal emergency.

And now this tie-up.

Already it had cost Mitch nearly forty minutes.

For what must have been the hundredth time he told himself to relax, take it in stride, do what Maddie advised to cope with such unavoidable irritating instances. Turn mentally inside out was the way she put it. Think flowers, for example, not a mere bouquet but a whole skyful, or think of finding a downy bird-belly feather that could be kept mid-air by the slightest breath for miles and miles over an ideal endless meadow. Think of a happy home run, a bases-loaded, tenth-inning game winner. Whatever it took to transcend, Maddie prescribed.

At times Mitch had been able to perform her inside-out trick. Not often and not easily, but he had.

However, this afternoon it was impossible.

The taxi seat was one reason. The foam rubber within it had given up ten thousand passengers ago. What the rump got now was practically all inflicting springs. What's more, the seat refused to stay in place, kept shifting forward from its proper slot beneath the back cushion. The ashtrays stunk, were stuffed with stubs and used tissues. No air conditioning, the uncloseable windows were cross-ventilating exhaust fumes.

Then there was the driver of the next car over. Emaciated, brittle-looking woman with a mass of hair an impossible red. She had her dough-white, crepey arm out the window, hung down lifelessly except for her fingers doing nervous flicks at a cigarette. She brought the cigarette to her sparse lips, took a long, ugly drag, exhaled from her nostrils.

Mitch imagined she had tusks.

She noticed him noticing and shot him a scrinched-up, superior look that called him a creep.

Ordinarily Mitch would have chalked her up as one of those inconsequential frays in the fabric of life. However, right there as she was, hardly more than a spit away, he was stuck with her.

He got out of the cab. The concrete surface of the parkway felt slippery underfoot. He stretched his back and limbs thoroughly, craned up, hoping to see movement ahead.

The taxi driver had gotten out earlier. He was on his haunches near the left front door, reading a tired copy of the *Daily News* that one of his morning passengers had left behind. The driver was a West Indian. His especially dark skin had a gloss to it. He stood, folded the newspaper and tossed it onto the front seat. Then he went back five or so lengths to a taxi that belonged to the same fleet, driven by someone he knew.

Mitch reached in and helped himself to the newspaper. He placed it on the left section of the taxi's hot, yellow hood, smoothed it out and stood over it.

During his wait in Boston he'd read most of that day's *Globe* and there'd been not a single line about what the *News* had chosen to front-page: the late-night frolic of an already notorious rock star who'd roller-bladed bare-ass around and around the Plaza Fountain so elusively it had taken six policemen to grab hold of her. The photo showed her looking stoned and gleeful, wrapped in a police jacket that had precisely slipped.

The Kalali murder.

It was on page seven. Just one of a dozen murders that had occurred in the tri-state area over the weekend. It did not involve anyone well-known, so page seven was generous positioning. Half a column bordering an ad for a Macy's sale of bras and girdles.

Mitch more or less read the Kalali item; anyway, got the gist of it:

A guy named Kalali had been slain night before last at his home out in Jersey. His wife was in a bad way. It looked to be robbery. They were Iranian people.

Mitch continued on through the paper several pages at a time, all the way to and past the sports section. A page just beyond sports offered a daily horoscope. Mitch put no stock in astrology, never had. He reasoned it was something thought up thousands of years ago when our solar system was considered the vast end-all. Now that we've had a look at Mars and Venus and so on and seen how arid, lifeless, hot or cold they were, and now that we know how huge the universe is and how this solar system is comparatively no more than a few motes in it, what basis was there for such beliefs?

Still, there on the page for contemporary consumption was the sign–characters of the Zodiac along with a bit of advice or prediction for each.

Purely for diversion Mitch read the horoscopes for Aries and Taurus and then skipped down the sign-by-sign listing for what might be said for Sagittarius.

It wasn't there. The list went from Scorpio to Capricorn. Why had they left out Sagittarius, his sign?

Mitch was amused at himself for feeling slighted.

He wouldn't mention the omission to Maddie, though. She'd make something of it.

The afternoon was practically shot by the time Mitch got into the city. The stingily filled egg salad, mostly chopped celery, sandwich he'd had at the Fidelity Eastern employees' lunch room and the packets of salted peanuts the airline had distributed weren't holding him. However, he'd persevere. In fact, it would be best if he did, because Maddie had said that morning, with a coating of promise, she'd be doing a cassoulet that night. He'd come close to telling her it was too warm for such a heavy meal.

Maddie had a fairly extensive kitchen repertoire, considering, but rarely was Mitch able to honestly compliment her on what she prepared. Cassoulet was her incessant nemesis. It never came out the same and never right. Too much thyme, or vermouth, or garlic, or cloves, one thing or another.

Anyway, tonight was supposed to be another cassoulet night and, maybe, if he stayed hungry and became even more so, hungry enough, he wouldn't have to fib to Maddie that it was delicious, wouldn't have to tell her he'd cleaned his plate when he'd hardly touched it, wouldn't have to perform appreciative sounds nor pretend he was helping himself to seconds.

He walked to the corner of Fifth Avenue, entered the Corvette Building and had one of the elevators all to himself up to the fourteenth floor to the corner office with his name on one of the two of its doors.

Shirley, his secretary, was at her desk not doing anything nor trying to appear that she was.

"You made it back," she said. "I was beginning to think you wouldn't."

"Any calls?"

"They're on your desk."

Mitch went into his inner office. Shirley following along, saying: "I lose the money I put down to layaway a pair of boots at Lord & Taylor if I don't pick them up today."

"Too hot for boots."

"It won't be soon enough."

"How much?"

"I put down twenty, I owe ninety."

"You're impossible."

"Otherwise I wouldn't be so ardently sought." Shirley arched as she accepted the hundred Mitch extended. Her smile thanked him. She had miraculous, rather large teeth, so white and even they looked a bit vicious. Her last name was Crowninshield. She was British but had been in America for half of her forty-two years. There was still considerable London in her manners and her manner of speaking and she could turn it on thick when she thought it advantageous, for herself or for Mitch. Guile she had, was smart as a skinned knee. She'd never been married, claimed she wouldn't be ever because why put an end to enjoyment.

One of Shirley's most apparent shortcomings was her weakness for layaways. At any given time she'd have small amounts of money deposited on things at Saks, Gallerie Lafayette, Bendel's, Bloomie's, wherever. All sorts of things that had spontaneously struck her fancy. She kept track of them on her calendar and nearly always waited until the final day before forfeiture to resort to having Mitch give her an advance.

After a number of such so-called advances she'd present Mitch with a detailed accounting, a printout showing she was a month or two behind in her salary. He'd keep it for a few days for effect then tear it up and drop it in her wastebasket where she was sure to discover it. Nothing said. She'd worked six years for Mitch. There'd been maybe a half dozen periods when she'd managed to resist layaways. Those times, Mitch noticed, coincided with hopeful love affairs.

Now, she'd already freshened her makeup, smoothed her panty-hose and was in the starting gate for Lord & Taylor's. "Anything you want done before I leave?"

"Nothing that won't keep."

"I'm all caught up with the Hyperion file."

"Good girl."

"Ta then," she said brightly to him and the whole place, grabbed up a soft leather tote that had, in its turn, once been a layaway at Bendel's and was gone.

Among the considerable number of pink *Called While You Were Out* slips on Mitch's desk were three from Maddie, the most recent only a half hour ago, two from Keith Ruder of Columbia Beneficial and one from Furio Visconti.

The latter caused Mitch to turn and look in the direction of the 580 Fifth Avenue building located diagonally across the intersection on the northwest corner of 47th. As coincidence would have it Visconti's place of business was also on the fourteenth floor.

Often, while gazing out merely to give his thinking more room, Mitch would catch on Visconti over there dealing away. Sometimes all he could see was the back of Visconti's head above his office chair. Other times, when Visconti had swiveled to face out, he and Mitch would peer across at one another, and once, Christmas week two years ago, Visconti had waved. Just a single, hand-up motion, and Mitch had responded rather automatically with the same.

That remote exchange across a city gorge was by no means the extent of what Mitch and Visconti saw of one another, although in Mitch's opinion both would have been better off had they let it go at that.

Seldom was Mitch on *the street* that he didn't run into Visconti. It wasn't altogether happenchance. In his particular way, Visconti was 47th. It was his allocated portion to chew on. Anyway, half his.

There he'd be, on the sidewalk outside an arcade or a jewelry merchant's window, talking to one of his minions or a fence. He'd stop talking or listening to make a point of saying hello to Mitch or sometimes more:

"How's it going?"

"Fine."

"Want to ask you something"

Mitch raises his chin, looks receptive.

"That a real Rothko I see over there on your office wall or just a print?"

"Real." A fib.

"That's funny. Thought I saw that one at the Museum of Modern Art a while back."

"I lend it out."

"You're a classy guy, Mitch."

Mitch agrees.

But this was the first time Visconti had ever phoned, wanted to be called back.

Mitch pressed the speaker button of his phone. He speed-dialed Maddie.

"Well, at last, there you are," she said.

"What's up?"

"No cassoulet tonight, darling. The inspiration deserted and left me lazy."

Mitch enjoyed the reprieve. "I'll pick up something on the way home."

"I'd rather go out," Maddie told him. "Maybe to Lespinasse or someplace."

She didn't mean the someplace. When she said Lespinasse Mitch knew she meant Lespinasse. His watch told him almost six. "Shall I come home first, or what?"

"Why don't you fiddle around there and I'll come by for you at seven."

"How did your day go?"

"Maybe I won't bother with putting on any makeup." She had this way of abruptly taking unrelated conversational side roads. Mitch had become used to it. "Would you mind terribly if I were bare-faced tonight?" she asked.

"I'll make reservations," he said.

"I already have. Are you okay? Your voice sounds a bit strange, sort of hollow."

She had hypersensitive hearing but he doubted she could pick up his empty, complaining stomach. "I've got you on speaker phone."

"I know, but that's not it. I did say seven, didn't I, precious?"

"If you want to make it sooner or later it's okay with me."

"No, just be out front. Billy already has the glove compartment crammed with parking violations and you know how he loathes having to circle the block."

She clicked off and was again up the avenue thirteen blocks away. But safe up there in the high apartment at the Sherry, way above the city's ordinary level and its dangers.

His Maddie.

Hung on the wall to his left were three framed, enlarged photographs of her. Ten years ago, five years ago, and last month. Any of the three were capable of causing him to lose his train of thought. Right now he was lost in the most recent, her pleasant, reassuring expression.

Mitch knew she ventured out more often than she admitted. He also knew she kept that from him to save him worry. Allowing her to take care of herself had from the start been part of their deal. For him it was the hardest part.

He dialed Keith Ruder, doubting that Ruder would still be in. The offices of Columbia Beneficial Insurance were located on Park in the twenties, in an imposing but spiritless building from which the drones of insurance stampeded out of each weekday at precisely five o'clock.

Ruder was there, said his last name instead of hello. He got right to it. "The file I had messengered to you, have you looked at it?"

"I was just going over it. I've been in Boston all day." Mitch reached for the oversize manila envelope bearing Columbia Beneficial's logo. He slit it open with the larger blade of a two-bladed Buck pocketknife that his father had given him because it had been his grandfather's.

As he removed the contents of the envelope he noticed the name Kalali but it took a moment for him to recall where he'd seen it before.

The files, besides Ruder's perfectly typed covering letter, consisted of a four-page itemized and numbered list of various pieces of jewelry, twenty pages of detailed descriptions and appraisals and a corresponding photograph of each insured item. Professionally taken photos. The appraisals were in order, done by Yavitz, a respectable upscale retail jeweler on Madison Avenue.

Mitch went to the bottom line. Replacement value for the entire lot came to six million one hundred thirty thousand. He purposely read the amount aloud, heard a disquieted grunt from Ruder.

"How long has the policy been in force?"

"Why do you ask?"

"Never know."

"Believe me, Mitch [usually it was Laughton], I've gone over and through every clause and all correspondence at least ten times today. It's tight."

"I'm sure if there's a way out you'll find it." Mitch was also sure Ruder would take that as a compliment.

"Our coverage began eight years ago," Ruder informed. "Before then Lloyds had it."

"Columbia is the sole underwriter?"

"Unfortunately."

"Smart bookies lay off heavy action," Mitch recited as though it was something from the Bible.

Ruder resented the bookie implication but let it pass. "From the start our coverage of the Kalalis was a package. Dwelling, cars, liability, the works. They tacked on the personal property coverage, which, of course, was their option."

"All these jewelry items right off?"

"No. To begin with the jewelry rider was for three million something. As they acquired additional pieces they let us know, complied with our requirements and we covered."

"Who paid the premiums?" At thirteen dollars a thousand, about eighty thousand a year.

"For the first five years the husband paid. After that the wife."

"Wonder why. Why do you think?"

"I don't see that it matters. The fact is the beneficiary is the wife. Columbia has the usual ninety days to settle with her."

"Maybe she won't live that long."

"No matter, somebody will pop up demanding to be paid. Of course, if we were to recover . . ." The prospect of that drew a long, full sigh from Ruder. "God, would I ever be grateful if we recovered."

Grateful would be nice for a change, Mitch thought.

Columbia Beneficial was one of his regular clients. He was on retainer to Columbia and to several of the other major insurance companies. Any one of them would have preferred having him on staff. At one time or another each had approached him with an offer, attractive numbers and numerous perks. Possibly he gave one thought to their propositions but never a second. At any price being among the tight asses in the gray atmosphere and paper pile of insurance didn't appeal to him. He was heart and soul a freelancer.

For the insurance firms that was an innovation.

Prior to Mitch, whenever cases came up that involved West 47th—robberies, usually, but often a robbery with a distinctive diamond district twist—the companies had no choice but to draw from their staff of claims adjusters. These fellows, capable as they might be in handling claims in the everyday world, were out of their element on 47th.

They got blinded by the sparkle, left behind by the vernacular, spun by the milieu to the point of vertiginous confusion.

Mitch, on the other hand, could hardly have been more streetwise. For years, actually most of his life, without being conscious of it, really, he'd been stoking up on the workings of 47th. His was not merely a familiarity with the street, nor was he like someone-come-lately hoping to be accepted, needing to earn a place. The street had already conditioned him to its ways and confirmed him. It had even exposed for his awareness the cunning peristalsis of its underbelly.

He was not to be fooled. The street liked that about him. His expertise of gemstones was equal to nearly anyone's. He could take a bare-eyed look at a stone, an emerald, say, and not only tell in which part of the earth it had been taken from but, as well, which part of that part. In many instances, even which mine.

He was just as adept when it came to finished jewelry. After a brief examination of a piece that bore no hallmark or signature, something that would stymie most people, he more often than not was able to date it within a few years and, from its style and the quality of workmanship, say where it was made and by whom.

"It's a sweet little bracelet, quite nice. Done by someone in Carlo Giuliano's shop. I'd say in the early 1880s, but not by Carlo himself. It's not that sweet. Besides it wasn't in Carlo's Neapolitan nature to overlook signing."

Such was the extensive know-how, know-where and know-who Mitch offered the insurance companies when eight years ago at age thirty he decided to sell them his services. They didn't snap him right up. Typically they pretended to be mulling it over for a month or two, tried to negotiate with him, claimed he was too costly and not really needed.

Mitch stuck to his conditions, sure they would come around. Fidelity Eastern was the first to retain him. Within a week all the others fell into line.

He'd done well by them. Columbia Beneficial especially. He'd worked ten of Columbia's major jewelry theft cases, made three total recoveries and two partials.

That wasn't to imply that his association with Columbia was close.

Anything but.

There was a bitterness towards Columbia in him, a personal thing that refused to be swallowed and digested by time. In Mitch's opinion all insurance companies were arctic-hearted, egregiously slick and one-way, but Columbia was the champion fine-printer of the bunch.

As for Keith Ruder, the person at Columbia he mainly dealt with, Mitch managed to keep him remote. He'd broken and parried so many luncheon invitations from Ruder that they'd finally stopped being extended, were reduced to the automatic and unmistakably insincere suggestion that they get together sometime soon.

At this moment there was Ruder on the other end of the line trying to sound buddy-buddy, forcing it, flavoring his tone with what he hoped was coming across as amiable conspiracy. It made Mitch think that this Kalali case, for some reason, was personally crucial for Ruder. Perhaps too many such large losses had piled up in Ruder's corner; maybe he was feeling the cold of an early, less compensating retirement hot on his neck.

"I assume you want me to get on this Kalali loss," Mitch said.

"I'd appreciate it."

"By now these pieces may have gone first-class carry-on to London or anywhere."

"Think so?"

Mitch really didn't but told Ruder: "Could be."

"Well . . ." A resigned sigh from Ruder. ". . . I suppose there's only so much to hope for. Can't expect a miracle."

"That's what it would take."

"Nevertheless you might as well sniff around a bit."

"What if I recover?"

"That would certainly be a blessing."

Blessings and miracles, Mitch thought. "I mean what would be in it for me?"

"Your usual percentage, of course. Three percent."

A hundred and eighty thousand. Fair enough, but out it came, pushed out by that old score that could probably never be settled by any amount: "I've raised my percentage to five."

"Since when?"

"I notified you. Surely you received my letter." There'd been no letter, but there would be.

Ruder reverted to type, got huffy. "Five is exorbitant."

"Not when you consider . . ."

"Five is out of the question!"

The money would be from Columbia's deep pocket, not Ruder's. Mitch figured that would come to Ruder in about ten seconds.

It took twelve.

Chapter 4

"Do you see him, Billy?"

"No, Mrs. Laughton. Wonder what color suit he put on this morning."

"It felt to me like one of his grays. Don't drive fast."

"I'm crawling."

"You are over on the left aren't you?"

"All the way."

"He should be there. What time is it?"

"I've got ten of. The car says twelve of."

"We're early. Go around."

"I could wait near the corner with the motor running."

"Do as you want but I'm not going to pay your damn tickets."

"They're as much yours as mine, Mrs. Laughton."

True enough, Maddie silently admitted. Billy got most of the tickets because he was so conscientious about waiting in no-standing zones for her.

They were now on Fifth Avenue in the black Lexus EL400. Only leftovers of the rush hour now. Lots of buses, though. One after another like elephants tusks to tails.

Despite the warm July night, Billy had on his uniform. Dove gray twill. Trousers and fitted, high-neck jacket, matching visored cap and gloves. His choice because he'd be doing some waiting out front of the St. Regis with other drivers. Otherwise he'd have worn regular slacks and shirt.

He committed the car to 46th Street and saw the way was clogged.

"Want some radio?" he asked.

She didn't want any radio.

He made conversation. "Which are you for, Mrs. Laughton, timber or owls?"

"Owls, of course."

"That's because you're not in need of any timber just now."

"Nor at the moment do I have occasion for an owl." Then, in the same breath: "Bet he was there and we missed him."

For her sake Billy held back saying he didn't think so. Billy knew when and when not to say things. He'd been Uncle Straw's driver for years.

Maddie made herself sit back. She measured her anticipation. Frequently at times like this she felt as though there was a sort of device in her, in her head or belly or pelvis, with which she was able to gauge how intensely she was looking forward to being with Mitch. It had been installed during their earliest time and now, after ten years of marriage, it was still there and she believed it always would be. Tonight it seemed to be on a cross circuit, arcing from her head to her pelvis, lingering at the latter.

Early. It would have pleased her if he'd been early, waiting on the corner of 47th and Fifth, his eagerness shifting him, making it impossible for him to stand still, his eyes searching up the avenue for her being brought to him. Him, her precious love, trying to hurry time, pacing, trying to bear the edge of his anticipation with pacing.

She adjusted her dark glasses. With a second finger reset them on the bridge of her nose. Gold wire-rimmed glasses with round magenta-tinted lenses. Chosen from her many pairs, an entire dresser-drawerful.

"Why are we stopped?" she asked.

"Garbage truck."

She pictured it and thought it wouldn't be difficult for her mind
to go from a garbage truck to blank. But her mind wouldn't mind.
It went from the garbage truck to the Manalo Blahnik navy satin
pumps she had on, which still felt somewhat tight and made her
wonder if her feet were getting fat, and from that to whether or not
she'd remembered to close the door of her aviary, to wondering
what Elise and Marian might be doing that moment in Spain
where it was now midnight or later. The last she'd heard from Elise
they'd wanted to move from Marbella back to Barcelona. Oddly
that desire had arrived by letter rather than the usual phone call. To
make sure Mitch was in on it, Maddie thought. "New stationery,"
Mitch had remarked before reading it aloud. Very fine, lined stationery from Armorial the Graveur on Fauborg St. Honoré. The
letter said (its only purpose, really) that Marian had located a darling apartment in Barcelona's better district, expensive but darling,
not all that large but sumptuous, more for intimacy than for enter-
taining. Why was it Elise couldn't communicate without using
words or phrases that were certain to conjure up sexual images?
Was it her intention to boast? It seemed so to Maddie.

"Phone him," she told Billy.

"I did, just now. No answer."

He's down on the street waiting, she told herself and then mentally told Mitch, *I didn't want you to have to wait tonight.* Fucking
garbage truck.

As though her cursing was what had been needed to dispel the
impediment the way was suddenly clear and Billy went ahead and
left and left and left around the block and pulled over for Mitch.

Maddie felt the air disturbed by his climbing in. She inhaled the
distinctive scent of him and leaned toward its source with her face
up to receive his lips briefly on her cheek.

"You weren't early," she accused.

"Would have been but I needed to freshen up."

"You didn't reshave."

"Maybe later."

"Maybe," she arched.

"Look at you! Thought you said no makeup."

"Changed my mind." She removed her dark glasses to expose her eyes.

Mitch knew how long it had taken her to get them so right. Both eyes equally and perfectly outlined and shadowed, lashes thickened.

Care had also been taken in what she'd decided to wear. Mitch imagined her standing before their bedroom mirror imagining how she looked. Her dress was an Isaac Mizrahi she'd recently bought at Bergdorf and shown to him on a hanger, telling him what it was. Large white polka dots on navy blue ground. The bodice of silk crepe de chine, the short, ample skirt of filmy silk chiffon. At the time he'd said he liked it with just adequate heart. Now he set that straight, told her enthusiastically, "You look smashing!"

"Think so?" She soaked that up and hoped for another helping and he didn't disappoint, told her: "Being with you tonight is going to be dangerous."

Instead of thank you she paused and extended her lips for him to bring his to. She was feeling extremely feminine. Her arms like wings, her thighs full of blossoms. She re-crossed her legs and the chiffon obediently floated and lightly settled upon and around her. "Navy is a helpful color for me, don't you think, for my hair and all?"

Mitch thought so, said so. Her heavy healthy hair was naturally blonde, naturally variegated. Plenty of shine but no brass. She had it styled fairly short and in such a simple way it practically disciplined itself, required only a vigorous swish or two and a combing with her fingers here and there to look right.

Billy brought the Lexus to the curb.

Mitch got out, extended his hand back in to Maddie.

She expected it, got it, used it as she aimed her left foot and found the sidewalk, placed her weight on that foot, kept her head down and then she too was out and up.

Stumble, as always, was her enemy. At such times as this her audacity challenged it. So far so good. She paused momentarily to gather her poise, glanced off as though to survey East 55th, then returned her attention to the direction that her highly honed senses told her was the entrance to the restaurant.

Mitch grasped her elbow firmly, started her.

She didn't shuffle or feel ahead with her feet. Took assured paces of a natural length, five to the held-open entrance door and twenty from it to where there were six steps up that she managed without so much as a toe bumping a riser. Mitch halted her while he dealt with the maître d'.

Mitch and Maddie had settled on this system years ago, his using her forearm like a tiller. By now they'd pretty much perfected it. She knew what each pressure of his hand meant, which signified to go left, which to right and to what degree each of those directions. Those for stop and start were easiest. Simply a restraining or slight forward shove. A little downward tug told her she'd reached the point where she could confidently sit. There were refinements, little squeezes of a certain number conveyed certain impending things. Stairs, for example.

Of course, their system wasn't infallible. Old enemy stumble often had its way and there'd been numerous collisions. One day, when attempting lunch at La Goulue, Maddie had misinterpreted a signal as the *sit* signal and taken an inelegant flop.

This night, however, no mishaps. She managed the zigzag course of tables and chairs and waiters without even a brush, and soon she was conspicuously seated on a banquette with the stem of a crystal wine goblet between her fingers, acclimating, actually sort of parsing, as she usually did, the sounds in the large, high-ceilinged room. The polyphony of conversations punctuated by trills of laughter and the effects of the waiters serving. She enjoyed Lespinasse, had been there numerous times for either lunch or dinner, and was acquainted well enough with the layout of the place to make a solo trip to the ladies' room.

"The stunning brunette two tables over," she said out of nowhere.

"Who?"

"The one who's hitting on you. Sneakily but nonetheless hitting."

"Two tables over?"

"Yeah."

"No brunette, just three paunchy businessmen at that table."

A waiter brought rolls and butter. Maddie told him: "That attractive lady, at the second table from here, the dark-haired one . . ."

"Yes, ma'am?"

"See the one I mean?"

"With a diamond clip in her hair, yes ma'am."

"Never mind," she said as though having a second thought. The waiter went about his business.

"You're tricky," Mitch said, wolfing a hunk of roll.

"You're a fibber," Maddie contended.

"Anyway, the brunette in question hasn't looked this way even once."

"Now how would you know that?"

Mitch retreated to the safety of silence.

Maddie went along with that for a short while, then let him off the hook by finding his hand and giving it three consoling pats. "Don't despair, precious," she said, "I was just guessing and happened to be right."

Again, Mitch came close to saying aloud.

Over the years there'd been numerous such instances, some so accurate it seemed she was able to recover her sight at will. She always claimed they were guesses; however they were too right and too frequent for Mitch to accept that. He thought a more likely explanation for these coincidental observations, as he called them, was she had developed an extraordinary ability that sometimes compensated for her blindness.

But wasn't that just as far-fetched as off-and-on seeing? Mitch's pragmatic side told him it was.

He'd gotten the first indication of this faculty of hers shortly after they'd met. He and Uncle Straw were out on the terrace of the Sherry Netherland apartment playing gin rummy for a penny a point. Maddie was sort of neutrally kibitzing, not commenting, just hovering around. Mitch drew the nine of diamonds. Discarded it.

Maddie moaned, she moaned before Uncle Straw picked up the nine. How could Maddie have known the nine was Uncle Straw's gin card, Mitch wondered. Uncle Straw evidently thought nothing of it, just gave himself points and gathered up the deck to shuffle for the next hand.

Mitch didn't puzzle over the incident. But neither could he dismiss it. He tried to mentally re-create it, the sequence of it, and became less certain it had happened as he recalled.

Still, he found himself on the lookout for such occurrences.

For example, the three sapphires. Mitch had purchased them as part of an estate. Three oval cuts, each about six carats. Maddie's birthday was a couple of weeks off, her first birthday since they'd been married, and he wanted to have one of the sapphires repolished and mounted into a ring for her. He brought the three sapphires home, told her what he intended to do and explained the differences between the three.

One had a distinctive lavender cast, threw pink and cornflower blue scintillations.

Another was a typical Burma tone, dark blue, inky.

The other was a bright Ceylon that just missed because it was ever so slightly zoned, that is, it was a lighter blue in one area.

"Which do you think is most me?" Maddie asked, pleased by his thoughtfulness.

"The Burma is the more precious," he told her, "worth more and will always be, but the lavender is far prettier."

At that point the stones, enclosed by cotton in individual glassine bags, were on the sofa table where Mitch had placed them. Maddie considered for a moment, then her fingers went straight to the lavender and took it up, as though she knew surely which was which.

"Is that one the lavender?" Mitch asked.

"Well, isn't it?"

"How could you tell?"

"Just guessed."

He watched Maddie raise her wine glass precisely to her lips. She'd ordered the house red. She took a sip preclusive to a gulp.

"Elise was always such a wine snob," she said. "It never failed to irk me, the way she went on about a wine's staying power or well-structured flavor or roundness of character and all that. What shit."

"Maybe since she's been in Europe she's been shamed out of that."

"Let's hope. That and all things like that."

Elise was Maddie's mother. Biological mother was how Maddie qualified her, not bitterly, just to be truer about it.

"What do you think about Elise and Marian wanting to move to Barcelona?" Maddie asked.

An indifferent shrug from Mitch. He sometimes forgot Maddie couldn't see such body language.

She went on. "For some ridiculous reason they seem to feel your approval is required, or rather that I need it."

"Has there been any mention of how much it would set you back?"

"Not yet, but if it's anywhere near what it cost for their move from Paris to Marbella or their one before that, from Capri to Paris, it'll be a small fortune. Why do you suppose they all of a sudden believe you have the power to cinch my purse strings?"

"I've no idea."

"Maybe I should nurture the fear. If I wanted to be mean I would."

Mitch couldn't imagine her mean. She could be tough at times but never mean.

"Would that appeal to you?" she asked.

"What?"

"The power to cinch."

"You've asked that before."

"Numerous times but you might have changed your mind."

"We should order," Mitch said. A waiter was standing at the ready. Maddie went right through the suggestion. "Sunday afternoon," she said, "afterward, when you were snoozing, I was remembering when the only kisses Elise and Marian exchanged were hello-goodbye, left and right pecks on the cheeks. Uncle Straw

contends that one night in parting they happened to put a lingering one smack in the middle and that was that."

Marian had been Uncle Straw's wife. Thus, Maddie's aunt by
marriage. She and Elise bore such a resemblance they were often
taken as sisters. They frequently fibbed about that, told people they
were fraternal twins.

Mitch had met Elise and Marian only once. Not at the wedding.
They didn't show for that. At the last minute Elise phoned to prove
by sounding hoarse and sniffily that she had a terrible flu. Said she'd
caught the bug while shopping in a chilly Paris rain for a wedding
present, said it didn't matter, that nothing, not even her near death
could keep her from attending, said they were merciful dears for
not insisting she fly considering what a mess her sinuses were, said
her heart would be with them.

The present, a pair of Christofle crystal candle holders, arrived
miraculously intact two weeks later. Carelessly packed in a regular
cardboard box rather than securely so in a Christofle carton. Reason enough for Mitch to suspect Elise had owned them for a while.

Two years after then Elise and Marian came over on the Concorde for a visit that actually was a combined inspection and refi-
nancing, so to speak. They came dressed in Ungaro suits and
matching matinee-length strands of ten-millimeter pearls.

From first sight, first cheek kisses, Mitch and Elise endured one
another. She talked through her teeth at him and only barely tried
to conceal her disdain. He, on the other hand, was tactfully polite
and amiable while finding her little more dimensional than the
photos he'd seen of her.

She was visually attractive, though. Mitch had to give her that.
Slender and conscientiously kept up. No doubt she'd had tucks and
redraping here and there. The sort of time-fighting, well-off
woman whom Mitch had known practically all his young life as the
typical client of the Laughton jewelry store up on Madison. Known
without knowing them. Those who came in to sell away what
they'd once cherished came in escorted by avarice and gossamer ex-
cuses for indulgence such as ennui, in need of a lift, deserving of
reward. The kind who never twitched a lash when told the price of

a piece, a diamond and platinum bracelet, say, that had struck their fancy, was a hundred thousand.

In Mitch's eyes Elise had that sort of cachet and whatever assets she presented were spoiled by both her smile and her laugh, which in his opinion couldn't have been more artificial. It was as though she had only a certain supply of sincerity and was afraid of running out.

Running out.

Elise and Marian were supposed to stay two weeks. After the third day it was apparent they wouldn't make it. On the sixth, having fulfilled the capital aspect of their mission (a six-figure wire transfer to their joint account at the main Champs-Elysées branch of the Credit Lyonnais), Elise and Aunt Marian each left three-minute messages of contrition on Maddie's answering machine, checked out of the Plaza and put to use what remained of their Concorde round-trip.

"Think they're happy?" Maddie asked.

"Sure, why not?" Mitch replied generously.

"The other day, to let them know for what must be the thousandth time that I don't give a rat's ass what they're up to, I had them sent a needlepoint pillow. You know those little pillows with sayings on them."

"What did it say, the one you sent?"

"Butch on the streets, femme in the sheets."

"That should do it," Mitch remarked wryly.

"I thought so."

"Let's order."

"Anyway," Maddie went on, "I'll bet anything that what Elise and Marian had, their sizzling, inconsiderate hots, have by now dampened down to a much less limiting arrangement, a mere sharing of preference. I picture them hitting on desperate young girls for one another." Maddie realized her spite, countered it by abruptly taking a bright side road. "Josie Jefferson was wonderful today!"

"I was wondering how it went."

"She arrived a quarter hour early, her lessons all practiced, a serious little artist eager to get tuned up and into Vivaldi."

"What piece?"

"Concerto in D Major, the Largo section. She virtually attacked it. For now she has more spirit than artistry but I heaped on the praise and asked her to solo next Sunday."

Maddie had been strumming and plucking at guitars since she could manage to hold one. She didn't become serious about it, however, until she lost her eyesight at age ten. Until the black, as she put it.

She'd taken instruction from an elderly Spanish man, a once highly recognized artist whose fingers had gone arthritic. Elise went along to his sixth-floor studio in the Carnegie Hall Building for the first few lessons, sat by the window in an ordinary folding chair counting minutes and turning pages of *Town and Country* and thinking why the hell didn't Maddie play something instead of doing those incessant exercises?

At fourteen she'd been accepted at Juilliard.

At eighteen she realized what a saving distraction the guitar had been.

She still played.

Various guitars and mandolins were propped around the apartment for her to take up whenever she was in that state of mind, and it pleased her whenever Mitch asked her to play for him. Some mornings, while he was shaving, she would sit on the edge of the tub and play pieces that she believed were sure to ignite him for his day. "How's this for a starter?" she'd say and go into a Stevie Ray Vaughan or a fandango by Rodrigo and he'd have difficulty keeping his attention on the strokes of his razor.

At other times, on Saturday afternoons or late after a night out, he'd sit close and watch, entranced by her fingers so deftly changing positions along the frets. How sure she was of the music she made no matter how complicated. If she made mistakes, which he doubted, his love prevented him from detecting them. What could he say to convey his appreciation for her performances? He, an audience of one, with thunderous applause and countless bravos in his heart.

His favorite pieces were from the "Castles of Spain" by Torróba, just about anything flamenco and the anonymously composed old piece called "Spanish Romance" or "Forbidden Games." He could only take infrequent doses of the latter as the melody line of it would get into his head and intrude there for a day or two.

To do her heart good Maddie gave guitar lessons twice or three times weekly to certain underprivileged children. She charged ten dollars a session and they often came pride in hand hoping she'd allow them to owe for a week or two. At one point Josie Jefferson had gotten two months in arrears. Her grandmother, who worked for a midtown janitorial service, got her caught up with six installments.

The reason Maddie charged for the lessons was to increase their importance and give them the strength of sacrifice. To more than even things out her pupils were paid (by her, though they didn't know who) to perform on every other Sunday afternoon at hospital wards and convalescent homes around the city.

The waiter had brought more rolls and replenished the butter.

"Why don't we order," Maddie said a bit plaintively. "I'm starved, practically skipped lunch, had only a roast beef and cheese on rye." She was a big eater, ate mannerly but a lot, and it was unreasonable that she was able to remain so ideally slender. Mitch imagined within her a roaring metabolic furnace, knew she wasn't bulimic, as some suspected and rumored.

This night she started with the *mille-feuille* of crabmeat with spiced mint vinaigrette, went clean-plate through the grilled yellowtail, baby carrots, baby turnips and all, and ended up with a lime soufflé.

As though saving best for last, she waited until the decaf was brought and she was stirring it cool and contemplating the tray of little, fancy gratuitous cookies the waiter placed on the cleared-off table, to ask Mitch: "How did your day go, precious?"

He was certain she didn't want to hear about his command appearance in Boston and all the routine waiting he'd had to endure. His need to bitch about that to someone had already receded and taken its place in that remote region in him where all his similar low-level needs to bitch resided.

No. Such dry stuff wasn't what she was after. She wanted to know what new had occurred on and around 47th. For years Mitch had been bringing the street home to her and the darker side of her was definitely hooked.

To Maddie the vagaries of West 47th were more intriguing and often more extravagant than those of New York's upper social layer.

Like the prominent diamond broker whose embittered wife knew his combinations and, while he was in London on business but really in Barbados for side kicks with a pretty, nineteen-year-old hard body, went to his office on 47th and helped herself to twelve million worth from his safe.

Like those sanctimonious 47th big dealers who kept three or four sets of books and got peeled down to the bone of evasion by the IRS.

"Allenwood's okay. If you got a choice take Allenwood. They got a kosher line at Allenwood."

And like the recent but already legendary misunderstanding between two partners that grew so heated one threw a whole trayful of their best goods out the fourth-story office window. (It's hail! No, it's diamonds from outer space maybe.) Causing, on the 47th sidewalk and gutters below, such a free-for-all that ambulances and an aggregate 152 stitches were required.

Such 47th Street tribulations appealed to Maddie. They were indeed larger than life and she, so dependent on imagination, dilated them even more.

Mitch also let her know when the more spectacular deals went down. She found them interesting and would have felt shorted had he left them untold. However, more colorful than the big deals were the raw deals and the double deals, the scams and swindles, petty and large.

So it followed that, for her, the most fascinating of all were the robberies, and the bolder the better.

Like the one last year, which had been premeditated a year before when a couple of guys bought a restaurant on the north side of 46th Street between Fifth Avenue and Avenue of the Americas. A narrow, short-order sort of place with no booths, just ten stools at a counter and a small, trap-doored cellar for storing supplies. The rear of the restaurant coincided with the rear of a major jewelry arcade on the south side of 47th. What separated the two was an air shaft one hundred and fifty feet wide where sumac grew and the raw earth surface glinted like pavé with decades of pieces of broken glass.

It took the two fellows and two others eight months to mole their way underground across the air shaft to be directly beneath the strong room of the jewelry arcade. That was where all fifty of the concessions of the arcade kept their goods each night and weekend.

With professional patience the guys waited two weeks for the advantages of a holy holiday. Took their undisturbed, own good time burning through the floor of the strong room. Emptied it of six million worth. Left behind not even a 14k bale.

Maddie knew that robbery inside out. First from what Mitch told her about it, the generally exposed scenario, then from the privileged intricacies she extracted from Mitch's detective friend James Hurley.

Mitch hung out with Hurley quite a bit. Their affinity was West 47th. As a captain out of Midtown North Precinct, Hurley's domain included the street. It was both a trouble spot and a centerpiece for him and he made the most of it.

So there they'd be having a whiskey and talking Knicks or something and Maddie would sideroad in with: "You'll never catch those guys."

"Which guys?"

"The ones who pulled off the mole robbery." The tabloids had dubbed it that.

"We'll get them," Hurley said.

"Never," Maddie contended, "those guys won't blow it. For almost a whole year they took turns frying over-easies and tunneling. I'll bet on them."

Nothing from Hurley.

Maddie went on: "A greasy spoon like that, you'd think their prints would be all over the place."

"We'll get them," Hurley maintained. "Won't we Mitch?"

"I suppose," Mitch said neutrally, "but Maddie's intuition is usually dependable when it comes to such things."

"We got a new lead this afternoon," Hurley said.

"From one of your slimy snitches, no doubt." Maddie scrinched her face. She loathed snitches, pictured them rodent-like, sneaking about furtively, keeping close to walls and living off waste.

"A really promising lead," Hurley added.

"Tell me about it."

Maddie pumped and Hurley imparted.

That was how it usually went.

This night at Lespinasse Mitch didn't have anything even approaching sensational to put into Maddie's ears. He gazed over his coffee cup at her, sensed the extent of her expectation and was tempted to fabricate a street story. He reasoned, however, if he made something up she wouldn't let him be brief; she'd want details and he'd have to keep on inventing and the fibs would pile up and that wasn't how he wanted to spend the better part of the night.

He wanted to go home and lie with her, remain perfectly still while she traced him with fingers and mouth, as she loved to do and as he loved her to do, drawing the precise picture of him in her mind, drawing that part of him that would occupy her so nicely.

His memory suggested the Kalali robbery and murder.

There was that, and it suited the moment perfectly, Mitch thought. It had the components but wouldn't take up much time because he'd stick to what he knew about it.

Which, at this point, wasn't much.

Chapter 5

The following morning there was no guitar playing while Mitch shaved.

He'd awakened at five and, although the face of his bedside clock suggested that he doze off for another couple of hours, he knew when he got up for the bathroom he was up for the day.

He'd slept fewer hours than usual but it had been a deeper sleep. Perhaps he hadn't even once changed position; his pillow wasn't punished, was still plump and showed only a head-size impression.

Such a good sleep no doubt because of good, long lovemaking.

Last night had been one of those like-minded times for him and Maddie, when their sexual wants not only coincided but were, as well, simultaneously above the reach of restraint, up in that lover's stratosphere where lust also has its place.

"How does that feel?"

"Marvelous."

"Tell me."

"Soon as I get my breath."

"It doesn't hurt too much?"

"You can't hurt me now. Nothing you can do will hurt now."

He shaved with the bathroom door shut, ran the water from the tap only when needed and only with enough force to rinse his razor. He took a brief, gentle shower and dressed as quietly as possible. Everything not to disturb her, conscientious of how supersensitive her hearing was.

He went noiselessly to her side of the bed for a goodbye look at her. His love in the black within her black. Her usual sleeping attitude, legs knifed up to herself, chin to her chest, one hand beneath a cheek. As though she were contained within the invisible shell of an egg. His love, her system had been so swamped with the neurotransmitters of pleasure that she was still under their influence.

He watched and listened to her breathing. The shallow breaths of sleep. He wished he could leave her a note declaring his love in some unique, adequately expressive way.

He went down the thirty-four floors and through the Sherry Netherland's breccia marble lobby. The uniformed doorman gave the brass-framed revolving door a vigorous spin. Mitch hopped into a quarter section of it and came out on Fifth Avenue.

The flag of Japan next to the flag of Germany limp over there above the entrance to the Plaza.

The gold embellishments on the building down the way, the one that had been confiscated from Imelda Marcos, celebrating the sun.

A taxi swerved in, offered itself to Mitch. He waved it on, glanced up at the Sherry's landmark clock, saw twenty to six and headed downtown at a pace that conveyed important destination.

Twelve minutes later he was in his office.

As he usually first did, he stood at the window and sighted down 47th. He wasn't able to see the entire street from this vantage, only about half the north side and none of the south; however that was enough for him to take in the temperament of it. It was as though each day his imagination expected the street to change, to be upheaved or thronged in a panic or roiled from end to end with visible avarice.

At times, depending upon what mood he was viewing the street through, he thought possibly his regard for it didn't exceed by much what he felt about insurance companies.

At the moment 47th's disposition was tranquil, nearly deserted. The precious goods, diamonds and such, that determined its nature were locked away, waiting in the incompatible dark for their keepers to come liberate them and allow them to do their daily dazzle.

It would be two to three hours yet.

The windows of the upper stories of the 580 building across the way were reflecting early sun. There was no activity or lights on in the offices and workrooms over there that Mitch could see. Except, of course, for those of Visconti.

Visconti's private corner office was dark, but the adjacent spaces on each side that comprised his operation were lighted and possibly doing business. Visconti's people seemed to be continually at it, Mitch thought, even nights, weekends, holidays. Especially nights, weekends and holidays. How many millions did they do a year?

He sat at his desk.

Before him lay the case file Ruder had sent late yesterday, the eight-by-ten color photographs and the corresponding loss list.

The Kalali loss.

Mitch had gone over it cursorily, intended now to thoroughly familiarize himself with the pieces that had been stolen, the swag.

Last thing yesterday, before going down to meet Maddie for dinner, he'd been studying the photograph of a ruby and diamond necklace and matching pair of ear clips. In fact, he'd been admiring those items and thinking how attractively designed they were, the way the diamonds and rubies integrated to create a flow that carried attention to the larger center stones. The loss list didn't indicate who was the maker. They looked good enough to be Van Cleef & Arpels in Mitch's estimation; however that was a value-increasing attribute that certainly wouldn't have been omitted.

What occurred to Mitch now, and bothered him, was that the photo of those diamond and ruby pieces wasn't where it should be. He'd left it on top of the other Kalali photos, was quite sure of that. Now he found it several photos down.

Had he, in his eagerness to meet Maddie, just stuck that photo in among the others? Possibly, but he couldn't recall having done that, wasn't really convinced he had. He pushed the bother aside.

On top now for his consideration was a photograph of two

emeralds. On the Kalali loss list these were described merely as two matching, unmounted emeralds of twenty carats each.

According to the photo they deserved more than that, Mitch thought, much more inasmuch as color was foremost when it came to emeralds. These appeared to be the ideal, deep, vibrant green that Mitch always compared to the green of crème de menthe.

Another thing. Their appraised value, indicated on the loss list, was one hundred fifty thousand.

Two stones at twenty carats each.

Forty carats in all.

That put them at only thirty-seven fifty a carat.

If they were as good as they looked to be in this photo they were worth several times that.

Strange.

Upon closer examination of the photo Mitch noticed what seemed to be scratches on the faces of the emeralds. Perhaps, although unlikely, unless they were deeper and more damaging than they looked, the scratches might be the depreciating factor. But then, they weren't scratches at all, Mitch realized. They were inscriptions, in what appeared to be Arabic.

He'd seen numerous carved emeralds, of course, but never any such as these. Usually the ones chosen to be carved were of lesser quality. These were fine. The only explanation for that would be they were old, Mitch thought.

The inscriptions.

It occurred to Mitch how they were going to cost some fence, how the buyer would contend that the emeralds, inscribed as they were and thus easily identifiable, were worth less than what the fence was asking. Mitch imagined the gist of the dialogue.

The buyer would make an offer slightly above the ridiculous level.

The fence would scoff and say the inscriptions could be polished away.

The buyer would say then go ahead and have them polished.

The fence, eager to have the incriminating swag out of his possession, would curse the inscriptions under his breath and take the buyer's offer.

So it would go.

Mitch looked up.

There stood Detective Hurley, a Styrofoam cup of coffee in each hand.

"Thought about calling but decided to come on up," he said, placing one of the coffees on a free spot of Mitch's desk. The pressure of his grip caused a puff of steam to come from the hole in the cup's lid. "You ought to keep your door locked," he advised.

"Thought it was."

"It wasn't," Hurley said. "What you working on?"

"Robbery over in Jersey, out of your jurisdiction."

"I got a call to help out on one over in Jersey." Hurley held his cup away from him as he snapped off its lid, so any spill would go on the carpet rather than him. He was wearing a tan summer suit fresh from the cleaners, a cotton and mostly polyester kind of suit. The jacket wasn't buttoned because Hurley had gained weight since the previous summer. He was thickly built to begin with and on him six gained pounds looked like a dozen. The tie he had on was an obviously old wide one, not a new wide one, and he hadn't tied it evenly. The narrow end was longer by a good four inches. He seldom got his tie even, and Mitch sometimes kidded him about that, told him: "Make a mark on the inside of your ties so you'll know where to start the knot. They have ties for teenagers like that."

"Who gives a fuck about a tie," was Hurley's attitude.

Now, as Mitch could have predicted, Hurley's attention went to the three framed photographs of Maddie hung on the far wall. He went up close to them, took in each for a long moment, seeming to draw from them, then nodded, evidently concurring with his private thoughts. "Some piece of work," he said. Nearly every time Hurley came to Mitch's office he paid the same homage and made such an observation. "You're a lucky bastard, Mitch," he said.

Mitch agreed.

Hurley grinned and took another lighthearted shot. "If Maddie could see how ugly you are she'd run." He blew on his coffee, gulped it and recoiled from the cup. "I apologize," he said, "not for insulting you but for bringing you this shit for coffee. To make it up to you I'm going to buy you breakfast."

Mitch gathered up the Kalali file, slipped it into a leather folio case and brought it along.

Hurley's city-provided Plymouth was parked at the curb with its engine idling, as though hoping to be stolen. With its black finish oxidized to gray and the numerous city scars on its body it looked like anything but a souped-up police car.

Hurley drove them up to Wolf's Deli on 57th. They took a table by the window. From there it was easy to imagine the outside was the inside confined by glass, and that they were outsiders, spectators of everything that passed. Sort of aquarium-like.

Hurley knew what he wanted for breakfast, quickly ordered a pastrami four-egg omelet and home fries. Mitch took longer, considered several such heavy entrees, but retreated to a bowl of oatmeal.

During the waiting period Hurley inquired: "How's your brother?"

"He's up in the Adirondacks somewhere with Doris. She has a place up there. I think it's near Canoga Lake. Ever been up there?"

"No."

"Nice this time of year."

"A real jewelry junkie that Doris."

"Yeah."

"She really so loaded?"

"I guess."

"From what I hear she married well and divorced better."

"Something like that."

"She's known around as the holdout's best friend."

"I've heard," Mitch said, not wanting to hear it.

"Must be a sickness, not being able to look at a piece of pretty jewelry without wanting to own it. Think it's a sickness?"

"I think guys exaggerate, especially swifts and fences."

"That's a fact. Still, there's something to what's said about this Doris. Andy's been close with her how long now?"

"Going on a year."

"That long, really? I didn't think it was that long. So, okay, I'll give them another six months."

"Who are you, the general in charge of romantic rations?"

"I'm being generous with six."

"I like Doris," Mitch said solidly.

"She ought to lose twenty, thirty pounds. She'd be a stunner."

"I like her because she's as vulnerable as she is smart and because whatever she's bringing to Andy is making him happy. Furthermore . . ." Mitch paused and emphatically aimed his next words, ". . . when it comes down to it, I also happen to be a jewelry junkie."

The breakfast was brought.

Mitch's bowl of oatmeal looked typically sad. A sprinkle of sugar improved it some, made its surface glisten, and a pat of butter cheered it up considerably. However, then the butter was unwilling to melt and Mitch had to push it under with the round of his spoon. He wished he'd ordered eggs Benedict.

Hurley, meanwhile, was putting away his big omelet.

Mitch studied him some, forgave him for his cynical forecast of only six months for Andy and Doris.

Hurley had never been married but been as good as. To a girl he'd helped out of a jam and quickly gotten to know and love. About eight years ago. He was thirty then, she twenty. They'd hit it off from the start. He more than her, but it seemed that she'd catch up. They lived together, did all the usual things that people hoping to couple do together: painted kitchen cabinets, bought shoes, adopted cats, kissed votively.

The one consequential thing they didn't do together was her habit. Despite his being an experienced cop he didn't realize she had a habit until her habit had her, until in her head her habit came before him and she resorted to being cunning. Used his love for her to provide that which she had to have.

He took to shaking down cocaine dealers and bringing their packets home to her. On his time off he'd cruise Brooklyn streets, preying on dealers. They got to know his car, knew him for what those in the underbelly call a take-off guy. They disappeared when they saw him coming.

She often complained about the quality of the dope he brought her, demanded better. He'd never done the stuff, didn't know what better was.

One very late night he shook down a young dealer out in Bensonhurst. He should have known. It was too easy. The guy was obvious right out there on the corner of 20th Avenue and 78th Street, didn't run or resist, just whined protests and motherfucked him a lot. Gave up two fat packets that Hurley brought home to her. Eager to please. He should have known.

She freebased the stuff and it killed her.

Exactly as the young dealer, on behalf of the other dealers around there, intended it to.

These days Hurley lived alone on the West Side in a two-window, fourth-floor, rear apartment. Said he didn't need anyone, and when he couldn't live up to that he called certain numbers and got professionally serviced.

He could have done better, wasn't a bad-looking guy, had all his dark brown Irish hair and agreeable green eyes that more often than not smiled when his mouth did.

He nudged Mitch. "Eat your porridge."

"Don't want it."

"Why'd you order it?"

"It appealed to me abstractly."

"Isn't that the way with so many things? Anyway, you should have had it with raisins. I knew you were going wrong when you didn't stipulate raisins. Does Maddie feed you oatmeal?"

"No."

"I wouldn't think so. She's not the oatmeal type."

"Shows how much you know."

"Tell me, what's this Jersey case you're working on?"

"A guy and his wife over in Far Hills took a major hit, over six million."

"And the guy got whacked."

"You read about it."

"Happens to be the case I'm on. The Jersey local and state people figure the swag might show up here. Which of your clients stands to lose?"

"Columbia Beneficial."

"That being that, maybe we shouldn't give it our best effort." Hurley was aware of Mitch's bad feelings towards Columbia and his reason for them. "On the other hand, if you recover you make a nice score, don't you?"

"Yeah."

"Count on me for help."

"I appreciate that."

"I'll throw leads your way, keep you up on any developments."

"Thanks."

"For a cut," Hurley added. "Say a fifth."

"A cut?"

"That way we'll be more in it together."

Hurley seemed serious, Mitch thought. He'd been helpful on a couple of Mitch's cases but hadn't asked for anything in return and had declined when Mitch offered.

"I've already got something for you," Hurley said. "Could save you time, might even ultimately lead to recovery."

"Like what?"

"A fifth," Hurley pressed.

"Okay, a fifth."

"Make it Jack Daniel's," Hurley laughed. "In fact make it a case of fifths."

Mitch regretted. "Really," he told Hurley, "I'll cut you in."

"Forget it. I don't need it."

"Who doesn't need money?"

"True, but I think it would be bad for us to go commercial. Down the line it could cost what we've got."

Mitch thought Hurley was probably right.

Hurley waited a beat, stabbed up what remained of his home fries, waited another beat. "When I stopped by the preese this morning word was the Jersey people were holding somebody."

"Who?"

"Puerto Rican by the name of Donnell Costas. He was the Kalalis' driver. Maybe they knew or maybe they didn't that he had a rap sheet."

"Any robberies on the rap?"

"No, but two burglaries back in the early eighties when he was seventeen, eighteen. One was suspended, the other cost him a year and a half. More recently he did serious time in Auburn and various other joints."

"For what?"

"Driving a van of hairs [furs] that had lost its way between a warehouse on 35th and a retailer uptown. Claimed he didn't steal the load, was just driving it for some guy, wouldn't give up the guy or say where he was taking the hair, just stood up and did the time."

"Not many stand-up guys like that anymore. Have they got evidence to connect him to this thing?"

"Not that I know of. When they picked him up at his apartment in Irvington he was packing to run."

"Can't blame him for that. He had to know he was jammed up."

"He was also packing a snub thirty-eight, which is enough to put him back inside."

"What's your guess?"

"Who the fuck knows with these kind. They go from the lightweight to the heavyweight division in a night. Anyway, we'll have a better picture of the whole thing when Mrs. Kalali comes conscious. If and when."

"What hospital is she in?"

"Right now Elizabeth Mercy but her doctor wants her moved over here to New York University, his hospital."

"Whoever popped her must have left her for dead."

"You'd think they would have put four or five into her to make sure."

"That could be the break."

"Yeah, but for now Mrs. Kalali is flirting with the angels."

Chapter 6

At that moment in room 1118 of New York University Hospital Roudabeth Kalali was headed above in the direction of consciousness.

Below lay oblivion, a dark red, vacant realm of immeasurable depth where she'd been effortlessly suspended. A pleasant state, really, as quiet as an agreeable thought and void of responsibility. It had been as much Roudabeth's preference to remain there as it had been to leave; however she was compelled to ascend, as though she was lighter than this atmosphere, an etheric shape made up entirely of will. How long would it take, this strange rise? Time was without consistent character, meaningful one moment, inconsequential the next. Forever seemed as possible as never.

Above was the surface, a plane between somewhere and somewhere, between within and beyond. Ungeometric, illusory, and yet she now came to be pressed lightly against some sort of substantial inner underside, contained by it. It was like being trapped beneath the ice of a frozen-over pond, although she was having no problem breathing. Each breath promised there would surely be a next.

Was it only to pass the interim, or was it to pay off debts with explanations that her memory began having its way? Numerous gates of her memory sprung open, experiences rushed out, impressions competed for recollection.

A date came to her, clearly, like a title.

January 16, 1979.

Mehrabad Airport, Teheran.

It was the bright but cool afternoon of Shah Pahlavi's departure.

She, Roudabeth, was there, along with husband, Abbas. Among the Shah's entourage of fifty or so.

The Shah took off his homburg—he kneeled, bent and kissed the ground. The built-up heels of his black shoes were evident. The humility of his arched back. Did his lips actually touch the ground?

Queen Farah Diba could not entirely conceal her disapproval of this, the Shah's final gesture. She waited close by. Perhaps she sighed intolerantly. She looked away.

The Shah stood nimbly, gave no attention to where the kneel had soiled his trousers. He was in black, suit and topcoat, with a black and white diagonal striped tie.

Queen Farah had on a gray cashmere coat, belted snugly. She appeared more detached than solemn. Her plain pearl ear clips were an intentional understatement. There was no way of telling how much extravagant jewelry was contained in her oversize shoulder bag.

They, the Shah and Queen Farah, continued onto the jet, the Shah's private 707. Most of the entourage was only seeing off. Roudabeth and Abbas were included in those going along. The plane already had the belongings in its belly, the many packed trunks and all. Precious layers between layers. Precious stuffings in the toes of socks and the fingers of gloves. It was a getaway, a haul.

The boarding stairs were in place. Queen Farah was first to go up and in. Then the Shah. His black back was the last of him. He would pilot. He would fly himself away.

There were no questions regarding what or how much was taken. There hadn't been the indignity of a search. Thus, at thirty-thousand feet it had occurred to her, Roudabeth, that the jet was rigged to explode, that it might never reach Egypt.

Memory is documentary.

A personal newsreel of sorts that now cut to November 28, 1978.

Roudabeth and Abbas were at the house of the Shah's sister, Princess Shams. Forty-five kilometers west of Teheran. Shaharazad, the Princess's daughter, was also there. The four were seated munching apricots and pistachios, pomegranate seeds and strips of sugared ginger, drinking a vintage sauterne.

A phone call was expected from General Nassiri, head of Savak, the secret police. He had arranged for another sortie, as such undertakings had come to be called.

Princess Shams specified what she wanted taken for her. She laughed and said her age required embellishment. She was sixty-one. Shaharazad rattled off what should be gotten for her, as though placing an order. Abbas was feeling important, telling jokes he'd memorized from *Playboy* magazine. His phlegmy laugh, wide-open mouth. There was nutmeat impacted between his tea-stained teeth. Roudabeth recognized the opportunism in his eyes. She knew his eyes.

The telephone chirped.

General Nassiri would meet Roudabeth and Abbas at the Niavaran Palace. Princess Shams' limousine transported them. Crystal vials hung on the uprights of the car's passenger windows contained wilted springs of lavender freesia. Night was coming on. The limousine outsped it to Kheyabun-e-Sa-ad-Abad. They were shown to a remote room in the old Qajar section of the palace where they changed into suitable clothing. Roudabeth into a much worn, faded blue chador and veil, so she was only eyes and hands. A chador with extra deep pockets. Abbas, meanwhile, got into old, ill-fitting trousers, shirt, jacket and poor shoes. He had the appearance of one of those cheap labor sorts who, hoping to be hired to do anything, gathered each morning in Gamruk Square.

The General arrived. Roudabeth hadn't seen him since the previous sortie three months ago. He seemed shorter and thinner, as though the imminence of deposal was depleting him.

Only three persons knew the most recent code and had a key: the Shah, the General, the Director of the Bank. Now the General handed over his key and revealed the code. Abbas repeated the code aloud several times to memorize it.

Within minutes Roudabeth and Abbas were under way in a poor, abused Peykan. Going south on Kheyabun-Vall-ye-Asr. That major street was deserted except for the military trucks that roared by. And the rebel factions that were bunched at corners. Black-hooded Shah-haters with automatic rifles and knives in their belts. Night was their accomplice. Overcome with fervor they charged across the street. All at once they were in the Peykan's headlights, hundreds pouring around and over it as though the little car was a boulder in a river. Roudabeth was terrified, grateful for disguise.

There were other similar incidents along the way into the center of the city. A left on Kheyabun-e-Takhit-e-Jamshid and a right on Villa brought them to Sevome-Isfand. Abbas parked the car behind the Officers' Club. If stopped they were to say they were janitors, lowly floor scrubbers.

They scurried through a maze of back alleys. From times before they knew the way to the rear of the Central Bank. It was a formidable, contemporary building, a fortress for wealth, normally impregnable but that night with a traitorous rear door.

The Director of the Bank was waiting just inside. He allowed them in. Not a word from him. His part done, he departed. As far as anyone was concerned, he'd never been there.

There were two vaults: one for money, the other for the hoard. The latter was subterranean, down a long, wide flight of hard-edged steps. There it was, with an electronic pad on the left: ten numerals and ten symbols.

Abbas entered the code. He got it right on his second try. The time lock deactivated, the bolts automatically retracted. Abbas pulled the vault door open. It was massive, steel two feet thick, but it swung open easily. Immediately inside was the steel gate. The key opened it.

They were in.

The lights were on. No need to hurry. They couldn't be caught. They were one with the catchers.

First, there on a pedestal was the Pahlavi Crown of State with a white aigrette sprouted above a diamond the size of an apricot, and that above an elaborate diamond and pearl diadem.

Paired with it on the pedestal was Queen Farah's crown, created eleven years ago by Van Cleef & Arpels. Huge carved emeralds, thirty-four rubies, one hundred and five pearls, one thousand four-hundred sixty-nine diamonds for Farah Diba's head.

Roudabeth and Abbas disregarded the crowns, as well as the numerous tiaras. Even the tiara that displayed the world's largest rose pink diamond. The size of a peach pit.

Nor was the famous Peacock Throne given so much as a glance. Never mind that it was gleaming all-over gold studded with twenty-seven thousand precious gems. It might as well have been a commonplace chair the way Roudabeth and Abbas passed it by to be deeper in the vault.

The vault was large, about twenty feet wide and twice that long. It had built-in drawers all around and glass cases containing solid gold goblets and bowls, swords and daggers with gem-encrusted scabbards and hilts. One long island of shelves held trays of polished uncut emeralds. Emeralds piled haphazardly like so many ordinary river pebbles. Emeralds, emeralds, loose emeralds by the thousands. They'd been so long undisturbed a fine dust had coated them.

Roudabeth took one up, just any one from the top of a pile. She rubbed it on the sleeve of her chador before appraising it. A beauty! The most desirable emerald color, a vivid, eloquent green. She dropped that one in her pocket and went on from tray to tray, selecting a few emeralds here, more there, more and more. She was a finicky shopper. Only the finest would do

Next she put to pocket two strands of priceless ruby prayer beads. Fulfilling one of Princess Shams' and Shaharazad's stipulations. Then there were pearls in a large gold casket. Such an abundance of pearls they overflowed, cascaded and swagged over the casket's edge. Cream and white and pinkish strands of huge, incredible pearls. Roudabeth looped her neck with strand after strand. She was lost in the Persian plunder, the booty, the hoard. A thief with permission.

She slid open one of the large cabinet drawers. It was lined with black velour to softly accommodate a thick layer of faceted emeralds. So thick a layer that when Roudabeth scooped up a handful the remaining plenty filled in the loss.

From another such drawer she took a handful of rubies. Then came a heaping handful of sapphires, double handfuls of diamonds of two carats, three carats and larger. Now her every move caused clicks in her pockets and she could feel left and right the heft and bulge against her thighs.

Abbas had been similarly busy. He too was laden.

They went as they'd come, locked as they went, and soon enough were again under way in the Peykan, again having to run the gamut of the incited black-hooded packs on Kheyabun-Vall-ye-Asr. If they'd been stopped with their precious cargo they would have surely been killed.

At Princess Shams' house the contents of their pockets were emptied onto a sheet. The Princess and her daughter were delighted. They eagerly picked through the spread of gems, were entirely caught up in them until Princess Shams remembered to reward Roudabeth with a few pieces, casually tossed them to her.

A few also went to Abbas. He had to feign his gratitude, did so excessively. Because secreted within the sleeve of his poor jacket, between its outer material and its lining, was a veritable fortune.

Hospital room 1118.

The duty nurse entered. She checked the intravenous infusion Mrs. Kalali was receiving, its drip rate and connection. All was well. The unconscious Mrs. Kalali lay unchanged, absolutely still, and, as far as the nurse could tell, not having a thought.

Chapter 7

Mitch had Hurley leave him off on 50th Street at one of those *while you wait* places that did graphic reproductions. He ordered six copies of the Kalali photographs. The clerk there, a paper-faced young fellow whose lips looked as though they were shedding, told Mitch it would take an hour.

Mitch didn't see why inasmuch as he was the only customer, asked why.

The clerk did the New York thing, deliberately crumpled up and discarded Mitch's work order invoice.

Mitch handled it, did a smile from his New York repertoire, the one that begged pardon and asked for leniency.

The clerk filled out another work order.

While you wait is right, Mitch thought on the way out.

He went to the corner. Bought two pounds of big black grapes from a street vendor. Sat in the mid-morning sun on the bank of the stream of Avenue of the Americas, that is, on the raised ledge that bordered the pool and fountain of the IBC Building. Come noon, office people would be on this ledge, having their brought lunches. Tuna salad and marijuana would be in the air.

At the moment Mitch was alone there, digging rather automatically into the brown bag for grape after grape, storing their seeds in his cheek until they were many and then, careful of passersby, jettisoning them with maximum force.

It occurred to him that despite his well-dressed appearance, his loitering there at this hour might cause people to take him as one of the recently unemployed, a guy whose clothes hadn't yet gone shabby or out of style, a jobless guy who was still shaving every day.

Three hundred thousand and some.

That, Mitch reminded himself, was how much he stood to make if he recovered the Kalali jewelry. Possibly those goods had already been sucked up and taken apart by the street. Maybe not. Maybe the street wouldn't ever get a look at them because they had gone to Los Angeles and on to Hong Kong. No, that wasn't how it would go, his optimism predicted, he'd be lucky, the stuff would practically fall in his hands.

His pager beeped.

He went to the pay phone down the way and dialed his office.

Shirley was in her strictly business mode, recited his messages without gripe or comment. There'd been another *please return my call* from Visconti and Ruder had phoned twice suggesting lunch or, if not lunch, at least drinks later. Ruder hadn't believed when told Mitch wasn't in.

Mitch wondered why Ruder was reverting. He'd thought he had Ruder conditioned. As for Visconti, now that could prove to be timely.

He'd left the bag of grapes on the ledge. It was gone. He returned to the graphics place. His photos were ready, had been for half an hour. He'd specified that they be collated in sets and placed in individual gray envelopes, and that was how they were.

He walked down Avenue of the Americas to 47th. He felt suddenly changed, more assertive. It was as though the sight of the street and its prospects had injected him. He crossed over against the belligerent traffic and turned in at the entrance second from the corner.

The Capital Jewelry Exchange.

A deep, narrow place strongly lighted by spotlights on tracks. Typical of 47th. There were identical, contiguous counters with display cases that ran its entire length on the left and on the right. Each section of counter was a booth-like space occupied by a separate business.

No major dealers here. The seller of pearls on one side offered mainly *biwas*. Opposite, the merchandise was 14k gold chains sold by weight. Next, wristwatches, various makes of inexpensive digitals. Then came gold charms: French poodles, tennis racquets, names such as MaryLou and Rosalie.

Nothing better.

The counter-to-counter carpet of the center aisle wasn't living up to the claim that its geometric pattern wouldn't show dirt.

Mitch walked on it, went straight to the back, ignoring the verbal hooks that were cast at him. *Let me show you something. How about a nice pendant? I need the money. Take your pick at half price.* He resented that in their practiced eyes he was being taken as a chump.

A door in the back gave to a steep, narrow stairway up. Lighted by a bare hundred watts. The vinyl-covered steps of the stairs were gritty and edged with nailed-on metal stripping that in places had come loose enough to trip. Fifteen steps up was halfway up. At that point was a landing with a shallow alcove.

Snugged into the alcove was a daybed covered in red Naugahyde. The guy who got up from the daybed was one of Joe Riccio's have-around guys. He wasn't tall but he was big, with such a gut his trousers in profile were triangular.

Mitch took it all in: cigarettes grounded out on the floor, a bag of Cheetos on the daybed along with an overhandled porno magazine that had on its cover a hard-faced blonde grinning around her foreshortened buttocks. On the wall above the daybed an intercom. The have-around in a pink, short-sleeve shirt wasn't wearing a piece, although no doubt there was one within easy reach beneath the daybed.

The have-around blocked the way. "What do you want?"

"I'm here to see Riccio."

"Sure you are. Got an appointment?"

"Yeah, Mitch Laughton."

"For this morning?"

"Yeah."

"I think not. Riccio ain't seeing nobody this morning. He told me."

"Look on his agenda."

"Okay, asshole, down you go." The have-around crowded Mitch with his belly.

Mitch avoided it. "Don't contaminate me."

"I'll break your fucking face, that's what I'll contaminate."

Mitch did a take that stopped everything. He focused his interest on the guy's eyes, craned forward a bit, scrutinizing more closely.

"You wearing eye shadow?"

"Huh?"

"It's smudged. Your eye shadow. The left eye."

"You calling me a fagala?"

"You're also quick." Mitch indicated the intercom. "Call up and tell Riccio I'm here. You're bad for business. When I see Riccio I'm going to tell him you cost him."

"Fuck you. All I got to do is press that red buzzer and three cowboys will come down and rip your head off."

"And all you'd do is watch, right? What is it, you afraid you'll break a fingernail or something?"

The guy fisted his fat right hand and swung.

Mitch easily sidestepped it.

The momentum of the miss carried the guy forward in a sort of clumsy lunge, spun him on his fat legs so now his back was to the stairwell. While he was trying to recover his balance Mitch brought his foot up to the guy's gut and shoved.

The guy grabbed at the air as he went over backwards, pitched down the steep stairway, caromed from wall to wall with the sharp edges of each of the fifteen steps hurting grunts out of him all the way to the bottom. He lay there face up.

Mitch peered down at him, thought the fat of the guy should have cushioned and prevented serious injury. Maybe not, though. The guy wasn't moving.

But then suddenly he was up and coming up, awkwardly clambering on all fours, gorilla-like.

Mitch had time to think how much he disliked this kind of guy, how this sort seemed to always bring out a mean part of him. It wasn't anything personal.

The guy's hands got to the landing. He tried to grab Mitch's leg.

Out of sympathy Mitch didn't kick him. A kick was in order and would have been easy, but, instead, Mitch merely gave the guy's face a push.

The fall the guy took this time was about the same, looked and sounded just as painful. He lay sprawled in a contorted position at the bottom of the stairs and, from the sounds of his moans, it was doubtful he'd attempt another climb.

Although the way was cleared now, Mitch had second thoughts about continuing on up to see Riccio. Before getting to Riccio there'd be more have-arounds to contend with and if he managed to get past those there would be Riccio's routine.

All Mitch had wanted was to exchange a few words with the man and leave with him a set of the Kalali photographs. But Riccio would never allow only that. He was an advocate of old-mob ways, slow, snaky, respect and all that. He'd insist on having espresso poured into merely rinsed cups and a couple of petrified anisette cookies placed on the saucers along with tiny stainless steel spoons.

Riccio would conversationally circle the reason for Mitch's un-scheduled visit with irrelevant observations and opinions and throw in a mob anecdote here and there. As though he had all the time in the world and Mitch wasn't suffering the place with its cheap, taste-less furnishings. Black synthetic carpet with such a high pile it looked like a million writhing worms and no telling what might be hiding in it.

At times Mitch had given thought to that carpet and how many loose diamonds and other precious stones must have been carelessly dropped to it out of the many thousands of carats Riccio took in and dealt out. Mitch could imagine Riccio down on his knees searching the deep black for several D flawless caraters he'd acci-dentally sent flying from their unfolded briefke paper diamond containers when he put his feet up on his desk. An agitated, grum-bling Riccio digging around in the tendrils, not finding, finally giving up and trying his best to put the loss out of mind. In that carpet a fortune lost.

Mitch looked up the stairs and knew what would be imminent. Riccio would sit there, backgrounded by a repaired wall enameled an avocado shade and punctuated by the faded prints of the Virgin and a De Beers magazine advertisement, and Mitch would have to endure Riccio's invitation of congeniality, his latter-day version of all the spaghetti suckers and mustache Petes he'd ever seen portrayed. Not for an instant admitting how anachronistic he was, he in his pointed, black, cap-toed shoes and white silk socks and over-starched shirt. A one-of-a-kind pinkie ring. Pavéd ruby, diamond, emerald version of the Italian flag.

Mitch had been up there in Riccio's lair maybe a half dozen times.

If he went up now he'd again have to stifle how amused he was by Riccio's voice. A voice too small, too thin, too high-pitched for any mobster, especially one who took such effort to come off as one. It was as though at age thirteen his pubes had refused to drop.

Riccio was well aware of this shortcoming, tried to overcome it by speaking breathily with as little throat as possible. So, Mitch, if he went up, would have to strain to hear him, would miss words and have a hard time keeping from laughing when Riccio's temper took over and he cocksuckered and scumbagged someone in his natural upper range.

Joseph Riccio.

He'd come quite a ways since back when he was an all-around, have-around guy for Nick Russo, when Russo was running the diamond district for the people who got answered to. For nineteen years Russo was the man those in the trade went to when the bank said no way. There was hardly a dealer on the street who at one time or another hadn't strung out what he owed the bank beyond the bank's tolerance. Many dealers were excommunicated for eternity by the bank's computer.

Such unfortunates were some of Russo's best customers.

Russo was also the man a dealer went to for fast money. When an opportunity came along that had to be jumped on right away or be lost. A packet of emeralds, for instance, nice Muzos that some coke mule from Columbia showed up with and was willing to let go at only slightly more than half what they were worth. Or a lot of nice-quality diamond rough that a black had carried in a white handkerchief all the way from Sierra Leone.

They came up, such chances, when going to the bank for a loan was out of the question. The bank would want to know all and require a week or so to process its forms.

Russo, on the other hand, wasn't interested in knowing anyone's reason for borrowing and there were never any papers. Ask for the money at eleven, it was there by noon, or sooner, politely delivered in a brown paper bag or a shoe box.

With the first week's interest of ten percent taken out in advance.

No matter, it was fast money, and also no matter that it was black money, the proceeds from pornography, extortion, numbers, bust-out bars, hijacking and the like. The important thing was it was there when needed, available with no more than a phone call. Forgive the usury. Whoever gave that illegal aspect much of a thought?

Thus Russo was a fixture on the street. In his criminal way a benefactor. Without him most of 47th wouldn't have been able to conduct business and many of those that could wouldn't have profited nearly as much.

That was especially true of the fences, guys on the first level of swag who worked teams of swifts. Russo was always there for them. He was the next level, a fence for the fences. He bought from established fences only, those that he knew, the dozen or so. He never bought from an unconnected swift or slick-looking jewelry crook.

"Someone told me you might be interested in something."

"Someone was wrong," Russo would say.

"Let me show you."

"Keep it in your pants."

However what the fences brought usually got bought. Russo was wise in the ways they did business and invariably he got the best of them. They were, he knew, like two-hundred-dollar whores who could be negotiated to lie down for fifty.

Swag.

Regarding it, Russo set some smart rules for himself. Like never keeping a piece of stolen jewelry intact for any unreasonable length of time, which to Russo meant no longer than an hour or two. Normally, a major piece that he'd acquired, say, a diamond necklace, would be broken up within minutes. It made no difference to him that the necklace was exceptional, made by Cartier or Van Cleef or whoever, he was merciless. Out came the stones, the gold and platinum tossed into the smelting crucible.

He had no appreciation for beauty.

And it was said of him that he could pop stones from their mountings by merely looking coldly at them.

Joseph Riccio was one of Russo's favorite have-arounds. One of.

Furio Visconti was just as much a favorite.

Russo played them against one another. Probably he figured that way he got more out of them. Eventually, when Riccio was made Russo's right hand, there was Visconti just as close on the left.

For years that's how it was. Russo telling Riccio he was number one in line and, practically in the same breath, telling Visconti the same. So, it followed that when Russo didn't have the heart to wake up one morning and forever, both Riccio and Visconti felt eligible to be allowed to take over the street.

It wasn't something they could settle amicably. They went at each other as early as during Russo's wake at the Scalise Funeral Home up on 188th Street, and again at the funeral. Scuffled and threatened around grave markers and consecrated ground and had to be restrained.

The suggestion was made that the way to settle the matter was the old way.

A sit-down.

On a sweltering Thursday afternoon in August Riccio and Visconti were transported in separate cars by guys they didn't know to the house of a man they'd only heard of. An unremarkable house on the Connecticut blacktop road between New Fairfield and New Milford. With a mailbox bearing the family name right on the road, as though that name didn't deserve to be self-conscious. House with aluminum siding and a screened-in rear porch overlooking a garden of zucchini and peppers.

They, Riccio and Visconti, sat on the porch in yellow canvas director chairs across from the old guy years past his days, who hooded his creamy eyes and did a great many nods and made a protruding lower lip so they would believe he was listening to their claims.

Riccio was in mob heaven. The only thing missing was an invisible orchestra playing O *Soave Fancinella*. Being in the presence of this fabled consigliere awed him, caused his little voice to go tremulous.

"I knew your uncle," the old guy said at Riccio, which made Riccio feel that he had an edge, until the old guy added: "Your uncle was a *spuce*.

"As for you," the old guy said at Visconti, "you probably think *bris-cola* is a soft drink."

Visconti knew it was a Sicilian card game but figured it best to let the old guy have his opinion.

The old guy announced that he had to take a leak. He went into the house, leaving Riccio and Visconti to ignore one another. Riccio craned up to get a better view of the garden. He would have stood but thought that might not be proper once one had sat at a sit-down. He considered complimenting the old guy on the garden and maybe make a point, but then he didn't know shit about gardens except that old guys like this one enjoyed fucking around in them and that was where he'd seen Don Corleone die six or seven times.

The old guy returned with the decision in his mouth. He'd had it in his head all along, even before they'd arrived, could have said it right off but knew some mob theater was expected of him.

He remained standing because to sit would probably give the impression that he intended to prolong this matter. He wanted to go down to Danbury and have the tires on his Lincoln rotated and get some fresh batteries for his flashlight so he could watch the raccoons try to beat the electrified fence he'd had put around his peppers and zucchinis.

He didn't say his say directly at either Riccio or Visconti. He aimed his words between and over their heads, focused on the screen where there was a blotch of bird shit. In a monotone that made it sound more like an indisputable decree he told them they were both good boys, they both deserved. Told them Russo had spoken equally well of them numerous times. (Actually, he'd only met Russo once about twelve years back when he needed a new stolen wristwatch.) Therefore, he concluded, it was fair that they both be promoted to caporegime and both have the territory.

Half each.

Riccio was to have everything from address number 39 to Avenue of the Americas and around that end of 47th.

Visconti would have everything the other way, from address number 38 to Fifth Avenue and around that end of 47th.

Shake hands.

Embrace left and right.

And the thing was done.

Except for the tribute, the cost of the sit-down, so to speak.

A hundred thousand was the figure mentioned, and to mention was like presenting an already overdue tab that would, if not promptly paid, be put into collection, so to speak.

Riccio and Visconti had to hustle around to come up with their parts of the hundred. The old consigliere got sixty of it. The two guys in the Bronx who'd arranged the thing split the rest.

Grazie.

Had Russo not died so soon this sit-down might never have taken place. The dispute between Riccio and Visconti over West 47th very likely would have fallen through the cracks of the old mob, because it was right about then that the old mob bosses— Persico, Salerno, Corallo, Rostelli and Castellano—as well as many of their minions, their underbosses, capos and soldiers, were being hit with federal grand jury indictments.

Unlike those times before when they'd been rounded up and brought in merely to rub them the wrong way or just for election headlines, this time what was at stake was serious time and there was a new thing called RICO, the Racketeer Influenced and Corrupt Organizations Act, to make the charges stick.

What a barrage of charges!

One hundred thirty-five counts against the top Genovese guys alone. One hundred twenty against the Lucchese leaders. Altogether, over five-hundred counts. Which, when translated into sentences, would mean consecutive lifetimes of time inside, would mean dying in the joint, getting out only after rigor mortis had set in.

Their mouths had brought them to this, their old-mob arrogance and their spillways mouths.

"How much he come up with?"

"Sixty-five, an extra five for being late."

"The piece of shit saying he was strapped."

"You smacked him pretty good. His fucking ear was bleeding. Fat Tony don't want him dead. He couldn't pay if he was dead."

"I hate poor-mouth late payers, that's all."

"Yeah. Listen, stop someplace when you see a place. I want to get a paper. You hear any more about Angelo?"

"Just that he's got to be done."

"I mean when."

"When Fat Tony says."

"You give a shit what happens to Angie?"

"No."

"You used to hang out with him a lot."

"What happens, happens."

"Makes no difference who it was that straightened him out. For what he did the cocksucker's got to get done, him and maybe his whole fucking family."

"Whatever Fat Tony says."

Mouthing, while all around was infested with bugs. The government had them. The old mob on over a hundred hours of tape. (What should they have done, become mutes and taken up singing?) They shouldn't have trusted the dashboard of their cars or the water tanks of their toilets, not even the heels of their shoes.

Worse, they shouldn't have trusted one another.

Soldiers and have-arounds who'd been theirs and in on all sorts of moves for years shed their covers and revealed themselves as having been federal good guys all along. Not only that. Guys they should have been able to be positively sure of, properly initiated guys they'd known since childhood whose legacy from made fathers and made grandfathers was to uphold that old-mob honor, old-mob respect, old-mob everything, were turning out to have been turned sometime along the way, were, behind their *goombah* faces, informers.

Cacchio! Shit! What was this world of theirs coming to? The silence that had been the code and, in so many instances, been painfully, sacrificially kept, had given way to giving up. Giving up people, places, amounts, killings, anything to the federal District Attorneys in exchange for not having to do all their remaining years in joints where the brightest prospects of any tomorrow would be a game of boccie.

Even the underbosses, counted on to be the most stand-up of stand-ups, decided they'd rather kneel and offer to plea-bargain. It got to be a matter of who had the most on who. Three of the older guys conveniently developed chest pains, were unable to get a deep breath.

Good riddance bad guys.

Arrivederci old mob.

Never to be the same.

Riccio and Visconti weren't among those held accountable. They got looked at and then were overlooked. None of their transgressions, terrible as they might have been, were mentioned on the taped conversations. They weren't notorious enough for anyone to use in plea bargaining and they hadn't been tight enough with the up-top mob guys for the government prosecutors to press out of them anything that might be helpful in those prominent cases.

Ironically, just as much a reason for the government not including Riccio and Visconti in the thick of it was the street.

The prosecutors regarded West 47 as a rather separate community with distinctive, shadowy ways. If they went digging and charging into it they'd be opening too complex a side issue, something, with its glittering appeal, that would surely distract from their main performances. They decided to leave 47th, including Riccio and Visconti, as it was and perhaps they'd take it on at some future time when their plate wasn't so full.

They never did.

Riccio loathed the transformation of the mob. The self-image he'd promoted all along refused to make room for any such change. He vowed that no matter what, even if he had to go it alone, he'd keep on keeping on, being loyal to the ways of his forebears. One day he suddenly claimed he was related on his mother's side to Albert Anastasia of Murder, Incorporated. He'd considered making it Meyer Lansky but that would have been contrary to the qualifying, pure Sicilian line and, besides, he favored Anastasia's legendary ruthlessness.

Riccio also enlisted only have-around guys with mentalities similar to his own.

Such as the fat one that Mitch had just moments ago shoved down the stairs twice. Mitch wasn't paying attention to him now, was hesitating there on the landing halfway up to Riccio, indecisive about those next fifteen steps. Thinking Riccio might want to again show off his new electronic money-counting machine, insist on demonstrating it, and Mitch would have to stand there and watch while in mere seconds the thing counted out a hundred thousand or two. "Just like they got in the big banks," Riccio would boast, which would cause Mitch to perhaps or perhaps not hold back cutting across Riccio's old-mob grain with a remark that the money counter was a *new* thing, a big improvement from the *old* days when it took all night for guys to count the take.

Mitch made up his mind.

Instead of going up he wrote on the face of one of the gray envelopes that contained a set of the Kalali photographs:

"Joe—take a look at these and call me."

He included his business card, tossed the envelope onto the daybed, gave the summoning button of the intercom a sure, long press. Went down where the fat have-around was expecting a kick, so sure of it he had his hands over his groin like a cup-jock.

Just stepped over him.

Chapter 8

Coming out of the Capital Jewelry Exchange, Mitch told himself that his passing on a personal visit with Riccio hadn't been a shirk.

The purpose of the visit had been to determine whether or not the Kalali swag had already found its way to and through Riccio. Not that Riccio would have admitted right out that he'd bought it; however, chances were, in keeping with his style, Riccio would have allowed Mitch to read him by replying with his eyes and doing an appropriate, lopsided, mob guy grin.

Mitch believed that the way he'd handled it, leaving the series of photos and a vague note, would accomplish the same determination. That is, if he didn't hear from Riccio he would assume the swag was gone, was no longer in its Kalali form and it would be a waste of him if he went chasing around hoping to recover.

On the other hand, if Riccio bothered to phone and wanted to know about the photos, it would indicate, at least as far as Riccio was concerned, the case was still alive.

Mitch headed east on the north side of 47.

It was busy now, normally so, its various elements into their usual concerns.

Carriers were out, dispatched by dealers whose offices were in the buildings above street level. Unexceptional-looking types, better for that reason, hurriedly threading through the crowd with gems on their person worth perhaps a hundred thousand or more, bound for the eyes of someone in the trade, another dealer who had a call for such goods, or a cutter or a maker.

Hasids stood out uniformed in their black long coats and trousers. Gone shiny in the seats and elbows. Home-laundered white shirts buttoned at the collar, no jaunt to the way they wore their wide-brimmed black hats, as though jaunt would be sinful. Black and white men shunning color and haggling in Yiddish. Their inventories in their pockets, their offices the curbs.

Swifts with residual stealth in their walks, given away too by their expensive running shoes, designer jeans, T-shirts printed with the name of exclusive resorts they'd never spend a night at or a university that wouldn't admit them. In pairs or threes they conspired, tried to agree upon which dealer might pay most fairly for the piece of swag they'd held out from last night's thievery. A two-carat diamond perhaps, freed from the prongs of an engagement ring that had been held dear for years and rarely taken off. A formerly meaningful diamond reduced now to impersonality, a mere stone.

East Indian dealers. Emerald and ruby melee their specialty, calibrated green and red nearly as tiny as Christmas glitter. On the sunstruck south side of the street their burnished complexions seemed to have a somewhat aubergine cast and, at a distance, they appeared well-dressed. However, at closer range it was apparent their suits were cheap, pressed while soiled, their cuffs frayed and the tight knots of their ties grimed. They were not well-liked in the trade because of their distrustful dispositions.

Sephardics, genuinely congenial but shrewd, and good-hearted but underhanded Armenians, and compulsively aggressive Israelis. More Israelis than ever, leaning insouciantly against the doorjambs of their shops, their dark eyes sharp to spot likely passersby that they tried to spiel in.

Wives from the suburbs. Dressed in smart numbers from Ann Taylor, clipping along on hardly worn heels. On their way with elevated heart rates to a recommended 47th gem dealer, a friend of a friend who they naively believe will show them the best and charge them the least.

Ex-wives past the point of keepsakes or sacrifice, merely wanting to divest themselves of the accumulations of ten to twenty anniversaries and other futile occasions.

Then, of course, there were the sightseers. How easy it was to pick those out, as they scalloped along from window to window, vainly trying to appear blasé to what seemed to them to be exhibited treasure troves. Everything placed just so under the most helpful lights. Numerous black or gray or white velour-covered shallow boxes propped up diagonally for advantageous display, symmetrically slotted to accommodate rings, twenty slots to a box, four rows, five across, every slot occupied by a diamond ring. Some of the rings had small hand-printed placards in their proximity, saying: *"radiant cut"* or *"one day low price"* or *"5 carats"* or *"visibly flawless"* or any of an assortment of exemptible 47th fibs. *"Not quality enhanced,"* was one the sightseers didn't comprehend. They whispered to one another: *"Can't be real, look at the huge one in the top row, I'd be afraid to wear it, do you think they're real?"* The precious stones sizzled their eyes, seemed to enjoy belittling the jewelry they had on.

Mitch, with his appearance and attitude, could hardly be mistaken for a sightseer. However, the way he usually walked that block was to some extent similar, the way he was seldom able to resist looking into a few windows.

This day was no exception.

About three-quarters of the way to Fifth his legs insisted he stop before a shop that he knew featured estate jewelry. Quite a few attractive pieces were displayed. Mitch appreciated a pair of chalcedony, black onyx and coral ear pendants, and a pair of ear clips of pavé set yellow diamonds, and a diamond and rock crystal jabot pin.

Then he spotted it, off to the right, recognized it immediately. The cushion-shaped blue sapphire. It greeted him with a flare of its eternal bright blue, and he mentally replied:

Hello, old friend. Where've you been? Haven't seen you around in quite a while. Remember when we first met? Must have been ten, maybe twelve years ago. You didn't have that calibré-cut diamond border then, but I know you. I must say you're looking sharp, none the worse for all you've been through. Bought, stolen, reset, sold at auction, stolen, bought, stolen, and so on. And now, here you are again, back on the street again, being offered again. Nice to see you. Maybe you enjoy being repeatedly bought and being owned and being stolen and coming back here, but it seems to me you'd be better off occupying one lovely finger for a lifetime. It's not your duty, of course, and, anyway, you're not alone in your transientness. Half the goods on the street keep making the cycle. See you around.

Mitch continued on to Fifth and entered the 580 building. He passed through the security checkpoint in the lobby and took an elevator up to the fourteenth floor.

At the far end of the corridor on fourteen was the substantial paneled door to Visconti's office. PARAGON GEMS, INC. gold-leafed on it. The door opened before Mitch was halfway to it.

A man stepped out.

A distinguished-looking man conscientiously dressed in a light gray gabardine vested suit and black and white wing-tipped ox-fords.

Mitch was at a range that permitted a complete look at the man. The swarthy, foreign complexion, the bushy black brows and the dark hair tight to the skull arranged straight back. He was in his mid-fifties or possibly in good shape in his sixties. He had a black-banded creamy panama hat in hand. He paused to put it on, was adjusting it just so as Mitch approached.

The man acknowledged Mitch with a single stranger-to-stranger nod. Mitch returned it. After going a short ways in their opposite directions they caught one another glancing back.

A foreign dealer, Mitch thought, or perhaps one of Visconti's wealthy Italian privates. Not anyone he'd ever seen around the district but certainly someone he'd remember if he ever saw him again.

Mitch entered Visconti's.

The offices had been redone since Mitch was last there about a year ago. The modest-sized reception area impressed. A pair of Louis XVI beechwood armchairs offered as seating on the left were upholstered in pale blue silk damask and were matched identically by another pair on the right. On the wall directly ahead hung a seascape so large and realistic that Mitch's imagination smelled ocean. Situated below the painting was a mahogany bureau plat inset with a blue leather writing surface and bordered by ormolu. Lighting was indirect and kind. The unobtrusive music was Stravinsky.

The surface of the desk was clear except for a dark blue intercom phone, a notepad contained in dark blue leather and a dark blue lacquer and gold DuPont fountain pen. The .44 caliber semiautomatic pistol in the right-hand drawer would probably also be blued, Mitch thought.

Behind the desk sat a young man in his late twenties. Another about the same age was sentried beside the closed door that evidently gave to where business was conducted. They had such mannerly ease and were so comfortably well-dressed they looked as though they were ready to pose for a *GQ* ad. Mitch knew them as two of Visconti's have-arounds and, as such, they typified the polarity of style between Visconti and Riccio.

New mob and old.

Mitch's intention was to elicit Visconti's cooperation at arm's length as he had Riccio's, by leaving a set of the Kalali photographs and a similar cryptic note. However, when he handed over his business card the young man behind the desk immediately got on the phone and announced him, and, before Mitch could say much else, the inner door was opened for him and he felt obliged to go on in.

Visconti's private office was buffered by an interior hallway. The door to it was closed and Mitch was left to open it on his own, a privilege of sorts.

Visconti came around from behind the desk, bringing a handshake and doing a smile that, even after the preliminaries, he didn't turn completely off.

"Nice of you to drop in," he said. "I called you a couple of times."

"I happened to be in the building."

"Great. I was about to have some tea. Have some with me?"

"Thanks."

"There's coffee too if you prefer."

"Tea's fine."

"Earl Grey?"

"Fine."

"I never used to drink the stuff but an English actress I spent some time with down on Mustique got me hooked on it. Maybe you know her." Visconti said her name.

Mitch knew of her, of course. A well-known. He wasn't surprised that she and Visconti had been socially or otherwise close.

"Ever been down there to Mustique?" Visconti asked.

"No."

"Lovely island, very exclusive. I wanted to buy a place down there but the fucks wouldn't sell to me. How do you like that?"

"Their loss," Mitch said liberally.

Visconti didn't resume behind his desk. He sat with Mitch on the visitor's side.

"My reason for phoning," he said, "was to invite you and your wife to my house in Watermill this coming weekend. I'm having a few people to dinner Saturday." He named a fashion designer, and a motion picture director who was in town to promote a major summer film that wasn't doing as well as expected. "You could come out Saturday and stay over."

"I'll have to consult Maddie. Seems to me she had something planned." Mitch's evasion wasn't meant to sound as obvious as the way it came out. He was a little embarrassed. He detected resignation in Visconti's expression.

Visconti eased the moment by calling attention to a painting on the wall to the left, a Jasper Johns flag. "Woman had it," he said. "Actually it was her husband's. When he died recently I traded her something for it."

Which meant to Mitch that Visconti had gotten it for next to nothing, just some swag material he'd paid little for.

The Jasper Johns was slightly awry. Visconti got up to straighten it, giving Mitch an opportunity to update the man.

He was slight-framed and of average height. About the same age as Mitch but looked older because of his high forehead and a hairline that was beginning to recede. He was wearing a white, amply cut silk shirt, triple-pleated cotton slacks tapered at the ankle and a pair of Superga tennis shoes. No socks. No jewelry.

It occurred to Mitch that he didn't really know Visconti as well as he thought. He'd never spent much time with him; there'd never been any discussions over drinks, or for that matter, any lengthy business dealings, just professional brushings every so often. Over the years it was actually their reputations that had mingled and thus, acquaintance was a sort of illusory effect.

On the whole, unless one was able to look close and long, Visconti didn't appear to be what he was. He had the demeanor of a successful, legitimate entrepreneur, someone smartly on top of his game, comfortable in his skin, nervousness never apparent. That was the impression he hoped to achieve. He promoted it, campaigned, ever trying to have the exposed side of him accepted as a sensitive human being with utmost regard for life's higher aspects.

For example, the poster he had hung in his office, better positioned than the Jasper Johns. Anyone entering would have to notice it right off. A large framed poster for a retrospective showing of films by the director Luchino Visconti.

The Leopard, The Damned, Death in Venice.

Furio Visconti claimed the director was an ancestor.

He backed up that claim convincingly with dates and places, fond memories and proved opinions gleaned from the extensive research he'd done. Luchino Visconti, the films and the man, was a topic Furio Visconti would cleverly bring a conversation around to and not allow to be quickly dropped.

Only once or twice was he questioned about the Visconti line that preceded *Uncle Luchino*. Each time he managed to parry and sidestep. He'd read and knew quite a bit about the Viscontis and how prominent they were in Northern Europe during the four-teenth and fifteenth centuries. Were, through the female side, re-lated to such dynasties as the Valois of France, the Hapsburgs of Austria and Spain and the Tudors of England. No, he didn't want to get into all that. It was too much of a better thing, too rich for his blood. And, regarding blood, while the Viscontis were a Mil-anese family, his own was Sicilian. Necessarily so for him to have been at such a young age conferred with the mob's coveted *made* status. His true legal name was Vescotini. His grandparents, like so many others who entered the country around the turn of the cen-tury, had lost the proper spelling to the impatient processing on Ellis Island.

From the various efforts Furio Visconti put out and kept up, it might have been thought he was trying to polish away his capo self. Quite the contrary, he was new mob. He wanted the duality. But if ever he were to be confronted with having to make a choice between sensibility and menace he'd have, without a second thought, opted for the latter. Because he enjoyed it. Just as much as did his old-mob-style counterpart at the other end of the street.

"Tell you what, call your wife now and find out about the weekend. That way, if it's okay with her, I'll be able to look for-ward to it."

Mitch did a glance at his watch. "She'll be in the middle of a lesson."

"What's she taking?"

"Giving. Guitar lessons." Actually this wasn't one of Maddie's les-son days. At that moment, Mitch thought, she was probably putting fresh water in the aviary and feeding her lady finches. He had no intention of mentioning Visconti's invitation to her, knew that if he did she'd want to accept, insist on accepting. Not because of the social amusement or the possibility of an after-dark beach stroll, for some extempory al fresco loving in the lap of a dune. Rather, the allure for her would be the prospect of sitting on a ter-race until long after dinner with Visconti and a couple of his have-arounds, drawing from them recollection of mob escapades, smart moves, big scores, justifiable paybacks, graphic tall tales and short from genuine mob mouths, underscored by wafts of alyssum and the concussion of crickets. She'd love it.

Visconti stepped back to see if he'd corrected the hang of the Jasper Johns. It looked straight to Mitch but Visconti gave the lower right hand corner of its frame a slight tap before he was satisfied. He returned to sit, asking: "Ever play the big casino?" Meaning, of course, the stock market.

"Used to some, not recently."

"Who's your broker?"

"The Bear."

"I get a good thing now and then, a can't-miss thing. Next one I get I'll give to you, as long as you promise it won't go any further. Most guys, when they get something sure can't wait to let others in on it. Like they've got a fucking list of people they want to have owe them. You're not that way though."

"How can you tell?"

"I got a sense about people. You, I want to get to know better. We'd get along."

Mitch thought actually Maddie might not be seeing to her birds at that moment. She'd be making the bed, stretching, tucking, smoothing the sheets and plumping the pillows by spanking them as though they'd been naughty. Before Maddie he'd been a one-pillow sort and more often than not that one ended up tossed to the floor during the night. She'd turned him into a steadfast, multi-pillow man. The head of their bed was piled with as many as eight European squares filled with finest goose down and cased in high-count shams. Each night he and Maddie sunk together. He sometimes wondered how it felt to her in her black, that soft, sinking escape. He'd closed his eyes to help him imagine but he was sure it wasn't the same.

"I've something I want to show you," Mitch told Visconti. He reached for his folio to take out a set of the Kalali photographs.

But just then the tea came.

It wasn't just tea, not just in mugs as Mitch had expected. One of Visconti's young have-arounds wearing a fresh white waiter's jacket brought it. On a huge silver tray, ivory handles. The matching silver service was of art deco design, unusually refined with hardly any surface decoration.

Mitch recognized the pieces as creations of Jean Puiforcat, believed by many to be the foremost French silversmith of the twenties and thirties. Worth plenty, Mitch thought, and wasn't it miraculous that the swift who'd stolen the tray and tea set hadn't banged them up? Usually such things were carelessly thrown into a knotted sheet where, in the lugging and all, they traded dents.

Also on the tray were several doileyed dishes precisely arranged with Sarah Bernhardts and cat's tongues and madeleinettes and a variety of crustless half-slice sandwiches. Altogether quite a load that the have-around, as physically well-conditioned as he appeared, was relieved to place down on the low table between Visconti and Mitch.

"I'll take it from here," Visconti said, dismissing the have-around. He lifted the lid from the tea pot, peeked in, sniffed, before pouring into the two elaborately hand-painted bone china cups. "Sugar?" he asked.

Mitch didn't have time to reply.

"You shouldn't, you know. Sugar is bad for the prostate, and . . ." he grinned conspiratorially, ". . . the last thing we want to go is the prostate."

"I prefer honey."

"There isn't any."

"Plain is fine."

They slurped. Mitch felt the rim of the cup click against his lower front teeth. Visconti seemed pleased to have company. Did he go to such elegant ritual when alone? Mitch wondered. It was certainly a far cry from Riccio's dirty espresso cups and stainless steel spoons.

"What was it you were about to show me?" Visconti asked.

Mitch handed him the gray envelope.

Visconti slid the photographs from it. He looked through them, giving each a moment but coming back for a second, longer look at the two inscribed emeralds. "So?" he said.

Mitch told him what the photographs were, how these pieces of jewelry had been stolen three nights ago, that one of the owners had been killed during the robbery. It seemed to Mitch that Visconti only half listened.

"What do you want me to say?" Visconti asked.

"Nothing if these pieces have already found their way to you."

"There's blood on the fucking stuff. I wouldn't touch it."

Mitch doubted that was a line Visconti had ever drawn. He got Visconti eyes to eyes for a long moment. The man wasn't easy to read. He was adept at hiding whatever he chose behind whatever he chose to reveal in his eyes and facial expression. Only when he allowed were his eyes and mouth in accord, so a person seldom knew which to go by.

Mitch decided to believe him in this Kalali matter. "All I ask is if these pieces come in or get offered you let me know."

"Why?"

"Only so I don't waste time trying to recover."

"That's it?"

"That's it."

"I got no problem with that. I'm not saying I'll call you up and tell you straight out but I'll let you know some way."

"However."

Mitch went for a couple of the madeleinettes. They were dusted with powdered sugar. He was sure his prostate could handle it.

"One condition, though," Visconti said.

"What?"

"If and when *you* recover the stuff you let *me* know." Visconti didn't give Mitch a chance to ask why. He stood abruptly. "Now I've got something to show you," he said and left the room.

Mitch poured more tea and had one of the Sarah Bernhardts and then two more by the time Visconti returned. Bringing a protective black flannel pouch drawn and tied by a scarlet grosgrain ribbon.

Visconti handed the pouch to Mitch, who gathered that he was expected to open it and that it contained something valuable.

Which turned out to be a *bonbonnière* or what was called a *boîte à bonbon* back in the 1700s. This particular one was circular, about three inches in diameter and an inch deep. It was finished in translucent pink mounted in borders of finely chased gold. The circumference of its lid was embellished with a row of old-cut diamonds. Such little boxes were used to hold dragées for sweetening the breath back then when most breaths were so badly in need of sweetening.

Mitch appreciated it, ran a finger delicately over the diamonds and pressed the one located at six o'clock. The hinged lid sprung open. Nothing inside.

"Lovely," Mitch managed to say, hearing his voice as though it originated outside himself.

Visconti waited for more. When he realized that was all the reaction he was going to get, he told Mitch: "Don't ask me. It's natural you'd want to know but don't ask. All I can tell you is it came in week before last and evidently the same guy, anyway the guy's daughter, has had it all the while."

Mitch did a shrug.

He clicked the *bonbonnière* shut and put it back into the pouch. Placed the pouch on the table. "I've got to get going," he said. "Can I assume we have an understanding on the Kalali material?"

"Yeah, sure. What's Kalali anyway? Sounds East Indian."

"Iranian."

"They've got a hard-on for us, the Iranians."

"Some do."

"Let me know about the weekend." Visconti did a goodbye smile. No handshake. They'd already done that and once a day was sufficient.

Mitch saw himself out, through the reception area with the eyes of the have-arounds on his back. He was about ten strides down the corridor when Visconti hurried out to catch up with him.

"I suppose you're aware of what your brother's into," Visconti said.

An immediate, purely reflex nod from Mitch. "Andy and I never keep anything from one another."

"I thought that's how it was but I wasn't sure so I didn't mention it."

"I wondered if you'd bring it up," Mitch said, fishing.

"But why Riccio," Visconti exaggerated slightly. "If he was going to run an errand, why not for me? Riccio's no friend."

"Andy's decision," Mitch said while thinking the long-shot wish that it wasn't true, that it was only something Visconti had heard.

The street was like that.

Along with its held tongue there was always a lot of bad-mouthing.

Chapter 9

The first pay phone Mitch tried digested his quarter but didn't give him a dial tone. On the next he and secretary Shirley could hardly hear one another.

"Where are you?" she asked.

He told her. He'd made it as far as the lobby of his building and almost into an elevator.

"You don't sound like you," she said, "not at all well."

"I'm okay."

"Perhaps, but you don't sound it."

"What's happening?"

"Just Ruder."

"So, close up."

"I've some filing and a couple of letters you think I've already done."

"Take off. Go somewhere and lay away something."

"I might. You've probably got a touch of the summer flu. Do your bones ache?"

"I'm going home," he told her, and within the minute he was outside heading up Fifth, dragging. He would, he thought, go straight home, get way up there in the Sherry with Maddie and forget there was a down here.

However, when he got to 50th and St. Patrick's he went in, and it seemed that radical change of atmosphere would be a palliative for his condition with its meek light, votive candles jigging, serious prayers barraging the altar with supplications.

He sat in the very last pew, distant enough from everyone and practically hidden by a fat pillar.

To take it on.

All at once rather than have it eat at him a bite at a time.

He gazed down at his hands. They were empty, relaxed on his thighs, but felt as though they were still holding the past.

That *bonbonnière.*

Twenty years ago it was among the estate pieces his father, Kenneth Laughton, brought back from a buying trip to London. At first sight Mitch had been attracted to the box and, when his father tagged it and placed it along with other merchandise in one of the store's display cases, he'd boyishly put a hex on it that he hoped would prevent it from being sold. At the same time he created a romantic story for the box, caring to believe it had early on belonged to a woman of nobility, a woman whose beauty and exceptional taste excused her numerous carnal caprices.

Mitch's attachment to the *bonbonnière* was not unnoticed by his father. Hardly a day passed that Mitch didn't wipe possible finger smudges and motes of dust from its pink and gold exterior, and press the six o'clock diamond on its lid to have it spring open, as though providing it with the exercise it required to keep agile.

His father understood.

Hadn't he at one time or another experienced the same sort of fondness for a thing so pretty?

Mitch expected any day the *bonbonnière* would be sold. He was prepared to accept that event, but weeks went by and it didn't sell and he noticed its coded price tag had been removed and he overheard his father inform a customer that it wasn't for sale.

Thereafter the *bonbonnière* was spoken of as Mitch's box. It hadn't ever been formally presented to him, was only possession understood, but it was his. He kept Läkerol lemon mint pastilles in it. Right up to the last.

It was about that time that Kenneth Laughton made the move of his dreams. From on Lexington in the fifties to on Madison in the sixties. A corner location. What's more, the oblong shape of the space and the relatively intimate size of it, only four hundred square feet, lent itself nicely to being made elegant.

K. Laughton and Sons.

Within a few months the business had established its cachet. No ordinary run-of-the-mill manufactured merchandise; it carried only estate jewelry and only the finer level of that.

Nearly every piece Laughton's offered came with an interesting or colorful or notorious past. Much more appealing was a one-of-a-kind diamond choker that had known the neck of a one-of-a-kind demimonde, pieces of another age in their original fitted cases that had been the conciliatory gifts to the wives of caught-straying robber barons, pieces from the not so long ago when the daughters of scions were marrying for titles and diamond tiaras and crotch-length strands of pearls were *de rigueur*.

The precious bijouterie of snooty English ladies and stars of the silent screen and Ziegfield show-offs who'd worn little or nothing else—could be found at Laughton's.

There was, of course, only a limited supply of such finer jewelry. Kenneth Laughton had to seek it out. He went on what he called hunting trips, sometimes accompanied by Mitch or Andy or both, to Geneva, St. Moritz, Milan, Monaco and other likely places. He and his sons were also prominent at the Sotheby and the Christie auctions. They'd be pointed out and when a particular piece was knocked down to them that usually verified its value. "Laughton got it," people would whisper and make that notation in their sales catalogues.

Often lovely pieces came to the store, brought by misfortunates embarrassed by the need to sell but rightly under the impression Laughton's would not take advantage of their plight.

A pair of Winston ear clips for instance.

"Why certainly Mrs. Whoever, we'll clean them for you."

"That's most kind of you."

"No bother, no bother at all. It will take only a few minutes."

"While we're at it, I was wondering, could you give me an idea of what they're worth? To you, I mean."

Others, whose fortunes had ascended, brought in pieces wanting to trade or leave on consignment. In fact, much of the Laughton stock was left by owners to be sold.

"Why in the world would you want to part with such a lovely bracelet. It's Van Cleef you know."

"I never wear it. It's a hand-me-down from my bitch-from-hell aunt. Anyway, I'm bored with it."

Many of those were frail, spindly-looking, overdieted women with scalpeled features, addicted to self-indulgence.

Mitch had learned to recognize their requirements. He knew how to wait on them. For one thing they didn't want him to be too well-mannered. Nor did they ever want to be called ma'am. At times he found them amusing, forgivable, and more often than not, his good nature was sincere.

All in all, Laughton and Sons was doing well, and there seemed to be no reason why it wouldn't continue to do so.

Came then the bitter cold morning, a Monday in February. The events of that day had had such a long run on the stage of Mitch's memory that he knew their every word and nuance.

To begin with, at about nine-thirty, a half hour before opening, Harvey Miner phones, to say his wife has fallen on the icy sidewalk. She has fractured her hip and he's at the hospital with her and won't be in until noon or one. Sorry.

Miner sounds unlike his usual laconic self, stressed, but considering his circumstances that's understandable.

Miner is the armed security man for the store, has been for several years. A retired cop of formidable height and bulk, intimidating even when he smiles. Normally, during business hours, Miner stands inside the entrance, from where he can watch over what's going on in the store and, as well, scrutinize and pass on those who wish to come in.

The entrance is arranged to prevent anyone from just walking in off the street. There's an outer and an inner door, both of thick glass heavily framed: and between the two is a vestibule that will accommodate no more than three persons at a time. The bolt of the inner door is electrically controlled. A button to activate the bolt and click it open is located inside within easy reach of where Miner stands. A second such button is located on the underside of the main display counter.

So, Miner won't be in until later and that's not important because its doubtful there'll be anyone out spending on this kind of day. It's punishingly cold. No sun and twenty degrees below freezing. The sidewalks and buildings along Madison appear brittle and depressed. There's no fast traffic to speak of and the cars and buses stopping and continuing along are coated dull with winter chemicals, their underneaths crusted with frozen muddy slush.

Still, like most other shops along the avenue, Laughton's is making ready. It is routine, the transferring of merchandise from the vault to the display cases and windows. Mitch and Andy and Kenneth pitch in and by regular opening time at ten the task is done.

At ten-thirty it's a welcome surprise when a customer comes from the street into the vestibule. A woman. Her impatience is apparent. It's as though she fears that if she's not immediately allowed in, the cold, like a monster, will catch up with her and consume her. And it is that impression, along with her qualifying well-off appearance, that prompts Andy to hastily click open the inner door.

Then she is in, standing there in calf-length sable, hunkered down, her head surrounded, nearly buried by the collar of the abundant fur.

"Damn cold!" are her first words.

She does a shiver, then sits and removes her expensive shoes. She rubs her feet vigorously to warm them. In front of strangers a self-confident, assertive act. She owns the world.

Through her sheer stockings Mitch sees the snug, enforced arrangement of her toes. Her toenails. Its seems too intimate. Her reddened nose and cheeks look as though they've been sharply pinched.

She's quite beautiful, Mitch thinks, anyway, a lot more attractive than most. Her hair and ears are contained by a black, wrapped turban which is pinned by an art deco period diamond, ruby and onyx jabot. A nice piece that Mitch's expertise makes out to be an authentic La Cloche Frères.

Also, she has on dark brown kid skin gloves. Outside the gloves on the second finger of her right hand is a large ring studded with various colored sapphires. Mitch appreciates that show of independent style.

A gasp from her, and another shiver. "I only walked over from Park," she says plaintively, "and I'm frozen to the marrow. One has to be mad to be about on such a day."

It's difficult to feel sorry for her, Mitch thinks, this lovely, privileged woman, temporarily uncomfortable. Her manner of speech is throaty, contains broad vowels with diphthongs here and there. An affectation that has probably become a habit. Mitch would never forget her voice. Later on, in one public place or another, he would hear a similar voice and be disappointed when he saw it wasn't her.

Kenneth asks her would she care for some coffee.

No thank you.

Kenneth suggests a glass of port.

She tells him archly that it depends on the port.

A twenty-year-old vintage finest reserve W. & J. Graham is presented, approved with an *mmmm* and poured into two finely etched claret glasses. Two because Kenneth won't allow her to drink alone.

In three uninterrupted swallows the port is down inside her and she is saying "Ah, that'll do the trick. May I have another?"

Kenneth obliges and that second portion limbers her. She ceases hugging herself. She slips back into her shoes and allows the sable to fall open enough to reveal a good, ample sling bag. The dress she has on is expensive but rather overstated, inappropriate for a winter Monday morning. Mitch thinks she should know better and must have her reason.

A paragraphic moment.

"What can we do for you?" Kenneth inquires.

"For one thing," she replies lightheartedly, "let my husband in. After all, he'll be paying the bill."

There's a man in the vestibule. Dressed in black. Well-tailored double-breasted topcoat, leather gloves, small-figured silk scarf.

Kenneth clicks the inner door open.

The woman calls the man Charles. He looks to be somewhere in his fifties. He gives her a brief hug and apologizes for being late. "Have you been waiting long?"

"Yes," she lies.

"I would have been on time but there was a call from Rome."

She forgives him with a smile and a slight shrug.

Mitch notices the man has a powdered face, aftershave powder that is a bit light for his complexion. Also, his shoes aren't up to the rest of his attire. They're round-toed, thick-soled, made to last ten or even twenty years with visits to a cobbler. Policeman shoes or those of a train conductor. Perhaps he has a foot problem, Mitch thinks.

Kenneth offers the man coffee or port.

The man declines with a gesture and asks the woman: "Have you chosen anything?"

She tells him she hasn't and he removes a pair of gold wire-rimmed eyeglasses from an inside pocket, puts them on and begins considering the pieces on display in the wall cases.

The woman, meanwhile, gives her attention to the main counter. She peers down through the glass surface to the items arranged just so. So many beautiful pieces. A diamond and ruby *sautoir* catches her eye and refuses to let go.

Kenneth is quick to realize her interest. He removes the necklace from the case and places it upon a cushiony square of black velour on the counter. "Exquisite, isn't it?" he says almost objectively.

She takes up the necklace, holds it up, enjoys examining it.

Kenneth pitches gently, informs that it once belonged to an heiress who, in her time, had been—how shall he put it?—a very free-spirited debutante.

A knowing grin from the woman. "I must have it," she exclaims.

It happens swiftly.

She drops the necklace into her sling bag. Her hand follows it in and comes out with the pistol. It has a silencer on it.

At once the man admits two other men. They go at it, methodically emptying the windows and the display cases, throwing piece after piece into Bergdorf Goodman shopping bags.

Mitch has never seen valuable jewels treated so harshly. He wants to tell the men to be more respectful.

The woman has moved to the open end of the main counter where she has a sure view of Kenneth, Andy and Mitch. The pistol she holds on them is barely visible, only the lethal tip of the silencer protrudes from the wide sleeve of her sable coat. Her expression has changed little. She's not apparently nervous and, although that's reassuring, better than having her jittery and overheated, Mitch believes it's best not to move.

There's an alarm button inset in the floor beneath the counter. Kenneth is making a try for it, inching his foot toward it. The woman seems unaware. The alarm is the silent sort, connected directly to the Nineteenth Precinct.

No warning from the woman.

She shoots Kenneth in the foot, the instep. It's almost as though the pistol has done it robotically, altered its aim, fired with absolute accuracy.

Pain clogs Kenneth's breath. What comes from him is a short guttural bleat. He slumps to the floor.

Mitch is surging with fury. There's an automatic pistol in the drawer to his left but his better judgment tells him he'd never get to it, his better judgment reminds him that he has always believed it would be best to not resist an armed robbery, that no amount of jewels would be worth dying for.

He and Andy and Kenneth are ordered into the vault, made to lie on the floor among the emptied vault drawers and trays and cartons. They're bound with their neckties and belts. Positioned as they are, right there before Mitch's eyes is the blood oozing from the tongue of his father's shoe.

He hears the robbers going. They are gone. Everything is gone.

The loss comes to twelve million. It seems an inordinate amount but the Laughton books prove it. About seven of the twelve is the value of goods that were Laughton-owned. The remaining five is the value of pieces that had been left on consignment.

There's insurance. A policy that all along promised complete coverage. For all its years Laughton's has paid the pricey premiums to Columbia Beneficial. However, now that there's been a loss, and such a large one, Columbia Beneficial says there are considerations.

A term in the fine print, not ambiguous or vague; it's right there, clearly a stipulation of the policy.

Keith Ruder, the Columbia Beneficial representative who handles the claim, is insincerely sorry to point it out.

In so many words what the term says is that security measures must include an armed guard inside the store during all business hours.

Which, of course, had not been the case.

No matter that Harvey Miner, the Laughton guard, had been under mortal pressure—a pistol held to the back of his head—that morning when he called in and recited the lie of his wife's injury.

Ruder seems to take personal pleasure in having found the loophole for Columbia Beneficial. Smugly, he says the extenuating circumstances make no difference. He refuses to budge from that stand, doesn't until Kenneth Laughton's lawyers get into it. Then Ruder budges only some.

The settlement.

Columbia Beneficial agrees to pay out six million. Kenneth must absorb the rest of the loss.

Five of the six million that comes from Columbia goes at once to make good on the jewelry Laughton's had on consignment. From what remains of the six Kenneth buys out of his long-term lease and pays his legal bills.

There's relatively little left. Not enough for Kenneth to start over. Besides, he's as empty as the store, can't stop grieving over all those precious pieces of jewelry, lovely tasteful pieces that he'd so carefully acquired, being put to death, so to speak, their gems extracted, their fine mountings sacrificed to some smelter's crucible.

He retreats, moves to the west coast of Florida, lives in a modest condo, sits in the sun, watches the sea, walks with a limp. He has a collection of canes, most of which Mitch and Maddie or Andy send him. His favorite and one most used is a nineteenth-century black-

thorn from the West of Ireland. Another that he treasures once belonged to Lord Byron.

A tinny clunk imposed on Mitch's self-communion. Then several more of the same.

Coins were being dropped through the slot of the brass poor box
situated a short distance from where Mitch sat in the most rear pew
of St. Patrick's.

He felt much better, in a way exorcised. The aftereffect of the
bonbonnière was gone from his hands and the performance for his
past that it produced on the stage of his memory was over, at least
for the time being, without so much as a curtain call.

Perhaps Visconti would sell him the *bonbonnière,* he thought, but
then maybe it wouldn't be good to have around. No. Leave bad
enough alone.

Off to his right where the pew ended at the main aisle Mitch
noticed the comers and goers doing genuflects that were actually
only slight bobs in the direction of the distant altar.

Ask for the moon but don't bruise a knee.

Chapter 10

The elevator attendant wasn't fazed by what he'd been hearing from the thirtieth floor on up. He was a New York serving sort with acquired terminal apathy, and if Mrs. Laughton was playing music so loud it went through the Sherry's thick interior structures like a sonic ray, he didn't care to know why.

Mitch, on the other hand, tried to imagine what Maddie might be up to this time. He recognized the music but didn't know the name of the piece ("Pena Penita"). It was a fast one by the Gipsy Kings.

Maddie played the Gipsy Kings frequently, but not like this, not at such a decibel that it caused Mitch's latchkey to veritably vibrate when he inserted it to let himself into the foyer of the apartment. Where the Gipsy Kings and their seven guitars were louder yet.

Usually, when Mitch arrived home, along with his first step inside he'd call out to Maddie, her name. Often she beat him to it, would call out to him to let him know which of the apartment's five rooms she happened to be in.

Mitch liked when that happened. It was evidence that her waiting for him hadn't been an ordinary wait but more a yearning honed and dilated with impatience.

There'd be none of that today, though. Not even a full-out

scream would do. He went down the connecting hallway, glanced into the kitchen on the chance that Maddie might be using the music for frame of mind while having a try at some complicated, loudly spiced Spanish recipe.

But no, nothing cooking.

On to the living room, the Persian carpets there were rolled up and the chairs and tables were moved aside, creating an expanse of hardwood floor. The same in the adjoining study.

Maddie was in the study, standing between the stereo speakers. At point-blank range of their blast. She had one foot up on the seat of a side chair. The most she was wearing was her favorite Spanish guitar, slung by a woven strap around her neck. Otherwise only sunglasses with mirrored lenses and a pair of black patent pumps with klutzy heels.

The double French doors that gave to the terrace were wide open. The white skin and the windows of the upper reaches of the General Motors Building were like a backdrop closer than across 59th Street. A rhomboidal shape of sunlight was striking the floor, barely missing Maddie's bareness.

Her aviary, situated against the wall opposite the balcony, was also open. All her beloved finches were out and around. Some were making passes at her, attention-seeking swoops and dives, fluttering her forehead and shoulders. Bishop Weaver finches from Sudan, orange and black and brown. Twinspot finches from southern Ethiopia, brilliant green and polka-dotted. Several exact look-alikes were in a row on the top edge of the draperies, an audience in the cheap seats.

Mitch was certain Maddie had no idea that he was there across the room from her. She was completely caught up in keeping up with the Gipsy Kings, the fingers of her left hand scurrying up and down the neck of the guitar, working the frets, the fingers of her right raking the strings with such swift force it seemed she was in-flicting punishment.

This afternoon interval was obviously meant to be Maddie's alone. Mitch felt the intruder; however, he rationalized, wouldn't it be wrong to interrupt, make his presence known? Either he should leave, return to street level and perhaps go to a Central Park bench, buy one of those bags of overpriced peanuts and shell away some time or, the other option, remain undisclosed where he was, play the peeper, the adoring thief.

Watching her. From the start of them it had been a pleasant diversion for him. By now it had become a need. The extent that he indulged in it was, of course, made possible by her sightlessness.

He thought of it as stealing, but had long ago exonerated himself. How privileged he was to be able to steal like that, to witness so much of her physical privacy, unlike most others to never be deprived by self-consciousness or shame. The thing about it that bothered him, though, was its one-sidedness. Many times he thought the wish that he and Maddie could exchange circumstances for a while, let her have the advantage of seeing him without being seen. To have her steal and steal, learn his most intimate and private self and still want and love him, would, he thought, even them up perfectly.

He removed his suit jacket, tossed it and his folio onto the nearest displaced chair. He admitted to himself that not for a moment had he really considered Central Park over this. He slipped his tie loose, unbuttoned his collar and cuffs. Arms crossed, nonchalantly leaning against the jamb of the connecting wide archway, he gave in totally to being the compulsive spectator.

Look at her, just look at her, he thought, what a remarkable love she was. He wouldn't have her be any less unpredictable. He fed, thrived on her eccentricities.

The music didn't seem so loud now. With her as she was in his eyes the complaint of his ears was being ignored. The rhomboid of sunlight was creeping up on her, had overtaken a lower leg. She stopped playing, raised the guitar in order to get at a place to the left of her navel. Three scratches there and she went on playing, picked right up with the tempo and chords.

A pair of lady finches, evidently overcome by the need to be more involved, flitted from somewhere in the room to light upon the upper end of the guitar. They weighed next to nothing, so they weren't a bother. They improved their grasp, settled and hung on through the various bobbing and dipping motions caused by Maddie's playing. Just as they would had they been perched precariously on a bough in an erratic breeze. Tiny participants, they weren't startled enough to fly off even when in Gypsy flamenco style she thumped and drummed on the guitar's soundboard. They took the ride all the way to the vocal.

One of the Gipsy Kings sang it. He got a head start and Maddie had a devil of a time catching up. The lyrics were too rapid and run together for her just passable Spanish. No matter, in this kind of singing the meanings of the words weren't as important as the wail with which they were supposed to be coated. An effect accomplished by creating a stricture at the outlet of the throat in order to more emphatically convey the excruciating possibilities of love: love cruel or prohibited, misunderstood or, for any of the countless reasons, tortured.

The requirement of flamenco singing to be somewhere off the notes and seldom on them suited Maddie. She had a dreadful singing voice, couldn't even carry "White Christmas." It was as though she couldn't hear herself. When she went around attempting Broadway numbers for example, such as something from *Phantom of the Opera* or *Evita,* Mitch would wince and look sick. "Don't cry for me Argentina . . ." Ughh. He was thankful that no words had been set to Ravel's "Daphnis and Chloé," although there was Maddie's humming, which also had the disease.

Now well into her flamenco duet, faking it, keeping a partial beat behind so she could imitate, she got reckless, missed one of the higher notes so badly that she kept veering with it and was unable to recover.

She segued into a laugh.

Broke herself up.

She took off the guitar and set it aside. Mitch thought that next she'd switch off the stereo.

She stepped forward onto the bare floor. The bright rhomboid was like an inaccurately aimed spotlight catching the lower half of her. She raised her arms above her head, straight up and stiffly like a gesture of surrender, then relaxed them a bit and formed them into an arch, the wrists gracefully rounded, the fingers close to touching. She tensed her buttocks, tucked them, causing a thrust to her pelvis. Raised her chin, put stretch into her neck, turned her head a quarter turn so her point of view was away, over that elevated shoulder. All her weight was on her left foot.

What sort of posturing was this? Mitch asked the situation. Did she have in mind some sort of yoga exercise?

She snapped her fingers like castanets and began.

First, a single stomp with her free foot, the substantial heel of her shoe brought down with such force it was like the report of a shot.

It was now obvious why the carpets were rolled out of the way.

Maddie tattooed the bare, hardwood floor with her heels, did a rapid-fire series of flamenco stomping with both feet.

What came to Mitch's mind was the demonstrative protests of a spoiled child who hadn't gotten her way; however the incongruity of that association was at once made apparent by Maddie's mature figure, the way her movements were causing her fully formed breasts to respond, the triangular forest of fair floss at her intersection.

Now she went into long, dipping strides, an exaggerated, haughty prance and some swirls. Punctuated with exclamation points of stomping.

Where and when had she learned this? Mitch wondered. She was no María Benítez but obviously this wasn't her first go at it. The people who lived in the apartment below had never complained. As far as he knew.

Fists on hips, elbows out, she flamencoed past him and on into the living room. Typically, her attitude shifted from aloof to defiant to sensually promising. She knew the apartment by steps, its dimensions, so there were no collisions (another of her enemies, collision), only near misses. Even though Mitch doubted she was entirely there. With make-believe overlaid upon her blackness, something that was ordinarily easy for her, made easy by the blackness, she was probably somewhere in Spain. Seville perhaps. Being a Carmen.

On her way back from the living room she paused to flamenco in place a short ways from him. Facing him, she came closer, and even closer and did five sharp stomps that seemed to Mitch to be expressions of reprimand. He saw himself in her mirrored lenses. Their convexity distorted him, gave him a big, lopsided nose.

Maddie snapped her head back dismissively and spun away, holding the imaginary hems of imaginary flouncing petticoats.

The music ended.

The Gipsy Kings were gone.

The apartment had been so full of sound it now felt vacant.

Mitch, the spectator, was stuck in place by the sudden quiet. It wouldn't take Maddie long to detect him, he knew. She had collapsed over the fat arm of a sofa chair down into its lap. Was breathing hard. Should he speak up, pretend he'd arrived that moment, hadn't witnessed any of her performance? He'd merely inquire about the furniture being out of place, the carpets, and accept any fib she offered.

He'd do better than that.

He silently removed his shoes and stocking-footed it out to the foyer. There he put his shoes back on and, imitating his usual arrival, opened the entrance door noisily. Called out to Maddie. Slammed the door shut.

"In here!" he heard her shout, which reassured him that his ruse had worked. On the way to her he exaggerated the sound of his walk on the bare floor, his own flamenco. For some reason he felt a flush of well-being and realized it probably should be attributed to the stealing he'd done, his brain having processed it and triggered some neurotransmitters. Overanxious endorphins, no doubt. He'd gotten about a two-thirds erection while stealing Maddie, which, he had to admit, was rather gluttonous considering how erotically sated he'd been with her little more than a dozen hours ago.

She was still in the sofa chair, knifed cross-wise, legs over one of its arms, head resting upon its other. She was perspiring. Her hair was damp and stringy. Her mouth let it be known that it expected a hello kiss.

Mitch delivered it. An upside-down kiss, noses to chins, brief, not so brief that she didn't get in a single dart of her tongue.

What a rascal she is, Mitch thought. He was such a fortunate lover.

"Home early," she said.

"Rearranging the furniture?" he asked.

She didn't reply.

"Felicia's been helping you, I hope." The live-out housekeeper.

Mitch still didn't get the fib.

"Warm in here," he said after watching a rivulet of perspiration run from her collarbone to an aureole.

"The air conditioning is on," she said.

"Won't do any good with the terrace doors open. Besides, aren't you afraid your finches might fly out?"

"They wouldn't. They'd never betray me." The birds had returned to the aviary, were chattering, sounded as though they might be commenting on the merits of the Maddie performance and having an after-show bite.

Mitch went to close the terrace doors. He caught a glimpse of office workers gathered at some of the windows of the fluorescent-lighted spaces across the way. Gapers, voyeurs. What were they expecting, an encore? He was tempted to flip them off. Instead, he decided what had been had been and just closed up.

Maddie was gone into the bedroom.

Mitch put together a vodka and tonic and took a couple of gulps before attending to the carpets and furniture. He got everything back in position by the time Maddie returned.

She'd showered. Was now in a long, pale silk kimono tied by a sash fringed on its ends. Mules of a matching shade with a pouf of Maribou on their insteps. She went directly to the sofa, as though knowing it was back in its familiar place. Sat and crossed her legs. The silk poured expensively around her.

"I'm having a drink," Mitch said, "want one?"

"Just a Perrier, thanks, and, as Mother Elise would put it, *avec glace.*"

While Mitch decapped the Perrier and poured he thought the wish that there was some way of obliterating Elise from Maddie's

mind, cauterize her, at least stick her in some way out of the way
sepulchral niche.

Maddie chug-a-lugged the Perrier and chewed on the ice. "I'm
too fair-haired for a convincing flamenco," she said.

"Huh?"

"A black wig might help but I'd still otherwise be blonde. Unless, of course, I wore a merkin and that would be a mess and a
bother. Anyway, you didn't seem to think much of my dancing."

Mitch tried to choose what he should say. Her teeth crunching
ice didn't help.

"You didn't applaud or anything, not even a bravo," she said.

"How did you know I was watching?"

"I sensed you were."

"Don't give me that."

"I always know."

"Come on."

"Okay, I usually know."

A dubious grunt from Mitch.

"Sometimes I know," she admitted in a tone that implied rock
bottom.

"Okay, where was I standing?"

She told him precisely. "I got a whiff of you when I went by and
on the way back I zeroed in."

"You have an uncanny sniffer."

"At times it can be less than a blessing," she said. "Like this morning in the reception at Ronald's office. As you know it's not all that
large, and a man waiting there smelled as though he hadn't been
able to wait . . . more than once. Phew." Ronald Albertson was her
attorney, an earnest fellow, who looked after the interests of the
Strawbridge family.

"So you went out this morning."

"Had to sign things."

"Couldn't they have been messengered to you?"

"I wanted to go out."

Mitch assumed her business with Ronald involved contributions
she was making to her causes such as the United Nations Children's

Fund and the World Wildlife Fund and AIDS research. She gave on a regular basis to these, and to numerous others when they appealed to her. It then occurred to Mitch that the Elise fund had made a pitch for a new apartment in Barcelona and decided that had probably been Maddie's business at Ronald's. What would happen, Mitch wondered, if she turned Elise down and instead gave to preserving the population of the Louisiana black bear?

"What was it with all that sneaking?" Maddie asked.

"Sneaking?"

"The way you snuck out to the foyer and slammed the door and all that?"

He was cornered.

"What a loony way to act."

"You should talk."

"Me? I'm unceasingly sane."

"I left my folio out on the landing," he fibbed.

She crunched more ice rather menacingly and then let him get away with it, did about a seventy-five percent version of her best smile; anyway enough of it to cause nice commas at the corners of her mouth. "I love you, precious," she declared unequivocally.

"Love you too," he said on the way over to her. They kissed a fairly lengthy one and held on after it. She told his ear: "I bought something for you today."

From her kimono pocket she brought out a small, leather-covered jeweler's box, gold-embossed and worn at its edges.

Fitted within the box's creamy velour interior was a pair of cuff links. They were Edwardian, guilloche green enamel and gold centered with rubies and diamonds. Even before taking them up Mitch believed they were Fabergé. And yes, there was the hallmark in Cyrillic on the underside of each line: **ФАѢЕРЖЕ** along with **Я.А.**, the initials of the work master Hjalmar Armfelt. "The man at the shop said they're the real thing."

"They are."

"He said people used to make Fabergé imitations and some still do."

"Yeah."

"He also said these had once belonged to Cary Grant, that they were a gift from Barbara Hutton when Grant married her in 1943. Believe that?"

Colorful provenance. Shades of the days of Laughton and Sons, Mitch thought. The cuff links must have set Maddie back at least twenty-five thousand. He took another admiring look at them before placing them back in their velour bed. "You shouldn't have," he said.

"Well, I have."

"Whoever you bought them from will take them back."

"No returns. He made a point of it. I'll bet it even says so on the sales receipt."

"How did you pay for them?"

"By check."

"Just stop it."

"No, you stop it. I know you like the cuff links. I heard your breath do a little catch right after I heard the box snap open."

"Not true."

"I listened for it."

"Whether I like them or not doesn't matter. The fact is you're way over your quota."

"It's a silly arrangement."

"It's what we agreed on."

"You bullied me into agreeing."

"I've never bullied you. Frankly I doubt anyone ever could."

"Okay, I'll put it another way; you suckered me into it. I was led to believe you'd eventually come around to seeing it differently."

Setting a quota had seemed to Mitch to be a solution. Until then Maddie had squandered money on him. Hardly a week passed that she didn't buy him something extravagant, something he himself couldn't so easily afford:

A thirty-four-thousand Gerald Genta perpetual calendar watch, a six-piece set of Hermès luggage (the overnight bag alone cost four thousand), ten suits in a range of fine worsteds and gabardines by the leading tailor in Milan (she sent his favorite-fitting one as a model and, for the while it was away, fibbed that it was misplaced at the dry cleaners), a Watteau sketch of a nude adolescent girl done in black and sienna charcoal which she hung to the left of his side of the bathroom vanity. For morning and evening inspiration, she said.

That was not to mention the less-costly things she splurged on, that she shrugged off as mere fripperies. Solid-gold Bulgari comb, Bucellati letter opener, Cartier lacquered fountain pens (everyone should have a spare) and so on. Necessary unnecessaries: antique English paperweight from Shrubsole, box of silver dominoes from Asprey, lots of things from Asprey.

Mitch enjoyed being the recipient of such largesse. Who wouldn't? However, for the sake of his male stuff, the health of that gender-conscious part of him that couldn't be merely a stand-in for the role of provider, he had to put a stop to it.

Maddie reasoned: What difference did it make whose money was spent? Why not just blend his lesser amount with her greater and let it be theirs? Sure, have Ronald put hers and his into a sort of financial blender and press the frappé button. Besides, giving to the one she loved as well as those who needed was a major pleasure for her. Would he deprive her of it?

Her contention was sensible. And comfortable for her. Her nature was to be generous. After the robbery of the Laughton store she'd offered Kenneth whatever it would take to restock and restart. Kenneth appreciated her willingness to help but couldn't see any direction other than out.

At various other times she'd also proposed putting up the money for an upscale store for Mitch. They'd be strolling upper Madison and come upon frontage space for lease and she'd ask his opinion on whether or not it would be a good location.

She'd slip in the topic during their pillow talks. Her insight told her that having such a store was his latent ambition. He never said it was something he craved. However he did contribute to visualizing a store with her, enjoyed doing so, often got carried away with that and allowed his enthusiasm to turn him inside out.

It had happened recently. Realizing how exposed he was at that moment she'd taken a shot. "We should stop talking about it and do it," she said.

Nothing from him.

"You deserve to be well-known for your taste in jewelry and all you know about it."

"Yeah." His enthusiasm having retreated.

She'd gotten exasperated. "What is it with you? Are you afraid people will point you out as a bounder who lives off his wife?"

"Bounder?" A new old one. Where did she dig that up?

"Bounder," she maintained.

"Maybe that's it."

"Another sample of double standard. A kept woman is entirely acceptable, even fascinating, but a kept man . . ."

"All men are kept in some way," Mitch asserted philosophically.

"As are women." Maddie shrugged.

They laughed at the truth.

So, a quota was the compromise. It put a cap on the amount she could spend on him each month. She abided by it diligently for a while but subsequently only once in a while, maybe half the time.

Mitch never made it a combustible issue. Actually, as time went on he became more reasonable about it, several times came close to admitting that he was macho stubborn and she was right. He shouldn't squelch her generosity.

But not in this instance with the Cary Grant–Fabergé cuff links.

He calmly insisted Maddie return them to the store.

She calmly told him before she'd do that she'd give them to just anyone. "You don't understand," he told her. "I seldom wear cuff links and I already own three pair. Only a couple of my evening shirts have cuffs that require them."

"That never occurred to me. So, we'll have to have some shirts like that made for you."

"I prefer regular cuffs."

"Oh," she acquiesced.

"But these links are exquisite, Maddie, and thank you anyway."

"No harm done," she said blithely. "I'll take them back and get you something else." And then, without a pause: "What'll we do for dinner?"

"Want to go out?"

"Not really. Did you have a proper lunch?"

"No."

"That's not smart. It's essential to us that you take care of yourself, precious. Can't have your energy level getting *diminuendo*, can we?"

Mitch tried to think of another way he should take that. He'd known men who were the last to know they weren't keeping pace. Just recently he'd read an article that dealt with the inequitable allotment of sexual potential to the genders. Maddie certainly had a wealth of passion, a swiftly replenishing fortune. Was free to spend all she wanted on him.

"I could whip up a tuna and something casserole," she said. "We haven't had one in weeks."

Mercy, Mitch thought. He resourcefully reasoned: "Felicia left the kitchen all tidy. Be a shame to mess it up. I'll go out and get something."

"Suits me," Maddie said, settling the matter with a loud, languid sigh.

Mitch changed into a pair of cotton tans and a sweatshirt worn once but not sweated in. When he returned to the study he saw Maddie was having a silent conversation with herself. He sat across from her in his usual chair and read much of that day's *Times* and a little here and there of last week's *New Yorker*.

Around six he put a bit of cash and credit cards into pocket and went down to find dinner. He had in mind some take-out from Barney's, a variety of delicacies, goose paté plentifully truffled, some kind of cold pasta maybe, certainly a loaf of well-done, crisp-crusted peasant bread. He'd munch on the heel of it on the way home. They'd eat on trays, find a movie on television, a Robert De Niro gangster or the like, one that on some previous similar night he'd narrated much of the action for Maddie so now she knew what was happening from the dialogue and sound effects.

Ruder was in the lobby. That was so unexpected that he didn't

register on Mitch right off, but it was unmistakably Ruder standing to one side of the way out.

Ruder was wearing a white cap, the sort most proper for golfing.
Perhaps that morning, when choosing how to present himself to
the day and those who'd be in it, he'd decided the cap was called for
by his blue and white seersucker suit, bought off the rack, of course,
at Tripler's, of course, six summers ago. Add on white, kilted loafers.
He'd lost sight of what he looked best in because he didn't look good
in much. There was slightly more than a hint of simian about him.
Short in the legs, long in the arms, a large head.

All in all he didn't appear to be what one might visualize as a
best-school person, which was what he was: Hotchkiss, Yale, Skull
and Bones and so on. He lived up in Rye in a handed-down house,
enjoyed a handed-down membership at Wykygyl, had been married only once but been left numerous times.

Ruder did a pleasant surprise. "I was having a drink here at
Harry's with a friend in from Philadelphia," he said. "He just now
left and I myself was about to."

Mitch thought Ruder deserved a fairly high rating as a makeup
man but then decided he'd probably had that line in his mouth all
the way uptown.

"I'd forgotten you live here at the Sherry," Ruder added on.

"I'd invite you up but my wife isn't feeling well," Mitch told him.
"I'm on my way to pick up a prescription for her."

"Nothing serious, I hope."

"Never know."

"Right. Friend of mine's wife went to bed spry that other night,
was dead at dawn."

"Your friend from Philadelphia?"

"No, another."

"You have a lot of friends."

"Who can have too many?"

He'll blow his nose any moment now, Mitch thought. Whenever
they'd been together Ruder had blown his nose repeatedly, although
he apparently didn't have a cold or allergy. It was like he was vainly

trying to expel something from his brain. His way of thinking, perhaps.

"Well," Mitch said, "I've got to hurry. Nice seeing you."

"I'll tag along if you don't mind. Give us a chance to talk. I've been trying to reach you all day. Didn't you get my messages?"

"Yeah," Mitch said, preferring not to waste a fib. He made for the revolving door, didn't wait for the doorman's assist, gave the door such a vigorous shove that Ruder had to let two compartments go by before he could confidently jump in and come out on Fifth. By then Mitch was a half dozen strides up the avenue.

Ruder jogged to catch up and then it wasn't easy for him to keep up because Mitch had about six inches of leg on him and was purposely using all of it.

"You're a strange one, Mitch. Really, I mean you have a twisted perception of how to deal with a client."

"An attitude."

"If I didn't like you so much I wouldn't put up with it."

What was this, like Mitch day? First Visconti, now Ruder, Mitch thought. "You wanted to talk?"

"Maybe we could stop in some place and have an iced tea. How about in here?" They were on 60th with the north entrance of the Pierre just ahead.

"I've got to get back to Maddie with the antibiotic. Can't what you want to discuss hold until tomorrow?"

"Certainly, but tomorrow it might have to keep until Thursday and Thursday it might have to . . . well, you know. My better judgment tells me while I've got you I'd better take advantage." Ruder did a smile that ended beseechingly. Both the smile and the beseeching were contrary to his nature and, knowing that, Mitch figured whatever Ruder had on his mind was of unusual importance.

"Okay," Mitch said, stopping on the corner, "but make it fast."

Ruder took out a bunched white handkerchief, found an unused section of it and blew his nose productively. He briefly examined what had been jettisoned from him before stuffing the cloth back into his rear trousers pocket.

It occurred to Mitch that some unfortunate had the task of laundering Ruder's daily hankies.

"I'd feel more at ease seated inside someplace," Ruder said. "I really would."

Mitch looked past those words to the drugstore located mid-block on the other side of the street. He hoped he didn't have to carry his pretense that far.

"I need you to save my ass," Ruder blurted.

"Huh?"

"My standing in Columbia is in jeopardy."

"I thought they loved you."

"They should. No one at Columbia has written more business with less risk. Hell, I've sold coverage with exclusions others have never been able to slip in." Ruder paused, blinked to show he was reflecting, swallowed to show he was distraught. Mitch let him go on. "We've had changes above my level. People have come aboard who don't know me. All they're seeing is where I've overstepped, those instances when I've had to put not only my toe but my whole foot over the line in order to write business. It makes no difference that I've often had to sacrifice my own ethics. No appreciation for that. The hard-hearted pricks. Losses are all that matter. Can't have losses, especially when they're sizable. One is too fucking many and I've had one right after another lately."

Ruder sagged, hung his head, like a man looking over the edge of an imminent long fall.

Mitch couldn't bring himself to do a sympathetic comment.

"The Kalali claim," Ruder said. "As it turns out the Kalali claim is the maker or breaker for me."

That brought back to Mitch the phone conversation he'd had yesterday with Ruder regarding the Kalali claim. He'd been right about Ruder being under critical pressure.

"You can save me," Ruder said.

"I don't see how."

"I've sorted through my chances and you come out as my most likely hope. You're going to recover the Kalali goods."

An amused scoff from Mitch.

"It's not just a hunch, more like a premonition, a foregone thing. You're going to make a total recovery, you're going to let no one, absolutely no one know that you have, you're going to hand the goods over to me and . . . I'm going to be off the hook."

"And grateful."

"Extremely."

"To what extent would extremely be?" Mitch asked less amused.

"Yesterday I quibbled with you over a five percent bonus. That was just a reflex, my spontaneous inclination to look after Columbia's interest. I should have been putting myself first. Now I am. Now I'm willing to agree for a ten percent bonus. That would make your end about six hundred thousand."

"Columbia won't go for that. Five would have been pressing them."

"They've paid five."

"Not to me."

"But they've paid it, believe me. You needn't worry. Anyway, whatever part they won't pay I'll personally come up with. It'll be worth it to me."

Mitch acted as though he was considering the proposal. He did a covered gaze, aimed it at the traffic contest out on Madison, particularly noticing the black messengers on bicycles, admiring how creatively they won out over the crams and pincering between bumpers and side panels. What was it that compelled those guys to give such flair to the menial?

Really there wasn't much for Mitch to think over. The extra that Ruder was offering him was pure windfall, inasmuch as he'd already decided to give the Kalali claim no less than his best effort. The only difference seemed to be Ruder's stipulation that if recovery was made he not mention it to anyone, hand the goods over and let Ruder take the bows.

That struck Mitch as a bit odd but not unreasonable. Ruder probably wanted to put a little extra drama into his vindication, perhaps wanted to choose the perfect moment to scatter the Kalali recovery across the desk of whoever it was at Columbia who was kneeing his neck. Shit, for three hundred thousand on top of three hundred thousand Ruder could bow until it got to be aerobic, and curtsy too.

"Can I count on you Mitch?"

"Yeah, start counting."

Chapter 11

For the rest of the week Mitch worked the district. Not just 47th but, as well, where the concentration had spilled the gem trade over onto 46th and 48th.

He didn't give away his purpose. He never did. There was no discernible eagerness or degree of prowl to him. He kept in apparent neutral, circulated casually in and out of places, as though he had time on his hands.

Of course there were those of the street who knew him so well they knew better. At the very least they could guess he was around with some interest. That was especially so in the major exchanges where many of the more established dealers had concessions.

"Simon."

"Mitch."

A meaningful handshake.

"What's new with you?"

"Nothing to sing about."

"You're looking well."

"I've got trouble with my eyes. A cataract or something the doctor says. Don't tell anybody."

"I won't."

"What would I do if I lost my eyes, even a little."

"You won't."

"One can't feel how good or bad a stone is. You ever know a half-blind gem dealer? My bones will be picked." A moan.

"Simon, my good friend, you'll be finding flaws bare-eyed when you're ninety."

"I should have such luck."

Thus, person to person, Mitch worked the labyrinths of the major exchanges in both Visconti's and Riccio's territories. He made his way from booth to booth, not expecting to come across the Kalali goods, or even a part of them. It hadn't ever been that easy, wouldn't be this time.

The most he hoped for was a shred of a lead, some little thing that might start an unraveling. It could be as subtle as a divulging quality in the eyes of someone who wouldn't inform outright but wanted to let him know there was currently an important swag deal going down.

He had at least that much coming from Miriam Birkus, who did business out of booth 32 in the Manhattan Exchange. Five years ago Miriam and her husband, Sid, were stuck in a losing streak. It got so bad they were forced to sell many of the special, better pieces of jewelry they'd put aside over the years to fall back on later on.

As so often happens, what Miriam and Sid's plight eventually came to was a week with a turnaround deal in it. Not a totally rectifying deal but one that might start things going the other way for them. A prosperous acquaintance of Sid's was opening a retail store in a large mall outside Chicago. He needed stock, particularly engagement and wedding ring sets in the three to five thousand dollar wholesale range. A New York manufacturer that Sid knew specialized in such a line. He allowed Sid to have thirty-five sets on memo. That is, Sid signed for them, assuming responsibility for their value.

What could go wrong? It was a sweet, quick deal. All Sid had to do was fly the goods to Chicago. His end would be eighteen thousand.

He took an early morning flight. At O'Hare he needed to use a men's room, found one and had his pick of vacant stalls. He covered the seat with a tissue and sat with his briefcase between his bare knees.

He was in the middle of defecating when they came over the top from the adjacent stalls, struck him once behind the ear with something hard and grabbed up the briefcase.

Later, Sid said dolefully that he must have looked too much the gem dealer. He didn't think there was such a look but what else would explain his having been spotted? Fingered by someone at the manufacturer's? Whoever, whatever, suspicions weren't going to change that he had to come up with $122,500 to cover the memo.

Visconti knew enough to not lend.

Sid considered suicide.

Mitch heard of the situation.

He went to the exchange and stopped by booth 32. Just Miriam was there. He was commiserating with her when a young swift came up beside him wanting to sell a swag ring he'd held out from a recent night's work. He was obviously an inexperienced swift, didn't know what he had or the value of it or any better than to bring it out and place it on the counter in plain sight.

An oval-cut fancy pink diamond weighing 4.58 carats flanked by tapered baguettes in a platinum mount. Appraised value: two hundred eighty thousand.

That was the description as it appeared on the Empire Mutual Insurance Company's loss list that Mitch had been going over just that morning.

No mistaking it.

The ring lay there on the counter. To Miriam it was salvation. To the swift some fast money. To Mitch a pat on the back from a client for the partial recovery and a few thousand bonus.

Three times the swift asked too loudly how much Miriam would give him for it. To his knowledge all diamonds were white.

A figure low enough to not contradict that impression was in Miriam's mouth; however she deferred to Mitch.

It was up to him.

He weighed the circumstances for a long moment and then turned his back on the transaction. He heard Miriam say two thousand in a typical 47th take it or leave it tone. He thought what a steal and, after allowing ample time, he turned back around to the counter. The swift was gone, the ring was out of sight. He resumed with a nervous but unburdened Miriam as though the interruption had been imaginary.

Thus, on this day, had the Kalali swag or, for that matter, any other heavy, hot material been on the move within the exchange, Miriam would have informed Mitch with a telling look. However, he didn't discern even a hint of that flavor in her eyes.

Nor was Mitch able to glean anything helpful from Saul Heimel, the cutter whose workshop was located fourth-floor rear of a building on 46th. Heimel, normally a wag who delighted in fertilizing any rumor, was too preoccupied with parrying an insult to his expertise. With the painful-sounding screech of faceting under way on a nearby scaif, a horizontal wheel charged with oil and diamond powder spinning at about twenty-five hundred revolutions per minute, Heimel wanted corroboration:

"Here, you tell me the girdle is thick." He handed Mitch a ten-power loupe and a four-carat brilliant-cut diamond locked in a pair of tweezers.

Mitch examined the diamond's widest part, that which divided its upper section from its base. "I wouldn't say so," he said, which didn't necessarily mean it wasn't.

"The son of a bitch claims I've ruined his stone. No thanks for the inclusion I've managed to hide with the bezel facets."

"Who?"

"Brings me an old miner piece of shit and expects me to recut it into the Star of India or something." Heimel was close to frothing. "I know his trick. He wants to pay me not so much. Fuck him. He pays or I keep his goods."

Mitch tried rerouting the topic but to no avail.

And that was how it went for him Wednesday and Thursday. For all his tactical nosing around, nothing. The less optimistic side of him suggested that what he had purely out of the torment suggested to Ruder was quite possibly the case. The Kalali goods were gone, out of the country perhaps, already sold off. He countered that thought with reminding himself how early it was, less than a week since the robbery.

Still, he knew from experience how brief was the expectancy of a recovery. Normally a couple of weeks at most. After that, kiss the goods goodbye.

Chapter 12

Friday morning.

Mitch first went to his office. He dictated a couple of letters, composing patiently to accommodate Shirley's sort-of-shorthand. He signed the checks she put before him and complimented her on the new silk blouse she'd recently liberated from layaway. He also called Visconti regarding the Watermill invitation.

"We have to go up to Maddie's uncle's place," was his true excuse. "It's his birthday and he hasn't been too well lately." Both fibs that when they'd been said Mitch knew they were overkill.

"Some other time then."

"For sure."

"You heard from Riccio?"

"As a matter of fact, yeah."

"I heard you'd heard."

Who was Visconti's wire at Riccio's? Mitch wondered. It had to be someone close in. What would be any have-around's good enough reason to take such a risk? If found out Riccio would tear him apart.

Riccio had phoned Mitch on Wednesday, wanting to know about the Kalali photos Mitch had cryptically left at his place.

"Good-looking material," was Riccio's opinion. "I take it somebody lost it."

"Yeah."

"Well, I ain't found it," Riccio said unhappily.

Mitch believed him. He asked of Riccio the same courtesy he'd asked of Visconti, which was to be told if the Kalali goods got fenced and became a dead issue. Riccio said he'd go along with that and, in the next breath, asked Mitch to let him know if the goods got recovered. That struck Mitch as odd. Visconti had also wanted to be notified.

"Why would you want to know?" Mitch asked Riccio, just curious.

Riccio's reply wasn't to be believed. "No big reason. I like to be on top of what's happening around, that's all."

Now it was Visconti on the phone, saying: "Look over."

Mitch swiveled his desk chair, looked out the window and across the chasm of Fifth to Visconti's office. Visconti was at his desk but turned to meet Mitch's view. He was holding something up to his face.

"You're a sharp dresser, Mitch," Visconti said. "Who picks out your ties?"

"My wife."

That stopped Visconti. His amiability had caused a blunder. He regained with "You make a great knot, small but not too tight, like today. I especially like the tie you've got on today. What is it, a Hermès?"

"I don't know. She cuts out the labels." Mitch now realized Visconti was on him with a pair of miniature binoculars. "You've got me at a disadvantage," he said.

"Not for long. I'm sending you over a pair identical with these. Zeiss ten by twenty-fives. They'll put you right in here."

Mitch nearly forgot how close-up Visconti was seeing him, almost allowed his true sentiments to show.

"By the way," Visconti asked as though just making talk. "Did you come onto those goods yet?"

"Which goods?" Mitch pretended.

"The Kalali goods."

Mitch couldn't recall having told Visconti whose goods they were, not by name. "No, but I'm getting there."

"When you do don't forget to let me know."

"Why?"

Visconti was faster and better with a reply than Riccio. "So I can help you celebrate," he said, "what else?"

Immediately after hanging up Mitch got up and drew the blinds. After a short while he went down and out to continue angling for a lead. That the Kalali goods apparently hadn't hit the district as of yesterday didn't mean they wouldn't today. He had to keep circulating and hope his going over the same tracks didn't give away how purposeful he was.

He put in two hours of moving around. Was, at that point, on the south side of 47th a couple of numbers over from Fifth Avenue, having a few words with an older 47th Streeter whose fingertip skin was stained black and eaten away by years and years of acid-testing things, stolen things usually, to determine their gold content. From his overconditioned point of view life was degrees of purity: 22k, 18, 14, 10, less. His eyes were zero k, gone creamy dull, tarnished, resigned to never being worth more. He had nothing for Mitch.

Across the way was the major West 47th building designated number 1. Mitch looked up the face of it to a certain set of windows. He'd looked up to them numerous times over the past few days. They'd always been dark. Now, however, there were lights on.

He crossed over, entered the building and went up to six.

His brother Andy's place of business was a short ways down the corridor. The LAUGHTON logo was gold-leafed on the door along with ESTATE JEWELRY in smaller letters. It was two adjoined rooms of modest size fixed up to give the impression that Andy could, if he needed, afford twice again as much space.

Mitch went in.

Doris, Andy's love and lover, was standing there with a smile already on, as though having foreseen Mitch's arrival. Perhaps she'd noticed him from the window, seen him cross the street, had positioned herself and waited. She greeted him with left and right cheek kisses, real contact ones, said his name fondly instead of a hello. "We got back only a few minutes ago," she told him.

The dress she had on looked long-journeyed in, Mitch noticed. Her makeup was fresh but her eyes seemed sleepy. She wasn't wearing any jewelry, which was rare for her. Usually she decorated herself with better pieces. Like several rings, as though the large selection she owned had all vied for her fingers and she'd given in to as many as possible. The same with bracelets. But now, for whatever reason, she didn't have on even simple gold ear loops.

Jewelry was Doris' addiction. She admitted it. She didn't really need it. Harry Winston had once told her that. Her beauty was enough, it accessorized her, Winston had fibbed for whatever reason.

"How was the trip?" Mitch asked. Standing aside were four pieces of luggage with first-class JFK destination tags attached to their handles.

"Andy will tell you," she said evasively, "when he gets off the phone."

The door to the inner office was not quite closed. Mitch's view of Andy was a slit and he couldn't hear what was being said. Probably he had Riccio on, Mitch thought. He could have gone in, crowded Andy, but he decided to wait, be easier.

"How about something to drink, a Coke or something?" Doris offered.

"A root beer, got a root beer?"

"You and Andy," she remarked and got a Hire's from the small fridge. Mitch watched her pop the tab. He hoped she didn't break a nail.

Andy came hurrying out, glad to see Mitch, demonstrating that with a strong hug. He was a six-year-younger and slightly shorter version of Mitch. Nearly the same smile, and eyes. A lot of his gestures and body language was imitative of Mitch's, picked up early.

"You didn't get any sun," Mitch said.

"No."

"Do any fishing? I had you in a stream making a perfect presentation to a big one."

Andy looked away, as though a second self was standing nearby to advise him whether or not he should continue the pretense. He came back to Mitch to be eyes to eyes with him for a long moment, during which he told the truth without saying it. "How did you find out?" he asked.

"Visconti. One half of the street always knows what the other half is up to. You should know that by now."

"Since when have you and Visconti been buddies?"

"It was a stupid move, Andy."

"Went off without a hitch," Andy said.

"This was your first errand?"

"Second."

Mitch exhaled a disgusted breath with an expletive on the end of it.

Andy needed to lift the situation to his own high. "Let me show you something," he said brightly.

They went into the inner office.

"I haven't delivered yet," Andy said as he opened his briefcase and from it removed an oblong black leather box with a snap closure. The box contained ten or so briefkes, those double papers folded eight times a certain special way, which gem dealers use to inescapably hold their precious stones. Andy chose one of the briefkes, unfolded it.

They lay in a crease like an accumulated ridge of the clearest frost. Forty pieces of D-flawless one-carat diamonds.

"Russian goods," Andy said, "electronically faceted, perfect makes."

Mitch took the briefke, rocked it slightly and ran the tip of his finger through the lot of diamonds, disturbing them, causing them to scintillate as though they'd been provoked and were resorting to that, their weapon.

"Stunning, aren't they?" Doris said rather covetously.

"Riccio should be pleased," Mitch remarked, holding back expressing his admiration. "How did you manage to get them?"

"Through a broker in Antwerp named Hamner. An older guy Dad used to deal with occasionally."

"You were lucky."

"It really didn't take much doing."

"You were lucky."

"We were careful," Andy contended.

"Very," Doris confirmed.

They'd flown to Buffalo, rented a car there and crossed over into Canada as though they were just part of the traffic bound for a Blue Jays night game in Toronto.

Three million was in the trunk, snugly packed in one of the pieces of luggage. Sixty-two pounds of used, untraceable hundreds.

The crucial banking part of it had been prearranged for by Andy on a previous trip to Toronto. The private bank on the fringe of the financial district was glad to handle such a sizable deposit. It specialized in such temporary transactions at a fee of one percent.

Next they'd flown to Brussels where they opened an account at another private bank. Then went on to Antwerp where the diamond broker, Hamner, and the goods were waiting. Andy hadn't specified Russian goods. That had been an unexpected plus. Russian diamonds, because of their ideal color and consistently perfect makes, had up to lately demanded a premium price; however Russia's needful economic situation had brought the price down into the more competitive range.

Andy had examined and chosen four lots of caraters: eighty pieces of D-flawless, sixty-four pieces of D-color VVSIs, thirty pieces of E-color VVSIs and twenty-five pieces of F-color VVSIs. An even two hundred pieces in all.

Prices had been discussed and after sufficient, rather ritualistic haggling, agreed upon.

The bank in Toronto was instructed to wire transfer $2,970,000 (the $3,000,000 less its fee) to the bank in Brussels, which immediately disbursed $2,479,021 to Hamner, the broker (that included his 8 percent fee). The remaining $490,979 (less the Brussels' bank charges) was Andy's margin. He had it wire-transferred to a bank in the Caymans.

Thus, Riccio's dirty three million cash, that unwieldy, incriminating bulk, had been transformed into the most lasting and dazzling of commodities. Negotiable anywhere, transportable in a shirt pocket, diamonds were a mob guy's best friend.

"Have to go some to make an easier, faster four hundred." Andy grinned.

A cynical grunt from Mitch. He folded the briefke to escape the influence of Riccio's diamonds. "Have you thought how it could have gone?"

"Sure, there was a downside."

"A way downside."

"You're going to piss on my score."

Maybe not, Mitch thought. Maybe, considering Andy's elation at the moment, he should back off, wait until a more neutral time. That was hard for Mitch to do because of the worry that had steamed up in him. "I'm glad it went okay," he said.

Andy read him. "You don't have to pretend you approve. I know you don't, I knew you wouldn't. That's why you had to hear about it the hard way."

"Let's drop it."

"No, you're primed. Go ahead."

"All right. Let's say it all went like it was computerized: the money across the border, the banks in Toronto and Brussels, the broker in Antwerp, the smear. Let's say you've got the diamonds and you're headed back to Riccio with them, but let's also say a take-off guy gets to you and you have to hand over the goods. You tell that to Riccio. He seems to buy it at first, but then he doesn't, he decides the take-off guy never was, that you're lying three million worth. He's insulted. He cocksuckers you twice in every sentence, tells you in otherwise-you'll-be-found-full-of-holes-off-Wards Island terms that you'd better come up with the three. What he doesn't tell you . . ."

"You surprise me."

"How?"

"The way you're not seeing me. You know what, you think you're the shaman of the street. While you've been going around dispensing cures and curses, where is it you think I've been, in a fucking trance?"

"Let me finish."

"I resent it."

"What Riccio doesn't tell you is the take-off guy is one of his crew, if not one of his have-arounds then a zip out to prove. You were set up. You owe Riccio three million and so much vig you'll never get to the nut. You're his. Do or die, his."

"I wouldn't let it get to that," Doris vowed. Unlike Andy, she'd been hanging on Mitch's every word. "I'd raise the three million," she said.

Andy went to the window and gazed down at 47th. At that moment to his eyes it had never looked greedier or grimier. Probably it would regain its more acceptable impression later on, he thought. It always had. The scenario Mitch had just depicted was by no means a revelation to him. He'd watched his back, been wary all the way. Several guys he noticed during the trip home he'd suspected of being take-offs.

He remained at the window. "I figure I could do a couple of errands before Riccio pulled anything like that. He probably had it in mind for next time."

Mitch took that to mean Andy didn't intend there to be a next time. He was relieved, told himself Andy hadn't really resented his concern.

They'd always looked out after one another. As youngsters they'd even gone so far as to play at doing that. For instance, at the cottage in Connecticut where the family spent summers, they'd be out in the lake, a long ways from shore.

"It's your turn to not be able to swim."

"You saved the last time."

"Like hell, but okay. Then I get two saves in a row."

Desperate thrashing of the water and credible cries for help. It alarmed their father at first but after he caught on to what they were doing he understood and enjoyed watching them.

In winter they'd create avalanches and take turns at digging one another out.

"Don't stop breathing. I'm almost to you!"
Realistic gasps for air. "Hurry!"

There was no mother to alarm. She'd died while giving birth to Andy. Thus he didn't own any memories of her, had to be satisfied with those he borrowed from those that were related to him and whatever he imagined by making photographs of her come to life.

Mitch didn't remember much about her, actually. Not her voice or her touch or her scent or any of the important things like that. However, early on, whenever Andy wanted to know about her, asked, Mitch passed on things Kenneth had told him at one time or another. A verbal legacy. For Andy's sake, and just as much his own he realized later, he elaborated creatively, invented various incidents to exemplify her caring. Mitch still believed that helped Andy cope with the presence of her absence. Perhaps even saved him.

Now Andy turned his back to the street, told Mitch: "I've over a million in the Caymans. Doris will match that and you and Maddie can kick in whatever you think would be fair."

"For what?"

"The only reason I ran Riccio's errands was so I'd have a large enough hunk to throw into the pot."

"I'm also throwing in my jewelry," Doris said. "Not all of it but a lot. I've got too much, just stashed away, pieces I was temporarily in love with but have been ignoring for ages. It's a crime. I bet I've at least enough to fill a whole showcase."

"There's a location on Madison in the seventies that's coming available," Andy said. "I've talked to the real estate agent about it."

He and Doris went on about what the new Laughton establishment on Madison would be like, how successful it would be. They jumped right over asking Mitch if he was for it or not. Their enthusiasm assumed he was.

What was it with everyone trying to get him back into a store on Madison? Mitch thought. Did it ever occur to them—Andy, Doris, Maddie—that he didn't want to be a goddamn shopkeeper, that he hadn't been cut out for it in the first place, that it had been something he'd fit himself into but not without having to squeeze and force the shape of his true nature? In fact, since there'd not been a family store, not had to kissy-kissy ass all those spoiled, well-off women every day he'd felt better about himself.

That wasn't to say he liked what he was now doing for a living. It was, as he secretly thought of it, something that kept him from doing what he didn't want to do, which was shopkeep. Put the goods on display every morning, put the goods back in the vault every night. Set the alarm. Pay the insurance company on time and hope switchers and lifters didn't pick you clean or some lady looking as though she could buy the place out didn't have a .380 automatic up her sable sleeve. Fuck no. Maybe he didn't know what he wanted to do and maybe it was a little late to be undecided about that, but for sure he wasn't going to be a shopkeeper.

He did a smile along with some nods that made him appear interested. "You're way ahead of me," he said. "Let me think about it some and catch up."

To change direction he took a set of the Kalali photos from his folio. Tossed it on Andy's desk. "Some things I'm hoping to recover for a client," he explained. "Take a look when you have a moment."

His pager beeped.

Hurley wanted to be called.

Mitch reached him at the precinct.

"What you up to?" Hurley asked.

"Just shagging around."

"And?"

"Nothing."

"I got an okay from the Jersey guys to take a look at the Kalali house. Who knows? Want to go along?"

"I'm having lunch with Maddie and afterwards I promised her the museum."

"Which museum?"

"The Met." She preferred the Met over the Museum of Modern Art and the Whitney. Whenever she'd sat aimed at the abstract paintings of either of the latter, she'd gotten low to medium grade anxiety attacks, sometimes even a bit nauseous; however the Fantin-

Latours, Whistlers, Cassatts and Boudins at the Met had a mollify-
ing effect.

"Bring Maddie along," Hurley suggested. "We'll stop and have
lunch at a place I know in Jersey City where the top mob guys used
to go and there's still a lot of what they once were in the atmosphere. It's very Maddie."

Chapter 13

Having had lunch they were again under way in the Lexus with Billy driving and Mitch up front with him, Maddie and Hurley in the back.

Billy sort of remembered the way they'd come. All through there was typical New Jersey waterfront and most of the ways weren't streets as much as cobbled or unpaved accesses from one unremarkable section to another. So Billy was to be forgiven for choosing a couple of turns that led to only the loading platforms of warehouses. He finally came onto Avenue E and a ramp that put them on the Turnpike Extension.

Bound for Far Hills.

"Anybody against some music?" Billy asked.

No one replied so he assumed, clicked the radio on and began scanning. He passed up some gloomy Mahler and a newscast that managed to get out the word *killed*. Some mellow jazz was what he hoped to find, some Oscar Peterson or John Coltrane. He went up and down the megacycles twice. The air was congested with the agony of heavy metal and the high school poetry and scratches of rap.

Shit, was what Billy thought of it and nearly said aloud. He gave up on the radio.

His patience this day was thin, stretched. He saw it as a sort of membrane with abnormal elasticity that ran sheet-like. Horizontally within his skull from his brow line to the stem of his brain. Impervious up to now.

He'd never allowed the tension of his patience to show. Wouldn't today. He'd be as expected, in the part of amenable Billy the driver, wait-here guy, on call and carry guy, a kind of satellite person the way his time revolved around that of others.

Before, when he'd driven Mr. Strawbridge, he'd done whatever was required to make himself indispensable, and there'd been no letup in that endeavor since he'd been driving Mitch and Maddie. Not once had there been a mention, not even a veiled hint of his being let go, nor had he implied that he might quit. By now the indispensability was mutual he believed. Wasn't he bound to them?

Admitted, he had himself a steady, soft spot. The salary was generous and the treatment liberal.

Those, however, weren't his reason for staying on. Not his way down inside reasons.

Years ago, over a series of lengthy waits for Mr. Strawbridge, particularly one of six hours at Kennedy because Mr. Strawbridge had missed his return flight from London, Billy had done what he considered to be some deep introspection. Opened himself up beyond his layers of ordinary motives and came up with why, despite the frequent urge to make a change, he should remain where he was.

The need to resent.

That was it. His need to resent.

Not devotion nor security, but the advantage of being able to resent with ease, confident that his resentment wasn't about to spill over (desert the Lexus and Maddie mid-traffic on 50th) or gather into a temperamental tornado and havoc everything in his vicinity to such an extent he'd have no recourse other than to hang head and remove himself to another vicinity.

It was a matter of counterpoise.

Mr. Strawbridge's genuine good nature and other personal merits, the various likabilities of Mitch and Maddie. Attributes that adequately outweighed (but not by much) his resentments, that kept the umbrageous side of him contained.

Where, he often asked himself remindfully, would he ever again find such suitability, such an accommodating ratio—never less than fifty-one percent honest-to-goodness consideration to offset his rarely more than forty-nine percent grudge?

He imagined having to endure employers who behaved less agreeably. He wouldn't put up with it. It wasn't in him to put up with it. He'd be forever deserting, escaping, quitting and being let go. There'd be too many trial periods, the begging for letters of reference.

Couldn't have that.

Couldn't risk having to have that, Billy thought.

So, what about this four-way pull on his patience today? What had brought it on?

Had to be the proposition.

Made to him Wednesday night when he was having his usual slice of pound cake at the narrow coffee shop around the corner on Columbus Avenue, when that guy came in and helped himself to the same booth. No introduction, no preamble, just the proposition straight out.

The guy was well-dressed. In gray. Had on a hundred-dollar tie. Seemed real enough, serious eyes, serious mouth. Talked like he had sense until the number came out of him. Twenty-five million.

From that point on Billy was sure what he had was another city crazy.

Still, as the guy had stipulated, he'd kept the proposition to himself, hadn't spoken about it to Mitch.

"What was it called, what I had to eat?" Maddie asked.

"Orecchio d' Elefante," Hurley told her.

"Which is what?"

"The literal translation is ear of elephant. Actually a loin veal chop pounded so thin it's floppy."

"The clams were delicious," she said. For a starter she'd ordered a dozen littlenecks on the half shell. Slurped them down without the disguise of Tabasco, Worcestershire or lemon. Mitch, a bit impressed, had visualized her stomach a pink resting place, albeit temporary, for all those homeless clams.

"Most women can't even stomach the idea of eating raw clams," he said now.

"It's a carnal thing," Maddie said and allowed that to hang in the air. "With me, of course, it's purely tactile, and I can accept the resemblance but why be so nasty nice? You know, Elise adores raw clams, oysters as well, always has. She fed me my first when I was three or so." Then, without a half beat or breath: "Did you happen to overhear those three men at the next table, I thought they were mob guys planning arson and a hit but it soon became apparent that two of them were trying to sell the third some fire and life insurance. Most disappointing."

"Used to be a guy couldn't get a waiter's job there unless he'd done a hitch in some joint."

"I'd have appreciated it more then," Maddie said.

"That's for sure," Mitch commented to the windshield.

At that moment they were passing over Newark Bay. It occurred to Mitch that once its water had been clean enough to drink. Black-hulled freighters were tied up like animals on short leash. The beaks of cranes picking their bellies empty. Then came Newark Airport on the left. A 747 on its glide path. Mitch imagined the collective quickening of the passengers' heartbeats.

He wished Billy would hurry the Lexus, get them to Far Hills sooner. He opened the glove compartment. It was stuffed with traffic citations, crumpled up malevolently and shoved in there. So many that some, as though relieved, flew out. A couple of years ago Mitch had paid off just as much of an accumulation, hoping a clean slate would inspire Billy to be more conscientious. All it did was set a precedent.

"I'm not going to put out for your goddamn tickets again," Mitch said. "You expect me to but I won't." He retrieved those that were on the floor.

Billy did a shrug.

"You'll get your license taken away."

Billy agreed with some nods that unmistakably conveyed it would be Mitch's loss.

Mitch noticed the black butt of a revolver in the compartment, no holster, just the weapon in among the cram of traffic tickets. He took it out. A Smith & Wesson .357 Magnum. A hefty piece.

"I recall you having a thirty-two automatic," Mitch said.

"A plinker. I traded it."

"This loaded?"

"Of course."

"You ought to keep it on safety."

"No one ever gets in there but me."

"I'm in there now."

"So you are," Billy said intractably.

Mitch put the revolver on safety and placed it back in among the tickets. He closed the glove sharply, closing the subject.

Maddie was back on the clams. "I'll bet I don't get hepatitis from them," she was saying. "Not in that restaurant. It's probably the safest place north of Miami to eat clams."

"Why?"

"If a mob boss ever got hepatitis the place would get bombed. Don't you think?"

They were on 78 now, headed west. New Jersey was sliding by, nothing pleasant. The city of Newark, off on the right, was aided by distance.

A wave of depression invaded Mitch. Not the deep sort, just a minor concavity, enough to be felt. It wasn't because of Billy's shaded insubordination or because Maddie was in the back with Hurley, Mitch told himself. Sure, Hurley had it for Maddie. That had been obvious for a long while but it was a long way from being active.

She used Hurley. Like right now, she was pumping the Kalali case out of him. Maybe Hurley thought it was conversation, but listening to it Mitch recognized it as pure Maddie, one-sided pump. By the time they got to Far Hills she'd know more about the Kalali case than he did.

He read, as though interested, what was displayed on the rear and side of an eighteen-wheeler that Billy passed doing a good twenty over the limit. He thought the wish they'd get stopped for speeding. By a hard-mouthed state cop. That would change the climate.

A green highway sign announced Irvington importantly.

Named after some guy Irving, Mitch thought. Never forget Irving what's-his-name. Irving Toplitz, that was it. A 47th guy who used to sell piqué goods out of his pocket. Dirty little diamonds in dirty overhandled briefkes. Got hold of an eighty-pointer (four-fifths of a carat) that was loupe clean, first quality. A held-back piece of swag popped out of an engagement ring. Irving showed the stone up and down the street. Turned down better than fair offers for it because once he sold it all he'd have to show was money. In his own way in love with that eighty-pointer, like an unfortunate-looking guy who'd come by a beautiful girl. One afternoon at curbside he was showing his prize possession to someone when he was accidentally jostled by a tourist. The eighty-pointer was flipped out of its open briefke. It bounced twice and found the sewer drain. Irv Toplitz felt victimized. He gave up on the street, was never seen upon it again.

Mitch thought a plaque should have been installed marking the spot, saying, for one and all to see forever, *here is where Irv Toplitz lost his spirit.* But then, if that was the criterion there'd be plaques all over the place.

"What time you want to get started tomorrow?" Billy asked.

"Early," Mitch told him.

"Not too early."

"Say seven, seven-thirty."

"Let's make it nine or ten."

"I want to be up there by then."

Billy didn't promise seven, seven-thirty.

Hurley now had out a set of the Kalali photos, was describing them to Maddie piece by piece.

Mitch adjusted his seat for more recline, closed his eyes and overheard: "A belle époque period diamond and pearl head ornament."

"What exactly is a head ornament?" Maddie asked.

"A comb."

"Why didn't they say a comb?"

They, Mitch thought cynically.

Hurley told her: "This one's made of real tortoiseshell mounted with a band of diamonds and bordered with natural pearls. Signed by Cartier."

"Sounds sweet. This Kalali lady had some lovely jewelry."

Had, Mitch thought.

"Wonder where she got it all. Maybe she bought swag."

Hurley went on to the photo of the two twenty-carat emeralds fitted in their ivory box. As he was describing them in detail to Maddie, Mitch visualized them, their Arabic-looking inscriptions and all.

"What do the inscriptions say?" Maddie asked.

"How should I know?"

"I'd think you'd want to," Maddie said. "It's probably important."

Mitch wondered why Hurley didn't tell her what the inscriptions said was irrelevant, that all that mattered was they'd been stolen and whoever stole them had killed one Kalali going on two.

Hurley went on describing other pieces.

Mitch wished he had earplugs.

But then Maddie reached forward and found his head, gave it a couple of loving strokes and mussed his hair some. That easily he was brought up to the brighter surface and the miles to the scene of the crime were made to seem not so many.

The gate of the Kalali house was open but the police crime scene tape was still up.

Mitch told Maddie he wouldn't be long, she was to wait in the car with Billy.

She did a brief, obedient smile.

Mitch and Hurley walked up the drive. It was lined with an abundance of blue hydrangeas at their peak. An oriole was enjoying ablutions in a cantilevered bath. Altogether a summer contentment about the place, not robbery and homicide.

They entered the house and immediately had to step around the outlined indication of where Mrs. Kalali had been shot down. The dried pool of her week-old blood dimensional on the slick, hardwood floor of the reception hall.

They proceeded to the study where shards of Persian glass crunched beneath their steps and books were heaped helter-skelter. Their attention was immediately drawn to the white sofa upon which was the dark red stain of Mr. Kalali's bleeding, a grisly Rorschach.

Now it was a place of robbery and homicide.

They went throughout the expansive house, absorbing the stark, cold, contemporary character of it. The master bedroom had been left as found, except for a lot of messy dusting for fingerprints.

Mitch and Hurley agreed that the condition of the dressing room was unusual, didn't look as though swifts had been there. Why hadn't it been ransacked, the dresser drawers yanked out, their contents dumped on the floor?

And the gaping, empty floor safe in the bedroom. A high-rated safe that would have taken considerable time and experience and special equipment to force open. What else could be assumed except that one of the Kalalis had opened it under duress?

"For all the good it did them," Mitch remarked.

"Getting any ideas?" Hurley asked.

"Could have been anyone's crew," Mitch said.

They went out to the rear terrace and further out on the grounds. The Jersey guys had already gone over the area but there was the chance that they might have missed something, something that had been dropped or whatever.

"Couldn't have asked for a more ideal setup with the easy wall, the overgrown grounds and all," Mitch commented.

"Here's where they came over. It was soggy so they left good, deep shoe prints. The Jersey police took impressions. According to them two of the guys weigh about one seventy-five, both had on Nikes. The other guy was a real lightweight, a hundred ten or so. Maybe not even that. Had on boots with pointed toes. Tiny narrow feet. Know a crew that has a swift like that?"

"Not offhand."

"At least it's something to look for. And the fact that they were a hard crew."

"That narrows it down some."

"Not much these days though. Would have ten years ago."

A hard crew was one that carried guns. Most swifts didn't used to and some still didn't because if caught the charge would be armed robbery rather than just burglary. Armed robbery carried a five-year-longer sentence.

Piano music.

Contradicting the moment with bits and passages of romantic Tchaikovsky. It seemed to be coming from somewhere neighboring but then Mitch and Hurley realized it was coming from the Kalali house.

They hurried in.

Maddie was seated at the black baby grand in the study. Her left hand struck three ominous-sounding chords, sort of Mozart. "This place is like a mausoleum," she complained.

"You were supposed to wait in the car," Mitch told her somewhat reproachfully.

"I needed to go to the bathroom." She did a lively, double upscale run all the way to the last ivory key, along with a Ray Charles chin up, head back. "I had no problem finding it."

Chapter 14

Such a summer Saturday!

Why, the very air was different from yesterday's. Not nearly so ladened nor polluted with responsibility. There'd be no Ruder, no Visconti, no Riccio, not a mote of 47th in this air, Mitch thought.

He lay on his left side on his side of the bed, curled enough so the base of his spine was pressed to the base of Maddie's. At times when they got into this position Mitch played with the illusion that they were permanently attached, like Siamese twins. The romantic fantasy was always spoiled by the inconveniences and impossibilities that would come with it. At other times he imagined their touching spines formed an erotic circuit for a current that would recharge them, in a sort of tantric way.

He'd been awake since five-thirty. It was now close to six.

If he got up now, didn't continue to lie there letting thoughts pass through his head like neutrinos, he'd be able to leisurely do whatever he had to do before Billy picked them up at seven-thirty.

He put his feet to the carpet.

Noise didn't matter. Maddie should get up. He said her name for the first time that day, softly. She didn't respond. He nudged her with it, twice, louder.

She did a torporous protesting *mmm* and reached with her legs to where he'd vacated. "Come back," she murmured.

"Billy will be here in an hour or so."

She burrowed in under her pile of pillows, pulled one of Mitch's to her, hugged it and was again taking the downward passage to sleep.

She'd be having to rush around later furious at herself, Mitch thought on his way to the kitchen.

Fresh-brewed Kona.

Well-buttered cinnamon toast.

He brought them into the bedroom. Placed the tray on the bed. The aromas would get to her. He compounded the enticement by pouring himself some of the rich, steaming black and crunching a bite of toast.

Maddie huffed and complained: "It's too fucking early."

"Maybe you'd rather not go to the country today."

"At a decent hour."

"You and Billy," Mitch remarked.

She sat up amidst the plump. "Coffee me please."

Mitch obliged and her first finger found the handle of the mug.

Mitch was used to her blind precision.

She helped herself to a slice of toast. Mitch didn't care for it all that much but he knew it was one of her every-so-often morning favorites.

"Are you dressed?" she asked.

"No."

"What do you intend to wear?"

"I don't know, why?"

"Wear jeans, a tight pair."

"It'll be too warm for jeans."

"And boots. You do have a pair of high-tops, don't you?"

She was up to something, Mitch thought.

"The Doc Martens I bought you. Did you leave them in the country?"

"Yeah," Mitch fibbed and thought he'd wear lightweight khakis, a T-shirt without a name or place on it and pair of sneakers. No matter what she was specifying or why, he was going to be comfortable.

She got up for the bathroom with a whole slice of toast clenched between her teeth. Mitch heard simultaneously the diametric sounds of the toast being crunched and the stream of her striking the water in the commode.

"I love you, precious," she called out from in there.

"Love you too," Mitch said, and with that exchange it seemed what had ensued up to then in his day had been merely overture.

Maddie was in the shower.

"We've about a half hour," he told her. Apparently she was being diligent about the time. However, when she was out and had dried herself she set about waxing her legs.

"You can do that up at Straw's," Mitch said.

She went on pressing the sheets of wax around her shins and calves. As she ripped them off it sounded and appeared painful to Mitch.

"Don't dawdle," he told her.

"Is that what I'm doing? I thought I was doing something that might please you later on."

Cheeks and thighs, he thought.

"Did you take in the paper?" she asked.

"No."

"Why don't you?"

He got that morning's *Times* from the landing. It was already quarter after seven and he wasn't yet dressed. Nor was Maddie. She was now before the mirror, leaning to it, fussing with her hair, picking at a tendril here, another there, as though she was seeing her image.

"I'll read to you on the way up," Mitch said.

"What are the headlines? Never mind, go to the fourth page. What's juicy on the fourth page?"

"Only a lot of wars."

"How about the Living Arts section?"

"That doesn't come on Saturdays."

"At least there must be some editorials."

There were two. She agreed with one, and the other having to do with the overfishing and the plights of Columbia River salmon made her temporarily irate.

Reading the *Times* aloud to her wasn't a daily must but something Mitch did fairly regularly. He enjoyed it. He often omitted or inserted words to make the articles more controversial or slanted more toward his views.

As he got into today's business section Maddie remarked *same old shit* and squirmed into a pair of black jeans. She sucked in, zipped up and ran an approving hand over her snugly contained buttocks. "What do you think?"

"You'll swelter."

Seven-thirty, quarter to eight.

"Where the hell is Billy?"

"He'll be along," Maddie assured.

"Think I should call Straw and let him know we're coming?"

"He'd rather we just showed up."

They spent one or two weekends each month up at Straw's. And nearly all holidays. A room designated as theirs was kept ready for them, plenty of changes for each season in its closet, a stock of personal needs in the adjoining bath.

Ready to go, they sat in the study.

More wait, more waste, Mitch thought.

There wasn't much of consequence one could do while doing wait, it was too distracting an activity in itself.

Maddie felt the hands of her special, exposed wristwatch. "Nine o'clock," she said.

Mitch's *Where the hell is Billy?* intensified to *Where the fuck is Billy?*

At nine-thirty Billy called up from the lobby. "I'm here," was all he said.

Maddie told Mitch to go on down. "I've a thing or two I want to take along."

"Like what?"

"Just a thing or two," she replied vaguely.

Now that Billy had arrived Mitch found his aggravation was anti-climactic. What, really, did a couple of hours matter? It wasn't imperative that they get to the country early, just a notion he'd fixed on. Still, he was going to have to do some reproach. He wasn't good at it, but Billy's attitude towards him, the client, had to be set straight.

Double standard, Mitch, double standard, he realized as he reached the lobby level. Nevertheless, he stepped out of the elevator, did an annoyed face and put some bite in his stride.

Billy, the Sherry doorman and their smiles were out front. A small flatbed trailer was hitched to the Lexus.

Mitch instantly revised his act.

On the flatbed was the reason Billy had been so insistent on nine-nine-thirty. Why Maddie had been taking her own sweet time.

At once, a gate of Mitch's memory sprung open and out for front and center came a certain night last winter during an afterwards among the pillows. He and Maddie had taken turns revealing things they'd at one time or another wanted and might again, material things.

He'd begun with the obligatory assertion that as long as he had her he wanted nothing more.

"As long as?" she'd arched.

"Okay, inasmuch as."

"Do I have to go first?"

"No," he said. "Let me think. I always wanted a hog."

"Really, a hog?"

"Uh huh."

"Are you sure, precious? You'd have to slop it. That's what they do, don't they, slop hogs?"

And now, there in front of the Sherry was the hog. Held upright on the flatbed by guy cables. Saturday New York walkers were pausing to admire it because it was up there on the flatbed looking exhibited.

What Maddie had gotten him in place of the Fabergé cuff links.

A Harley-Davidson no less.

A new Heritage Softail Classic in serious black with chrome-laced wheels, chrome fishtail mufflers, a shotgun style exhaust, fat boy tank, everything. Even black cowhide fringes with chrome beads dangling from the hand grips and chrome studs and conchos that played up the black, harness-leather saddlebags.

Mitch and Billy were wheeling it down the ramp of the flatbed when Maddie came out.

"How's that for a cycle?" she said brightly.

"Where's yours?" Mitch said.

"Don't I wish," she laughed. "Man, you're just going to have to pack your bitch." Evidently while buying the bike she'd made them throw in some vernacular. "You're not going to insist I take it back, are you?"

That hadn't entered Mitch's mind. It would be his next two Christmases and birthdays. "You're much too good to me," he said.

"Just trying to keep even," was her nice comeback.

Mitch rolled the Harley to parallel with the curb and leaned in on its kickstand.

Billy got two visored helmets from the Lexus, full-face, mean-looking black Arai Quantum/s helmets. Identical his and hers. They'd been custom-fitted with two-way intercoms that allowed helmet-to-helmet conversation. Billy also distributed pairs of black cowhide gloves.

The helmet and gloves suited Maddie's black jeans and short black jean jacket with a genuine club insignia on the back. STAMFORD STEALTHS, speed-lined skull and all, stitched in acid green. Her box-toed construction worker's boots were also right. The jacket was far from new, had been bought by phone from a far downtown military surplus and second-hand clothing outlet. Maddie had called a half dozen such places. The store man had thought she was another New York nut when she wanted the jacket delivered to the Sherry. He'd hung up on her twice but right off on her third call she blurted that she'd pay double what he was asking and that made it worth the chance.

All in all Maddie looked every bit the biker.

Mitch, on the other hand, in his T-shirt, khakis and bare feet in sneaks came nowhere near the image. His bare neck, forearms and ankles were going to be graveyards for airborne insects.

"There's an owner's manual somewhere," Maddie told him. "But you don't need instructions now, do you precious?" She was anxious to get on and get going.

"I really ought to go back up and put on some jeans and a different shirt," Mitch said.

"You'll swelter," Maddie mimicked.

Mitch went up to change.

Billy drove the Lexus and flatbed away.

Maddie removed two pistols from the waistband of her jeans. She put them in one of the Harley's saddlebags. Also four spare clips and a couple of boxes of cartridges.

She wasn't furtive about it. They were, after all, legally her husband's guns, and to hell with any passersby who were made apprehensive by the sight of them or, even more, by the sight of her, the bad-looking biker, with them.

On her own she found her way onto the Harley's rear seat, so when Mitch came down he had only to show her where to place her feet. He kneeled and positioned them for her.

He legged over and got settled in the saddle. Paused a minute to enjoy the initial feel of having the Harley under him.

He started it up and allowed it to idle.

Potato, potato, potato.

The unmistakable Harley sound.

"C'mon man," Maddie urged, "put the pedal to the metal."

Mitch waited for a break in the Fifth Avenue traffic to cut across and get on Central Park South. He decided not to go up through the park because there'd be so much roller-blading and other kinds of rolling in there. He continued on to Columbus Circle, went up to the west side of the park to 72nd and then made all the lights to the Henry Hudson Parkway.

It was jammed with headed-out traffic, but, in this instance, Mitch wouldn't have to wait in it. He put the Harley in the narrow between lanes and, defying exhaust and the possibility of abrupt lane changers, ran the gauntlet doing fifty.

He heard Maddie's breath catching. Maybe she was sensing the risk. "How is it back there?" he asked.

"I've never been so carried away!" she exclaimed.

Actually, Maddie wasn't certain how she was faring. Part of her was exhilarated by the open speed and tenuousness, while nearly as much of her wished she'd stipulated a back support for the seat she was on. Her black heightened the sensation that any moment she might go flying off to oblivion. The Harley salesman had suggested a back support; however, he'd referred to it in the vernacular as a *sissy bar* and that had settled it for her.

It took about twenty miles of wind and Harley growl to chase most of her trepidation. Her normal existential attitude took over. "Swerve some," she told Mitch.

"Huh?"

"Do some swerves. I like it when I'm made to lean."

"There'll be lots of corners."

"Don't deprive me."

He waited until there was a clear stretch. He covered all two miles of it with back-and-forth full-width swerving.

Maddie's squeals of delight and fright were appropriately diphthonged.

He went back to going straight.

"Why?" she asked.

"There's a car just ahead."

"Cop car?"

"No."

"What kind of car?"

He anticipated her, told her it was a Porsche.

"Which model?"

"Looks to be a nine-eleven."

"Blow it away."

"We're already doing eighty." Actually sixty-five.

"What the fuck, crank it!"

Mitch added just enough throttle to snap Maddie's head and roar past the four-year-old, laboring Toyota Tercel.

And so it went as they proceeded up the Saw Mill and got on the Taconic, headed for upstate. Maddie did about ten miles of humming and then got to singing a Mary-Chapin Carpenter and

Mitch was relieved when instead of a third chorus she asked how much further.

"About fifty miles, a little less. You okay?"

"Yeah, but you know what this thing is?"

"What thing?"

"This hog of yours. It's a seven-hundred-pound vibrator."

"It's having its way with you?"

"I may get off before I get off," she laughed. "It's almost as relentless as you are."

"Oh?"

"At times," she added, tempering the compliment.

"Everything you say is true."

"But you're a big fibber."

Don't admit, don't deny, he told himself.

"I've caught you in more fibs than there are beans in a jar," she said. "It's part of your charm. Did I mention that when Straw phoned the other day he said he had a surprise for us?"

"Big or little surprise?"

"He tried to make it sound little but my hunch is it's big-time."

Maddie leaned forward, pressed against Mitch's back, put her arms around and invaded his jeans. It was a tight squeeze for her hands but he helped by sucking in his abdomen.

Chapter 15

Claverack, Austerlitz, Kinderhook.

And there, at noon, the private drive of Uncle Straw's place was beneath the Harley's wheels.

An unpaved drive.

Numerous times there'd been inclinations to have it black-topped and once, two Strawbridges back, that so-called improvement had come as close as a bid from a local paving company. The morning the workmen arrived with their graders, rollers and macadam cookers, it was decided paving would be too costly a change, too costly to the eyes.

The alternative was a gravel of a compatible shade.

A mile-long drive, it serpentined through an apple orchard. Sixty of the orchards' eighty-five trees were still encountering seasons. Many of the sixty were old survivors with major amputations. They'd seen the trunks of neighbors topple over from interior rot. They resolutely continued to bear.

In return for their loyalty they were tended, pruned severely for their own good each spring and sprayed at the first sign of blight or rust or leaf hopper.

Further in on the drive the apples gave way to pines. A prevenient comfort zone, thick above, refreshing below. Carpeted with needle drop.

After the pines came openness, lawn, a gently sloped expanse of it. Cared for but by no means manicured or formal. Lawn like a wide green skirt arranged around the sit of the house.

The Strawbridge house.

It had never been otherwise known. Unlike so many of the residences up there along the Hudson, manor houses and such, it hadn't once belonged to the Stuyvesants or the Rensselaers or any other of those early New Amsterdam families with a Van between their names.

Nor was there any Dutch in its architectural personality.

It was a Georgian revival, almost a replica of a house Nelson Strawbridge, Maddie's great-grandfather, had admired in 1910, while spending a weekend in Surrey. Nelson was so taken by that Surrey house that he filed it in his ready memory and, fourteen years later, when he decided to build on what he called his patch of four hundred acres up in Kinderhook, he sent his architect to England to sketch the lines of it.

The architect did him one better. Made acquaintance with the owner, who happened to be in a financial squeeze and therefore considered it a blessing that he was able to realize ten thousand for anything so dispensable as a set of the original plans.

The Strawbridge rendition was a large house by ordinary standards but much less than what was considered a mansion by those who owned mansions.

Sixteen rooms.

The majority of which were situated in the three-story main section. The exterior was of clean, aged brick with a sharply pitched, blue-slate roof. Crisp white trim at every opportunity. Nine over nine sash windows eared by black shutters. A house of elegant proportions and details while escaping pretension.

There it was now, coming into Mitch's view and Maddie's mind. The pines had notified her. Being family, they ignored the front entrance and went around the side to the apron of the four-car garage.

It was good to have the helmets off.

Maddie thought that might be what it was like for a chick to
come out of incubation. Stop thinking weirdly, she chided herself.
Her thighs and pelvis were tingling.

Mitch stretched his back and shoulders and came close to complaining on behalf of his rump. Such a long ride first time out had
been asking too much of it.

Where was Straw? Usually he heard them arrive and came out
right away to greet them. Not today for some reason.

They entered through a side gate which gave to a herringbone-
patterned brick wall along the rear of the house. The service and
kitchen areas were located in the wing opposite, about a hundred
feet away. They'd gone only a few steps when someone came out
from the kitchen, causing a hitch in Mitch's stride.

"What is it, precious?" Maddie asked.

"I believe it might be Straw's surprise," Mitch told her.

"What's she like?"

"How do you know it's a she?"

"Straw told me."

"I thought it was to be a surprise."

"I mean what he said with words didn't tell me, his voice had
some gratified mischief in it. There's no mistaking gratified mischief. Describe her to me."

Where to start, with what words? "She's tall," Mitch said.

"How tall?"

"Quite tall?"

"Nose to nose with you?"

"Possibly."

"Why am I having to drag this out of you? Is she attractive? How
old would you say? Say, for Christ's sake."

"I didn't get that much of a look at her." Which was true. He'd
only gotten the merest glimpse of the woman's face, and apparently,
she hadn't noticed them at all. She'd come out intent on a destination in the opposite direction. Was now on her way.

The fingers of her right hand had two bottles of Heineken by
their throats. The way she was swinging those beers spoke her
frame of mind.

Mitch guessed she was about six-one, maybe two. Her slender-
ness made her appear even taller, and, give and take as physiques
often do, her height made her look all the more slender.

Hers was indeed a remarkable and fortunate body.

At the moment she had it adorned by only three things, two of
which were green mucking boots, Wellingtons. The other was the
bottom of a thong bikini, the merest triangle of silvery material.
The boots were too large for her. She had to scuff along, hardly raising her feet. Straw's boots, Mitch surmised. There was something
candidly intimate about her being in Straw's boots, undressed as she
was.

Wherever this woman was headed, no doubt there would be
Straw. Mitch steered Maddie's elbow and followed along. It wasn't
lost to him that again he was observing someone unaware.

He maintained an accommodating distance, not so far behind
the woman that he couldn't make out the quality of her skin. Ivory
pale, too pale to risk exposure on such a sunny day. Her hair was
black as crow feathers, and as shiny. Styled close to her skull, somewhat like a bathing cap.

There was something unique about her bearing, Mitch noticed.
For one thing her head was taking a level ride on her neck, as
though it was attached by some motion-absorbing device. And her
buttocks with that silver string out of sight between them, materi-
alizing above. Tight, ideally sufficient buttocks, they too seemed like
passengers left and right not required to be affected by her walk.

With Mitch and Maddie in her wake, the woman went along a
brick wall that served as backdrop for a crowd of craning double
hollyhocks. Through the allée formed by eight paired seventy-year-
old maples. Close by and past the thousand panes of greenhouse.
Out to where Straw had his vegetable garden, and into it.

The woman stopped there. Where was Straw? Her eyes sought
him. She called out. His name on the undulate of the mid-day,
mid-summer air. It seemed a cue he'd been awaiting. Certain leafy
stalks in a row of corn were like a curtain that Straw parted and
stepped through.

The woman handed him one of the beers. Was paid for it with a peck of a kiss on her mouth.

As Straw swigged he spotted the approach of Mitch and Maddie. He stood his ground, allowed them to come to him, so he could feed on the full-length sight of them together.

He gave a hug to each, hugs with their names said fondly in them. Mitch's also contained two comradely pats on the back.

"I came out to cut some Bibb for lunch and got challenged by some weeds," Straw said. He introduced the woman.

Wallis Wentworth.

Assumed or not, Mitch thought, both the Wallis and the Wentworth suited her. Cindy, Amy, Chrissie or whatever would have been unfortunate. Straw called her Wally. He put his arm around her, drew her to his side possessively. "I sent Wally in for beers," he said. He extended his. "Have a swig."

Maddie's reach went right to the bottle. She took three swallows and pressed the cold sweating green glass to her hot sweating forehead before handing it on to Mitch.

Wally apparently thought nothing of standing there so nearly nude. She had her arms crossed, which partially covered her breasts; however that was a natural aspect of her stance, not self-consciousness. Her breasts were small but not meager. Firm, almost adolescent-looking with pink nipples like the tips of a baby's finger. A slight, nice pooch to her abdomen.

Mitch guessed Wally was beyond her thirties by maybe four or five years. A time-fighter. Well-boned features that wouldn't give up easily. She reminded him somewhat of the late actress Kay Kendall. He appreciated the way her smile annihilated her aloofness. How could he describe it to Maddie? An explosive smile, he might say, and probably Maddie would quip that she hadn't heard it.

Straw and Wally.

A good physical match, and perhaps not only that, was Mitch's early impression. Straw had the size and substance such a woman would play against best. Her black cap of hair counterpoint to his straight, thinning gray and white. Her lengthy leanness, Straw's above average height and bulky build. Her forties, his sixties. And yes, his wealth and her urgency to be underwritten.

Need for need, they were a pair of providers who had evidently opened up supply lines.

Gratified mischief, Mitch thought.

"I've yet to cut the lettuce," Straw said. He was effortlessly aristocratic-looking. It was incongruous that his hands and forearms should now be so caked with dirt, that soil was impacted beneath his fingernails. A transfer of lipstick was discernible on his nearly white brush mustache. He had on frayed cutoff jeans and ruined moccasins.

"Why don't you all go inside," he said, "and I'll be along shortly."

Chapter 16

Lunch on the upper terrace.

Everyone freshly bathed and changed into whites. Pleated linen shorts, sheer shirts hardly buttoned, oversize tank tops with loose ventilating armholes.

Straw had on a creamy Ecuadorian hat, its brim shaped just so for maximum jauntiness. It was new.

"Coveting my hat, are you? Here!" He put it on Wally before she could dodge. Like his boots it was too large for her, slipped down over her forehead to her brows, caught on her ears.

She laughed gorgeously, went along with it as though the hat was now hers and she intended to wear it. Then, suddenly, as though it was her right, she flung it anywhere. Her hair had gotten mussed. She didn't bother with it.

Above the table, well above them, a stretch of bleached muslin tamed blaze into shadowless flattery. The scents that had been atomized on wrists, throats and ankles competed with the fragrance of the sweet williams in the close-by Versailles planters. The food appeared too beautiful to disturb.

Everything cool.

Green beans, red peppers, white Argenteuil asparagus, magenta beets. Poached salmon sprinkled with dill, a legion of identical and equally decapitated Brisling sardines, tomatoes, cornichons, a paté. And that wasn't all.

The wine was a vintage Gewürztraminer.

Aside on a serving table, to be anticipated throughout, was a *tarte aux poires* and something else layered that was extremely chocolate and a silver platter of fresh green figs so perfectly ripe they required a bed of cotton.

Straw tore at a crusty loaf of French peasant bread. He used the hunk to sop up some olive oil, then dabbed it into a saucer of grated parmesan. He'd be a vigorous eater this day. In keeping with his state of mind.

Mitch had noticed the change in Straw. Not that Straw had been so evidently heavy-hearted before now but it seemed as though an encumbering skin had been shed. Straw's eyes and hands were quicker, his posture higher, his voice rounder and coming from deeper in him.

Mitch had mentioned it to Maddie.

"Told you," she'd said, "but no need to be concerned about Straw."

"Who's concerned?"

"He could never be an old fool," and after scarcely a half beat: "but we'll keep on the lookout for symptoms, won't we?"

The conversation at lunch, which was really the main course, skipped and skimmed along randomly and landed on Wally.

"I was once married to a golf hustler," she said. "He was terribly good at it, would purposely slice and hook his drives, thrash around in the rough and miss easy putts to sucker whoever happened to be his opponent into betting really big on the last couple of holes. Then, of course, he'd play up to his game and make the killing."

"When was that?"

"Oh." Wally smiled. "Too many years ago to divulge. I was practically a child."

"Do you golf?" That from Maddie.

Wally didn't miss the implication. "Never have," she replied.

She went on to tell of her days as a runway fashion model in

New York and in Europe. She'd been a regular for Geoffrey Beene, Cardin and Valentino. When that silly business had had enough of her, she'd certainly had her fill of it. She got into something similar, became a Las Vegas showgirl, one of those detached walking displays, costumed in a few sequins, a feather or two and an enormous headpiece. Eyelashes out to here, she laughed, a self-penalizing laugh.

Mitch stole from her left breast by way of the armhole of her tank top. Earlier he'd seen her a mere triangle short of naked, he thought, and now here he was stealing. What a thief he was. He ought to be caught and convicted. That Wally had been a runway fashion model and a Vegas exhibitionist explained her haughty head, ass control and physical audacity. He liked her.

"That's where Wally and I met," Straw said, "in Vegas. About a month ago when I was out there. She won at baccarat, for me."

"Nine hands in a row," Wally said.

"Ten," Straw corrected. "Then one thing led to another."

Mitch imagined the another.

Hooray for Straw, Maddie nearly blurted. She augured that this Wally would prove to be more forthright and beneficial than all the *mal mariées* that had been circling Straw for years.

Maddie popped nine tiny Niçoise olives into her mouth, stored them in her left jaw. Her tongue conveyed them consecutively to her chew and helped collect the pits in her right jaw. She had an urge to eject the pits forcefully, machine-gun them out. She spat them into her hand and deposited them on her butter dish. She did an interested-in-all-things face and kept it on until there was an adequate break in the conversation. "Mitch is going to teach me to shoot," she announced.

"Splendid idea!" Straw said.

As though his niece's vision was twenty-twenty.

"Good thing for a woman to know," Wally contributed.

"You are going to teach me, aren't you precious?" Maddie said.

"One of these days," Mitch replied.

"Tomorrow," Maddie scheduled.

"With what? Straw doesn't have a pistol, do you Straw?" Mitch signaled Straw should say no.

Straw fibbed reluctantly. "A shotgun or two is all."

Maddie vetoed shotguns. "But say we had a pistol for tomorrow, you'd teach me wouldn't you?"

"Sure," Mitch told her, believing he was on safe ground.

"Marian was an excellent shot," Straw said. "Really, a veritable sharpshooter. She owned a forty-four magnum. Whenever we had a squabble she'd go out and shoot at something. As you can imagine, it unnerved me." He grinned and shook his head as though remembering a close call. "By the way," he told Maddie, "I received another request for foreign aid this past week."

"So did I," Maddie said.

"There's a house in Aix-en-Provence that Marian says she must have."

"To me it was in Barcelona. How much did she hit you up for?"

"Three hundred. What about Elise?"

"The same. I've had it sent."

"So have I."

Better they had given the money to an elephant or rhino cause than to that pair of girl-eating piranhas, Mitch thought. He imagined Elise and Marian with six hundred thousand to blow, and blow it they would.

The same amount Ruder had promised him if he recovered the Kalali goods. Don't think about that, Mitch told himself. It hadn't been on his mind all day. Anyway, not featured.

He backed his chair away from the table some and turned it to better his view. A pair of sparrows were on the terrace railing nervously considering the tray of figs. If the birds got up enough courage to make a go at the figs, how long, Mitch wondered, would he pretend to not notice?

Fig, he thought, and associated *figa,* which was an Italian gutter term he'd often heard Riccio use. Why didn't Riccio just say *cunt?*

Strawbridge land.

Mitch gazed over the railing at it. To his left, south of the house, was about two hundred level acres of pastures. A scattered herd of Holstein-Friesian cows in it. Black and white all-day munchers. The cows didn't belong to Straw but to the dairy farmer whose complex of barns, silos and such were miniaturized in the distance. Straw just allowed the cows.

Mitch had walked over to the dairy farm a few times. He learned from the farmer that Holsteins gave more milk than other breeds. On the average a butterfat content of 3.7 percent. But the milk from Guernseys was higher in protein.

In the opposite direction, north of the house, the terrain was uneven and mainly wooded. Oaks, elms, maples and pines vied for sunlight with their heights. A few hickories. Numerous inexplicable clearings and patches of wild blackberries. Also several energetic springs with runoffs that insisted their ways to lower terrain and spread into a marsh, mysterious, inviolable.

Straight west was the river, the Hudson. A Strawbridge mile and a half between the house and it. That distance made easier by traditional paths. It was something always there to go to, the river, to spend a while on the three-hundred-foot-high granite bluff that overlooked it. Admiring the river's perpetualness, expending some worship on it in a way as probably the native Americans once had, the Mohicans for instance.

Those bluffs high above the river had become a favorite place for Mitch. He'd explored them up and down, gotten to know their obscure traversing ledges, their deceiving crevices and dead ends. They were a long ways from West 47.

Gazing out from the upper terrace, Mitch thought how at one time this land had been an incidental part of a vast Dutch land grant and how smart of great-grandfather Nelson Strawbridge to have acquired it. It was said he won the parcel in a one-on-one croquet match while spending a Fourth of July in Newport.

Grandfather Gordon Strawbridge had also demonstrated his judiciousness by passing the house and land on to his son, Martin (Straw), rather than to his daughter, Elise.

Elise hadn't been entirely omitted from her father's will, but she had good reason to feel slighted. She was left two million, an erotic sketch by Mihaly Zichy that she never knew Gordon owned (why not one of his Fantin-Latours?). And two balls, baseballs autographed by Babe Ruth and Bill Dickey.

The remainder of the estate, estimated to be in the five hundred million range, was divided equally between Straw and Elise's fatherless thirteen-year-old daughter, Madeline (Maddie), whom Gordon had always doted on. Maddie's portion would be looked after by the family lawyers, Albertson and Albertson, otherwise there were no restricting conditions.

Elise was more irate than hurt. She'd never gotten along well with her father. The most that could be said was they'd been fairly compatible for brief periods now and then.

Elise had always taken perverse pleasure in disappointing him. She'd promote herself in his eyes to the point where he'd begin to count on her, then let him down. He often told her she was selfish. She never denied it.

A psychiatrist suggested she was using her negative behavior to test the extent of her father's love for her, to determine how much he would put up with.

She parried the suggestion. "What shit. I'm not that scheming."

She seemed to believe that candor was the fee for indemnity. "It's just not in me," she'd say. "I don't have what it takes to endure even the merest self-deprivation."

No wonder, then, that inheriting only two million was tragic for her. She'd counted on so much more. As sure as she was of her own blood she'd believed it would be coming to her.

She spent close to a hundred thousand on legal fees, trying to invalidate the will. On the basis that her father had been mentally disturbed, a bigot, unbalanced by his extreme intolerance. She claimed the sole reason he'd shorted her was she'd been honest in disclosing her sexual preference for women.

A lady lawyer with whom Elise happened one night to be sharing a three A.M. afterwards ceiling forthrightly advised her to drop her legal action. No court would find in her favor. Even if she won sympathy, which was unlikely, hadn't her father's will been drawn up eleven years *prior* to her *coming out?*

Elise withdrew but not for a moment would she be resigned. She went on a bitter fling. Ran through the two million and was left with no bearable option other than to go on Maddie's dole.

It was difficult for her but she managed to feign affection for Maddie. Brushed her hair, took her to Bergdorf for new shoes, tucked her bedcovers. To her way of thinking it was a sort of self-deprivation. She couldn't sustain it and was greatly relieved when she found she didn't need to, that Maddie would never refuse her.

If Elise had any redeeming qualities she kept them obscured. Was it possible that she was completely without parental conscience? It seemed so. For her, conceiving Maddie had been unpleasant, carrying her had been disfiguring, delivering her had been painful, and having to care for her was over the top.

She didn't keep these justifications to herself, sardonically articulated them for the amusement of her cohorts, most of whom could not feel sorry for her because they needed their full supply of pity for themselves.

About then Maddie had gone blind.

It wasn't really a going. That is, it wasn't gradual.

She awakened one morning believing she hadn't awakened, that the black she was experiencing was still the black of sleep. She often had very realistic dreams, so she lay there awaiting where this one might take her.

She touched her eyelids, caused them to blink. She felt them slipping up and down over her eyes. It was weird. How many million times before had she blinked and never felt that. The tip of her finger felt the flickings of her lashes.

As swift as her realization a volt of panic shot through her. She sat up. She cried out, an unrestrained bawl. When no one came she fell back on her pillows.

Black.

There was no reason for it. She hadn't gotten anything harmful in her eyes.

It was temporary, she assured herself, would go away in a while. Calm down, calm down.

She regretted having cried out, hoped no one had heard her. She wouldn't again no matter what. If this inability to see didn't go away, she'd stay in bed, say she felt achy, had caught a virus, was feverish.

Perhaps she'd be brought some water and antihistamine capsules and a thermometer but other than that there'd be no concern.

She would be alone in the black.

It frightened her but, at the same time, its possible advantages occurred to her. What if she plunged into it, floated on it. What if this black was something she could bring on at will. How useful that could be. If it went away, as it surely would, she hoped she'd be able to get it back.

She lay there listening to herself. Her breathing was a private wind, her heartbeat a friendly, signaling drum. She scratched an itch from her cheek, clicked her teeth, sniffled, swallowed. Her insularity was amplified. With a little more concentration she might be able to hear the coursing of her blood.

Look! Weren't those angels? Angels outlined by trails of glittering effervescence, moving about against the black? If not for the black she wouldn't have been able to see them.

Her black.

She claimed it and felt suddenly serene, as though she'd been granted a wish.

On the third such day when Elise looked in on her, Maddie was up and dressed.

"How are you today?" Elise inquired dutifully.

"I'm blind," Maddie replied matter of fact.

"What nonsense."

The initial examination of Maddie was conducted by an elderly ophthalmologist at his office on East 72nd. He found nothing wrong with her eyes and said in Maddie's presence it was his opinion that she was malingering, faking it.

Uncle Straw took Maddie to see specialists at Johns Hopkins and Mayo and the Hermann Eye Center at Texas Medical. Many of the country's most reputable ophthalmologists, neurologists and neurobiologists had their go at her.

Her head was scanned repeatedly. Each doctor didn't seem to want to rely upon the diagnostic procedures done by the doctor who'd preceded him. Time and again Maddie was placed on a stainless steel tray and, like a torpedo, slid into a tube. Sandbags on each side of her head to keep her from moving, while not only her visual system but her entire brain could be looked at dimensionally and in slices.

Computerized axial tomography, positron-emission tomography, nuclear magnetic resonance, biomagnetic imaging. Scanning laser ophthalmoscopes mapped her retinas in three-tenths of a second.

All diseases that cause blindness were detectable, but the reason for Maddie's loss of sight eluded the specialists.

Had she ever had meningitis?

Meningoencephalitis? Birds carry it.

Cat scratch fever?

No, no and no. Of course, she'd owned a few parakeets and fed pigeons in the park countless times. She adored cats, had had several over the years. There might very well have been scratches, but fever?

Each doctor who beamed into Maddie's eyes and viewed as deep in as he could saw normal, healthy-looking retinas. Nothing wrong with those vital slivers of neural tissue located at the back of the eyeball. No degeneration or even inflammation.

Where the optic nerves stemmed from the retinas also appeared normal. Beyond that point couldn't be seen with an ophthalmoscope. The cause had to be in there, somewhere beyond.

At the optic chasm, perhaps, where the optic nerves split and ran to the left and right like an intersection of a four-lane highway. Or possibly further on in the thalamus, where the optic nerves fed into the switchboard-like geniculate bodies.

The search for a diagnosis proceeded into the visual cortex and on into the cerebral cortex, a region of the brain that still baffled medical science when it came to the part it played in seeing and processing what was seen. All sorts of astounding things could be going on in there that the scans weren't picking up.

Despite their sizable fees the doctors were at a loss.

Maddie's visual system had just shut down, turned off, closed shop.

And Lord knows why.

Maddie vowed to kick the shins of anyone who proposed another scan.

Early on, at one of the most prestigious eye clinics, a young female neurobiologist, relegated to a third-team silent observer, had
dared to speak out of turn with the suggestion that Maddie's blindness might be psychologically caused.

Her words were lost to everyone but Maddie, and she only recalled them when the rummage for a pathological reason ran out of
steam.

Could the psyche block a person's ability to see? It wasn't a common occurrence but neither was it unheard of. In fact, over the past
fifty years, the number of reported cases of *hysterical blindness,* as it
was called, had increased considerably.

According to psychiatry, the condition was brought about by
chronic emotional stress. The unconscious, overloaded with such
stress and tired of putting up with it, converted it into a physical
disorder, such as blindness.

It fit. The more Maddie thought about it the more comfortable
she felt with it, although the *hysterical* label bothered her some. She'd
never been in a state of hysteria, there'd never been any tantrums or
uncontrollable anxieties. Of course, those things could have been
going on in her unconscious, couldn't they?

Possibly.

Anyway, no more doctors, no more scans. She was tutored in
Braille. She also learned to tap about with one of those long white
canes and to trust the guidance of a specially trained dog.

It wasn't so terrible, being blind, she tried to convince herself.
Consider all the ugliness she wouldn't be visually subjected to. Still,
blind was blind, and she hadn't seen enough beauty to satisfy her.

Normally, a person who couldn't see couldn't do much, wasn't
expected to. There were traditional limitations.

Maddie was determined to surpass those limits, stretch them as
far as her black would permit, and then some, if she could. It was,
she believed, much a matter of spirit. Her spirit was her ally, just as
stumble and fumble were her enemies.

She exercised her functioning senses, her hearing, smell, touch.

They became increasingly enhanced. Eventually she found, as she'd hoped, that she was able to consolidate them into a sort of super-perception.

See, her spirit said, *told you so.*

The white cane stayed propped in a corner next to her dresser. The guiding dog was contributed to someone who needed it.

Elise was seldom around. Maddie's blindness would have deprived her even more.

Maddie lived with Uncle Straw.

And now, this remarkable, valiant, spirit-charged woman lives with me, Mitch thought, as there on the upper terrace of Straw's Kinderhook house, he turned and gave his attention to what she was into at the moment.

She was putting on a little show.

She had Wally blindfolded with one of Straw's neckties. The luncheon plates, glasses and all had been moved to one side so about half of the tabletop was clear. On the cleared part lay a black and white hundred-dollar baccarat chip, a keepsake from the night Straw and Wally had met at the Golden Nugget.

"Find the chip," Maddie told Wally. "Go ahead, find it."

Wally reached out with her right hand. She changed her mind three times before deciding where she believed the chip was located. She was way off.

"I don't think it's possible," Wally said, "not for me, anyway."

"You weren't seeing with your fingers," Maddie said. "As I told you, you have to see with your fingers. Try again."

Wally missed again. She laughed and pulled off the blindfold.

Maddie would show her it could be done. Of course, no blindfold was needed. "Place the chip anywhere," she said.

Wally kept the chip in her fist. She winked at Straw. "Okay," she challenged Maddie, "now, you find it."

It was something both Straw and Mitch had seen Maddie do numerous times. *Spatial reckoning* was her label for it.

At first it had been a notion inspired from having heard all those neurologists and neurobiologists speak about the vagaries of the human brain, how one special process of it could override another special process, how it was frequently forced to be cross-worked, how impulses and signals from banks of hundreds of millions of rods and cones circuited information back and forth at the rate of a quadrillionth of a second.

Thus, Maddie visualized her brain as a tremendous tangle that might not always function as perfectly as it was supposed to. Trade-offs of responsibilities could be going on in there, especially between the sensory cells.

For instance, occasionally, hearing cells might smell and smelling cells might hear.

Touching cells might see.

And, maybe, rather than mutually agreeable switching like that, certain more aggressive cells took over doing things they were not supposed to do on their own.

Whenever they felt the urge or were asked to emphatically enough by the landlady.

Spatial reckoning.

Seeing with the fingers.

A way for Maddie to know things were where they were.

She couldn't do it at will. It wasn't something she could absolutely depend on, as she wished it would be. Nor did she believe that her fingers could literally see. However, from all her practice at it and the many times she'd been right, she felt there was something to it. The neurobiologists would scoff at her notion, but by their own admission, they didn't know everything.

Maddie held her hand above the tabletop and concentrated. After about a minute she gave up. "No fair," she said.

Wally was impressed that Maddie had perceived that the chip wasn't on the table. She was further impressed when she suddenly flipped the chip into the air heads or tails fashion and Maddie somehow knew she had and made a mid-air stab at it.

The sparrows were pecking at the figs.

Mitch shooed them away. Less than a minute later they were back on the railing getting set to make another foray. Like me and 47th, Mitch thought.

Maddie pinched his earlobe, as she often did when she wanted his entire attention to what she was about to say. "Be a love," she said, "and fetch the things from the saddlebags of the Harley."

Mitch realized almost immediately what the things would be. He knew her, what a tricker she was, the beautiful, all-time, undefeated champion rascal of the world. He did some exasperation and shook his head incredulously because it was unbelievable that he could love her so much.

"And while you're at it," Maddie told him, "why don't you show Straw your new hog."

Mitch and Straw went down to the Harley. Straw admired it all around, ran his hand over it in places. "Great-looking machine. I've never been on one."

"Never too late."

"For many things. What do you think of my Wally?"

"I think you're almost as lucky as she is."

Straw appreciated that nice way of putting it. They traded smiles, were eyes to eyes for a suspended moment.

Mitch took a bank check from his shirt pocket, handed it to Straw.

"What's this?" Straw asked as he always did.

"The mortgage payment."

"Don't you think it's time we did away with this nonsense?"

The apartment of the Sherry had been Straw's. He'd wanted Mitch and Maddie to have it as a wedding gift. Straw insisted, reasoned that the apartment was territory familiar to Maddie, from the go she'd be at home in it. Mitch compromised. Straw could give half the apartment to Maddie, he'd buy the other half. Thus, the monthly mortgage payments. They were sizable and with interest included.

"Really . . ." Straw protested.

"June and July are also in there," Mitch told him. He'd gotten that much in arrears.

Straw didn't look at the check.

Mitch felt three months lighter.

He unbuckled the saddlebags and took out the two pistols. One was a Glock M-22, a real stopper, the pistol preferred by Secret Service and Drug Enforcement guys. The other was a Beretta 92F Centurion, a backup weapon but also one that had good take-down power.

As a jeweler Mitch had been licensed to carry. Still was but hadn't for years.

He did a little scoffing grunt. "Next," he grumbled, "she'll be wanting to take up knife throwing."

Chapter 17

The following morning, while Maddie helped with the breakfast dishes, Mitch went out to find a place to shoot. He wanted to be done with it so he and Maddie could devote the rest of the day to sloth and passion.

He had in mind the old barn out in the middle of what the Strawbridges had always called the West Meadow.

The undisturbed meadow made it appear as though it would be an easy half mile; however, it turned out to be more of a wade than a walk with the perennial rye grass as it was, thick and crotch high.

Good for the legs, Mitch told himself as he pushed ahead, noticing the contradictions of Queen Anne's lace, less romantically known as wild carrot, and huge hydra-headed purple clover

He, the intruder, was the cause of countless grasshoppers to bound about, for red-winged blackbirds to be flushed up. Garter snakes were running ahead of him.

The sun hadn't yet gotten to the dew deep down. He was soaked to the knees. He paused mid-meadow to look skyward. The moon was a leftover piece of tissue.

The barn was large and lonely. No one visited it anymore. The elements were having their way with it, peeling its coats, bleaching it, promoting rot and rust in places. A dying barn. Its roof looked healthy, though, Mitch noticed. That would help prolong its stand.

He'd intended to use one of the exterior sides for the shooting, but now it occurred to him that considering Maddie's handicap it would be more prudent to do it inside where there were walls all around.

He went in. He saw right away the roof actually wasn't all that good. Sunlight was shafting through it in numerous places. No loft. It wasn't that kind of barn. It had high rafters. An owl was asleep in one. Bats were hung from others.

On the left was some farm machinery past use. A hay rake with its big, curved intimidating prongs. Next to it, a hay baler that looked as though it resented obsolescence and would like nothing better than to compact something or someone.

There were other abandoned items. A lot of rat droppings. Mitch heard the scuttling of mice claws on the wooden floor, hornets whizzing.

He returned to the house for Maddie. She had the weapons and everything in a plastic shopping bag that she refused to give up. She slung it over her shoulder and followed Mitch across the meadow.

She'd been in the barn many times when she was sighted but not since. She had a vague recollection of it. Outstanding was the time Uncle Straw had come as close as a trouser leg of being bitten by a copperhead there. The snake had sprung and gotten its fangs snagged in the woolen fabric.

Mitch tried to move the old potbelly cast iron stove that was in one corner. It was too heavy but he outwitted it, disassembled it and put its manageable components back together where he wanted it, out in the open before the rear well.

He counted off ten paces from the stove and placed at that spot the enamel-topped kitchen table with one leg missing and another wobbly. He covered the grimy surface of the table with some news-paper he'd brought along. Laid out the pistols, clips and cartridges.

"You're too good to me," Maddie remarked.

"Just trying to stay even," Mitch said, which made the next turn with those words hers. "Hold out your open hand."

She did.

He slapped the Beretta into it.

"Is it ready to shoot?" she asked.

"No."

"So why are you giving it to me?"

"So you can load it. A shooter should know how."

"Give me a clip."

"They're on the table."

She found one. "It's empty."

"Load it."

She fumbled around before she found the carton of nine-millimeter cartridges. She sure hated fumble. She removed a round from the carton and felt it for shape and size.

Like a tiny, hard penis, she thought, and then, upon second thought, like a not so tiny clitoris. She often thanked the power in charge of handing out such equipment that she hadn't been given a shy, find-me-if-you-can sort.

Mitch told her how to load the clip. A couple of times he was tempted to guide her fingers but knew she'd be miffed if he did.

Finally, she had in all the clip would hold. Fifteen rounds. "Now I put it into the handle, right?"

"The butt."

"Okay, the butt."

She inserted the clip partway.

"Ram it in," Mitch told her.

"That's what the actress said to the bishop," she quipped. She rammed the clip into place.

Mitch showed her how to break open the barrel of the Beretta so a sixteenth round could be put into the chamber. She did it the second time without his help. "Now?" she asked.

"You ready?"

"In which direction do you suggest I shoot?"

"Wherever except at me." Letting her shoot the first load on her own would teach her a lot, Mitch figured. She might even want to quit after a taste of it.

She held the Beretta slack-armed, didn't have much of a grip on it. She pointed it at anything and pulled the trigger. Kept it pulled as though that was her only option.

The pistol nearly jolted itself out of her hand. As the sixteen rounds fired in rapid succession her aim was snapped further up-wards. The last couple of rounds splintered boards at the peak of the roof.

The owl fluffed itself and turned its back on the disturbance below.

The bats tightened their talons.

The mice scurried to the fields.

Maddie was astonished. She hadn't expected such ferocity. It was as though the Beretta was a lethal infuriated creature on the end of her arm, one that would do her bidding. She liked the smell of the exploded gunpowder, the way the concussion caused her ears to ring.

Now Mitch taught her. The importance of a solid stance, rigid arm, a tight two-hand grip. The advantage of holding her breath and squeezing the Beretta's trigger rather than jerking it.

She improved with each load. The cast iron stove became her target, her adversary. Her sense of direction was uncanny. Mitch spun her around several times to try to confuse her, but she brought her aim to the stove and fired at it.

Her hits rang and ricocheted. Eventually, almost as many hits as misses.

The smoke from so many explosions layered in the air in the barn. The carton of ammunition for the Beretta was depleted. Mitch told her it was.

Again, she'd astounded him, he thought, and again he'd enjoyed it. His blind love, on her way to being a sharpshooter. However, enough was enough. They should go out to the bluff, its mossy spot, do anything to one another. The proposal didn't get out of his mouth because . . .

"Now," she said, extending her arm, "hand me the Glock."

Chapter 18

"The patient's name."

"Kalali." He spelled it for her.

"First name?"

How many Kalalis could there be in this hospital, Mitch thought. "Roudabeth," he replied.

"Are you a relative?"

"Brother-in-law."

"Her condition is improved."

"How much improved? Is she conscious?"

"All I'm allowed to tell you is her condition is improved and that she's no longer in intensive care. For anything else you'll have to speak to her doctor."

"What room is she in now?"

The middle-aged woman with the teenage hairstyle and nearly no chin had already caused her computer to escape from Kalali. She took a persevering New York breath and punched it up again. "Room eleven eighteen east," she informed Mitch in a tone that conveyed that was the last he'd get from her.

He gave her a New York ambiguous thanks and went from patient information to the last-minute gift and other stuff shop off the lobby. Not especially to buy anything, only to sort of hyphenate what might be his next move.

He hadn't intended on being there at New York University Hospital this morning. On his way downtown he'd admitted how much he wasn't looking forward to another day of poking around 47th. At practically that same instant someone vacated a taxi right there and Mitch climbed in. He'd allowed his intuition to tell the driver where to go.

All along he'd been hoping for a conscious Mrs. Kalali. She'd seen the swifts, might be able to make them from the police photo files. At least she could describe them. Mitch had kept up on her condition, phoned the hospital to inquire twice each day, even during the weekend from Straw's. Each time he'd been told there was no change.

But now on Monday morning apparently there'd been a change. Mrs. Kalali was improved. That might mean she was no longer unconscious, perhaps well enough to talk.

He put back the butterscotch Life Savers he was about to buy and went out to the elevator. The up one he chose made a lot of stops. By the time he got off on eleven he was disguised in an attitude of belonging where he was and knowing where he was going.

Everyone at the nursing station of 11 East was busy. Mitch didn't stop and wasn't stopped. Room 1118 was at the far end of the corner. A private room with its door closed.

Maybe, Mitch thought, Mrs. Kalali was being given a sponge bath or was using a bedpan. He prepared himself for any such encounter, would do a medically blasé face, say he was Dr. Laughton, beg pardon and retreat.

He went in.

Mrs. Kalali was face up, eyes closed, head bandaged like a turban. Oxygen leaders were clipped to her nostrils. The only animated thing was the registering of her vital signs on the monitor above her bed.

She might be only sleeping, Mitch thought, might respond if he called out her name. He went close to the side of the bed, stood over her. She appeared insubstantial, still in the throes of trauma. Would it be dangerous to startle her? He'd arouse her gently with a whisper, was about to when the toilet was flushed in the room's private bath.

A young man came out. Preoccupied with himself, the hang of his suit jacket, buttoning it, correcting his shirtsleeves. He was fair-haired and somewhat on the pretty side. When he became aware of Mitch his composure deserted him.

Mitch was experienced with awkward moments. "Has she come to?" he asked with impersonal interest.

"Not yet."

"But anytime now, so the doctor told me."

The young man acted like someone being cornered. He evaded Mitch's eyes and left without another word.

Mitch wasn't about to lose him, whoever he was. He followed him down the corridor and into the same elevator. They didn't speak during the descent. Mitch allowed the young man to exit first, then tagged along behind him to the hospital cafeteria there on the ground floor. At this morning hour all but a few tables were vacant.

The young man took a carton of chocolate milk and a plastic-wrapped egg salad sandwich to a table next to the window. Mitch got an iced tea and closed in, chose the table next over.

Outside on practically the same level was the East River Drive. The hurrying traffic on it was distracting, a lot of taxi yellow. The river beyond contaminated-looking.

Continuing to avoid with his eyes, the young man said: "You're the police, aren't you?"

Mitch did a shrug that could have been taken for a yes.

"I knew you'd be showing up about now."

"Why didn't you run?" A good prompt, Mitch figured.

"Why should I? I didn't do anything."

"Depends."

"What do you mean depends?"

"Eat your sandwich."

"I intend to."

"Tell me about you and Mrs. Kalali."

"Nothing to tell."

"Why were you up there with her?"

"Just looking in on her."

"A concerned visit."

"That's all."

"Your first time here probably. You been here before?"

"Could I see some police identification? I refuse to say anything more until you show me identification."

Mitch complied, went into his jacket pocket, but, as though diverted by a sudden realization, he brought nothing out. "I just now made you," he said. "You work girls at a bust-out bar on 43rd."

"Not me."

"I'm sure of it."

"That's ridiculous."

"What name do you go by?"

"Roger Addison."

A dubious grunt. "That's not a real name."

"It most certainly is." Roger presented his driver's license.

Mitch pretended to examine it suspiciously front and back. "Guess you only resemble the guy who works that bust-out," he conceded.

"It so happens I work at Saks."

Mitch let him suck up some of the chocolate milk before telling him: "You're in deep shit Roger."

"I didn't do anything."

"Tell me about you and Mrs. Kalali."

"Like I said, there's nothing to tell."

"If she comes out of the coma there'll be plenty to tell, won't there?"

An indifferent shrug from Roger. His flushed complexion didn't go along with it.

"Maybe what you're hoping is she doesn't come out of it," Mitch said.

"That's not true."

"Then why are you hanging around here claiming you're family so you can sit bedside at all hours?"

An accurate assumption.

"I've been keeping a sort of vigil," Roger admitted. "I want to be the first person she sees when she comes conscious."

Mitch could relate to that.

"Besides," Roger went on, "one of the doctors told me it's possible that things said to her may be registering."

"So you've been having one-sided conversations."

"It's frustrating."

"I'll bet. What is it you say to her?"

"Mainly I want her to understand that what happened wasn't my fault. There wasn't supposed to be any violence." Roger dropped his head and remained downcast for a long moment. He came up with: "I should have a lawyer, shouldn't I?"

"Can you afford a good one?"

"Not really."

"You claim you didn't do anything."

"I didn't."

"Tell me what you did do and I'll tell you if it's anything."

"I have to be at work at noon," Roger stalled.

"That gives us a couple of hours. Is your story longer than that?" Mitch threw in a smile because it was so evident Roger could use it.

Roger began on the sandwich. Took small bites and chewed slowly. Each swallow brought him closer to disclosure. He had such a need to vent that once he opened up it came pouring out.

He told how he'd met Mrs. Kalali at Saks. He hadn't taken up with her for what he could get out of her. At least that wasn't his only reason and, after a while, as they became more involved, he hardly gave a thought to what he might gain. She was dreadfully unhappy. Her husband was vilely abusing her. There was such satisfaction in being meaningful to her, Roger said. Besides, he had always been physically attracted to mature women.

She would leave her husband. They would go somewhere, anywhere kinder, and be together. No longer would they have to sneak afternoons.

They would. If they had the money.

Mrs. Kalali had little of her own. A few thousand was all.

There was, however, the jewelry.

She proposed they sell it. It was worth far more than they'd get for it. That was the way with jewelry. Buy dear, sell cheap. The dealers on 47th, for example. They feasted on misfortune. They seemed able to smell one's need to sell and, once they got the scent, they started grubbing.

New music, old words, Mitch thought.

Anyway, Roger continued, there was the jewelry. And there was the insurance on the jewelry. He wished now she'd never mentioned the insurance.

She brought the policy to one of their afternoons at the Plaza. It was like a catechism. Questions and answers. Clearly, if the jewelry was stolen the insurance company had to pay Mrs. Kalali the appraised value within ninety days. The future contained a check for six million.

"So, you arranged for a gimmie," Mitch said.

"A what?"

"You made a deal with someone to steal it."

"What did you call it?"

"A gimmie. It's a street term."

"Oh."

"Did you or Mrs. Kalali make those arrangements?"

It was like Roger hadn't heard the question.

Mitch asked again.

Still nothing from Roger. He got up. It seemed he was going to leave; however he went to the cafeteria counter. He returned to the table with a plastic container of bread pudding and, evidently, a decision. Between the second and third spoonfuls of the pudding he mumbled something.

"What?"

"I took care of it," Roger repeated.

"The gimmie?"

"Whatever you call it."

"You know those kind of people?"

"I didn't. I happened to know someone who knew someone of that sort."

"Who?"

"I'd rather not say."

"I mean who did this acquaintance of yours hook you up with?"

"I met the man. I met with him twice."

"Where?"

"The Four Seasons."

"Really, the Four Seasons?"

"He bought lunch. With a platinum American Express."

"What was the man's name?" The key question.

"He introduced himself as Frank Melton."

Frank Melton didn't ring a bell with Mitch.

"But," Roger said, "I got a glance at the name on his platinum card. It was Crosetti. I didn't get the first name."

Crosetti? That rang all kinds of bells. Sal Crosetti.

Roger continued: "He wasn't very receptive until I told him the jewelry was valued at six million. I gave him the layout of the Kalali house, the alarm system and everything. He told me more or less how it would go, assured me there wouldn't be any violence. Just a nice, quiet robbery were his words. I believed him. I'm in trouble aren't I?"

"You're in trouble."

"But I didn't do anything."

Mitch sat back and took a moment to study this Roger Addison. His hair was well-cut. His ears had an almost translucent quality to them. Mitch still hadn't gotten a direct look at his eyes. There was a small birthmark, purplish, like a berry stain on the back of his neck just above the collar of what was probably this Monday's version of his daily fresh shirt. In a better world this Roger would never have stepped into the stream of 47th and been carried in over his head.

"I didn't do anything," he was again insisting.

Mitch wondered if he should level with him, tell him he was an accessory to murder for one thing and would probably do ten to fifteen on that count alone, tell him he wasn't the sort who'd do well in the joint, that he'd get fucked to death.

No use spoiling his day, Mitch decided.

Chapter 19

Salvatore Crosetti had been an outside-insider of 47th for going on twelve years. At one time he'd been just a have-around guy for an underboss in Providence, which was his hometown. Back then, when he wasn't just being around, he was out collecting from or paying off people who bet on sports. Mostly collecting from. He got paid a fixed amount weekly for doing that.

He saved a few thousand. Chances for scores came along and he'd had the money to take advantage. Like a certain race on the Saturday card at Narragansett that he knew the winner of the Thursday before. He also handled a little side action from suckers on football and baskets. No telling to what extent his boss wouldn't have appreciated that.

The big break for Crosetti came when a friend of his Uncle Mario developed emphysema and was advised by the doctors to go live as long as he could someplace where the air was easier to breathe and he wouldn't have to move around much. This friend was an established New York City fence with a crew of swifts and numerous 47th Street contacts. He sold out to Crosetti for fifty thousand. Twenty-five on the handshake, twenty-five on the come.

Crosetti was a fence to be dealt with from his first week at it. It was as though he was spontaneously transformed, the way he assumed the image. Probably it was the way he'd had himself in mind for years. No more acrylic in his suits. No more once-a-month haircuts. He dressed tastefully conservative, bought his suits and accessories at Dunhill. His knowledge of gems and jewelry was limited, but he bluffed convincingly while he picked up on them quickly.

He had an instinctive sense of how to handle his swifts, when to be hard or lenient on them. His crew consisted of three blacks and two whites. They all lived in Mount Vernon.

Early on, Crosetti caught one of the whites holding back and got rid of him. Refused to take him on again. Another was apprehended in the closet of a house and was sentenced to three years. For the year and a half the swift was inside Crosetti kept true to the code, provided for the guy's wife and kids. An envelope containing cash every month.

Crosetti wasn't married. He always had a juggle of women friends, both straights and hooks. He preferred hooks who looked straight and straights with a hooker semblance to them. He had a physical reputation that, according to persistent firsthand testimony, must have been deserved.

During his first few years on 47th Crosetti did business with both Riccio and Visconti. Then he had a falling out with Riccio over a piece of swag Riccio had bought from him. A ring with a fair-sized stone in it that looked for all the world to be a good ruby. Refractive tests proved it was a spinel, and, as such, wasn't worth a tenth of what Riccio had paid.

Typically, Riccio old-mobbed. Didn't merely ask for his money back but demanded and insulted, claimed for all the street to hear that Crosetti had intentionally cheated him.

Crosetti took exception. His reputation was at stake. Out of resentment rather than deceit he counterclaimed he'd sold Riccio a ruby that was a ruby and that Riccio was trying to fuck him out of both the ruby and the money.

The bitterness between the two men reached its apogee one noontime when Riccio was out on the street and happened to spot Crosetti across the way. "Piece of shit!" Riccio shouted.

"Dirty prick!" Crosetti fired back.

What ensued was a name-calling battle that continued for the length of the block. Riccio on one side of the street. Crosetti on the opposite side. A crowd followed each along as they *scumbagged* and *cocksuckered* at one another. Spit sprayed the air, fists were raised. Every so often Riccio did a meaner face and feinted a charge across. Crosetti sneered defiantly, extended his arms and beckoned Riccio to come ahead.

How many times and ways could they shout *asshole?* When they'd exhausted such everyday defilements, they found fresh ammunition in calling down venereal diseases on one another.

At various times in the past there'd been other al fresco arguments on 47th, but never one to compare with Riccio versus Crosetti. It was an event still being recalled. People who'd been nowhere near 47th that day claimed to have witnessed it.

Mitch was one of those who missed it; however both Riccio and Crosetti told him their conflicting versions of it—what brought it about and who got the best of it.

He preferred to believe Crosetti.

Because he enjoyed disbelieving Riccio.

In Mitch's opinion, of all the fences, Crosetti was the least slippery. That was not to say Crosetti was entirely lacking in that unctuous quality. He had a reserve of it in him that he could apply to help him squeeze out of a tight spot; however, slippery wasn't his everyday way.

As yet, Crosetti and Mitch hadn't needed to confront one another head-on. They'd only sideswiped a few times.

Like five years ago when Mitch was out to recover a pair of Van Cleef & Arpels diamond bracelets that were the major pieces taken in a robbery up in Larchmont. Mitch was on the corner of 46th and Fifth having a hot dog and a Hire's at a street vendor's wagon. Crosetti came up. He had an unlighted seven-inch Cohiba Robusto protruding from the left corner of his mouth. An element of his cachet. Mitch had never seen him light up. He literally conducted conversations with it, held it between his first finger and thumb and wielded it like a baton.

The color of the cigar was a perfect match for the beaded-stripe, double-breasted suit he had on that day. A blue paisley silk square puffed stylishly from his breast pocket.

"I'll have what he's having," Crosetti told the vendor, "except for the kraut, no kraut."

He removed the cigar from his mouth so he could put in a third of the dog and roll. He hardly chewed before swallowing.

"How's it going, Mitch?"

"Okay, Sal, how about you."

"Good and bad, you know. A little of each and not too much of either. That's what keeps things interesting, right?" Another bite and then, as though the exchange had been going on for a while, "By the way, the two similar Van Cleef pieces you been looking for."

"What about them?"

"They ain't anymore."

"You know that for sure."

"Why should I shit you? They went three days ago. I personally saw them go. Personally."

Crosetti was letting Mitch know that the diamonds of the Van Cleef bracelets had been plucked from their platinum settings and the settings had been melted down. It wasn't good news but being told was a sort of favor.

Mitch thanked Crosetti for it.

Now was another time. Now was the Monday when Roger Addison had revealed Crosetti's involvement in the Kalali robbery and it looked as though a head-on between Mitch and Crosetti was inevitable.

Mitch went directly from New York University Hospital to 47th. He worked the street, on the lookout for Crosetti, inquiring here and there in an offhand manner.

"Crosetti."

"He was around."

"When?"

"Last week. Tuesday I think it was. He hasn't been around since."

"I understand he hasn't been offering much lately." A leading remark from Mitch.

"Not to me anyway."

"He usually throws you a little something, doesn't he?"

"Very little and not usually."

Crosetti hung out, when he hung out, in the Monarch, a large exchange located mid-block on the north side of the street. His spot was the concession of a somewhat hooked-up guy who was seldom there. A narrow spot in the left front corner of the exchange. No display cases, no merchandise. Business was done pocket to pocket. Crosetti would sit in there at the window and watch the street, as though it was an all-day movie.

But he wasn't there today.

He wasn't around.

Mitch pay-phoned Visconti, who immediately came on. His excuse for the call was to thank him for the binoculars.

"How was it up in Kinderhook?" Visconti inquired.

"Fine."

"Nice country, especially this time of year."

How, Mitch wondered, did Visconti know Straw's place was in Kinderhook, not just upstate somewhere, but specifically Kinderhook? Just as puzzling, why did he know?

"You missed out on a great weekend Mitch. Besides the people I told you would be there, there were some others you know."

"Such as?"

"The dealer, Ben Ziegler, for one. He dropped by. You know Ben, and Sy Plansky, the colored stone guy from L.A."

Mitch knew Plansky from the Laughton and Sons days. A business acquaintance of his father's who, when a better piece was missing one of its colored stones, could be depended upon to come up with a close enough match.

"Sal Crosetti was also out," Visconti said. "You know Sal, of course, but I bet you didn't know he could do magic."

"He's never done any time. I guess that's magic." Mitch did a little laugh.

So did Visconti. "Sal dazzled us with his sleight of hand. The only thing he didn't make disappear was his hard-on. You should have seen the quality bimbo he had with him."

"What else did he have with him?"

"Like what?"

"Like anything?"

"We didn't do any business if that's what you mean. Shit, Mitch, you want to know you should ask. I'm not saying I'd tell you true, but, you and me, we're close enough for you to ask straight out."

Such bullshit, Mitch thought.

"What is it," Visconti wanted to know. "Does Sal have something you're after?"

"No."

"Like the Kalali goods?"

"If he did you'd know it," Mitch said. "You'd be the first to know, wouldn't you?"

"Fucking right. If he didn't bring it to me I'd shove his tongue up his ass."

Silence in reverence for that image.

"Come to think of it," Visconti went on, "the Kalali thing isn't Sal's style. There's never been blood on any of his goods. His crew never carries."

"You're making too much of this. I just inquired and you stretched it."

"You're right, Mitch. Yeah. Hey, you play squash or handball?"

"Used to."

"How about one of these afternoons going with me to my club? Later this week maybe."

"It's possible."

"Pick a day, I'm yours."

"I'll let you know."

"If you don't happen to be in the mood for a match we can just take some steam and a plunge. They got a special pool they keep at around forty degrees. Turns any size dick into an acorn."

Mitch nearly winced. He struck the pay phone's push button panel with the heel of his hand, clicked down the cradle a couple of times and hung up. It would sound as though electronic trouble had disconnected him. He'd heard enough. Evidently Crosetti hadn't moved the goods in Visconti's direction. Not yet, anyway.

He went to the intersection and was crossing when Hurley's police Plymouth turned the corner and intercepted him in the crosswalk.

"Where you headed?" Hurley asked.

"The office."

"Fuck that."

Crossers were having to go around Hurley's car, were grumbling about it being in the way. Some pounded on the trunk.

"Get in before I get lynched," Hurley told Mitch.

He hung a left on 46th and went north on Park. While stopped at a light, he glanced out at a talker. A young guy who looked three times his age, wearing clothes he probably hadn't had off in a year. Matted hair and a long-ignored beard. He was striding along hard, ranting hatefully to someone in his head.

"Sal Crosetti . . . " Mitch began.

"A loonybin," Hurley said. "That's what we got, a fucking open zoo for crazies, know what I mean? Someday I'm going to get uncommitted."

"Sure," Mitch said indulgently.

"What I could go for is a place down on the Maryland–Chesapeake shore. Plenty of land with a keep-out sign every five feet. Have some horses. Ever been down there, around Prince Frederick, that part?"

"No. You ever owned a horse?"

"A piece of a claimer once. Wiseguy bookie talked me into it, the fuck. I owned a tenth or something like that. The horse never won, never. Dropped in class and ran out three times."

Mitch tried to imagine Hurley on a Maryland horse farm. It was most unlikely. "Take a lot of money to own a place like that. If you had that much you probably wouldn't want to."

"Probably not," Hurley said dourly. "I'd go live in Monaco or some such place. Lay around and get waited on."

Hurley was about as down as Mitch had ever seen him. Maybe,

Mitch thought, hearing about Addison and Sal Crosetti would lift him. Those would have been Mitch's next words, however . . .

"How about this?" Hurley said. "A lady, a well-off type, shops at Bergdorf. Buys a few things, walks over to the park and up to her apartment house in the sixties. Goes into the lobby, gets into the elevator. A guy gets in with her. Another guy is covering the lobby attendant. These two cowboys had spotted her in Bergdorf, and the ring she's wearing—a six-carat diamond, emerald-cut, a Tiffany stone. The guy in the elevator orders her to hand over the ring. She refuses. He doesn't tell her a second time. He takes out a pair of pruning shears and lops off her finger."

"This happened?"

"Saturday."

"Christ!"

"Yeah, Him, Mary, Joseph and the rest."

"Promise me something."

"Sure, what?"

"Don't tell this New York true romance to Maddie."

"I won't."

"Promise."

"I said I won't."

Mitch did a grin and kept it on, challenging Hurley to decipher it.

"What did you do, find the Kalali swag in your Rice Krispie box this morning?" Hurley said.

"Not quite."

Mitch related the question-and-answer session he'd had with Roger Addison that morning, how Addison, on behalf of Mrs. Kalali, had arranged a gimmie with Sal Crosetti.

"Crosetti?" Hurley considered that dubiously for a long moment. "I guess there's always the possibility that one of his swifts lost it and began whacking out people."

"Going to have him picked up?"

"How do you want to play it?"

"You know. I'd like the chance to shake him down before you start shaking him up." Mitch was concerned with making the recovery. According to the terms of his agreement with Columbia if the police recovered he got nothing. Hurley knew that. "Do what you have to," Mitch said resignedly.

"You want a first shot at Crosetti, you got it," Hurley told him. "Just don't take all week."

"A couple of days."

"Maybe not even that. I have an idea where Crosetti might be later tonight, around eleven or so."

"Where?"

"I'll come by for you."

Those were possibly six-hundred-thousand-dollar words, Mitch thought. Things were falling into place. "Want to go have a coffee?"

"Can't. Got another case and paperwork up to my ass at the preese."

Hurley dropped Mitch off outside his office and continued on crosstown. He didn't know by memory where Crosetti now lived, had to look it up in the directory he kept on such people, a small, simulated-leather-covered address book badly in need of a refill. Soiled pages, smeared and crossed-out entries, alphabet tabs missing.

He drove uptown on Tenth Avenue. Tenth became Amsterdam. At 71st he took Broadway for two blocks and parked on 73rd. He entered the Ansonia.

Crosetti's suite was on the fifteenth floor of the old, face-lifted, renovated hotel. Hurley called up on a house phone, allowed a full minute of rings. To make double sure he also dialed Crosetti's number on one of the pay phones and let it ring twenty times.

He took the self-service elevator up to fifteen, located Crosetti's suite and went right to work on the three locks. Two old, one new, all three relatively easy for Hurley to tumble.

The suite was two rooms, a bedroom and a sitting room. A bathroom but no kitchen, just a small refrigerator in a closet.

Searching wasn't difficult. There weren't many hiding places and Hurley was familiar with all the usual ones: the flip-top trash pail, the air conditioner, the ice trays, the toilet tank, toes of shoes. He went through each room swiftly and methodically, not being overly careful because no matter how careful he might be Crosetti would know someone had been there.

On a table in the sitting room positioned close to one of the windows was a millimeter gauge, a Mettler PC 400C electronic scale, some tweezers, a triplet ten-power loupe, a jar of diamond-washing alcohol, a bottle of sulfuric acid and its companion piece of slate for determining gold content. A fence's usual essentials.

A brown paper bag contained a handful of gold and platinum ring and bracelet mountings. Bereft of their stones, they appeared merely metallic, forsaken.

No sign of what Hurley was hoping for.

He took a last look around and went out.

Chapter 20

At twenty after eleven that night Mitch was waiting outside the Sherry. He'd been there for over a half hour, talking bygone baseball and recent violence with the doorman.

Hurley's police Plymouth pulled to the curb.

"I was about to give up on you," Mitch told Hurley.

"I said around eleven. Twenty after is around."

Wait had again chafed Mitch. "Where we going?"

"Hopefully to get you your six hundred large. Does Maddie know you're with me?"

"Sure."

"You tell her everything?"

"No, you do."

They took 59th over to Third and went uptown. To a high-rise apartment house on 70th. Thirty-six stories trying for the impression of upscale. Its oversize lobby contained a lot of overstuffed furniture, mirrors and several hanging light fixtures comprised of clear plastic unsuccessfully imitating crystal.

Both of the lobby attendants on duty knew Hurley by name. They also assumed to know what he was there for. The elevator was self-service. Hurley punched in the button numbered 22. The coalesced smell of diverse food preferences was pronounced. Even more so in the corridor of the twenty-second floor. Various sounds leaked through the many closed doors.

All the way down the corridor and around another to the last possible apartment. Hurley pressed the square chime button in the face of the door. They were looked out at through a peephole.

The woman who admitted them acted a bit too glad to see Hurley, gave him a quick hug. She was a one-name person that Hurley introduced as Gloria. Chunky and plain-faced. The cotton print dress she had on concealed her shape. Her shoes were black flats.

There was a narrow table in the entryway. Business cards on it. Mitch picked up one of the cards on the way in. It had the word INTERIORS and a phone number.

No doubt about the place. A typical, twenty-five-hundred-a-month unfurnished. Three bedrooms, living room, dining alcove, narrow New York kitchen. Effortlessly decorated in black and beige and chrome. Two eight-foot sofas were separated by a low glass table. An artificial ficus with lima bean–shaped pebbles around the base of its trunk. Framed $19.98 prints of tropical scenes: a black native's head eternally burdened by a stalk of bananas.

Mitch was on the sofa that was vacant. The sofa opposite was occupied by two working girls. One was blonder but the hair of both was a mass of split ends and done to death by repetitive chemical warfare.

The two were neither pretty nor ugly. One way or the other would depend on the light, the angle and the degree of arousal that had been attained. They were overdressed, as though there was to be a party. Their long fingernails were rectangular-shaped and enameled white.

Interiors, Mitch thought. Evidently this was one of the places Hurley came to get serviced or called for a delivery. At the moment he was off somewhere having a few private words with Gloria.

The girls did smiles at Mitch. It was Monday night slow. Any action would be a godsend.

"What's your name?" the less blonde asked.

Mitch told her his first.

"What do you do Mitch?"

"I have a business on 47th Street."

"You a diamond dealer?"

"Yeah," Mitch fibbed for the hell of it.

"Can you get me a diamond?"

The predictable question. Mitch shrugged.

"Actually, what I want is studs. Two-carat studs, although I'd settle for one-carat."

Said as though her wanting was enough. Mitch doubted she was
really that spoiled. "What's wrong with those you have on?" he
asked.

"These? These are fakes. You can tell can't you?"

"They look okay," Mitch told her.

"No shit, can you get me some studs?"

"He's a stud," the more blonde put in.

"Keep out of this," the less blonde snapped.

The more blonde didn't. "A guy I saw a few weeks ago told me
he was a diamond dealer," she said. "He promised me a ring but
didn't come through." She did a pout.

"You gave it a try but he gave it a lie," the less blonde smirked
competitively.

"Mitch wouldn't do that, would you Mitch?"

"Never know," Mitch replied.

"I'd like to find out what you're made of, so to speak," the less
blonde said.

As though it was an unpremeditated, brand-new, marvelous idea,
the more blonde proposed that they go into the bedroom for a
triple.

"Not tonight," Mitch said.

From that point on, as far as the girls were concerned, he wasn't
there.

Hurley came and sat, told Mitch: "He's here. Getting his oil
changed."

"We're not going to confront him here, are we?"

"No. I promised Gloria we wouldn't."

They waited nearly a half hour. To Mitch it seemed much longer.
Crosetti came from one of the bedrooms, tie and jacket off. He

looked as though he'd just gotten well-laid. There was a sort of loose, slow float to his head.

He was surprised but not taken aback to see Hurley and Mitch there. He greeted them amiably. Hurley suggested they go someplace for a talk.

They went down to the lobby and settled in armchairs in the far corner.

Crosetti took out one of his Cohiba Robustos. It fit perfectly into the hole he shaped with his lips. He worked it in and out a few times, rotated it, licked it, went through the entire ritual except for lighting up. He looked to Mitch, looked to Hurley, asked, by raising his chin, what this was about.

"Saturday before last," Hurley began, "there was a robbery over in Jersey."

"Where in Jersey?" Crosetti asked.

"Far Hills."

"Where's that?"

"Don't shit us."

"I'm strictly Westchester," Crosetti said. "You both know I'm strictly Westchester. Yeah I might reach up into Greenwich or someplace once in a while but as a rule I don't cross state lines."

"Far Hills," Mitch insisted.

"Believe me, Mitch, I wouldn't go all the way over to Far Hills for the fucking crown jewels in a bureau drawer."

"That's not what we're getting, Sal."

"From who are you getting?"

"How about a young civilian named Roger Addison?"

"The name means nothing," Crosetti replied too quickly. "Some snitch is playing with your heads. When did you say this Far Hills job was?"

"A week ago last Saturday."

"I was in A.C."

"But where was your crew?"

"I gave them the weekend off."

"Sure you did."

"They didn't do Far Hills," Sal said unequivocally.

"I want to believe you, Sal, but I don't," Hurley said.

"How much swag is involved?"

"Six million."

"So I heard," Sal admitted.

"With blood on it."

"That I also heard."

"Sal . . ."

"Jimmy, honest to Christ, me and my crew had nothing to do with Far Hills."

"Let me bring you up to speed," Mitch told Sal. Told him point by point the information he'd extracted that morning from Roger Addison. The two lunches at the Four Seasons, the gimmie that was arranged, all of it.

Sal listened level-eyed and expressionless. Then came a moment of decision, a silent, paragraphic moment during which he cocked his head and looked off to his left as though a prompt would be forthcoming from that direction.

He held his cigar upright. "Okay," he said, "there was a gimmie. At least there was supposed to be. Why the fuck not? Gimmies are good for the economy. The people make out; I get, my swifts get, whoever buys gets, the street gets. The only one out is the insurance company and they already got so fucking much they don't deserve. Know what I mean? Circulation, good for the economy."

Mitch had to admit to himself there was some validity to Crosetti's reasoning. Long ago he'd arrived at a similar philosophy. Of course, that the insurance companies lost appealed to him.

Crosetti continued:

"This kid what's-his-name and me made an arrangement. I had it scheduled in my head for Friday night. That was the Friday before last. But my best swift's wife is having a baby, the Lamaze way, you know, and he's got to be there, and another got punched out pretty bad Thursday afternoon and he's a mess. I'm shorthanded. So, I reschedule it in my head for sometime the following week and with nothing happening take off for A.C. I'm back on Monday and I drive over to Far Hills to take a look at the job. The place is all tied up with crime scene ribbon and there's all kinds of law all over it. Needless to say, I don't even stop."

Mitch looked at Hurley to see if he was buying it. Hurley did a *could be* shrug.

"You're saying the thing never came off, somebody got to the place ahead of you?"

"That's it," Crosetti said. "You're blaming me for something I would have done but it got done before I could do it. *Capish?*"

Mitch and Hurley didn't let it go at that. Crosetti glanced from one to the other for reaction, but they gamed him, just sat there silent and blank. Which pulled the story out of Crosetti again.

He repeated it in part or entirely three times more. Each time he omitted something or added another detail, but, basically, he stuck to the same version and each time both Mitch and Hurley found the gimmie that never happened more acceptable.

"Sure, Sal, but let me ask, personally, in your professional opinion, who do you think did the Kalali thing?"

"I got no fucking idea. Honest. Nobody has put even initials in my ear. I do know the street wants the goods bad. I know that for sure because of the way I've been pressed. This past weekend I got pressed hard by certain people and they got pissed at me, but what the fuck, I can't come up with goods I ain't got."

All the while Crosetti kept time and jabbed for emphasis with his unlighted cigar. As though he was in front of the New York Philharmonic.

"Anyway," he went on, "why is everybody making such a big fucking deal out of these particular goods? They show up, they show up. They don't, they don't. It ain't like there's never going to be more."

Mitch watched Crosetti go.

He felt somewhat drained. That made him realize to what measure he'd been counting on the recovery, actually the six hundred thousand. Unconsciously maybe but nonetheless counting. Having big money of his own wasn't really all that important, he fibbed to himself.

A resigned sigh. "Well," he said, "back to the starting blocks."

"Yeah, false start," Hurley said.

They stood up to leave.

"By the way," Hurley said, "I forgot to mention, I have to go out of town for a few days."

"When?"

"Tomorrow morning. I'm going to Maryland."

"To look over some properties, I suppose," Mitch said wryly.

"Don't I wish. I have to testify on a case in Baltimore. I gave a deposition but they want me on the stand."

"How long will you be gone?"

"I'll be back Thursday. Friday, the latest. Anything turns up give me a call at the Chesapeake Motel."

Chapter 21

Lois Mae Dayton, more frequently known as Peaches, had dire needs again.

Like a place to go back to. She had been sharing a fourth-floor, one-and-a-half-room walk-up on Cebra Avenue in the Stapleton section of Staten Island. With a girl about her own age named Debbie something. During the past week, while Peaches was hanging out with Floyd and others in Brooklyn, Debbie had taken off, and that same day the walk-up had been rented to someone else.

Debbie had taken everything with her. Along with her own stuff every stitch and shoe and possession of Peaches.

Considering what little Peaches was left with—the dress she had on and whatever happened to be in her shoulder bag—she took the loss fairly well. She'd asked for it, she believed, as she had more or less times before. It was her fault for having trusted a size-seven roommate. No use wasting anger on Debbie. She was gone to somewhere.

Peaches was now on the Staten Island Ferry, returning to Manhattan. Out on the upper deck on the portside seated on one of the fixed benches. The ferry trip was a time-out. The next phase of her life and having to cope with it wouldn't begin until the ferry pulled in. In the meantime the vessel was growling and shuddering under her and she didn't have sunglasses to offset the late morning glare on the water.

She closed her eyes.

To sort of celebrate the beginning that lay ahead, she restricted her thoughts to things she would like. Foremost, a place of her own. Entirely hers, no roommate or guy staying over longer than a night or two and then moving in. A place on the Upper West Side not far from the park, or, even better, a loft in the TriBeCa area. She'd furnish it with truly new furniture, not a single broken thing retrieved from the street or lugged out of some second-, third-, fourth-hand store.

It wasn't unthinkable that she'd have a car. Sure, a convertible she'd go like hell and look outstanding in. A driver's license with her photo on it, a genuine Social Security number rather than just nine numbers she made up. A checking account? A credit card? There'd be lots of dinners out. She'd know all the best eating places.

As for clothes, she might go DKNY. At the very least Calvin. The shoes she'd have!

She opened her eyes. Yawned. Her teeth needed brushing. The ferry still had quite a ways to go. The water didn't look like anything she'd care to swim in. Once she'd almost learned to swim.

She got up and went inside to the restroom. It smelled like what it was mainly for. She pulled off her panties and threw them into the trash basket. Tore open the packet of three she'd bought for a dollar off an outside table of a store on Orchard Street that morning. Put a fresh pair on and felt that much improved.

Her makeup needed repair.

She brushed her hair, and used her fingers to give it the desirable muss.

She dug into the very bottom of her bag for the loose change she'd thrown in at various times. Made sure she got every penny. Three dollars forty-three cents. She put the change into her small, inside purse, which then contained altogether sixteen dollars and some.

Also in that inside purse were the earrings.

She decided to put them on.

The light in that enclosed space was yellow and dim. It cost the diamonds nearly all their glitter. The rubies looked more black than red.

Peaches had had a falling out with Floyd over the earrings. After the robbery she wouldn't take them off, contended they were hers, her part of the swag.

That wasn't how Floyd saw it. He tried to sweet-talk and fondle them off her. Offered her a hundred for them. Finally he lost patience and set about to rip them off. They were made with locking French backs and held fast to her ears.

She managed to struggle free of Floyd, made a dash down to the street. He wasn't about to chase after her and cause a public fuss. Little kicking, honky ass bitch with bleeding earlobes: swag earrings with much more serious blood on them.

The ferry was bumping pilings, lining up with its slip.

Peaches returned the earrings to her inside purse and hurried out to the unloading ramp to be among the first off. Next was the subway. She believed it a significant positive sign that she was exactly on time to catch the Lexington Avenue express, and, after long stretches of unsteady, noisy speed and seven screeching stops, she came up out of the ground at 59th Street.

There were numerous jewelry stores in the area, including Tiffany and Winston and Van Cleef & Arpels. She decided against those imposing establishments, settled on a small shop on 60th because it felt comfortable to her.

She went in with one of the earrings in her fist and what she believed was her most winning expression. She made it immediately understood that she was a seller not a buyer.

The jeweler was an ordinary-looking man named Eli Phelps. He had pale, pampered hands. He examined the earring with a ten-power loupe and concealed his interest.

"Where's the other?" he asked.

"I lost it."

"How unfortunate."

"One ought to be worth something."

"Not nearly as much as a pair."

"So, what's one worth?"

Phelps counted the diamonds and rubies, realized their superb quality, estimated their size within a point or so. At the same time he took stock of Peaches, gauged her knowledge and concluded that she was too young to know the true value.

"Five thousand," he told her.

"Is that all?" Peaches scrinched her face. Actually, five thousand was more than she'd expected.

"I might be able to do six," Phelps conceded, "but that would be cutting it painfully close. Painfully," he repeated because he enjoyed using the word for such circumstances.

Peaches pretended to rummage around in her bag. She did a gasp of surprise. "What do you know, I found it." She brought out the other earring, placed it next to its match on the black velour square on the counter. "Now how much?" she asked straight at Phelps.

He was both impressed and rubbed the wrong way by her artifice. No matter, he was going to make out. "Twenty thousand," he replied.

Peaches was sure her eyes were dancing. See how good fate can be if you just slap it on the ass, she thought. "Cash," she specified.

"I'm afraid that's impossible."

"Why?"

"It just is, impossible."

"I won't take a check," Peaches stated unequivocally. At least two out of every five checks she'd ever accepted had been the no account or insufficient kind. She wasn't about to get stiffed this time.

"Okay," Phelps said, "here's what you do. Take the earrings to this person." He wrote the name and address on the reverse side of one of his business cards. "I'll phone him and tell him to expect you. He'll pay you cash."

"Twenty thousand."

"Without a quibble. I guarantee it."

It was what Phelps had in mind all along. The way he preferred to handle such matters, not lay out any money, just refer. In return he'd get a ten percent cut of the difference between the twenty thousand this girl would be paid and the hundred thousand or so the earrings would bring at auction or wholesale.

Peaches' walk to twenty thousand down Fifth Avenue seemed to take hardly any time. She was in a state of extreme personalization. Just about everything in sight, especially handbags, shoes, compact disc players and such, had a new attainable significance for her.

Twenty thousand.

Two hundred hundreds. One thousand twenties.

Her imagination exaggerated what a stack it would be. A far cry from the paltry amount she'd earned from nearly bare-ass dancing. Those dollar bills and rare fives slipped in under the elastic of her G-string by male fingers in appreciation of the convincing way she squirmed and snapped her crotch and performed make-believe fucks with an upright pole.

When she reached 47th Peaches turned right and entered the first major building, designated number 1. The name that had been given to her by Phelps was on the directory in the lobby. And on the sixth floor she also found it on one of the doors.

She went in.

There was Andrew Laughton.

At the desk in the outer office going over invoices. It took a moment for his expectation to adjust to the sight of Peaches. Eli Phelps had said a *young lady* would be along momentarily wanting to sell some fine earrings that she didn't understand. Meaning she had no idea of their value.

Young lady.

Not an apt description of this person in a flimsy halter dress of pink that barely reached down to her crotch, this gangly-limbed, not yet entirely developed creature whose eyes were way overexaggerated by makeup, whose lower lip appeared swollen and incapable of meeting her upper, a mouth that looked ready to suck on whatever might be offered.

Andrew stood and introduced himself.

Peaches said she was Miranda Turner, a name she'd used before. She gave Phelps' business card to Andrew. "This guy told me you'd give me cash for my earrings."

Andrew offered her a chair.

As she sat, the crotch of her white panties was exposed and remained in sight. She got the earrings from her inner purse, handed them to Andrew.

He took a quick look at them. "They're quite lovely," he said. "And they'll be ever more so once they've been cleaned. May I do that for you?"

"Just give me the money and you can do whatever the fuck you want with them later."

"How much are you hoping to get?"

Peaches thought that had been settled. She didn't want to go through it again. She did a persevering sigh. "Twenty thousand," she said firmly.

The amount seemed incongruous coming from that mouth, Andrew thought. "They certainly appear to be worth that much," he said, "but I'll need to take a closer look."

He placed the earrings on the desk and went into the inner office, ostensibly to get a loupe. Doris was there. He quickly looked through the photographs of the Kalali swag that Mitch had left with him the previous Friday. His experienced eyes had almost immediately recognized the earrings and he was now checking to be certain. And, yes, there, without question, was the photo of them. Was it possible the earrings the girl had were coincidentally the same design? Exactly? No they had too much quality for that to be the case: one-of-a-kind quality.

Andrew whispered swift instructions to Doris. She accompanied him to the outer office. Peaches accepted a Pepsi and Doris complimented her on her fingernails, which had kitten faces enameled on them. "They were nicer," Peaches said, "but now some are chipping off. I had them done by a Korean woman two weeks ago. She also does great palm trees and flags."

Andrew, meanwhile, was examining the earrings under ten-times magnification, noticing the insurance registry code number scratched on the backs near the base of the posts, so tiny it was hardly visible. "How much?" he asked again.

"Twenty thousand," Peaches replied again.

"And you want cash you say?"

Will he ever get it? Peaches thought. She nodded.

"At the moment," Andrew told her, "I don't have that much in the safe . . . "

"Shit," from Peaches with a lot of *sh*.

" . . . but Doris will go to the bank for it."

Peaches brightened. "Where's the bank?"

"I won't be ten minutes," Doris assured and hurried out.

She was true to her word. She returned in eight.

Mitch was with her.

Peaches took a quick look at him and then tried to not look at him. Her instinct told her he could be a problem: he could be a cop. Or perhaps he was only a guy who naturally had that don't-fuck-with-me look. She also noticed Doris had come back empty-handed. "Hey, how about my money?" she demanded.

Andrew introduced Mitch as Investigator Laughton. Mitch went right at it. "Where did you get these earrings?"

"I found them," Peaches said.

"Where?"

"In a taxi. I got in and there they were. Lucky for me, huh?"

Mitch pretended he was believing her, then shifted. "Who gave them to you?"

"I told you I found them in a taxi."

"I know, but someone gave them to you."

"Actually, yeah, someone."

"Who?"

"My aunt. She left them to me when she died."

"On her deathbed."

"How did you know?"

"She took them off and tossed them to you."

"Something like that."

Mitch did an amused laugh. "Where else did you get them?"

Peaches thought for a while before saying smugly: "I blew a guy for them." She enjoyed that explanation because there was a degree of truth to it.

"Generous guy."

"Great blow job." Peaches grinned.

"Who was the guy?"

The truth again. She saw no harm in it. "A guy named Floyd."

"Floyd what?"

"A lot of people don't have last names anymore."

"Is he from around here?"

"Brooklyn." Once more she told herself no harm. There had to be ten thousand Floyds in Brooklyn. What fun it was telling truths this cop was taking to be lies.

Mitch had noticed the boots Peaches was wearing, their pointed steel-capped toes. He'd also guessed her weight to be around a hundred five or ten. He mentally placed her in the footprints he'd seen on the rear grounds of the Kalali house. She fit. She was the lightweight swift.

"You're full of stories," he told her.

"Is that a nice way of saying I'm full of shit?"

"Yeah, now let me tell one. Saturday night, week before last, around midnight, you went with some guys out to Far Hills, New Jersey, to do a robbery. You got left off on the road that runs along the rear grounds of the house. You climbed over the wall and made for the house. Big, white contemporary house. Remember it?"

Don't say anything, Peaches told herself.

Mitch kept on. "The owners of the house had just gotten home from dinner. A man and his wife. They were the only ones at home. They were held at gunpoint while the jewelry was gathered up. The wife was cooperative. The husband wasn't. He got out of line and was killed. The wife panicked and was also shot." Mitch paused. He could almost see his words sinking in. "How am I doing?"

Peaches tried to conceal her astonishment. This fucker knew everything, she thought. It was as though he'd been there when it happened.

She glanced at the way out. Should she try to make a run for it? She could outrun these people. She looked at Mitch and knew she'd never make it.

Keep on lying, her instincts advised.

She glanced at the earrings on the desk. Fucking earrings. She wished now she'd never seen them, that she'd let Floyd have them. She wished now that the only problem she had was having only sixteen dollars to her real name and no place to live.

Keep on lying, her instincts insisted.

She reached down into that place in her where her lies seemed to originate. She chose one but didn't believe it would get her out of this. She was jammed up, seriously jammed this time. Not like before. Those minor offenses such as shoplifting when she was juvenile. If she was still juvenile she'd tell this cop to kiss it.

What to do?

Her instincts told her to twist the truth.

She did a lengthy frown and bit her lower lip crookedly before giving in with a smaller, fragile voice. "It was supposed to be just a joy ride," she said. "Floyd talked me into going along. I had no idea they were out to rob a house."

Andy went into his inner office and phoned the police.

By the time they arrived Mitch had drawn it out of Peaches, the identity of Floyd. Mitch knew that particular Floyd, knew the crew. What's more he knew the fence that crew belonged to.

Chapter 22

"I'll wait up."

"No," Mitch told her, "go on to bed."

"You won't be long."

"I may be a while." He was in the Lexus talking to her on the no-hands cellular. It was like she was a mid-air spirit.

"No matter, I'll wait up. I'll listen to something. One of those Dashiell Hammetts you got me."

"I thought you'd already heard those."

"Why are you still in the car?"

"I'm just sitting here."

"I don't like tonight," she said.

"Got the jeebies?" One of her resurrected words. She had others such as *nifty* and *hunky-dory.*

"Some," she said vaguely, and then, more pointedly: "I felt around in your bottom drawer."

"Oh?"

"You took the Beretta. You should have taken the Glock. And you didn't take a spare clip. Why did you take the Beretta?" Rapid firing at him.

"No particular reason. Just in case."

"Nine to five should be enough. I want you home nights."

"I usually am."

"This is the second night out of four that you've been out. We should find you a nice, safe nine-to-fiver. Even better, how about a sleep-til-nooner?"

"Sure."

"Sex and sloth. Doesn't that appeal to you?"

"I have to make a living Maddie."

"Same old same old. When should I expect you?"

"Go to sleep."

"Can't. I'm wired. You should have taken a spare clip. You should have taken the Glock. Where are you?"

"New Rochelle."

"Hurley called a while ago."

"What did he say?"

"He'll be back in town tomorrow."

Mitch had spoken to Hurley on the phone around dinnertime. He'd told him about Peaches, the Kalali earrings and all, and Hurley had agreed with him on which crew and which fence was involved. Hurley had made him promise to put himself on hold, to wait, not make a move until he got back. Hurley had been adamant about that, so much so he'd drawn that promise out of Mitch three times during the course of their phone conversation.

For naught. Mitch couldn't possibly wait, knew he couldn't, gave it a halfhearted try and was still trying when he changed into some jeans and sneakers, and strapped on the holster rig for the Beretta next to his bare skin so the weapon would be out of sight beneath a lightweight chambray shirt. "Where did you tell Hurley I was?"

"Out. Just out. What else could I tell him? I didn't know where you were and now all I know is New Rochelle, which you've got to admit isn't very specific. Are you hungry?"

"No." She'd made fresh gaspacho for dinner and had unintentionally inundated it with cayenne. "I had two helpings," he fibbed. They'd gone down the disposal.

"Did you now?" she said skeptically.

"I could have gone for three."

"Still, anytime you're out adventuring, you ought to carry along a snack. So you don't get low blood sugar. Low blood sugar could be a fatal handicap."

Fatal, he thought, indicated where her mind was. "You have to give some lessons tomorrow, don't you?"

"One. I did have two but Georgie Watson had to cancel."

"Which is he?"

"The three-card monte kid who works on that cardboard box outside Winston's. He showed me how he does it. It's just a way of lying with your hands. Know the difference between lying and fibbing?"

"Yeah, but what?"

"Mercy."

"I would have said consideration."

"Same thing, sort of. Do you ever lie to me with your hands?"

"Never."

"I love you, come on home."

"I will in a while."

"Whatever it is you're doing it's not worth it."

"Not to you maybe."

"Worth was the wrong word," she said a bit apologetically. "What I meant to say was it's not essential."

No comment from Mitch.

"Seriously, have you given any thought lately to not doing what you do?"

"And becoming a shopkeeper?"

"No, I agree you're not the shopkeeping sort. We could travel. We could go lots of lovely places and you could describe them to me. You know, like you did when we went to Florence."

"Think so?"

"You weren't reading from a guidebook when we were in Florence, were you?"

"You asked me that at the time and I believe I told you I wasn't."

"I know, but sometimes, not often, but sometimes when I ask you the same thing twice you give me different answers."

"Can't put anything over on you."

"Except yourself."

Mitch tried to imagine what that would be like, just traveling around, going anywhere first-class with first-class her. Maybe he'd do it if he had the money, that much.

"You ought to see what I have on," she said.

"Nothing?"

"Uh uh. A little silk something and four-inch heels. A little silk something is more effective than nothing. Especially with four-inch heels, wouldn't you say?"

Effective, he thought.

"It wouldn't take you long to get home. I could be doing sensational things to you only a half hour from now."

"Stop worrying."

"I'm not. I know you can take care of yourself, no matter what."

"Keep thinking that."

"I'll try. You're on the Kalali case, aren't you?"

"Yeah."

"I wish you were just out playing poker. I'd even settle for out playing around," she said and clicked off without a goodbye because, as usual, when it came to them, she disliked the word.

Mitch was parked off the corner of Paine Avenue where it intersected with Lyncroft. Ralph Lentini's house was diagonally across the way. There were no streetlights; however Mitch was able to see the house well enough.

Two stories topped by a shorter third and a wood-shingled roof that looked as though wind, with the help of rot, had made off with more than a few. Around the base of the structure scraggly, slighted rhododendrons were expressing their discontent, and along the property lines on each side were wild-looking twelve-foot-high boxwood hedges. On the right was a double-width concrete driveway.

Mitch had been parked there for nearly an hour and nothing about the house had changed. On the first floor there was still only one paltry light on, which Mitch guessed was a hall light, and there was still the variegated flickering of a television screen reflected upon a wall of the second-floor front room that Mitch believed was most likely a bedroom.

He'd decided not to make a move until there was a change, something that would tell him more definitely what the situation was. He had to contend with his impatience, told it to hang on, that this wasn't ordinary, wasteful wait, the difference being it had a high degree of anticipation in it, as well as imminent reward.

He punched in the CD player. Of the eight-disc load the most compatible with the moment was a rendition of composer Carl Maria von Weber's romantic concerto *Konzertstück* for piano and or-chestra. Mitch was well-acquainted with the piece and its four movements: a lady's longing for her absent love, her fears for his safety, the excitement of his impending return and the passion of reunion.

A car went by, and, five minutes later, another, then a huffing, overdoing, middle-aged jogger and a woman walking a brace of pugs to all their pissing places.

Mitch fast-forwarded the Weber to the last movement. Wait was getting to him. He felt to see that he had his all-purpose knife, and his tiny waterproof Mag Lite. He made sure his sneaker laces were tied. He checked that he had a round in the firing chamber of the Beretta.

He took the Beretta off safety, snugged it back into its holster. It felt reassuring.

He got out of the car. It was good to stand. He walked to the corner and down Paine at a strolling pace, hands in the back jean pockets. There were no sidewalks. He crossed over and after a short ways was directly in front of Lentini's house. From that vantage the television was reflecting on the ceiling in that upper room. Maybe Ralph was up there asleep with the television on. Maybe he'd gone out and left it on, Mitch thought. There were various maybes.

He went up the drive. The grass at the rear of the house was high, dry and gone to seed. There was a swimming pool enclosed by a five-foot-high steel wire fence and a shed that Mitch surmised contained the pool heater, filter and maintenance equipment. The pool looked like a rectangular swamp. Its surface was coated with green scum. Algae upon algae. The smell of organic decay reached out beyond its boundaries.

Mitch surveyed the back of the house. Ground floor left to right: two-car garage, rear entrance, cellar door, window, window, two bay windows, glass-enclosed porch. Second floor right to left: balcony above the porch, window, window, six more windows, balcony over the garage.

He was looking at the house for a way in, as would a swift. He was a swift. A stealer. Out to steal from the stealers. Wasn't this the reason he enjoyed what he did, moments such as now? Wasn't this why he was reluctant to give it up, this more fitting and fulfilling payback for the lady with the automatic up her sable sleeve? His secret heart fed on it, was eating it up now at a hundred and twenty a minute.

He tried the rear door, the windows, the cellar door and the door to the porch. He didn't expect it to be that easy but sometimes people were careless and forgetful.

Not Ralph, though.

How about the second-story windows? People rarely locked their second-story windows. As though that much height was protective. Considering Ralph's profession he probably had his double-bolted and nailed shut, Mitch thought. Then again, maybe not. The only way to find out was to go up and try them. There was a rain gutter that would give him access. He'd be able to sidle along on it once he got up. There was a wisteria vine gone crazy at the corner of the garage. It would be an easy climb for a second-story man. He was a second-story man.

He'd chosen his first grip and made his first foot placement on the vine when the garage door started opening. An elongated rectangle of light struck the concrete turnaround section of the drive. It became wider, brighter as the electric door opener performed its noisy function.

Ralph started the Pontiac. As he backed it out, its headlights raked the foliage of the wisteria at the corner of the garage.

Mitch remained perfectly still. Ralph shifted out of reverse, reached up to the sun visor and pressed the garage door's remote-control switch.

The door commenced its descent.

Ralph took it for granted, didn't wait for the door to be entirely closed before he got under way down the drive.

Mitch realized the chance. He dove for it, rolled in under the descending door, just made it.

He lay there on the garage floor for a moment. The boast he'd heard over the years from so many swifts was true, he thought. There wasn't a house, old or new, that couldn't somehow be gotten into.

The first part of the house Mitch entered was a narrow utility area. Determined to be thorough and systematic, he reached down into the top-load clothes washer and felt around in the clothes dryer. Nothing. Nor in a dirty laundry bag was there anything but offensive socks and underwear and such. Across from the washer and dryer was an upright freezer. It contained numerous wrapped, labeled and frozen veal and pork roasts and an assortment of the cheapest sort of frozen complete dinners. Mitch examined a few of the roasts. They were all about equal size and felt about the same.

Possibly a certain two or three of them were layers of meat around a stuffing of jewels. Was that too much cleverness to expect? Mitch chose at random a couple of the frozen roasts, took them into the adjacent kitchen and placed them in the microwave on high.

He swiftly searched in the kitchen, the obvious places: cabinets, refrigerator, canisters, and the not so obvious, such as down in the belly of the waste disposal unit.

In the adjoining room, which was meant to serve as a dining room, he was made to realize what he was up against.

Ralph's cumulate of swag . . .

Swag upon swag in front of swag beneath swag. The only way to get from room to room was to stay within the narrow aisles that cut through it.

It would be impossible for Mitch to search the many hiding places it presented. How could he determine which of the fifty or more television sets in sight contained the Kalali jewels in place of electronic guts? Which among the legion of vases and lamps and statues should he suspect?

Considerably disheartened he proceeded up the main stairs to the second floor. There was less of an amassment of swag up there but still far too much. Only what was evidently Ralph's bedroom, the room in which earlier Mitch had seen television reflections, was reasonably furnished. Two cartons of VCR porno tapes at the foot of the bed. Precarious stacks of the same on top of two side-by-side giant-screen television sets. Could Ralph's concentration handle two at a time? Under the bed only a pair of wayward panties, another pair shoved between the mattress and box spring. In the top dresser drawer about twenty wristwatches in a neat row, good gold ones, well-known makes, several with diamond bezels and numerals. On the bare floor of the next room a waist-high pile of fur coats with their labels and monograms cut out.

Mitch went up a short flight of lesser stairs to what evidently had once been servants' quarters. Small rooms, low ceilings, one long-abandoned bath. Empty rooms except one, which contained a haphazard heap of luggage. An assortment of overnight bags, suitcases, valises, satchels. No street vendor rip-offs. These were the real expensive things. Vuitton, Hermés, Morabito, Bottega Veneta, Mark Cross and the like. Ralph's swifts had, week after week, brought swag in them and he'd just thrown them in this room.

The many burglaries they represented, Mitch thought, the amount of jewelry and other precious things they had helped carry away. He happened to look down. There, practically at his feet, was a blue Fendi satchel stamped with the initials RK.

Roudabeth Kalali.

Mitch took up the satchel. Its emptiness taunted him. What had been brought in it was most likely still somewhere in this house, hidden among the overwhelming stolen. He hated the house. Ralph and it had beaten him.

A wipe of light, headlights.

Ralph had returned.

Mitch could hear the grind of the garage door, the car pulling in. What should he do? Try for the first floor and a door out? Go down a flight and out one of the windows? Now he heard Ralph in the main part of the house, Ralph and someone, their voices.

They came up to the second floor and down the hall and into Ralph's bedroom.

Ralph and a woman.

They were directly below.

Why, Mitch wondered, should he be overhearing them so clearly?

He spotted the register inset in the hardwood floor. Such registers were commonplace in older houses. Made of cast iron with a grille-like arrangement of adjustable louvers, their purpose was to allow heated air to rise from one level to another. An unadvertised convenience was they allowed a person in the upper room to view what might be taking place in the room below.

Mitch kneeled to the register. He saw it was located above Ralph's unmade bed. By getting down closer to it he widened and improved his vantage.

They were undressing.

Ralph quickly, the woman just as much so. She had a face that appeared twice as old as her body, and considerably harder. Not a genuine blonde by any means. Her lower hair was dark and plentiful. Every sound she and Ralph made seemed to rise amplified: the unzipping, the slipping down and out of, the tumbling discard of shoes. It was apparent to Mitch that Ralph was anxious to get to it and the woman was anxious to get it done.

"You didn't happen to find a barrette, did you?" she asked.

"A what?"

"A barrette. You know, to hold my hair in place. I think I lost it here last time."

"I ain't seen nothing like that."

"It was gold."

"I would have noticed."

"A nice one."

An amused grunt from Ralph. "Next you'll be telling me it was eighteen K."

"Maybe it was," she arched.

"You want I should put on a couple of helpers?"

"Whatever puffs your panties."

Ralph inserted a porno film into each of the two VCRs at the foot of the bed.

The audio preceded the picture by several seconds, long enough for some moaning and a few *yeses*. Ralph turned off the sound. He got settled on the bed, adjusted a pillow, laced his fingers and placed his hands behind his head.

Ready to receive.

From Mitch's point of view Ralph's flaccid penis looked like a butchered chicken neck lying in a nest of steel wool. In another moment it was obscured by the woman's head, which immediately started pistoning.

Ralph's eyes began to glaze.

Mitch stopped watching, kneeled up, ignored the register. Now was a good time to leave, he thought. Any incidental noise he might make on his way out, such as a creak on the steps or whatever, wouldn't be heard. No use staying here while some passé suburban hooker serviced a fat fence. He might as well forget tonight, go on home empty-handed.

Another, less pragmatic part of him insisted on having its say. It told him not yet, told him there was still a chance that he might overhear or see something that would aid his cause. This woman wasn't about to stay all night. Ralph would be alone later. Maybe then, inadvertently or otherwise, he'd give away the hiding place. Stay there, Mitch, keep an eye on him.

Mitch returned his attention to the register and what was happening below.

The woman was still at it. And doing a lot of obligatory *humming* along with it to fake enjoyment.

Ralph's eyes were shifting from porno to porno.

The woman stopped abruptly. She got up and lighted a cigarette. As though she had no intention of continuing, had gone on strike.

"What're you doing?" Ralph asked, perturbed.

"Nothing."

"Why'd you stop? I was right there, for Christ's sake. Didn't you know I was right there?"

"Yeah."

"So why?"

"You don't treat me right," she complained matter of fact.

"How don't I?"

"You never give me a little something extra."

"I give you a hundred. I can remember when you were fifty."

"I'm not talking about money."

"What are you talking?"

"You gave Maxine a nice bracelet. You haven't given me shit."

"That was over a year ago with Maxine. I don't even see her anymore."

"All the more reason."

"You want a bracelet?"

"Sure."

"I'll give you a fucking bracelet," Ralph voiced gruffly. He got up. His erection was half lost. From a drawer of his dresser he got a pair of heavyweight leather work gloves. He put them on and went across the room to a Japanese ceramic planter that contained, of all things, a cactus. A variety generally known as a barrel cactus due to its stumpy, symmetrical shape. It was about fifteen inches in diameter at its girth and had countless needle-sharp prickers protruding from its skin. Not at all a friendly plant.

The leather gloves permitted Ralph to painlessly lift the cactus out. He placed it on the floor while he rummaged around in the bottom of the planter. Finally, he replaced the cactus. It looked none the worse from having been disturbed.

"Here's your bracelet," he said begrudgingly, tossing it to the woman.

It was a man's ID bracelet.

With SHORTY engraved on it.

The woman hardly looked at it before tossing it back to Ralph. "Keep it, Ralph," she said derogatorily, "it describes you."

"Don't be such a smart-ass cunt."

Silence was the extent of her apology. She reached for her panties, determined the back from the front.

"Okay," Ralph said, "you really don't want a bracelet. What is it you really want?"

"A Rolex. An eighteen K blue face, oyster with diamonds around the dial."

"I ain't got a Rollie right now, but I will, sooner or later. First one that comes in is yours."

"Yeah."

"I'll save it for you."

"Yeah."

"You don't believe me what the fuck can I do?"

"I'll settle for a hair," the woman said.

"How about a mink jacket?"

"How about a full-length chinchilla?"

"Let's take a look."

They went out of the room, out of Mitch's view. When they returned the woman had on a full-length silver fox coat.

She didn't know furs. While going through the pile she'd passed over a Russian sable and a Russian belly lynx. If she'd latched on to either of those Ralph would have had to throw her out and neither of them would have gotten satisfied. As it was the fox was worth about thirty-five hundred off the rack new, which it was about six years from being, and Ralph figured he'd be lucky to get five hundred for it come cold weather. As swag, it had cost him a hundred.

She didn't take off the coat.

Ralph got back in position on the bed and she went about getting him a second hard-on. When she'd accomplished that she swung a leg up over him, found herself with him and settled on him. "Full length," she uttered and did some blandishing gasps and exhales.

It wasn't going to be that easy for her. Her extortionate intermission had cost Ralph much of his mental momentum. At about the fifteen-minute mark she was still in a straddle, sliding back and forth and performing her best pelvic ovals.

Both Ralph and the woman were so caught up in trying they were unaware that three guys had entered the room.

Three of Riccio's have-arounds.

They appeared so all at once it was as though they had materialized, Mitch thought, as he observed from overhead. He knew these three from their having been around with Riccio on 47th.

The tall, extremely round-shouldered one was Bechetti. The equally tall heavyweight with boxer's ears was Caselli. The shorter Fratino was slick and nervous. Like all Riccio's minions they came off as old-mob sorts with old-mob ways. They wore wide trousers with overly roomy seats, sleeveless knit shirts and sports jackets too one thing or another: tight, long, loud.

"Get rid of the bimbo," Bechetti said. Evidently he'd been given charge of this business.

The woman had already dismounted Ralph. She'd instantly taken the temperature of the situation and knew it was too cold for her. She thought about asking Ralph for her hundred. Only thought about it, as she gathered up her things and was hurried off, barefoot in her fur.

Ralph remained face up on the bed. He reasoned he'd be less liable to be knocked down if he was already down. He felt exposed and more vulnerable however because he was naked. His cock had rapidly retracted. What little could still be seen of it was glistening wet.

Bechetti stood on one side of the bed, Caselli on the other side. Like they were visiting a hospital patient. They just stood there without saying anything for a while letting Ralph's imagination get up speed.

Bechetti did a smile. "Where you been, Ralph?"

"I been here. What do you mean where have I been?"

"You ain't been on 47th lately."

"I been nowhere. I got food poisoning or something."

"People wonder why you ain't been around."

"I was going to be down on 47th tomorrow." Ralph managed some indignance. "What is this, you come busting into my house?"

"People figure you're stiffing."

Ralph knew who *people* was. "I didn't promise anything to Riccio," he said.

"Who said anything about a promise? Promises don't mean shit," Caselli said.

"Riccio expects," Bechetti recited.

"Tomorrow," Ralph said, "I'll be on 47th tomorrow."

"That's a promise," Bechetti pointed out.

"Tomorrow is late, Ralph."

"That's why we're here tonight."

"For what?"

"For what you haven't been to see Riccio with."

It occurred to Ralph that these guys might be there on their own. That they were just cowboying, shaking him down. Possibly Riccio didn't know anything about this move. Not that that improved the situation. Anyway, he wasn't about to give up swag that would bring him a million and a half or two. "I ain't got much," he said, "just a few things, nothing big."

Bechetti reached quickly and took a clamping hold on Ralph's upper lip with his thumb and first finger. He pulled sharply upward. Ralph went with the pain rather than resist and cause more of it. He came up like he was on springs. It hurt so much he skipped two or three breaths. Now they had him standing.

Bechetti hardened about a thousand percent. "Listen you piece of shit. We know what you got. What we want is where you got it."

"How can I show you where I got something when I ain't got it," Ralph contended. "What am I, a fucking magician, I can make things right out of the air?" The inside tissue of Ralph's upper lip was ripped from where it joined his gums. Blood was filming his teeth. "Look around all you want. Take what you find," he told them.

Mitch, meanwhile, peering down, hoped Ralph would stick to the lie. How was it, he thought, Riccio knew Ralph had the Kalali swag? That was easy: Peaches was now in police custody, the police had taken her statement, and that information, quick as a phone call, had found its way into Riccio's ear.

A more puzzling question was why should Riccio be so eager to get hold of that particular swag? Sure, he'd enjoy having the goods, but it wasn't like him to use so much lean. Normally, he tried to keep on good terms with fences such as Ralph and, although the fences didn't consider Riccio *good people*, they brought to him peacefully and he paid peacefully. What was happening in the bedroom below was definitely out of order and definitely for some important reason, Mitch decided.

Fratino returned to the bedroom from having seen to the woman. "He tell yet?"

"No."

"He's a fucking *spuce*. I'll make him tell."

"I ain't got nothing big," Ralph insisted. "I don't know who said otherwise but I ain't got nothing big."

"He's a lying scumbag."

"What is it you want Ralph, you want Frat to give you a fifteen-minute fist fuck?"

"Bend him over," Fratino said.

"You want him to ram his fist up your ass?"

"See if there's some cold cream or something in the bathroom," Fratino said, as he took off his jacket. He also took off his wristwatch. "Bend him over."

Nothing from Ralph. He'd heard about Fratino. He never thought it would happen to him.

Caselli grabbed Ralph by the back of the neck, needed only one of his huge, broken-knuckle hands to shove Ralph's upper half face down on the bed. Ralph's knees buckled and went to the floor.

"That's good," Fratino said. "Just like that is good. And never mind the cold cream. I'm going to fuck him dry all the way up to my elbow."

Bechetti was amused. "Maybe that's where he's got the stuff, up his ass. That where you got it Ralph?"

Ralph was out of struggle. "Please," he pleaded.

"Where you got it?"

"I'll show you."

Goodbye recovery, Mitch thought. So long six hundred thousand. Once the Kalali swag was in Riccio's hands it would be reduced to mere precious stones and disappear into that abyssal aspect of 47th dedicated to refashioning.

Mitch hated to see it. Ralph was going to go over to that planter and remove that fat cactus.

However, Ralph didn't. He didn't give that hiding place as much as a glance. He asked could he put on his trousers and Bechetti said no and he asked why and Bechetti told him forget it and called him a piece of shit again and Ralph went obediently from the bedroom and Bechetti and the others followed along.

It occurred to Mitch that they might be coming up. He was relieved when he heard their steps on the main stairs as they went down to the first floor.

Ralph was stalling them, Mitch thought. Playing them for time, probably hoping for a chance to bolt. If Ralph could just keep them on the first floor long enough . . .

Mitch went swiftly but stealthily down to Ralph's bedroom. The leather work gloves were right there. As he put them on he realized how charged he was, now so close to stealing the swag. No matter that he was stealing it back, it was stealing.

The cactus was heavier than it appeared. It almost slipped from his hands. He placed it on the floor and looked into the planter, Ralph's secret repository.

Apparently it wasn't Ralph's only secret repository. On the inner bottom of the planter were a few modest pieces of gold jewelry, manufactured stuff with a touch of diamond pavé, and a couple of rings set with semiprecious stones. Altogether not worth more than three thousand.

So, *where was* the Kalali swag?

Ralph really was leading them to it, Mitch thought. He might as well find the safe way out and head for home while everyone was distracted.

He pulled off the gloves and threw them across the room. He felt like kicking the cactus. He went from the bedroom and down the second-floor hall. He didn't feel like being sneaky. He had to repress the urge to stomp. He could hear them downstairs. Ralph doing a lapse of memory, saying he was trying to remember where he put the swag, then a commotion as they smacked him. There was the smell of meat cooking. The roasts in the microwave. What if he'd been right about the swag being inside that meat? Jewelry roulade. To hell with it.

At the end of the hall he unbolted the door that gave to the balcony above the enclosed porch. The porch railing was weathered rotten and a section of it broke away when he leaned over it to see what he'd have for help. No vines, nothing, and no shrubbery below.

It was about a sixteen-foot drop. He hung on to the edge to make it a nine-foot drop. At the very moment he let go he heard them come out. Perhaps that's what caused him to land wrong.

He got up quickly. In a moment they'd be rounding the corner of the porch. He had only one way to go. He made a dash for the swimming pool area. It was possible they'd seen him. He crouched behind the small shed that housed the pool equipment. What a night, he thought, he'd be glad to get home. What a way to make a living.

They were headed for the pool area, coming straight at him. The naked Ralph leading, complaining when he happened to step on something sharp. What were they doing out here?

They kept coming. All the way to the shed. They were on the other side of it, no more than six feet from Mitch for a moment, when Ralph threw a switch that turned on the pool light.

The scummy green surface of the water, now illuminated from underneath, looked deceivingly attractive. Like an emerald of impossible size. There was no clear opening. The bottom of the pool wasn't visible. The scum covered from side to side and end to end. It had such a putrid odor in its calm that surely it would smell a lot worse if it was ever churned up.

Ralph gazed down at the water and walked back and forth along one side of the pool. The have-arounds waited. Ralph walked around the pool. Four times.

"How about it, Ralph?" Bechetti pressed.

"Give me time," Ralph said.

"I'll give you maybe another breath."

"He's fucking with our heads," Fratino said. "There ain't nothing out here. Why are we out here? What a stink. In a minute I'm going to throw up."

"This is all just shit," Caselli said. He'd had enough. As Ralph passed by him on the fifth time around the edge of the pool, Caselli grabbed him by the throat, got him with one of his huge, broken-knuckled hands.

Ralph didn't resist, knew better, just suffered it, stiffened and went up on his toes.

Bechetti interceded. "Let him go. Don't kill him yet. Let him go."

"Maybe the fuck wants to go for a swim," Caselli said. He released his grip with a shove.

Ralph went into the deep end of the pool backwards.

Into the green scum.

There was no splash. The scum was like an instantaneous healing membrane the way it came together to mend the place where Ralph's weight had torn through it.

Surely he was drowned.

Trapped beneath a surface as unified as ice.

But then, he broke up through it, flailing at it, fighting it, coughing and spewing. "I can't swim," he managed to shout.

The have-arounds laughed.

Ralph only knew how to float. In desperation, he brought his legs up and kicked little kicks, extended his arms and worked his hands. His thirty pounds of overweight helped his buoyancy. He wasn't however going anywhere. The thick blanket of scum had him locked in place.

"Okay, Ralph, tell us where," Bechetti said.

"I was trying to show you," Ralph told him.

"You don't have to show, just say."

"Get me out," Ralph begged.

"We will, after you say."

Ralph knew better. Perhaps he suddenly accepted his doom. "Fuck you," he shouted with bite.

"What kind of attitude is that? I always took you for smart. All you got to do is say."

"Fuck you," Ralph said again more emphatically, as though he enjoyed the words.

Fratino took out his pistol. So did Caselli. They hurriedly threaded on silencers.

Fratino got off the first shot. It caused a sharp sucking sound as it struck the scummy surface close by Ralph.

"Don't pop him yet," Bechetti said behind his hand.

Fratino nodded. "I'll just put a little lead in his pencil."

They aimed for Ralph's genitals. They fired rapidly, as though competing for hits. Each used up an entire clip.

Ralph realized their target. He shielded his genitals with his hands. His upper body sank. He used his hands to keep afloat. His genitals were exposed. It was either-or like that for him until the slugs slammed into his upper thighs, groin and lower abdomen.

He went under, started breathing water.

The bright red of blood bubbled up amidst the green. Ruby and emerald.

"I told you not to pop him," Bechetti reprimanded.

"I was trying not to," Fratino said.

That was also Caselli's excuse.

"Now we got to find the stuff on our own."

"No sweat. It's in the house some fucking place. We'll find it."

Bechetti turned off the pool light. They headed for the house.

When they were surely inside Mitch came out from around the shed. He'd had some difficulty not feeling sorry for Ralph. He'd even considered doing the heroic, stepping out with Beretta leveled, confronting the three, rescuing Ralph. His better judgment asked if he disliked living that much. Ralph wasn't the kind he should put himself on the line for.

So, it had been a perverse, one-act play that he'd experienced from the wings. His view had been the back of the performances, the mistakes.

Something peculiar he'd noticed about Ralph: the way Ralph had walked around and around the pool and each time around when he came to a particular spot there'd been a slight hitch in his walk, the merest hesitation, as though he was ambivalent about whether to stop there or continue on.

If there was one thing Mitch knew about fences such as Ralph it was how they loathed losing swag once they had it in their possession. Sell it, yes. That was their reason for being, but to have it taken from them or having to give it up was unthinkable. Attesting to that attitude was Ralph dead beneath the scum.

Those hesitations of Ralph's had been very subtle, but now Mitch's recollection expanded them, made them obvious, definite. And possibly, meaningful.

He went around to the other side of the pool to where he believed the hesitations had occurred. He kneeled and ran his hand along the tiles just above the scum line.

He found it.

A cleat cemented to the tile, the sort of small cleat to which normally a drop line and thermometer would be attached to ascertain water temperature. A length of twine was tied to the cleat. It was ordinary, hemp packing twine. Mitch tried pulling at it. It wouldn't just come up. There was something much more substantial than a thermometer attached to its submerged end.

Mitch got a good grip on the twine and began hoisting slowly hand over hand. He couldn't see because of the scum but something was coming up.

But then it wasn't.

The twine had broken and whatever had been on the end of it was now on the bottom of the pool.

Mitch cursed the cheap twine and cheap Ralph. At the least the twine could have put off breaking until he'd determined what was tied to it. For all he knew his hope had him pursuing an old bucket.

He tried to see what it was, pushed aside some green scum to make a patch that was only water. He shined his Mag Lite down. Even when he extended it below the surface its beam was defeated by the murk.

There was no doubt about him going in. Reluctance, but no doubt. The only question at the moment was whether he should go in clothed or naked.

He chose naked, undressed quickly and placed his clothing and the Beretta out of sight behind the shed. In case they returned to the pool for some reason. He could hear them inside, rummaging around roughly, breaking vases and such. They were searching in vain, he told himself, the house might be full of swag but the swag wasn't in there. Maybe.

He tried to bring himself to dive. It would be a swift slice down through the layer of scum. He stood on the edge, poised to spring, even went up on his toes a couple of times. But he couldn't bring himself to do it.

He turned and slipped in feet first, lowered himself slowly, told himself the scum was imaginary, that his bare skin wasn't feeling the slime of it, he was going for a dip in a pristine pool, sparkling, clean water. Mind over scummy, green matter.

He couldn't, however, shut out the stench. The malodor of organic decay invaded his nostrils and lungs and got to his brain. It made him retch. He was in up to his chin. To escape the air he took a deep breath of it and went under.

He was about midway between the deep end and the shallow. At the point where the bottom began to slope. He felt with his feet along the coving. His feet came in contact with something. He maneuvered down to beam his Mag Lite on it.

The woman.

The body of her. Her arms caught in the sleeves of the fox coat. The ampleness of the coat spread out wing-like on each side of her. She had the appearance of some lazy, hairy water creature, unwilling to exert itself unless stirred.

The mere touch of Mitch's foot had impelled her. She coasted along the bottom, bound gradually for the deepest part.

Ralph's body was also in there somewhere, Mitch thought. He was bathing with the dead.

He shined his light around in various directions. No sign of whatever had been tied to the twine. It should have been right here. He reasoned that it, like the dead woman, must have slid down the slope of the bottom.

He needed a breath, had to go up for some of that awful air. He'd need a big deep breath of it. He expected to go up where he'd gone in; however, the top of his head met the resistance of scum. It was gelatinous, tight layers upon layers of decomposition and algae, several inches thick. It gave way, and as Mitch's head emerged, it seemed to slip down over his face like he was putting on a heavy turtleneck sweater, but putrid.

He gasped. Took the breath as quickly as possible and went back under.

He swam for the deepest part. Felt the pressure increase. He came to the body of the woman. His bare thigh brushed the fur as he passed by, and a moment later he saw he was headed for the body of Ralph.

It was at the drain on the bottom, appeared to be hovering over the drain, trying to escape by way of it. Ralph's legs were crouched, his back bent forward, his arms encircling.

Mitch swam closer.

He could have easily missed the twine. Merely the frayed end of it protruded from beneath Ralph's body. He shoved the body away and saw attached to the other end of the twine, tied securely, closed by it, a white plastic kitchen trash bag.

He grabbed it by its neck and sprang for the surface.

Chapter 23

It was a little after three when Mitch arrived home.

There were no lights on. Lights were of no use to Maddie, of course, and often, when she was home alone at night, she simply neglected to turn them on.

Mitch went directly to the bedroom. The bed was only ready to be occupied, the top sheet folded down as precise as an envelope, the goose-down-filled pillows plumped and piled in place, but no Maddie. Mitch's eyes needed her . . .

. . . found her in the living room.

She was on the sofa in an awkward position, as though sleep had suddenly won out over her and toppled her. Her eyes were closed. Sometimes, contrary to normal reflex, she fell asleep with her eyes open and Mitch would gently lower her lids like shades. But her eyes were closed now, and, according to the rate and sounds of her breaths, she was surely sleeping.

Mitch stood there, taking her in, replenishing, replacing the make-do image of her with the actual her. Why hadn't she minded him, gone to bed as he'd told her? She'd tried to wait up.

She had on headphones. A Walkman was somewhere on the sofa with her. Cassettes were scattered about on the floor. Mitch gathered them up to not step on them. He carefully removed the headphones and believed he'd done so without waking her. He'd leave her as she was for the time being, would carry her in to bed.

"How about a kiss?" she murmured.

"In a minute," he said and went into the bathroom. He undressed, threw everything into the laundry hamper, then turned to the familiar mirror.

Look at me looking at me, he thought. What a mess. There were remnants of the green scum caked here and there on him. A lot of it in his hair. His nostrils were green. So were his eyelashes and ear holes.

He grinned. For what may have been the fiftieth time since he'd pulled over beneath a New Rochelle streetlight. Before then, actually as soon as he'd gotten out of the pool, he'd squeezed and shaken the white plastic trash bag and believed what it contained felt right, had the right weight. It wasn't until he was well away from Ralph's house, and all, however, that he cut the twine from the neck of the bag and took a look.

No trash in that trash bag.

The Kalali swag.

He deserved to grin. He deserved to tell himself *nice going* along with telling himself that it had been twenty, maybe thirty percent his resourcefulness and seventy percent luck, but it was also okay if he transposed those figures. Wait until Hurley heard how it had come off. He'd love it. There'd be no need to exaggerate. It had been bizarre enough. For instance, Ralph's typical fence paranoia, his using the scummy swimming pool as a hiding place. And the way Ralph, even after death, had seemed to be trying to hold on to the bag of swag.

Mitch relaxed the corners of his mouth so he could watch them form another grin.

"What's with this 'in a minute' stuff?" Maddie demanded to know as she padded somnolently into the bathroom leading with her lips. "I've been deprived all night and now . . . " She stopped short of reaching within range and cringed. "You smell awful," she said, "worse than a grave robber."

"You've known grave robbers?" Mitch jested.

"Don't you dare come near me."

Maddie backed off four steps. Mitch got into the shower stall. It took three all-over lathers and rinses for him to feel free of scum and death. Maddie had two big towels waiting. He dried his upper half while she kneeled and tended to the rest, not slighting any part or crease. She even had him lift his feet so she could dry between his toes. There was a degree of ritual to it but nothing of dominance-submission. It was simply something she sometimes did and always enjoyed doing. At first, years ago, he'd resisted, felt awkward and rather embarrassed by having her toweling him dry as though he was a child, but then he tried turnabout and understood and accepted the adoring, caring quality of it.

Now she was done. She remained down, pressed her cheek to the socket of his groin and said: "You must be hungry."

He was, but wouldn't her suggestion be a helping of that gaspacho from hell? "I'll just get a glass of milk," he said.

She insisted on getting it for him, brought it and several ginger snaps to him in the bedroom, and, while he stood and drank and munched, she got into bed so she'd be there when he got in, would be sort of receiving him.

She'd made the bed fresh and allowed it to remain fresh so that he would experience that pleasure now: the chaste sensuality of fine, imported sheets. He sighed luxuriously when he'd inserted himself between them. She let him acclimate before claiming her kiss, a brief, sweet one.

They lay face up, side in touch with side, silent for a while. Finally she said what he expected: "Tell me."

He didn't want to. He was being shared by exhilaration and fatigue and he favored giving in to the latter. "Tomorrow," he told her.

"Promise?"

"Yeah."

"You'll remember everything? You won't leave anything out?"

"Promise," he fibbed, knowing he'd omit telling her what Fratino had wanted to do to Ralph and that he probably wouldn't reveal the extent he'd been repulsed by that putrid pool and having to swim with those bodies. She'd most likely detect his omissions, however, and pump them out of him, he thought. "What time is it?" he asked.

"I don't know. You've got the sight. What time do you have to get up?"

"Eight or so," he replied. His bedside clock told him it was now quarter to four. He set its alarm for eight. When he clicked off the light it was as though he also clicked himself off.

Maddie let an estimated ten minutes go by before she got up and went around to his side to mercifully un-set his alarm.

Chapter 24

Pickings on a mandolin.

The accompaniment to Mitch's ascent to consciousness that brought him face to face with his bedside clock, its arms indicating frantically, mutely, five to eleven. What happened to eight o'clock? Mitch complained, feeling betrayed.

He got up quickly. This was supposed to have been one of those rare days of days, he thought, a full course of glorious victorious hours, a six-hundred-thousand day. He'd wanted to enjoy every minute of it and now, here it was, nearly half over. No matter about the alarm, Maddie should have awakened him. He'd told her eight.

He rushed through his ablutions. Put on a suitable suit and a tie of celebratory color and pattern. As somewhat of a payback he merely peeked in on Maddie in the study giving the mandolin lesson. She'd have to discover him gone.

With the throat of the white plastic trash bag inescapably in his grasp, Mitch taxied down to 47th to his brother Andy's place of business. Andy was delighted when Mitch emptied the Kalali swag onto the work bench in the inner office. The bracelets, necklaces, rings, brooches, strands, pins and all. A six-million-dollar array.

Andy congratulated and gave Mitch a prideful, well-done slap on the back.

"Fine goods," Mitch admired, holding up an intricately worked diamond and calibré-cut sapphire art deco bracelet.

"It looks Boucheron. Is it signed?"

Mitch louped the bracelet, saw that it did indeed bear the Boucheron hallmark.

"You still have the good, fast eye," he said.

"You don't?" Andy smiled. He nudged certain of the Kalali pieces, urging them to show more life. "A shame to see these beauties not looking their best," he said. Precious stones, particularly diamonds, have an affinity for grease. The swifts and Ralph had handled this jewelry so much that it was considerably dulled by their body oils.

"I thought I'd clean it up," Mitch said, "if that's okay with you." Andy had the needed professional equipment there on the work bench.

It wasn't merely okay with Andy; he was glad to help.

Piece by piece the jewelry was placed in a wire basket and immersed in a Bransonic 521 ultrasound cleaning tank filled with a degreasing solution. It was rather like deep frying but with sonic vibrations instead of heat and degreaser instead of oil.

Next, each piece was held by tweezers while it was exposed to pressurized steam from the nozzle of a box-like appliance called a Steamaster HPJ-25. That to get rid of any stubborn residue that might be lodged in the mountings. Time and again, the mundane steam seemed to hiss spitefully at the special beauty it was being forced to enhance.

Andy and Mitch worked in tandem, as they once had when there'd been a Laughton store. They were done in less than an hour. Now the Kalali swag lay there in its utmost brilliance, its numerous facets barraging the air sharply with scintillations.

The pieces were put into individual clear plastic, self-sealing envelopes. There was just barely enough room for the lot in Mitch's attaché case.

It was still lunchtime when Mitch arrived at his office. Shirley was eating in at her desk.

"There you are!" she said with a chiding tone countered immediately by a smile. "I've been beeping you."

"I haven't been beepable."

"You lost your beeper?"

"Either that or Maddie hid it."

"You've never been a loser," was Shirley's opinion. "Have you had lunch? You don't look as though you've had lunch."

"No, what are you having?"

"My more or less usual. I'd be glad to share."

Shirley more frequently than not brought her lunch from home. Her more or less usual was a cream cheese and watercress on raisin wheat, London tea room style, the bread sliced extremely thin and its crust amputated. Mitch didn't think it qualified as a sandwich. Shirley often said she'd rather starve than subject herself to one of those feeding troughs New Yorkers line up at.

"Order me a roast beef on rye, fries and a Mountain Dew," Mitch told her. "Has Ruder called?"

"No, but George Bickford has, twice."

Bickford was a client, Ruder's counterpart at Northland Providential, a Philadelphia insurance company from which Mitch had been receiving a retainer every month for six years.

"And Hurley stopped by about an hour ago," Shirley went on, "said he'd be back. And," she added pointedly, "*I* need to talk to you."

"About a layaway?"

"No. Anyway, my need can keep until you have a free moment."

Mitch did a fast read of Shirley and believed what he saw was either she was getting married, needed money for an abortion or wanted a raise.

"You want a raise," he said.

"A rise," she corrected.

"A raise," he corrected back. "In this country a rise is something else altogether and I'm sure you've caused a great many but what you want in this case is a raise."

"Whatever."

"Please order my sandwich."

Mitch went into his office. He cleared his desk and moved the two visitors' chairs aside to make enough room on the carpet. He wanted to do this alone, indulge in the doing.

He placed the Kalali file on his desk. The four-page numerically itemized loss list, the twenty pages of corresponding descriptions and appraisals and the eight-by-ten color photographs of each of the forty-eight stolen, now restolen, items.

He arranged the photographs on the carpet. According to their loss list numbers in four orderly rows, twelve to a row with space in between to move about from row to row.

He paused to consider and appreciate what he was doing. No need to hurry, make it last, he thought, although at the finish there'd be the phone call to Ruder, the six-hundred-thousand phone call. He thought the wish that he'd made the recovery for someone, anyone, other than Ruder.

Shirley came in with his lunch. She laid it out nicely on the ledge behind his desk and he sat upon the ledge while he ate. He invited her to join him and she got her thermos of tea and sat with him.

"About the raise . . . " he started.

"It's nothing that has to be decided right off," she told him. "I mean, it's not critical."

"Oh?"

"If you say no then no it is and none the worse."

"You won't quit on me?"

"Lord no. I have the best job in the district. Working elsewhere would be bloody painful. It's just that I'm so far behind on my lay-aways that it seems I'll never catch up. Saturday last I went over-board, put twenty down on a silk blouse at Saks and forty more on a jacket that hooked me with its reduced sign at Bergdorf." She did a sag. "I'm incorrigible."

Mitch had the urge to give her an encouraging hug as well as a raise. A mere, platonic hug couldn't be misconstrued as sexual harassment, could it? "Would a hundred more a week help?" he asked.

Shirley's sun came on. "It would just about free me!"

"Then make it a hundred and fifty."

"That's too much."

"Today it isn't."

Shirley kissed him. On the cheek but close to the mouth. He noticed she was wearing an expensive scent. She immediately gathered up the remnants of his lunch and went out to her desk. Mitch hadn't thought it possible that he could feel any better but he did. Not hugely, but he did. Generosity is therapeutic, he thought, especially when it's affordable.

He returned his attention to the Kalali swag. He removed it all from the attaché case, and referring to the loss list, used a black magic marker to note the designated number of each piece on the outside of the transparent envelope that contained it.

That done, he set about to place each piece on its corresponding photograph. He was busy at it when Hurley showed up.

A gesture was Hurley's hello. No smile.

Mitch would let Hurley have the first word, sure it would be congratulatory, something such as *hey, nice going.* But Hurley just stood there taking in the rows of photos on the carpet and the swag. His expression had some glower in it, as though he resented what he was seeing.

"What's your problem?" Mitch asked.

"You didn't wait."

"I couldn't."

"Yeah, it was right there and so easy you had to make the move, couldn't help yourself, had to."

"You know me and having to wait." Mitch shrugged nonchalantly, trying to lighten the moment.

"I practically perjured myself down in Baltimore in order to make it back here today. You should have waited."

"What's the difference?"

"None," Hurley replied too quickly.

Mitch was disappointed by Hurley's reaction, but then Hurley made it right, grinned as though he'd been kidding. "You did good," he said exuberantly.

"I got lucky," Mitch said modestly. He related some of his previous night's adventure. The high points and a little of the in-between. He'd gradually dole out the details. "You'll probably want to let the New Rochelle police know about the bodies in the pool."

"Maybe," Hurley said, "or maybe somebody should just find them sooner or later."

Mitch didn't understand that but let it go. He was about half done with correlating the pieces of jewelry and the photographs. Hurley showed mild interest as Mitch returned to that task. "What's with this piece?" Hurley asked, indicating a yet vacant photo of a diamond-encrusted bangle bracelet.

"That one? It's here. I saw it. I just haven't gotten to it."

Hurley continued perusing the rows of photographs. "And these?" he asked offhand. "Did you happen to notice these?" The two enscribed emeralds.

Mitch was distracted, barely glanced to see which photo Hurley was referring to. "Probably," he replied.

A grunt from Hurley, a sort of deep subversive sound that seemed to emanate from a Hurley within Hurley. He walked to the window and looked down at 47th. "You'll be turning over everything to Ruder."

"Yeah."

"He know you've made the recovery?"

"Not yet."

"I guess you can't wait to tell him."

"Six hundred thousand."

"Anybody know you've got this stuff, other than you and me? Maddie, I suppose she knows."

"Not even Maddie."

Hurley unbuckled his belt and retucked his shirt, to offset with preoccupation the directness of what he was about to suggest. "How about fuck Ruder," he said as though it was an impetuous notion that shouldn't be taken seriously. Unless, of course, Mitch chose to jump on it.

"Sure," Mitch played along.

"How about you were never in New Rochelle last night. You were anywhere other than New Rochelle. We pop the stones from all this shit, melt down and Ruder gets fucked."

That last part appealed to Mitch.

Hurley knew that. "How much do you think we'd be looking at?" he asked.

"Two, maybe three million."

"So, I get my horse farm in Maryland, you can have an all-paid-for place on Martha's Vineyard or somewhere."

In the various recoveries Mitch had made over the years there'd never been an opportunity such as this. Everything about it was right for doing wrong. No one except Hurley knew he'd made the recovery; Mrs. Kalali and Roger Addison would get their six million from Columbia Beneficial; Ruder would be out on his ass.

"Could you handle it?" Hurley pressed.

"Nearly."

"I don't think so," Hurley challenged, "you're too fucking straight. How anyone in this twisted business could stay so straight is beyond me."

"You're right," Mitch said, his tone letting Hurley know as far as he was concerned the subject had ended. He continued correlating the swag and was soon done. When he went down the loss list he saw every piece was accounted for.

Except one.

Number 32.

The two enscribed emeralds.

He mentioned that to Hurley.

"Are they actually *missing?*" Hurley asked.

"What do you mean *actually?*"

"Just that maybe they appealed to you."

"You must be kidding."

"I wouldn't blame you."

"Hurley, go out and come in again."

"Nothing sinful about helping yourself to a little hold-out."

"Make up your mind. One minute I'm too straight, the next I'm holding out. Shit, if I was going to hold out something from these goods it wouldn't be those two scratched-up emeralds."

"I guess."

"No guess to it."

"Then maybe the emeralds got accidentally dropped someplace. In your car or at home. That possible?"

Mitch considered it. Car? No. Home? No. Andy's during the clean-up? He didn't think so, no. But it was strange that only one item should be missing and that it should be this one. Might Ralph have taken a fancy to them and put them aside? He could have, but would he? Why would he? They weren't the sort of things an experienced fence such as Ralph would keep. They were too identifiable.

"Anyway," Mitch brightened, "forty-seven out of forty-eight isn't bad."

Hurley agreed. "Want to go have a beer?"

"I've too much work to do."

Hurley almost let it go at that. He looked off thoughtfully, as though weighing what had ensued during the last quarter hour. When he brought his look back he did an amending face. "Sorry about the attitude," he said. "I'm on the rag. My room at the motel in Baltimore was right next to the ice machine."

"Forget it."

"Sure about the beer?"

"Maybe later."

"Later's not good for me. See you tomorrow."

With Hurley gone, Mitch decided on a time-out. He left the photographs and the swag on the floor, switched off the light and shut himself in. Seated at his desk, he tried to blank his mind. It had been overaccelerating since yesterday and Peaches.

He wished his was the sort of mind that *could* be turned off and on. Some people claimed they could do that. The meditators. He'd never been good at meditating. Once, years ago, he'd attended a transcendental meditation class and given it an open-minded

month. At least once each day, sometimes twice, he'd sat quietly
with eyes closed and chanted the nonsense syllable that was his
mantra. But always some aspect of 47th Street came jabbing in, as
though the mantra had usurped its place.

Now he drew in deep breaths, relaxed his shoulders and defeated the urge to turn and peek through the slats of the drawn
blinds at Visconti's office across the way and 47th below in its
Wednesday summer afternoon mode. Instead of the peek, Mitch
imagined it, which was, really, as compulsive as a peek.

The back of Visconti's head above the back of his expensive
leather chair. The Luchino Visconti movie poster on the wall beyond. A silver salver of fruit on the side table? On the street below
two-thirds of the people would be tourists. Obvious because of the
way they were dressed and their stop-and-go walks from window
to window, diamonds to diamonds. Tomorrow, Mitch told himself,
he'd walk the street, down one side and back up the other. By tomorrow the street would have heard of the recovery. He wouldn't,
however, be taking any bows. The street didn't like being deprived.
Swag was grist for its mill.

The telephone.

Were his eyes caught on it or was it staring at him? Why hadn't
Maddie called? He regretted now not having given her a depart-
ing hug. Maybe she was out shopping, defying curbs and bumpers,
or maybe at that moment she was seated on a hard bench in the
Grecian wing of the Metropolitan absorbing vibrations from ancient marble nudes. He should have hugged her, put some love in
her ear. There should never be any should haves.

Why hadn't Ruder called? It would be better if Ruder called
him rather than . . .

It was as though he'd launched the wish and it had been immediately granted. Shirley came on the intercom with:

"Ruder on one."

Mitch didn't get on the line for nearly a minute, then opened
with a busy: "Yes, Keith." He rarely called Ruder by first name,
never thought of him that way.

"How are you, Mitch?"

"Depends on who you ask. What's up?"

"Having not heard from you I was wondering how things were going."

"You sound as though you've got something," Mitch told him.

"What do you mean?"

"Could be it's your sinuses. I seem to recall your telling me you had a problem with allergies. A lot of ragweed in the air this time of year. And pollen." Actually, Ruder sounded the same as ever, stuffy and dry.

"It's probably the connection," Ruder said a bit exasperated. "Anyway, do you have good news for me? The situation here is getting rather squeezy to say the least."

"Hang on a second." Mitch held the receiver at arm's length and covered the mouthpiece lightly while he pretended to be giving instructions to Shirley regarding a letter that had to go out today. The figure two million eight hundred thousand was nonchalantly mentioned. "Now," he got back to Ruder, "where were we?"

"I was asking if you had any news for me."

"Oh, yes. I guess you mean regarding the Kalali case."

"Of course."

"Didn't you get my message?"

"Message?"

"Yesterday afternoon. Come on now, Keith, you're toying with me."

"I don't toy!" Ruder snapped, his true disposition coming through. He controlled. "You left a message with my secretary?"

"No."

"Then with whom?"

"Your secretary must have been out. The electronic answering system was on. You know, that press one if, press two if thing."

"I didn't get the message."

"Goes to show that system isn't infallible. Really Keith, you sound raspy. It could be your throat. You ought to have it looked into. I had an acquaintance who sounded similar. He ended up in Sloan-Kettering."

"What was the goddamn message?" Ruder was only a few nerve ends from losing it.

God, how much he disliked this man, Mitch thought. Why not do what Hurley had suggested: not mention the goods, pop the stones and let Ruder take his fall?

Moment of truth.

"I've recovered the Kalali swag," Mitch said so rapidly and run together it sounded like nonsense.

"What? What was that?"

"What you wanted to hear."

"I didn't get it."

Mitch did an impatient exhale and said again what he'd said, but this time disconnecting and drawing out each syllable.

Ruder was overwhelmed, overjoyed, couldn't hold in a short length of laugh. "You're remarkable," he said. "I knew you'd come through for me, Mitch. You're remarkable."

"Yeah."

"So, where's the jewelry?"

"I have it."

"Bring it down."

"You'll cut me a check."

"First of the month."

"Okay, first of the month I'll bring it down. That's only ten days."

"Be reasonable Laughton [now it was Laughton]. This is a large, structured organization. A check of that size takes some doing. Certain people have to approve, certain signatures are required. You understand."

"Certainly."

"Bring it down."

"Cut a check."

In the silence Mitch could hear capitulation. "I'll do my best," Ruder told him.

Mitch hastily gathered up the pieces of jewelry from the floor. Shirley helped.

She also supplied an Henri Bendel shopping bag with another

of the same inside it for Mitch to carry the jewelry in. It would be safer than his attaché case. There had been a rash of snatch-and-run robberies lately involving 47th Street dealers. Thieves waited around the district, spotted a likely-looking dealer with his case in hand, followed him and, at his least wary moment, sideswiped him full speed.

Just another variation in the perpetual foray between West 47 dealers and stealers.

No one, however, went about with six million worth of jewels in a shopping bag. Shirley topped the jewelry with layers of tissue paper, tucked the paper in well around the edges.

Mitch was in high spirit during the taxi ride downtown. The shopping bag on his lap. He forgave the cramped, cage-like back seat and the suicidal Israeli driver. He forgave the buses for their bullying and sooty exhausts. A happy hello to that mix of marvelous New Yorkers crossing at 39th. The same for the well-off obscured by the dark-tinted windows of the chauffeured Rolls-Royce equivalently stopped for the light.

He gave the taxi driver an undeserved two-dollar tip and entered the thirty-two-story gray fortress that was the Columbia Beneficial building.

The elevator was like a pneumatic box with its soft, long stops. The reception area had nothing on its gray walls except the company name. The receptionist, a prototypical older aunt, once married forever divorced, didn't have even a New York smile for Mitch, told him it would be only a minute. He believed her and remained standing.

At the five-minute mark he opted for one of the gray leather sofas. It wheezed as he sat. The magazines on the low table were only *Sports Afield, Reader's Digest* and *Life.*

At the seven-minute mark Mitch realized this qualified as a wait and at twenty minutes his needle was nearing the red.

Ruder's secretary saved the moment, came out to lead Mitch in. She was professionally pleasant. Mitch didn't know her by name, just by sight. She had a wide, humpy ass, and, to make it worse, it was in a tight, white flannel skirt.

Mitch followed it down the corridor past executive offices to the one that was Ruder's.

"Mr. Ruder has been called into an emergency meeting," the secretary said. "You're to leave what you've brought with me." She extended her hand to receive the shopping bag.

"Nothing doing," Mitch told her. "I need to see Ruder."

"That's impossible."

"Call him out of the meeting."

"It's not being held here. It's an outside meeting."

"When will he be back?"

"Not this afternoon."

The dickhead knew about this when I spoke to him, Mitch thought. Or else Miss all-ass here is fibbing for him while he hides in the executive toilet.

"My instructions are to put what you've brought into Mr. Ruder's safe, to give you a receipt and an appointment for ten tomorrow morning."

She said it straight, it sounded straight.

Mitch glanced at the safe inset in the wall to the left. It was open, empty. He didn't relish the prospect of having this six million in a shopping bag on the end of his arm any longer. Besides, rush hour was about to occur and he'd have a problem getting a taxi uptown. He pictured himself on the subway with the shopping bag.

"What kind of receipt?" he asked.

"The loss list."

Mitch's reluctance had its say: "I don't think so. Are you absolutely sure Ruder isn't coming back? Is he where I might reach him by phone?"

"I've already revised Mr. Ruder's schedule to accommodate you at ten tomorrow morning."

Mitch's compliance had its say: "May I please see that loss list?" The secretary handed it to him. He saw it was identical with the one he had, in fact, the original. That each page was separately signed and dated as received by Ruder was reassuring. Ten tomorrow morning wasn't unreasonable.

"Who knows the combination to that safe?" Mitch asked. "Do you?"

"No, only Mr. Ruder knows the combination. He had it changed only a few weeks ago."

Mitch's trust was not total. He wouldn't permit the secretary to put the jewelry into the safe. Saw to it himself, inserted the shopping bag and all into that steel hole. It was a tight fit. He closed the safe door, twisted the handle which slid the bolts into place and locked it by rotating the combination dial four times around.

For a while that night was a sensational night for Mitch. Despite his less-than-satisfactory trip to Ruder's office, he climbed back up to the altitude of his high of that day and stayed up throughout dinner and afterwards.

Maddie soared with him.

In keeping she chose to wear a next-to-nothing, a red silk satin number by Alberta Ferretti that was bare on top and bottomed out mid-thigh.

"It calls for a strong mouth, don't you think?" she said while getting ready.

"By all means a strong mouth," Mitch insinuated.

"Oh, you," she admonished archly.

The center drawer of her dressing table was fitted with a slotted rack for her tubes of lipstick. About a dozen tubes arranged according to shade left to right from nearly naive to saturnalism. This night she went straightaway to the extreme right for Yves St. Laurent's *Mischievous Rose,* spun it up and began applying.

She paused from that effort to ask: "Do you think it's absolutely essential that I wear panties?"

"Yeah."

"Were I eighteen and going out to a rock club I wouldn't. It's okay, though, isn't it, that my titties are on their own?"

"Yeah."

"This fabric shows off my nips."

"You're treacherous. I don't think you realize how treacherous you are. Want a refill?"

They were having some blanc de blanc as an overture. The bottle was only about two drinks from empty. Mitch poured and Maddie started on her lips again. She paused again. "Did I mention that Straw phoned today? From Kennedy. He and Wally are off to London to give the Cleremont a try. Something tells me they'll come back married. That would really scorch Marian."

"How long will they be gone, did he say?"

"I suppose as long as it takes."

"It," Mitch thought aloud.

Maddie stared at the mirror, intensely, as though she could see her image. "Tell me true, precious," she said, "am I beginning to look as though I've been around the garden a few times. All I have to go on is what you tell me. Do I? And don't fib."

Mitch leaned and delivered a mere touch of a kiss to the round of her bare shoulder. "You look like you've just found the path and are still amazed by the blossoms."

"What a sweetie you are."

They were slightly sloshed by the time Billy dropped them off at Le Cirque. Everything was pleasant to amusing. Even things that ordinarily weren't so pleasant or amusing. The dinner was superb. They shared some *moules*. Couldn't decide on dessert so they ordered six of the offerings and took only nibbles of each.

During coffee and calvados doubles Maddie brought up the Kalali recovery. She'd been saving it, the real dessert.

Mitch started by relating the Peaches episode. Then proceeded to his adventure at Ralph's house. His intention was to omit certain gruesome things; however it was all linked and he got going and it all came out. From his first impression of Ralph's swag-laden rooms to his repulsive but rewarding dip in what had to be the world's scummiest swimming pool.

The part that especially amused Maddie was Mitch on the uppermost floor peering down through the register at the give and take routines of Ralph and the woman. Mitch performed all their dialogue in a Cary Grant manner. Then, of course, there'd been the cactus.

After dinner, feeling the calvados, they went to the cabaret at the

Russian Tea Room for an hour of Liliane Montevecchi singing about the varieties and vagaries of love.

Then they went home and made a few of their own versions.

Normally, following such late night lovemaking, Mitch slept like he was in hibernation. This night, however, his consciousness gave him a jolt after only an hour. His eyelids refused to remain shut. He lay there fixed on the blade of light on the ceiling from the night bulb in the bathroom.

A plentiful dose of endorphins were yet at work in his bloodstream, doing their best to make him feel well-being. Sleep should have been easy.

Finally he gave up trying for it, got up and went quietly into the study.

He would read, make use of the wakefulness by catching up on the last few issues of *Gem and Geology*, the quarterly journal of the Gemeological Institute of America.

The first article of interest to him was entitled "Update of Mining Rubies and Fancy Sapphires in Northern Vietnam."

One of Mitch's secret someday things was to spend time at a gem source such as that mentioned in the article: the mining areas around the town of Luc Yen located in the Bac Bo mountains two hundred kilometers northwest of Hanoi. Mitch read sections of the article twice so his fantasy was well-nourished.

He would be there. He would traipse around the small, likely valleys with head down, eyes scanning the gravelly ground. It would be tropical, sweltering. He would have on suitable boots, fang-proof leather fortresses. His shirt would be ten times its weight with sweat. Rivulets of sweat would roll down his torso and pool at his beltline. He'd have on his Glock in a holster rig. And an old, good-enough hat.

How sure-eyed he'd be! Any ruby or sapphire in his path would end up in his pouch. Here and there as he ambled along he would suddenly stop and squat and poke at the alluvial gravel where the merest bit of red or pink had peeked up at him. It would turn out to be much more than a hint when it was in his fingers and he spat on it and held it up to the sun.

The next article he got into was entitled "Gem Wealth of Tanzania" and off he went to a diamond-bearing stream bed a few miles south of Mwadui. Africa! Natural pink diamonds! Worth a fortune.

Dawn intruded.

Mitch went into the bedroom and lay next to Maddie, drew her to him.

A complaining moan from her. She shucked off his arm and wiggled away. She was having her own pleasant mind trip, wasn't ready for realities. "Go to work," she grumbled sleepily.

Might as well, Mitch thought. He got up and dressed and left a loving note Scotch-taped to the flushing lever of the toilet commode where she would surely find it. He'd read the note to her when he got home.

He arrived at Columbia Beneficial at twenty to ten. Self-imposed wait was a lot more bearable. The thirty-first floor reception area was unchanged, same gray atmosphere, same auntie receptionist, same magazines.

Mitch yawned.

He felt like stretching out on the sofa. He could say he was having a dizzy spell. His right foot was keeping time to some internal composition.

At precisely ten Ruder's secretary came out to fetch him. Today her prodigious rump was worse off in black and white plaid. She escorted him into Ruder's office. Ruder wasn't there. "Mr. Ruder will be with you shortly," she assured and, before going out to her desk, suggested that Mitch sit.

He remained standing. Sitting might imply that this was a meeting. He was there only to pick up his check. Ruder, being Ruder, wouldn't let it go at that, Mitch thought. There'd be small talk, cordial bullshit.

He glanced around the office. The wall safe was closed. The Kalali jewelry was in the dark, unable to scintillate, impotent. One of the framed photos on the cabinet behind Ruder's desk was of ex-president Gerald Ford. It bore Ford's hurried signature, just the signature, no best wishes. Possibly Ruder had forged the signature, Mitch thought. He decided that was what he'd believe.

The brass nautical-looking clock next to Ford's photo said it was ten after ten.

This was the most inflicting kind of wait, Ruder-caused.

At quarter after Ruder showed up. He closed the door, went directly to his tufted leather desk chair. He acknowledged Mitch with a curt good morning, the *good* barely audible. He put on his reading glasses. They were strong, made his eyes appear hyperthyroidic. He gave routine attention to some papers on his desk.

Mitch had expected Ruder would be all grin and gratitude. Not that it mattered.

Finally, Ruder removed his glasses and focused on Mitch. A hard, contemplative stare. "You're a slick son of a bitch, Laughton," he said.

"What's the problem?"

"I expected more of you."

"You shouldn't have," Mitch quipped just to keep up. He guessed perhaps the recovery of the Kalali jewels hadn't been enough to save Ruder's ass. What else could account for his being so sour-tempered?

"As of now, neither I nor this company want anything more to do with you," Ruder said. "I dictated our notice first thing this morning. You'll receive it in the mail."

"What the hell did I do?"

"You're not to be trusted."

"Evidently there's some misunderstanding."

"No misunderstanding. You've defined yourself quite clearly. Underhanded greed is something we won't put up with."

Mitch wasn't about to beg for an explanation. If Ruder had a bug up his ass he hoped it stung him. "Okay," Mitch said, "just give me my check and I'll be out of here."

"You'll get your check on the first of the month. According to our agreement with you we're required to give you thirty days' notice of termination. Our retainer check on the first will more than cover that thirty days. However, we're through with you as of now, is that understood?"

"I'll be getting my retainer fee on the first as usual."

"Yes."

"And a check for ten percent of the appraised value of the Kalali recovery."

"Five percent," Ruder corrected.

"We agreed on ten."

"Ten if you made a full recovery, five if you made only a partial."

"There was no such stipulation."

"Perhaps you failed to hear it. Your mind is usually elsewhere."

"Not when it comes to a six-hundred-thousand deal."

"I distinctly recall the condition," Ruder insisted, "you would receive an extra five percent for making a full recovery." He took up a copy of the Kalali loss list. He didn't need to refer to it, did so only for effect. "Item thirty-two was not included in the goods you left here yesterday."

The two enscribed emeralds.

Mitch realized now what Ruder was up to. He intended to pull the old insurance trick: invent a loophole and squirm out of paying by way of it.

"Evidently you've taken quite a liking to item thirty-two," Ruder remarked snidely.

"Those emeralds are not in the recovery because they weren't in the recovery. I've never seen them." It was the second time he'd been accused of holding back. Hurley yesterday, today Ruder.

"What gets me is here you are quibbling over a paltry three hundred thousand," Ruder said.

Why had three hundred thousand suddenly become paltry? Mitch wondered. He told Ruder straight across and unequivocally: "I want what I've got coming, what you know fucking well we agreed to. Ten percent, ten. The loss list total is six million one hundred thirty thousand. The appraised value of the two emeralds according to the loss list was one hundred fifty thousand. Deduct that one fifty from the six million one thirty and the recovery total

comes to five million nine eighty. At ten percent Columbia Beneficial owes me five hundred ninety-eight thousand. Now, why
don't you cut the insurance bullshit and go to whoever you need
to in this penitentiary and cut me a check for five ninety eight."

Ruder just sat there with upper-hand complacency.

"I'll wait," Mitch said.

"I've a good mind to not pay you a damn cent."

"I'd sue."

"Sure you would. You'd run the gauntlet of our lawyers and end
up bloodied and broke." Even before those words were out Ruder
was giving his attention to the paperwork of some other matter. As
far as he was concerned Mitch was no longer there.

"You're a prick," Mitch said.

"You're a thief," Ruder retaliated without so much as a glance
up.

Mitch turned to leave. He took three steps in the direction of
the way out. The fuse in him, already lighted, reached its detona-
tion point. With an explosion of rage he spun around and went for
Ruder. Dove across the desk.

Ruder might have evaded if he'd seen it coming a second sooner
or if Mitch hadn't been so quick. Mitch didn't get him with his
hands as he intended. His shoulder caught Ruder beneath the
chin.

The desk chair toppled over, sending the two men sprawling behind the desk.

Ruder landed on top. He tried to get off and get up.

Mitch grabbed Ruder's shirt front with his left hand. Such a furious, twisting grab that the placket of the shirt ripped and the but-
tons were torn off. Keeping that hold, Mitch punched with his
right.

One, two, three, straight jabbing punches.

The first two were glancing, but the third landed solid on
Ruder's nose, and Mitch's fist felt both the give of the fleshy part
and the more resistant cartilage and bone.

He let go.

Ruder rolled off and scrambled to the nearby corner, where he

remained down, his hand cupping his nose. Blood seeped from between his fingers. Most likely his nose was broken. "I'll have you
arrested," he muttered and made a move to reach the telephone.
Mitch feinted a lunge.

Ruder flinched and drew back.

Mitch wouldn't hit him again. He didn't need to. That one perfect punch on the nose was enough. He stood, took his time,
straightened his jacket and tie and shot his cuffs. He felt great. His
heart was zapping. There was a laugh in his chest. It was as though
some sort of elation-causing body chemical had been released into
his bloodstream.

It had been in him for years, that punch in the nose.

It had cost a fortune.

Three hundred thousand.

But it was worth it.

Chapter 25

It seemed to Mitch that the order of his life was immutable.

Each moment called for a decision, and whenever he decided to act contrary to what appeared to be the expected, the unavoidable, that contrariness became what had really been inevitable.

Fate was convenient to itself.

Why not just boat the oars and ride the rapids?

Thus, Mitch told himself he was only doing what had been predetermined, when, right after breaking Ruder's nose, he phoned his office and told Shirley to close up, take what remained of that day off. And while she was at it, she might as well also take tomorrow, Friday, off. And Monday. He'd see her Tuesday morning.

"You're off center," she said. "Did someone smack you on the head and make off with the shopping bag?"

"No."

"You left it in a taxi?"

"No."

"Then why are you hyperventilating so? You ought to hear how hard you're breathing. Like you've run a mile. I'll wager your heart rate is up. Place the mouthpiece to your chest so I can have a listen. Better come back to the office and I'll make tea. You're in no condition to be out there in the wilds. Bring some shortbread cookies. You know the kind."

"Go layaway."

A four-and-a-half-day hiatus.

He wouldn't set foot on 47th, wouldn't give it so much as a thought. To hell with it. He wasn't addicted to the street. It didn't have him psychologically tethered. He could take it or leave it. After all, do away with its glitter and what was it? A hive swarming with traffickers who were constantly trying to out-hondle one another.

"*To you, my friend, twenty-two a carat. I paid twenty.*"

"*You have a receipt?*"

"*Am I not entitled to make? Let me make two a carat.*"

"*I'm short at the moment.*"

"*Who isn't? I should be asking twenty-four and getting it, even twenty-five. Look at the goods.*"

"*I have already.*"

"*Another look.*"

"*I know the goods.*"

"*Tell me they're not worth twenty-five.*"

"*They're nice goods. Not for twenty-five but nice goods.*"

"*All I'm asking is twenty-two.*"

"*Why?*"

"*I'm ashamed to tell.*"

"*So don't tell.*"

"*Truthfully, I went in on something that went bad. I need cash to cover. You know how it is. My reputation is at stake, everything.*"

"*I told you, I'm short right now. I'd help maybe if I could but . . . .*"

"*Tomorrow maybe. I have been given until tomorrow.*"

"*I offer twenty-one today.*"

"*Twenty-two.*"

"*Twenty-one.*"

"*You're taking advantage.*"

For instance.

Mitch was reasonably true to his pledge. He stayed away from 47th, and each time it threatened to enter his mind he barricaded as best he could with distraction.

Friday night he and Maddie were on their way down to China-town to alleviate her craving for *dim sum*. Billy was driving them. Mitch was seated in back on the left. They were at 50th. Mitch felt 47th coming up. He would demonstrate his irreverence by closing his eyes.

However, when they were stopped by a light at that intersection, Mitch leaned forward in order to look past Maddie and out the window.

Forty-seventh was in its dormancy. The city streetlights along that chasm illuminated its inactivity. Every upper window of its outdated, shoulder-to-shoulder buildings was dark, every street-level window was barren. The sidewalks were vacant. Only a few cars were using the way for passage to the theater district. Forty-seventh had the appearance of a street stricken, commercially for-saken.

Perhaps a day would come when it would be, Mitch thought. As for now its impoverishment was an illusion. Within its numerous safes, vaults and strong rooms lay a collective hoard of gems worth millions upon millions. Precious stones that begged for light, re-quired it. In the darkness now but not sleeping. They never slept. They with their facets, their tables and pavilions, girdles and cutlets. It was as though they were being punished for their brilliance.

"What is it precious?" Maddie was asking.

"Hmmm?"

"You're being awfully quiet."

"Just thinking."

When they were first married Mitch believed, because Maddie couldn't see his eyes or his facial expression, the only way she could discern his disposition was by the tone of his voice. In time he learned that silence didn't always conceal, that she was often able to sense what was brewing in him.

"Just thinking ahead to some sweet and sour soup," he told her.

"It's the three hundred thousand, isn't it?"

"Not really."

"I must say you're being courageous about it. Any number of men have leaped from very high floors after losing a lot less."

"Not me."

"Just checking."

Saturday they went to the park and sat on a rock. Listened to Borodin's Symphony No. 1 in E Flat Major and some old Fleetwood Mac.

Sunday he read her most of the *Times* and they then took a growling ride around town on the Harley.

Monday he met Hurley for a drink at Harry Cipriani's, the intimate restaurant situated off the lobby of the Sherry. Their table next to the window was about the size of a Frisbee. By craning up Mitch had a clear view of the passersby out on Fifth. When he sat relaxed the sheer café-type curtains transformed those into transitory ghosts.

Harry's was crowded as it usually was from four on. Show people, cheaters, wives in pairs putting off having to go home from shopping, business sorts who'd given only an hour to the office since the last drink at lunch.

Mitch had a scotch and water.

He was down to the cubes before Hurley told him too coincidentally, just dropped it on him: "Ruder is missing."

"What do you mean missing?"

"Just that. He hasn't been seen or heard from since last Thursday."

"You know what happened Thursday?"

"Yeah, you gave him a nose job. You heard from him?"

"No."

"Around noon last Thursday he got an emergency appointment with his doctor on 65th to have his nose set. According to the doctor Ruder said he was going to sue you. After the doctor's he disappeared."

"I need an alibi?"

"He fucked you out of how much?"

"Three hundred for sure, maybe six."

"You need an alibi." Hurley did a serious expression, then nullified it with a grin. "Ruder had a slight concussion. He was advised to go home and rest. He didn't. Anyway, he didn't get there."

"Maybe he went blank, you know, got amnesia."

"Yeah, at this moment he could be shuffling in and out of the men's toilet at Grand Central."

"What a break for him not knowing himself."

They ordered another and drank to that.

When Hurley was gone, Mitch went out onto Fifth. He decided against a walk over to Lex. Instead he just stood out of the way to the left of the Sherry's canopied entrance. The late afternoon sun was yellowing the city. Soon it would go to orange. The air was thick and unsettled, redolent with hurry. Across the way, runners were funneling into the park by way of its southeast corner. They seemed to be people with less-complicated lives.

Really, where was Ruder? Mitch asked.

Wandering mindlessly, a blank among the scribble, a someone whose identity had sprung a leak and drained?

More to it than that, Mitch suspected.

A dog came along, a black and white of an oriental breed with a pushed-in face. Its walk had some proud prance in it, not at all a lost walk. It stopped at the water main that protruded from the exterior wall of the Sherry just above street level. Gleaming brass, double-headed pipe, diligently kept polished. The dog appraised it with several discriminating sniffs, then lifted his right hind leg to it.

No piss.

He was out of piss from having dispensed on the many corners, posts and such he'd encountered along his way.

He glanced in under at his genitals, as though to say he was doing his part, they should cooperate. He sidled into perfect position, lifted. Failed again. Sniffed at the brass to make sure he had or hadn't and continued on up the east side of Fifth.

Mitch watched the dog go. When it reached the intersection of 61st it was lost to the legs of pedestrians and cars making the turn. Mitch regained sight of it mid-block to 62nd. By then, the rear-end view of it at that distance was no longer a dog shape.

Smart little guy, Mitch thought, the way he accepted being on empty and headed nonstop for his bowl and probably the lap of a Scalamandre covered sofa chair.

Within a split second of his having made that opinion, Mitch saw the receding creature break from its straight course and revert to a dog shape in profile as it veered to the left, to the curb, to the hub-cap of a Bentley.

Mitch went inside. He stopped at the lobby newsstand for a magazine and just did catch an elevator that was closing to go up. There were two other passengers: a man and a woman. That was the extent of what Mitch made of them, no special regard, no reason to take particular notice, just that swift impression: a man and woman. The upward ride began. Mitch minded his elevator manners, faced forward and kept his eyes fixed ahead on the grain of the walnut paneling. To stare or even to briefly glance aside at a stranger in the confines of such a cubicle might be considered, according to unwritten New York law, an invasion of person, a potential nosiness.

The woman got off on twelve.

During the minor commotion of her exit Mitch happened to glance down at the shoes of the man.

Black and white wing-tipped oxfords.

It registered immediately, when and where Mitch had recently noticed someone wearing black and white wing-tips. They weren't shoes one saw every day, not even twice in two weeks. He was ambivalent about turning and taking an obvious look at the man, and by the time he'd decided he would, the elevator reached the thirty-second floor, leveled and opened.

Mitch stepped out onto the landing.

So did the man.

There was no doubt about it now. The black-banded panama hat, the impeccably groomed appearance. Not a gray-vested gabardine suit today, a vested black one of equally fine quality and cut. Bushy brows. It was definitely the man Mitch had practically collided with entering Visconti's office the week before last. The man Mitch had then thought from appearance was one of Visconti's wealthy foreign clients.

"I believe you must be Mr. Laughton," the man was amiably saying now. "Mr. Mitchell Laughton?"

"Yes?" Wary as usual.

"Might I have a word with you?"

"Depends on the word."

The man produced a calling card from out of a black alligator leather card case.

Mitch expected it would be a business card; however it had only the man's name tastefully engraved on it. Centered in small letters.

Manonchehr Djam.

What kind of name is that? Mitch thought.

The man pronounced it for him. He was always having to pronounce it. "I've been trying to reach you at your office since last Thursday afternoon," he said. "I was beginning to fear that you might be away on vacation."

"How did you find out where I live?"

"I inquired," Djam said as though that was plausible and sufficient. "I apologize for the intrusion but the matter I wish to discuss with you is most pressing."

"Couldn't it hold until tomorrow?"

"Yes, of course . . . "

Mitch had his key out, was finding the cylinder hole with it. What he'd had in mind was an old movie night. A certain channel he and Maddie often turned to had a triple feature of *Thin Man*'s scheduled and such a dose of Loy and Powell solving crimes between martinis would be just the palliative he needed. He and Maddie would get naked and hunker down among the pillows with an exorbitant bottle of vintage Graves and, as usual, he'd narrate the action for her between the lines of dialogue.

He had the apartment door unlatched and open a crack. His curiosity hadn't really been oblivious. Now, at the last moment, it jumped up to ask: "What's it about, this matter of yours that's so important?"

"It concerns the Kalali jewels," Djam replied.

"Come on in."

Mitch took Djam's panama and showed him to the study. The aviary door was open but all the birds were perched inside. One, a lady finch, came winging out as though dispatched by the others. It circled three times around Djam like it was on a reconnaissance mission. Djam didn't know quite what to make of it. He finally decided he should be amused, stopped ducking and broke out into a wide grin that exposed large, tea-stained teeth.

The lady finch's return to the aviary caused a lot of bird chatter.

Djam accepted a chair. He crossed his legs somewhat gracefully. A waste because he immediately stood up as Maddie entered the study.

She was fresh out of a shower, had washed her hair. The blonde of it was darker wet. She hadn't yet toweled it, so it was a mass of short tendrils.

Nor had she belted the full-length white terry cloth robe she had on. It hung open.

Djam respectfully averted his eyes. Maddie sensed there was someone other than Mitch in the room. She insouciantly sashed the robe, exercising her contention that one of the advantages of being blind was it forgave most immodesties.

Mitch introduced Djam, mispronounced his name three different ways.

Would Djam care for something to drink?

"I'd thoroughly appreciate a glass of tea," he said.

That was more bother than tossing some ice cubes into a glass and sloshing in vodka or whatever; however Mitch managed to be hospitable. "Any preference to the kind of tea?"

"Black tea, thank you. Any good kind of black tea."

"I don't think, in fact, I know we're all out of black," Maddie said. A fib because they never drank it. "But I believe we have some jasmine."

"That will do fine," Djam told her. Actually, he deplored such fragrant teas, considered them too feminine for his taste.

"And I should warn you," Maddie added, "we do our tea with bags. We used to ritualize. You know, preheat the pot, measure exactly and steep and all that but lately it's been merely bags."

What bullshit, Mitch thought. There'd never been any steeping.

"Any way you fix it will be fine," Djam assured.

"Did I understand that you wanted a glass of tea?"

"Yes."

"Iced tea?"

"No, hot, thank you . . . " Djam regretted that he hadn't declined. Now he was going to have to suffer a glass of dreadful, prissy jasmine that was not even correctly prepared. Oh well.

Mitch excused himself, left Djam seated there and went into the kitchen to help Maddie make the tea. He looked into the cupboard while she put water on to boil. "I don't see any jasmine," he said.

"We don't have any. I only said we did in the hope that he wouldn't want it and settle for an easier scotch on the rocks. Who the hell is he, anyway?"

"I don't know."

"What do you mean you don't know?"

"I just met him."

"That's not like you, bringing home a total stranger."

"Here's some tea bags."

"What's got into you? He's not British you know."

"Not with that name."

"Nor that accent."

"He doesn't have an accent, other than British I mean."

"Hell he doesn't. Most of it's been schooled out of him but it's there. Cambridge probably."

She was always hearing things most people missed.

"Anyway, he said he wanted to have a word with me," Mitch said.

"What about?"

"The Kalali jewelry."

"Oh?" Maddie had an instantaneous rise in interest. In place of the ordinary glass for the tea she got out a Waterford goblet, Celia pattern, and wrapped one of her best linen napkins around it so Mr. Djam wouldn't burn his fingers.

Mitch carried in the tray.

Maddie announced: "No jasmine I'm afraid but some scrumptious lemon zinger."

Djam was on his haunches examining the underside of a corner of the room's main carpet. "A very pleasing Tabriz" was his opinion of it. "I assume you realize that other carpet over there, though much smaller, is the better of the two." He was referring to the prayer-size carpet near the bookcase.

"You must mean Killer," Maddie said. She'd named the carpet that because of the numerous times it had tripped her. She'd often verbally admonished it for its behavior and even threatened to throw it down the trash chute.

"A fairly fine nineteenth century silk Heriz," Djam said. "It deserves to be hung rather than trampled on." He had resumed sitting with legs crossed, the glass of tea resting on his knee. Lemon zinger. He glanced down at it. It appeared insipid, attenuated. Perhaps he could get away with a single sip and then place it aside and forget about it.

"Is that your metier, carpets?" Maddie asked.

"In part," Djam replied. "My responsibilities require it. During the two or three years that preceded the revolution, especially when the revolution became imminent, a great number of our finest carpets were shipped to the West. Planeloads went by way of Syria, others were sent overland by truck to Germany and Switzerland. I regret we shall never recover the greater part of those national treasures; however we continue to do what we can. Only last October I spotted a pedigreed sixteenth century carpet in the exhibition prior to sale at a major auction house in London. The reserve on it was ninety thousand pounds. You can imagine how delighted I was that it had come out of hiding, so to speak. I proved provenance and the carpet is now back where it belongs."

It sounded to Maddie that Djam expected applause. "And where's that?" she asked.

"In the Bastan Museum. Of course."

"Did you say Boston?"

"No, Bastan," he said, his long A's making it sound as much like Boston as it had before. "In Teheran," he added.

The lemon zinger was on its way to his lips when suddenly something occurred to him. He placed the glass on the side table next to his chair. "How remiss of me," he uttered sharply, "I haven't yet introduced my professional self." From that same elegant black case he slipped out another card, identical in quality to the first but bearing, along with his name:

Committee of Cultural Reclamation
Islamic Republic of Iran

Mitch read the card aloud for Maddie's benefit. Now they realized with certainty which revolution Djam was talking about.

"So you see," Djam said. "You and I, Mr. Laughton, are involved in the same sort of business. We are both bent on recovering precious things. You for your reasons, myself for quite another."

Mitch saw the comparison but what was the point? Whatever it was, if this Djam got to it quickly enough, there might still be time to catch the *Thin Man* triple feature. Anyway, two-thirds of it. "You mentioned the Kalali jewelry," Mitch prompted.

"Yes."

"What's your interest in it?"

"Substantial," Djam replied. "What are your chances of making a recovery?"

A shrug from Mitch. Evidently Djam was unaware that the recovery had already been made. Rather than inform him of that, Mitch decided he'd take this a little further. Not far, just enough to get some of the intrigue out of it. He told Djam: "I guess you feel the same towards the Kalali jewels as you do about those contraband carpets you spoke of."

"Even more strongly."

"They once belonged to your government and it wants them back."

"Exactly."

Mitch had known about the Iranian hoard for many years. At various times he'd read about it in trade articles and books on gems. There had been photographs illustrating the extent of this treasure. Tray after tray on shelf after shelf piled with precious stones. Chests filled to the point of overflow with emeralds, sapphires, rubies, diamonds. It infected the mind with fantasy. It was the stuff of impossible fables, and yet, there it was, as real as could be, causing more than mere fascination, an ache to get one's hands into it, to fill one's pockets, a lusting that just about anyone, but especially a dealer in gemstones, would be susceptible to.

Djam relaxed his gaunt face and did a slight smile to help the impression that he was a pleasant-natured Iranian. While inwardly he was annoyed by having just noticed a scuff mark on the white area of his right oxford. It was tantamount to a bruise. He looked to Maddie, who was comfortably situated in the corner of the deep sofa across from him. Her legs doubled up so the soles of her bare feet were directed right at him. He'd been informed that Mitchell Laughton's wife was blind and, thus, he'd expected that would be apparent in all the ordinary ways. Up to now, however, Mrs. Laughton seemed able to get about as well as any sighted person. No uncertainty in her walk, no hesitancy in her hands. Nor did her eyes have a fixed functionless quality. Her eyes appeared to be involved with whatever was taking place, reacting reflexively as normal eyes do to what was being said and who was saying it, and, somehow, incredibly, to what was being done and who was doing it. Djam believed it was probably an affect she'd perfected. It and the affront of the bottom of her feet caused him to be uneasy.

He redirected his attention to Mitch. "Imagine, if you will, what a temptation the Iranian treasury must have been to a certain privileged few in nineteen seventy-eight. By then it was inevitable that the Shah would be ousted. Various members of the Shah's family had already fled, were residing in France, Switzerland, this country and elsewhere. Many prominent government officials had done likewise. Not to feel sorry for them. Hundreds of millions in currency had preceded their departures.

"For those of the elite who remained in Iran but knew they would soon take flight, the national treasure was impossible to ignore. It couldn't be merely left behind. At least not all of it. Such a trove of precious stones. Worth billions, was the guess. How accommodating that it had never been properly inventoried and appraised. The task would have taken five, maybe ten years, and then been obsolete. The attitude had always been no need to know more about it other than that it was there.

"During those final months of the Shah his relatives and close associates discreetly pilfered the treasure. They were allowed to get

to it and take nibbles and bites of it every now and then. A handful of diamonds wouldn't be missed, nor would a pocketful of rubies, sapphires or emeralds. Abundance covered up each little
ransacking.

"Abbas Kalali and his wife, Roudabeth, were among those who
paid such visits to the vault in the Central Bank where the treasure
was kept. Not that the Kalalis were high in favor with the Shah or
within the coterie of the elite. Kalali was never more than a mid-
level official assigned to one bureau or another. His well-being was
dependent on a remote and tenuous connection: the wife of one of
his uncles happened to be the cousin of General Nassiri, the head
of Savak, the Shah's secret police.

"Perhaps the most accurate measure of Abbas Kalali's standing
was his bribery price of only a million dollars. Only? you say. Remember, this was at a time when the going rate for influence by a
member of the Shah's family was a hundred million. Prime minis-
ters were slipped fifty million, generals went for thirty.

"You might wonder, then, how it was that Abbas Kalali got to
dip into the treasure, what was it about him that gave him access?
Why him? Well, Abbas Kalali was the apotheosis of sycophancy. He
knew when to laugh and when to commiserate, when to take a side,
which side to take, when to lose, when to appear or disappear. Thus,
it was often agreeable for the coterie of the privileged to have him
around. You know the sort."

Yeah, Mitch thought, he knew have-arounds.

"Kalali was obviously willing to be used and use him they did.
Especially during the final months of the Shah when it was dan-
gerous to be making trips to the vault at odd hours. They enlisted
Kalali to go for them. He was their designated thief and carrier."

Nothing so unusual about that, Mitch thought.

"No doubt," Djam went on, "they expected that while Kalali
was at it he would help himself to a helping. That didn't matter to
them as long as it wasn't too much and he didn't embarrass by letting them know about it. And, as long as he brought from the vault
whatever it took to satisfy them."

Djam paused. Evidently he had more to say. He shifted his position in the chair and transposed the cross of his legs.

"Your tea must be cold," Maddie said.

Djam wondered how she could know he hadn't drunk it.

"I can heat it up for you."

"No, please, don't bother," Djam said. "I prefer it lukewarm."

A nearly inaudible grunt of disbelief from Maddie.

"So," Mitch said, "according to what you say, I gather you believe the Kalali jewels are made up from gems that were taken from the Iranian treasury."

"Mainly they are, yes," Djam replied. "Of course there was more, much more, loose cut stones and quite a bit of rough. Diamonds and rubies mostly. Kalali sold those in various lots over the years. He must have realized plenty for them, plenty."

"How come you're just now laying claim?"

"As reluctant as I am to admit it, we were never able to catch up with him. He was like a damn cricket. You know, one of those elusive bugs. Pounce to capture it, think you have, open your hands only to find you haven't. When he first came to the United States, which was in August of 1980 after the death of the Shah, he lived in northern California under an assumed name, always under a document-supported assumed name. Then it was Arizona and South Dakota of all places. We never gave up on him altogether but after a half dozen years we more or less left it to God's will that he would somehow, someday turn up. Which he did most recently, turned up dead."

"Not under an assumed name."

"No. Apparently time caused him to believe he was forgotten."

"And all was forgiven. You still want them back, those gems, what's left of them?"

"We do."

"The Iranian treasure must be getting pretty paltry."

"I assure you the Iranian treasure would still make you momentarily forget to take a breath."

Mitch was thinking of a lady in a coma and her vigilant lover, their hopes. "Strikes me as greedy," he told Djam. "Those piles of gems you have and here you are eager to recover these relative few. Greedy, wouldn't you say, Maddie?"

"How about hoggish?" Maddie enjoyed replying.

If Djam was either embarrassed or insulted it didn't show. He did another pleasant Iranian smile and several thoughtful blinks and said: "Actually, I would be satisfied with the recovery of just one piece of the Kalali jewels."

"You would?"

"Yes."

"Any piece?"

"One particular piece."

"Name it."

"It appears on the insurance company loss list as item number thirty-two."

The loss list. When, where, Mitch wondered, had Djam become so familiar with the loss list? As for item number thirty-two, what a bane it had been.

Those two enscribed emeralds.

"Instead," Mitch suggested, "how about a pair of diamond and ruby ear pendants, an exquisite pair, Burma rubies, clean E-color diamonds. They might even be D's." Selling.

"Only the emeralds will do," Djam told him.

"Why?"

"Must I tell you?"

Mitch sensed a long wind coming up. He almost got to say his *no* before Maddie's *yes*. She, with her usual penchant for accounts that might smack of thievery or any sort of sharp practice, was all ears.

"Very few people in this country are knowledgeable when it comes to Iranian history," Djam said. "I don't suppose you're the exception."

Oh Christ, Mitch thought, how far back will he go?

As though answering Mitch's mind, Djam began with: "Seventeen thirty-six was the year that Nadar Shah took over the throne of Iran from the Safavids, who had ruled for more than two hundred and thirty years. He was an Afsharid Turkman from northern

Khorasan. At the time, Iran was by no means a wealthy country. Its primary source of revenue was the silk trade, and carpet weaving. What's more, being remote from Europe, literally cut off from Europe by Ottoman territory, any trade in that direction was sporadic at most.

"Nadar Shah was not the sort to remain content with such marginal solvency. His was an aggressive nature. He was also obsessed with treasure and jewels. Thus, in seventeen thirty-eight, only two years after taking rule, Nadar and his army went plundering."

Now, this is getting good, Maddie thought.

Djam went on: "He didn't go charging around grabbing up whatever he just happened upon. He knew where the real riches were and went straight for them. The Moghul emperors of India were then the wealthiest of the world's wealthy. No one had more. They hoarded nearly all the fine diamonds from their prolific mines at Panama and Cuddapah. They merely had to reach out to neighboring Burma and Ceylon for whatever rubies and sapphires they desired. With the same ease they acquired the choicest pearls from the Andaman Sea located immediately to the east.

"The Moghuls were especially fond of emeralds. The finest came from the mines of distant Colombia, those that the Spanish conquistadors discovered north of Bogotá in the region of Muzo. Spain had the emeralds, the Moghuls had the money. Spain preferred money, the Moghuls preferred emeralds. It couldn't have been a more agreeable arrangement. Spanish ships carried the emerald rough from Colombia to the Philippines where it was cut and polished before being delivered to Delhi.

"So, thus were the riches Nadar Shah was set upon. The Moghul armies fought but were no match. Nadar's forces overran all of Delhi. They appropriated the treasure and headed home.

"Picture if you will that victorious homeward-bound trek. I have, numerous times. What a sight it must have been! What jubilance must have occupied Nadar's heart as he led that caravan laden with booty! Literally hundreds of thousands of precious stones! Layer after layer rolled up in leopard and tiger skins, caskets of pearls, a dozen pack horses needed to convey the emeralds!"

Djam realized he was getting carried away. He checked his exuberance, sort of shook it off and elevated his torso to recapture his previous dignity. "The Iranian treasure that we spoke of before, that which the Kalalis and others dipped into, is, of course, comprised mainly of the spoils of Nadar Shah's Delhi campaign."

"You hardly touched on the best part, the robbery," Maddie complained.

"Robbery?"

"Nadar Shah might have appropriated, as you put it; however it was robbery."

"It wasn't thought of as such in those days," Djam told her.

"I suppose not; however he was a swift, big-time but no less and swift, and the stuff he stole was swag."

Mitch assumed the two enscribed emeralds that were on the Kalali loss list had been part of Nadar Shah's Moghul booty. But so what? If that was their only significance it was trivial, considering the enormous amounts of emeralds in the Iranian treasury. What made those two that, from what Mitch could see weren't special, so special? He asked Djam.

"That is the most salient part of what I'm telling you," Djam said.

"There's more?"

"Yes, what I've just related is only background. I thought you would enjoy it."

Mitch was now about eighty percent restive, twenty percent curious. He looked to Maddie, thinking she might have had enough and would do an excuse such as having to get ready for a dinner party out; however she was distracted, vigorously roughing up her hair with her fingers to help it dry.

"Husayn al-Qasim Muhammad ibn Hashid," Djam said with an ethnic, gargling-like quality that, because of its change, sounded exaggerated, "was a poet who lived in a province of Esfahan. An admirably devout man. He was a descendant of Iran's most revered mystical poet, Jahal Ad-Din-Ar Rumi."

"When was this?" Maddie interrupted.

"The precise year is a matter of controversy," Djam replied.

"Some accounts have it as eighteen ten, others at eighteen eight. It surely was around that time, the early eighteen hundreds. Anyway, Husayn al-Qasim, as I said, was a religious person. Pious would be a more accurate description. He placed his own contentment and even his meager requirements second to his worship. His most joyful pursuit was in composing verses of devotion to God, and praying, of course.

"Esfahan is for the most part an arid province. Except for the provincial capital it is sparsely inhabited. The small village where Husayn lived was far from any other settlement. Such remoteness suited him. He had no desire or need to associate or experience what lay beyond his view.

"The radiance of such a pious man transcends distance. He was known of, spoken of. That was how Ali-Bin al-Nizami, who at the time was the Imam of the most important mosque in Teheran, learned of Husayn's ailment. Husayn was going blind.

"There were those who said that Husayn's swiftly progressive blindness was a result of his having seen the heart of the sun while staring directly into it. Probably the less mythic cause was a condition we now know as macular degeneration, wherein the macula part of the retina leaks fluid which destroys the retinal nerve tissue. It is untreatable.

"As a gesture of sympathy and hoping to ease, the Imam selected two large emeralds from the treasury and sent them to Husayn along with the suggestions that Husayn hold them up to his eyes and gaze through them whenever he felt inclined. According to the Koran green is the color of heavenly bliss, the color of paradise."

Djam paused.

Mitch believed he could save words and time. "So," he said, "those enscribed emeralds are the two you now want to recover."

"Please, you're getting ahead of me," Djam said and went on: "Husayn was grateful for the Imam's concern and followed his suggestion. For forty days, at intervals throughout each day, he brought the two emeralds to his eyes, and through them, as well as he was able, saw the colorless aridity of the Esfahan countryside transformed into a blessed verdancy.

"That he did so for forty days was not just arbitrary. In our Koran as in your Bible the number forty is given mystical significance. It is the stipulated length of time for a period of mourning or repentance, for example, or steadfastness.

"Husayn spent the fortieth morning of those forty days composing verses in praise of the Khider, the figure spoken of in sura twenty of the Koran as the unnamed companion of Moses. The Khider is the patron saint most frequently related to the green color of paradise. Husayn was especially inspired that morning and his verses flowed so freely from him it seemed as though he was a mere conduit, a go-between. To this day they are considered to be his best.

"Came noon Husayn performed his ablutions, and, after saying his mid-day prayers, he had a little to eat. Almonds, pomegranate seeds and goat cheese. There, seated on the bare ground on the shady side of his modest house, he treated himself to the enjoyment of gazing through the two emeralds. Within a short while he became drowsy and could not resist falling into a deep sleep.

"When he awakened it was late afternoon. The sun had come around to him and there were independent fluffs of clouds in the sky. He could see those clouds clearly. He was able to make out their edges, layers and forms. He saw that the line of the horizon was distinct, and everything, all the way to it, each shape and each variety of hue, was no longer obscure, but sharply visible to him. The eyesight he'd lost had been returned.

"Husayn looked down at his clenched hands and opened them. Each contained one of the emeralds. Just as he had undergone a change so had those green stones. The flat surface of their faces had been plainly polished. Now, however, each bore a finely engraved inscription in old Farsi, the original Persian language. The inscriptions pertained to what we call *yagin*, the light of intuitive certainty by which the heart sees God."

"Oh, what a fascinating story," Maddie said.

"And true," Djam assured.

"Could be," Mitch compromised.

"I'm sure you can now understand why we are so anxious to

have those emeralds returned," Djam said. "They are sacred to us, an affirmation of our beliefs. It's as if you had in your possession one of the commandment tablets of Moses and someone made off with it."

Mitch thought that was stretching it. Maybe it was true that Husayn what's-his-name's eyesight had improved to some extent for some more earthly reason and maybe it was also true that someone had realized the advantage of the circumstances and had the inscriptions done. The shroud of Turin came to mind, that contrivance.

Mitch's thoughts in that direction halted and went another way. Why was he such a doubter? he asked himself. Nearly every time, right off, a doubter. Why couldn't he be more often spontaneously receptive, at least a potential believer? It wasn't a new question. The answer, the excuse, the explanation or whatever had always been that it was something West 47 had done to him, as ambiguous and abstract as that. Also, more specifically, some of the blame belonged to the woman with the pistol up her sable sleeve. "Kalali probably took them unknowingly," Mitch reasoned. "He probably thought they were just ordinary emeralds."

"No," Djam told him. "Kalali was well-aware of what he was taking. Those emeralds were kept in a special glass case in the vault. He knew their religious history, how much they were valued. That was what he was counting on, how much we would be willing to pay to have them back."

"How was it you knew Kalali had them?"

"We didn't at first. It could have been any one of the Shah's entourage who had swiped from the vault. There were dozens. It could even have been the Shah himself, considering it was such an audacious act. We learned that it was Kalali when he made an overture in a roundabout way to negotiate a price. That was early on during his California days. His trepidations must have gotten the best of him. He broke off contact and disappeared."

"One would think with your resources . . . "

"This large country is inhabited by diverse people. It's much less difficult for someone to get lost than it is for someone to be found."

True enough, Mitch thought. His curiosity asked Djam: "How much would you have paid Kalali for the emeralds?"

"Kalali was a condemned man."

"Say he wasn't, how much?"

"The same amount we're now offering."

Had Mitch heard right? "What do you mean offering?"

"I am authorized by the Committee of Cultural Reclamation to reward whoever recovers the emeralds for us with twenty-five million dollars."

Wishful hearing, Mitch told himself, the guy hadn't really said twenty-five million. "How much did you say?"

"Twenty-five million."

"American dollars."

"Naturally."

Oh how that would fit, Mitch thought. If true, his pessimism reminded. "To whom have you made this offer?" he asked.

"I would rather not say. To several people." Djam did that smile again. Unfortunate teeth. "And now you," he said.

Riccio, Mitch thought. It explained why Riccio had resorted to such extreme, old–mob violence with Ralph. Rather than wait for the Kalali swag to possibly come his way he'd gone after it. It also explained why Ruder had done such a quick change when he realized the emeralds weren't in the recovery. Item thirty-two, missing. Sure, Ruder was looking at a nice, fat twenty-five-million score. Out of which he was going to give Mitch, for doing all the work, a skinny extra three hundred thousand. Big-hearted Ruder, the prick. And since Mitch had seen Djam coming out of Visconti's office, no doubt Visconti was in on it. "Why didn't you come to me first?" Mitch asked.

"You were on my agenda," Djam replied. "However, I was told you wouldn't be amenable to such a proposition."

"Who told you that?"

"You were described as . . . I believe the way they put it was . . . too straight. Also, it was said you wouldn't be motivated, you didn't need the money because your wife was wealthy."

A chuckle from Maddie. "Mitch was your best shot," she told

Djam. "He probably would have recovered your precious emeralds for nothing. Isn't that right, Mitch darling?"

Mitch turned partially away as though to deflect Maddie's words. The numbers got into him, took over and ran across the front of his mind like a repetitive electronic sign, starting with a two, then a five, then a comma and all those zeros.

He could handle that.

Chapter 26

He was in his office on the phone with Hurley.

"Is the guy real?" Hurley asked.

Mitch had just told him about Djam, the emeralds and the twenty-five million offer. "Hard to tell. It looks it, sounds it." In the cooler light of Tuesday morning Mitch had allowed his skepticism to snap back into place like a filter.

"Could be he's a throwback," Hurley said.

"What do you mean throwback?"

"The Arabs had their day. Was a time when any prototype Arab who could afford a good suit, impressive luggage and a suite for a week at the Pierre was someone who got his ass kissed. Remember? A lot of them were into it only for that reason."

"Yeah."

"Then came the Japs. Same thing. Next maybe the Chinks coming out of Hong Kong. So, could be your guy . . . what did he call himself?"

"Manonchehr Djam." Mitch still had trouble with the name.

"Could be he's a throwback."

"You're probably right. I'd prefer that you weren't but probably you are." If so, Mitch thought, the Iranian was also fucking with Riccio's head, and Visconti's. Djam hadn't struck him as that foolish but who knows how far someone doing such an ego scam might dare to take it. "This morning," he told Hurley, "just for the hell of it I was going over the chain of possession of the Kalali goods. The link that's missing is the swift, Floyd."

"We picked him up."

"What's his version?"

"We picked him up in a body bag. He had a mouth-first hole in his head. Now, I ask you, when you want a guy to give up something how can he say what you want to hear when he's got a throat full of pistol?" A short inured laugh from Hurley.

"How about the other swifts?"

"We got the one called Tracy. He's about as stand-up as a paraplegic. We only sort of promised a plea and he laid the whole thing out for us. Says the girl Peaches popped Mr. Kalali."

"Believe him?"

"Yeah."

"He mention the emeralds?"

"Come to think of it I did ask him about them. He never saw them. Everything except Peaches' earrings went to Ralph."

"How's Peaches getting along?" Mitch inquired.

"I should be such a lie artist. So far she's changed the scenario eight times. You heard from Ruder?"

"Why should I?"

"No reason. He just might get it in his head to call you . . . from the spot on the floor where he sleeps in the West Side bus terminal. How's Maddie?"

"The same, perfect."

"Give her my best. No, give her *your* best."

"I try."

While Mitch was on line one with Hurley line two had started blinking, and Shirley had picked it up. She'd brought in a message slip. Mitch read it now. Originally her precise handwriting had said: *Riccio wants to talk with you.* She'd crossed out the *talk with* and replaced it with *see* and an exclamation point.

Twenty minutes later Mitch was climbing Riccio's gritty, vinyl-covered stairs. The same fat have-around was on duty on the landing halfway up. He wanted no part of Mitch this time. He backed aside awkwardly and sat on the edge of the daybed. "You got an appointment?" he asked.

Mitch ignored him, went on up to Riccio's rooms. He had to go through Bechetti to get in to Riccio but there was no problem: he was expected. Riccio was at a Formica-topped table against the wall, going over some swag that had come in from the preceding weekend. In a small adjacent room off to the right a couple of have-arounds were watching a television talk show.

Riccio didn't usually get up to greet someone but now he did. He came at Mitch with a big smile, a two-handed shake and flattery. "Nice to see you, Mitch. What is this with you? How come you're looking so good. You just get a haircut or something? Come on, sit. I was just going to have some coffee."

"None for me, thanks," Mitch said, mindful of the billions of bacteria there would be on the rim of one of Riccio's dirty cups.

"How come no coffee?"

"Doctor's orders."

"What is it, the belly?"

"Nerves."

"Nerves can lead to an early death," Riccio recited as though it was sky-writing.

They were seated at the Formica-topped table, diagonally across from one another. Folding metal chairs that didn't match. Eight skinny black twists of cigars bound by a rubber band. The swag. Three separate lots. Mitch assumed one lot was that which would be broken up. Another was what would be kept, the third awaited Riccio's decision. Mitch tried to disregard it.

"What do you think of this?" Riccio asked, tossing Mitch a piece from the unsorted lot.

Mitch thought, for one thing, that it didn't deserve such rough handling, especially when he held it up and realized how fine it was. A *sautoir* consisting of natural seed pearls and tiny diamond rondelles suspending a frosted rock crystal hoop that was delicately bordered with bagettes of calibré onyx and tasseled with ruby heads. Mitch's appreciation was obvious.

"Like it?" Riccio asked.

"It's nice," Mitch understated. Not to waste his expertise, he held back telling Riccio it was Mauboussin circa 1910.

"It's yours," Riccio said.

Mitch placed the *sautoir* on the table. It didn't belong here, he thought, not in this ugly, smelly place being mishandled by coarse hands. It deserved to be around the neck of a lovely, high-fashioned lady, to give her fingers something to fuss with, during the public phase of a rendezvous at the bar of the Ritz in Paris.

"What's the matter?" Riccio asked.

"It's not my taste," Mitch told him.

"That's not right. You don't like it you should still accept. If it was anybody but you I'd consider it an insult." Riccio gathered up the *sautoir* and relegated it to the break-up lot.

To Mitch that was a kind of murder.

"Let's be more comfortable," Riccio said.

They moved to a nearby couch. It was new but cheap, the sort that would soon go lumpy. "I take a nap now and then," Riccio explained. A regular foam rubber bed pillow had a pink and yellow floral case. A crucifix over the bed. "I hear you had some good luck," he said.

"How's that?"

"The stuff you brought me the pictures of a couple of weeks back. You found it."

"Who told you?"

"That insurance guy. What's his name?"

"Ruder."

"That's it, Ruder. He said you found the whole package and made a nice score. I'm happy for you. You deserve."

"When did you talk to Ruder?"

"Last week sometime. I think it was Wednesday. Yeah, Wednesday." Riccio called out to Bechetti who immediately showed himself in the doorway of the television room. "Wasn't it Wednesday we talked with that insurance guy?"

"Yeah, Wednesday," Bechetti corroborated.

If Riccio and Ruder knew each other it was news to Mitch. One thing for certain: if they had talked and Ruder had mentioned the recovery it couldn't have been Wednesday. Ruder didn't know about it until Thursday. "I heard that Ruder is missing," Mitch said off-hand.

"No shit. You mean he ain't been around anywhere?"

"Since Thursday afternoon."

"So, who gives a fuck? Guy like that gets missed for a while, month or two it's like he fucking never was." Riccio inserted a finger behind the top button of his shirt. He stretched his neck. The shirt was overstarched, the collar like a blade at his throat. "Tell the truth, I didn't like the guy. He was a piece of shit."

Mitch noticed the past tense.

"Know what happens to a guy like that?" Riccio went on. "He fucks with the wrong people. They take exception. He keeps on fucking with them and they have to hurt him. They could pop a cap into him but that ain't satisfying enough, they don't want to just do that. Know what they do? They hold his mouth open and pour diamonds into him. Then they give him four or five shots in the belly, hard right hands right in there. He's an asshole. He's coughing blood but he's still fucking with these wrong people. What can they do? Throw him in the river? Not yet. First, to make sure he sinks, you know, that he doesn't gas up and bloat and come to the top someplace, they slit him up the front and rip his guts and everything out like he was a fish. That way they also get back the diamonds. Happens to a guy like that who fucks with the wrong people."

Mitch had never disliked Ruder to the extent that he'd wish him such a fate. He knew, however, as sure as he'd just heard Riccio's horror story, it had probably happened. A shiver climbed the ladder of his spine. His facial expression remained unchanged.

"Anyway," Riccio said, "Ruder told us when you handed over that swag to him you held out."

"I turned in all there was."

"Except a pair of emeralds."

"I never had them."

"Look, I don't blame you for putting those emeralds aside, not when there's this sand nigger moving around saying he'll give twenty-five extra large for them."

Riccio's phone rang. He went over to his desk and answered it. A grunt instead of a hello. It wasn't a conversation, at least not from Riccio's end. Just a series of flat *yeahs* and *nos*. Mitch looked past him and saw Fratino in the television room, the doorway framing him. Like a tableau, Mitch thought. Have-around in a short-sleeve wrinkle-proof shirt with pistol rig on. Hyper reality. He should be exactly done in acrylic and exhibited at the Whitney.

Riccio returned to the couch. "I'll make you a deal for the two emeralds," he said.

"I told you, I don't have them."

"Sure you do."

"What can I say?"

"You can say what kind of a deal like the sensible, straight guy I think you are and I'll tell you I'm willing to give you one extra large for them and you can think about it for five or ten seconds in order to look smart before you say okay, Riccio, that's what you can say."

While those were Riccio's words, Mitch was asking himself why was he there? Breathing the same air as this man and the others. He wasn't one of them. He would never be one of them. No matter how the street shaped him. They happened to be inhabitants, an ingredient of the mix. They tolerated him. He tolerated them. The bubbling coo of pigeons in the eaves. Transmitted television voices. Precious stones lost in the high-pile weave of the wall-to-wall rug. Riccio farted without apology. What am I? Mitch asked himself, a social chameleon?

"I don't get it," he told Riccio.

"What don't you get?"

"If I had the emeralds why should I give them to you for a million when I could get twenty-five million for them?"

"Because you're not greedy. Because the million I'd pay you wouldn't come with any bad feelings along with it, no hurt, nothing like that. Because you don't need the money. You got a rich wife, who, by the way, you should worry about when she goes out shopping and places. Even in the daytime, on any street, you should worry about the wrong people fucking with her."

Riccio's brain was rotten, Mitch thought. There were calluses on his eyes. He was eaten with pathology, putrefied by habit, perhaps by birth. The air that had the misfortune of being sucked into him came out contaminated. He had a wife and children he kissed, a priest he confessed to, holy water went to his head, the chamber of his rottenness, each week.

"How about it?" Riccio pressed.

"No deal," Mitch replied unequivocally. He was surprised how much pleasure he got out of telling Riccio that, how angry and yet calm he was. "And, as for my wife," he said, "I'll look out for her. Anyway, no need for me to worry about her for a while." He paused and did a smug punishing smile, "She's leaving tonight to spend some time in France . . . with her mother."

Chapter 27

Shortly before nine that night she came out of the Sherry. Her luggage had preceded her and Billy and the doorman had loaded it into the trunk of the Lexus.

She was wearing an outfit suitable for traveling: slacks and a pullover and an amply cut, lightweight, long coat. Her hair was contained in a latter-day cloche.

When she reached the curb she hesitated in order to adjust her dark glasses. The open, rear door of the Lexus awaited her. Her right hand searched and found the upper part of the car's frame along the roofline before she ducked down and got in.

Caselli and Fratino, Riccio's two have-arounds, were parked across the avenue. When the Lexus pulled out they followed along behind. Crosstown to the FDR Drive and up to and over the Triborough and all the way to Kennedy to the TWA terminal.

"Maybe she really ain't going," Fratino said.

Caselli agreed.

They watched Billy help get her luggage checked at the curb. A TWA courtesy attendant showed up with a wheelchair. She refused it. The attendant guided her. Through the automatic doors and on into the terminal.

Caselli stayed with the car.

Fratino got out and followed her. That she had checked some luggage didn't prove anything. The luggage could make the trip without her.

Fratino followed her to the security pass-through and on to the gate. The attendant remained with her. She was traveling first-class, could board then or later. She waited to be last, then she and the attendant entered the boarding ramp and were out of sight.

Within a short while the attendant emerged and the doors to the boarding ramp were closed.

Fratino was beginning to believe. He watched from a window as the 747 disconnected and pulled away. As it taxied out to the runway he thought he caught a glimpse of her in a window seat of the first-class section.

Still, he waited, allowed more than enough time for a takeoff before going to the nearby bank of telephones to call Riccio.

"The cunt's gone," he said.

"What did you do to her?"

"I didn't do nothing to her. I'm at Kennedy. She got on a plane and it took off."

"You sure?"

"Positive."

Chapter 28

At that moment Mitch and Maddie were going seventy-five through the heavy night air, northbound on the Taconic State Parkway. The unrelenting growl of the Harley beneath them seemed strong and reassuring, as though declaring *make way, I'm carrying my owners to safety*.

They arrived at Kinderhook and Uncle Straw's house at half past eleven. The house was summer stuffy from having been shut up for several days, so, first thing, they went about opening windows to allow the slight breezes from the west across the Hudson to flow through.

Maddie turned down the bedcovers in their usual room, second floor rear. Mitch, meanwhile, made some toasted cheese sandwiches and brought them up on a tray. Oven-warmed potato chips, two sweating bottles of St. Pauli Girl.

"Want some music?" he asked.

"Got some," she replied, meaning the chorus of the pastoral night being performed by the tiny creatures moving about enormously brave deep among the grasses and perched higher upon the platforms of leaves.

Mitch placed the tray upon the table by the window. He lighted an old glass oil lamp and switched off the electric ones, thinking it would lend to the mood. He was immediately reminded that lighting did not matter to Maddie. It had been a while since he'd made such an oversight.

"I smell an oil lamp," she said.

"Yeah."

"That's one of the countless things I love about you," she smiled, "you have a sense for the appropriate."

Somehow she knows when I need to be saved, Mitch thought. The oil lamp was smoking, blackening its glass chimney. He reduced the wick.

They ate in silence. Mitch observed her. Actually, it was more an examination the way he employed his sighted advantage, took lengthy notices of her various features, appreciating them so much and focusing so intensely upon them that at times they seemed magnified. The left corner of her mouth, the perfect crease of it that made a faultless transition to her cheek. It alone momentarily occupied his entire visual field. As did the textures of her various parts. The space between her eyelid and brow. Her instrumental hands.

He rode her finger up to her teeth. Caught a glimpse of the slick pink pillow of her tongue. His thought came with an ache. I won't let anyone harm her, he vowed. They'll have to go through me, over me.

He loathed being reminded by his practical side they would probably do just that.

He left the oil lamp burning when they went to bed. Its captive flame projected a shadowy ring upon the ceiling. Maddie snuggled into the cave of his arm and fell asleep quickly. He was left awake with his worry. Shirley was thirty-five thousand feet over the Atlantic. Riccio's have-arounds had bought the impersonation. They wouldn't be coming this night. This night was a stay; he could rest easy.

Still, when he finally gave in to sleep he remained in the shallows.

The birds woke him at dawn with their chirping. He got up, dressed quietly and went down to grind some coffee and set it to brewing. He stood there at the kitchen counter as though caught in a spell by the explosive hisses and drips of the automatic coffee maker. His mind felt dull and vulnerable, a heavy head. The glass pot seemed to be purposely slow to fill. He couldn't wait for it, went out onto the covered rear porch, intending to go back inside shortly and pour himself a cup.

His legs, however, as though they were independent and, at that moment, in charge, took him down the porch steps and across the wide rear lawn to a gated opening in the neatly masoned brick wall on the south. That gave to a buffer of mowed meadow and a piled rock wall beyond which lay the expansive area where the neighbor's cows were permitted to pasture.

The cows.

The sight of them caused both his mind and body to brighten and snap into alignment for this day. They were mere black and whites in the distance, being let out; however there was no mistaking they might be other than cows.

He had patience for them, could have stood and waited for all the time it would take for them to make their slow amble to him. A large herd. How many? Fifty at least, more.

He strode right at them and soon was among them. They with only slight or no acknowledgment of him, the most meager curiosity. Their huge dark eyes. Their barreled girths and bony rumps. Tails switching out of habit.

Mitch was lost in them, their simple worthiness. They were so removed from diamonds, emeralds and such, and above all, threatless.

He circled back to the piled rock wall and walked along beside it for quite a ways. He climbed up onto it and sighted across the West Meadow, that large gently undulating open area of crotch-high grass that he'd waded the weekend before last. No trace of his trek through it now. The grasses and the Queen Anne's lace that his weight and motion had injured had fully recovered.

He traversed the meadow by the old equipment barn where he'd taught Maddie to shoot, and entered the woods. The sun was not yet high enough to cause dapple. Patches where the branches did not umbrella still had some night wet on them. Offsprings of maples and oaks were submissive whips. The chatter of a squirrel. The metallic cry of a jay. The leaves of last year, superficially dry, damp a layer down, especially slippery on the inclines. And, underneath, the accumulated drop and rich decay of countless autumns, spongy.

About a quarter of a mile in ledges broke the regularity of the woods. Blocks of nearly black granite, more massive than high. A modular series of those individualized by their varying heights and defining faults. Water, from what seemed their secret source, seeped from them, ran down their faces, preferred the grooves of their fractures. Mitch's mouth was dry. He stood at the base of a ledge, leaned to it for his tongue to catch some of the trickle. He pressed his forehead against the rough wet. Closed his eyes and imagined his brain being bathed.

With his face dripping and shirt-front soaked, he followed one of the runoff gullies down to the lower land. The marsh there was at its summer low, having receded and left all the clumps of skunk cabbage standing on their roots like columns. The water of the marsh was no more than a foot or two deep out in its middle. It appeared blacker because of that, its surface closer to the black silt of the bottom.

Mitch found a fallen branch and used it to poke at the bottom. The branch went down into the silt easily, penetrated nearly a foot before it met resistance, and that was just there at the edge.

The bass croaks of frogs. Their frantic leaps for underwater. Mitch knew, of course, that he was not out on some empty-stomach, early morning hike. It was reconnaissance, looking at the lay of the land in a way that he had never perceived it. A battleground. If Riccio's have-arounds came, and chances were they eventually would, they'd outnumber him. He was desperately in need of allies. Possibly, he was finding some.

He crossed several clearings. One was particularly wide, had blackberries growing in a thorny patch. He picked as many as his hand could contain and ate them on the way out to the bluff overlooking the Hudson. The wide river, two hundred feet below, was silvery green. It seemed to be at a standstill. The deceptive river, hiding its currents. It was too formidable to be friendly, Mitch thought. He climbed down the bluff by way of the unapparent, back-and-forth trail that he was certain had once been used by the Mohicans. There was a more accessible, roundabout way down to the Strawbridge boathouse but Mitch had seldom used it.

The boathouse was a well-preserved wooden structure situated on a float that allowed it to adjust to the rise or fall of the river. It consisted of three slips below a room used for storing boating equipment, life jackets, oars, seat cushions, pennants and the like. Its interior smelled of oil and gasoline and baked wood. There were three boats:

Two were Chris-Craft speedboats: a relatively new one and a sixty-year-old classic. The other boat was far more ordinary: an outboard with a fiberglass hull. Mitch had been out in the Chris-Craft several times with Uncle Straw, but the outboard was the one they used to go upstream to fish the mouths of the tributaries for trout.

Mitch took a comprehensive look around the boathouse. Then climbed the bluff and went straight home. Maddie was in the kitchen, barefoot and half dressed. Her hair was spiking every which way. She was about to scramble a half dozen eggs. The butter in the pan was scorched. She poured the bowl of disturbed eggs into the pan and overdosed them with Worcestershire.

"Great coffee!" she said, raising her mug to the level of her smile.

Mitch poured some. It was a little too strong, on the bitter side. He was hungry, tempted to settle for a bowl of cereal and raisins; however he waited for her eggs, endured them with large bites and quick swallows. "Good eggs," he fibbed.

She knew better. "You're nice," she told him.

"What would you like to do today?" he asked.

"You," she replied wickedly, "but later."

There were three phone calls that morning. The first was from Shirley to say she was staying at a charming hotel off Boulevard St. Germain and that if she wasn't so worried about them she'd be having a marvelous time. When would this crisis be over? She'd met an extremely attractive businessman on the plane. Please let her know as soon as all was well so she could breathe easy and take full advantage of him.

The second call, not a half hour later, was from Uncle Straw and Wally, both on the line at the same time, so it was a four-way conversation. They'd done well at the casino in London, although actually, they hadn't spent all that much time at the tables. Now they were in Monaco, staying at the Hôtel de Paris, had been there two days and hardly been out of the suite. They had some surprising news, Straw said, and Maddie tried to drag it out of him, but he remained cryptic, would only say it was happy news, which caused Wally to confirm that it couldn't be happier. Maddie had all she could do to keep from guessing aloud that they were either married or had agreed to be. She was sure that was it, that Straw wanted to wait until he got home to more intimately share it. When were they coming home? They weren't sure, thought they might go on to Baden-Baden or somewhere or anywhere. They sounded so up. *Pick the tomatoes* were Straw's words before disconnecting.

The third call came an hour later. Mitch picked it up. His several hellos got no response. He heard background sounds and what he took to be breathing and then only dial tone.

"Who was that?" Maddie asked.

"A wrong number," he told her.

While Maddie went out to the garden to pick some tomatoes, Mitch went into Straw's study. A cabinet there was where Straw kept his guns. Three shotguns, a rifle and four pistols. Mitch settled on a shotgun. The one he liked the weight and feel of was a Mossberg 500 pump-action 12-gauge with a short eighteen-and-a-half-inch barrel. It wasn't loaded and there didn't seem to be any ammunition in the drawers of the cabinet.

He took the shotgun up to his bedroom and placed it on the bed. Also his own two weapons, the Beretta and the Glock. He examined each in turn, saw that they were clean and in surely reliable working order. He cocked and dry-fired the automatics, released and inserted clips.

Then the shotgun. He'd never fired a pump-action, never even

GERALD A. BROWNE

had one in his hands, but how complicated could it be? The forward hand operated the action by pulling back to eject the fired shell and pushing forward to position the next round into the firing chamber. He snugged the butt of the gun to his shoulder, pumped and dry-fired it until he was comfortable with the required rhythm. Did the same from the hip, got really good at it from the hip.

Maddie walked in on him. "What on earth are you doing?" she asked.

"Nothing," he told her, "just . . . just trying to get this door latch to work properly. It seems to be sticking."

"Sounded to me like you were pumping a shotgun," she said wryly.

"Any tomatoes?" he veered.

"Plenty."

He wondered how she could tell the ripe ones, asked her.

"Squeeze," she told him. He held back telling her that two of those she'd picked were green.

"I have to do some errands, get a few things. Want to stay here?"

"No, I'm with you." Exactly what she'd said yesterday, when he'd tried to get her to fly to Paris to stay with friends, out of harm's way until this Riccio thing simmered down. No words, not even his adamant, angry ones, could sway her. "I'm with you," was how she wanted it no matter what.

They were in Straw's blue Chevy pickup. Into town and then north on Route 9, the highway to Albany. First stop was at a building supply place for the planking. Mitch found that the widest they had in ready stock was fourteen inches. If he wanted wider it would be a special order. They'd have to mill it. That would take two days, maybe three. Mitch couldn't count on having two days, maybe three. So, in place of planking he got four sheets of four-by-eight half-inch plywood and had the mill hand-rip them lengthwise down the middle to make eight pieces two feet wide, eight feet long.

In the hardware and paint section Mitch bought a battery-charged professional stapler and a supply of one-inch staples, three gallons of latex enamel, two black and a green and a couple of rollers and roller pans.

A mile or so further up Route 9 was a strip mall dominated by a nervous red neon that declared RICK'S GUNS AND AMMO. While Mitch went in Maddie waited in the pickup, scrunched down with her bare feet up on the dash and a Clint Black playing.

Rick's offered just about everything imaginable for ordinary and fancy killing. Assault rifles on the left, power bows on the right. Ostensibly for animal hunting and benign target competitions. Rick was the man behind a locked glass counter crowded with handguns. He had a shaved head five days in need of a shave.

Mitch ordered up two cartons of double-ought buckshot shells and a carton of 12-gauge slugs. A couple of cartons of 9mm 115-grain Starfire balloon points and an equal number of 180-grain .40 calibers. "Want those forties in hollow point too?" Rick asked.

"Yeah."

"A lot of shooting," Rick commented passively while figuring the tab.

"Just stocking up."

"Smart. Season will be here before we know it."

Was there ever not a season for the Riccios? Mitch thought.

"Got a special on throwing knives in case you're interested," Rick said. "Ever throw a knife?"

"No." But Hofritz steak knives taken from a dining room drawer to the backyard and, inspired by James Coburn in *The Magnificent Seven*, thrown from ten feet end over end at the tough trunk of an oak. Set of eight knives in a fitted case. Four for himself, four for Andy for alternate tries. Not enough force to make them stick. Only one out of every twenty or more throws hitting point first. Kenneth rightfully giving them hell for having broken the tips off two.

"Not as hard to do as you think, throwing a knife," Rick said. "Guy used to part-time here got about as good as anybody could at it. Word got around and nobody would mess with him."

Mitch realized Rick wasn't selling as much as he was merely telling.

"Another advantage with having a throwing knife for a weapon is you're not required to be licensed to carry it," Rick said.

Mitch had noticed camouflaged combat fatigues stacked on a table in the rear. He went to them and held up a pair. They were the leaf-mottled type with a great many different pockets. Evidently they weren't marked for size. He grabbed up any two pair and a couple of matching beaked caps.

On Mitch's mental shopping list next was an audio cassette player-recorder. A store on Elm Street in Kinderhook had one that would do. It was about the size of an average hardcover book, could be battery-powered and had outlets to accommodate two auxiliary speakers. Not that Mitch would need two. The speakers he bought were the miniature, cube-shaped sort about four by four by four. He also bought a fifty-foot length of speaker wire that had the appropriate male adapters on each end, a half dozen size C Duracell batteries and a Maxell XLII ninety-minute high-resonance audiotape cassette.

He had thought he was leaving the most surely available thing until last. Red poster paint. The stationery and art supply store there in Kinderhook had poster paint in quite a few colors but was all out of bright red. Mitch had to drive the ten miles to Chatham to get it. It came in four- and six-ounce jars. He bought three of the sixes.

They arrived home mid-afternoon. Mitch went right to work, carried the plywood sections and the latex enamel to the large shed situated on the back side of the four-car garage. He transferred the enamel into a five-gallon plastic pail. One part green stirred into two parts black created what Mitch believed was a close enough murky shade. He leaned the eight plywood sections separately against the side of the shed and was about to start on them when Maddie came humming and *da-da-tee-da-ing* off key, bringing tomatoes in a basket and a shaker of imported LaBaleine sea salt. She made him stop and sit with her. The basket in her lap. The base of their backs against the shed's warm boards.

She handed him one of the tomatoes and took one for herself. He hesitated. He watched. He suspected she knew he was watching, as she, not altogether subtly, ritualized, commencing with the twist and painful-looking plucking out of the star-like stem, followed by a long efficient lick up one area of the red skin to leave it wet. So the sprinkle of salt would adhere.

Mitch's vision again seemed capable of magnification.

The intricacies of each motion he observed seemed slowed.

Her mouth opened, exposing her teeth, perfect and sharp, white unrelenting blades. The taut red skin no match for their incredible erotic precision. Juice tried to escape, was captured. The red pulp and seeds were at her mercy, chewed and sucked out.

Mitch forced himself to look away. How much he loved her, he thought against the blank sky. So much that everything about her had become extraordinary. Madly in love. That seemed to fit. Did all extreme lovers experience such close encounters with this special, pleasureful insanity or was he an anomaly, cursed and blessed? No doubt, he decided the imminence of danger, the possibility of losing all, was having its effect.

Two tomatoes eaten, Maddie dabbed at the corners of her mouth with the sleeve of her T-shirt.

"I'm ready to paint," she said.

He'd promised she could help. He poured some of the enamel into one of the roller pans while she located the plywood sections and determined how he'd leaned them in a predictable row. She was anxious to begin, went at it enthusiastically.

"No need to do both sides, right?" she said.

"No."

"But we have to do the edges, don't we?"

"And the ends."

"We mustn't overlook the ends. Am I putting it on too thick?"

"No, you're doing fine."

"Why don't you do something else? I can handle this."

He went into the shed. It was where Straw kept his tools, gardening implements and other odds and ends. It wasn't very orderly. Each spring Straw put it neat and from then on allowed it to become cluttered. For the past several years Mitch had helped with the annual straightening, so the place wasn't unfamiliar to him.

He immediately spotted the lopping shears and the gasoline-powered hedge trimmers. He'd need those.

He might also put to use one of those sash window weights that Straw kept for old time's sake. Shaped like a summer sausage with an eye on one end where a line could be tied. Mitch had to climb up onto the work bench to get one down and it was while he was up there that he noticed the trap. Heavily rusted old thing hanging on a nail by its anchor chain. He took it down and saw it was a leg trap, the common sort, that would, when sprung, clamp together two sets of steel teeth. At one time it must have had six, perhaps ten feet of anchor chain which would be secured around a tree or whatever to keep the caught varmint from making off with the trap. Now, for some reason there was only about four feet of chain. Along the base, barely readable because of the layers of rust, was ARMSTEAD WOLF TRAP and a patent number.

Mitch tried to work the trap. Its parts were frozen in place. He searched around and finally found an aerosol can of a substance that was especially meant to penetrate and dissolve rust. He sprayed the trap thoroughly with it and waited a couple of minutes. The trap's parts still wouldn't give. No matter, he thought, it wasn't, after all, something he'd counted on but rather an added innovation. He gave the trap another spraying and left it for now.

Maddie was finishing up on the last section of plywood. She gave it a couple of final rolls. "How did I do?" she asked. "Did I miss a lot of places?"

"No," Mitch fibbed. Later, when he had the chance, he'd touch up the areas where raw board was visible. Actually, considering, Maddie had done well.

She put down the roller and roller pan. Her white sneakers were splattered, her hand coated to the wrist. "What's next?" she asked, ready for anything.

They went into the house. After washing up in the kitchen sink they sat at the table there and saw to the guns. Mitch was undecided about which shells he should load into the pump shotgun, the buckshot or the slugs. Both had advantages, depending on circumstances. The slugs had more range and penetration, made one big hole. On the other hand, closer in with the buckshot it was almost impossible to miss. The shotgun could hold eight rounds. Mitch loaded in some of each in no particular order.

Meanwhile, Maddie was loading the clips for the pistols. Four for the Glock and the same number for the Beretta. She inserted a full clip into the butt of each pistol and rammed them home.

"We'll each have three extra clips," she said. "Think that'll be enough?"

Mitch didn't reply.

Maddie knew why. "The Glock is yours but the Beretta is mine," she said.

That wasn't how Mitch intended it. She wouldn't be doing any shooting and no one would be shooting at her.

"The Beretta is mine," she repeated, unequivocally.

"Yeah," Mitch said as though that had been his understanding all along. There'd be clashes enough he figured.

The day was making its slow exit.

They went out and sat on the front steps. There were deer down in the apple orchard. Mitch counted eight. Two with antlers, four does and a pair of fawns. Foraging for windfalls, intent on that, but yet, alert, untrusting, bringing their heads up high, sniffing, glancing around frequently.

Mitch described the deer to Maddie. He couldn't make out their eyes at that distance, and no doubt she realized that; however she allowed him to make much of their huge black pupils, dilated by possible danger, the way they didn't dare blink.

"I could live on your descriptions," she said gratefully.

What he didn't describe to her was what he was foreseeing as he gazed down at the winding gravel drive. That was how they would come. They wouldn't be stealthy, wouldn't come sneaking from various directions. Their arrogance wouldn't allow that. They would drive in and park just about there, he thought, settling on a spot about a hundred yards away. They would be so sure of themselves, the killings they'd been sent to do. They would get out of the car, nonchalantly re-tuck their shirts and straighten their suit jackets, and probably talk about something extraneous, perhaps about a meal they'd eaten or planned to eat, as they proceeded up the rest of the drive to the house. Mitch despised how sure of themselves they would be. Sure of his death, of Maddie's.

The emeralds were no longer Riccio's first issue, Mitch believed. The emeralds had been superseded by the call for old-mob satisfaction. That Mitch had had no choice but to refuse Riccio didn't matter. Riccio hadn't believed it and turning Riccio down was like wounding him, like throwing pepper in his eyes. It prevented him from seeing reasonableness. To put up with it, to just let it pass, would, according to Riccio's code, shrink him. He'd be smaller inside himself for it. If he allowed it once he might allow it again and he'd become small enough inside himself to be stepped over, if not on.

The emeralds? If they came with the thing all the better. Twenty-five extra large was twenty-five extra large. However, in Riccio's world the void left by lost money had a way of being surely and swiftly filled by other money. Riccio would consider himself ahead when his have-arounds returned and told him the thing had been done.

"That twenty-five million . . . " Maddie said.

"Which twenty-five million?" Mitch quipped.

"If you'd had those emeralds and if the Iranian had come across with the twenty-five for them as he said he would, what difference would it have made?"

"Who knows?"

"For you, I mean."

"No use speculating."

"Oh? I say speculation is next best to a sure thing."

"I've never heard you say that."

"You probably weren't listening. Quite often speculations *are* sure things; they're just not apparent."

Mitch was amused. He kissed her a short, adoring one high on her cheek.

"With that twenty-five you'd no longer have to endure West 47th."

"I don't endure it," he contended and immediately realized that was only partially true. "Not all the time," he added.

"Naturally, you'd miss it for a while."

"I'd miss it," he admitted.

"But only for a while, and it would go on and on missing you." He scoffed.

"We'd be miles away, wouldn't we?"

"Like where?"

She didn't have to give it even a moment's thought. "You'd be picking up big tabs at lots of extravagant places. Maybe we'd have a sort of permanent place on the lake to convenience your going to the Geneva auctions. You'd have clients in Milan and Paris. Maybe a small, flawless office in Zurich with a secretary who'd know the perfect way to say you weren't in, in ten languages. You'd only dabble in fine jewelry. You'd temperamentally dole out your expertise to the huge spenders. We'd motor the Loire and you'd describe. You'd keep me from dancing off edges into canals in Venice and St. Petersburg. You'd walk me into the rose fields of Grasse." She paused a digestive beat. "What do you think?"

"Sounds good," Mitch replied as brightly as he could manage, and, rather than allow futility to further blunt his edge, he asked, "How would you like me to read to you tonight? Some Carlos Fuentes perhaps."

"Uh uh," she said emphatically, "this morning I told you what I wanted to do but later, and later is now."

Chapter 29

The summer night embraced the house, pressed it with fragrances and every so often sent a scuff of wind to the open bedroom windows to play spectrally with the sheer curtains. All was dark. The nearest prevailing light was a moon distant, and that but only the merest silver, unproviding.

Thus, even when Mitch was open-eyed he was equally blind.

Her hands were vessels, nearly weightless. They skimmed along him, his sea of flesh. She knew his courses and currents, where she was most likely to encounter maelstroms. Her hands drifted, here and there and here, persistently under way but avoiding destination, just barely, tacking at the last moment.

He lay still, as he knew she wanted. Already his cock did not seem to have enough skin to contain itself. It would burst from sensation when her mouth enclosed it, when her tongue lashed and her teeth made brief, inflicting visits.

She was such a greedy lover, greedy taker and greedy giver. Or, wasn't it generous giver and generous taker?

Frequently she removed her mouth, all at once, and breathed upon the warmth and wet she'd caused. Cooled his cock before resuming. Her hands never stopped. Burrowing, gliding, fingernails threatening.

Having her way with him.

She was sopping, puffed apart by the time she legged over and found herself with him. She did not ride him. She did not move at all immediately. The slick, tight channel of her held him sur-rounded. Oppositely, she had impaled herself all the way to her belly. The sop ran from her.

She did not ride him. Did not need to. She leaned forward up over him, just so, to become more parted below, just so, and helped herself to as much sensitivity as she wanted.

Her want. She took it in portions, marveled at his restraint, shared the sixth time she came.

With him.

Chapter 30

Nudged by all he had to do, Mitch came awake at first light. He got up immediately, dressed and went downstairs and out to the shed. Temporary diamonds on the grass. Much of the sky a funereal mauve. Sparrows frightened to fly from under the eaves.

He applied paint to the places on the plywood sections that Maddie had missed, and then went into the shed to check on the wolf trap. The trap appeared unchanged but, when he picked it up, flakes and clumps of rust fell from it. The solvent had lived up to its claims. The parts that made the trap a trap, its hinges, spring and release, now worked freely, easily. Mitch set the trap and sprung it with an old hardwood broom handle. He sharpened the trap's double set of triangular teeth. First with a metal file and then more with a whetstone. He set the trap again, sprung it again. The razor-sharp teeth crunched clear through the broom handle.

The plywood sections weren't yet thoroughly dry but he didn't want to wait. They were heavy and unwieldy. Once he got squatted beneath them and got them balanced he could manage three at a time layered on the bend of his back.

He had to pass through the woods to get them to the marsh, through the underbrush, the crazy vines and young trees. The young trees seemed capricious the way they hung on to his legs and the edges and corners of the plywood. He felt like telling them this wasn't a game.

Three round-trips with plywood sections. He placed them down at the edge of the marsh. He'd get back to them when he was done with the blackberry brambles.

The width of the bramble patch varied from twenty to fifty feet. It was wider across and thicker as well where the growth was new. Those greener, more vigorous canes were five to six feet high, thousands in the collective competing for the sun with familial strangle. Thorns on them like the spurs of a fighting cock.

Mitch put on the tough, leather gloves and began with the hedge trimmers. Before long he had cut a short ways into the patch, creating what appeared to be a shallow lair. It wasn't easy going. He was on his knees, having to crawl along hunched, being snagged and scratched at every turn. The canes seemed to resent his intrusion. Even the thorns dropped by those long dead stabbed through the fabric of his jeans.

What had appeared to be a lair became the tunnel that Mitch intended. He shaped it with the loppers, leaving the overhead canes as they were, intricately meshed.

Forty feet of bramble tunnel. He would add the final elements to it later.

He returned to the marsh, to the plywood sections. He sighted across and estimated that from where he stood the distance to the opposite bank was too great for his purpose. He moved along the edge where the summer had receded the water, leaving the silt dry and black like gunpowder. The huge green leaves of the skunk cabbage and the tufts of swamp grass were chest high. After a short ways he came upon a place where the temporary shore was somewhat elevated and jutted out. He went back for the plywood sections and got busy on them.

He laid two of the sections end to end, painted sides up and overlapped about six inches. He joined the two sections by driving two rows of one-inch staples into the overlap. He stapled the coiled length of quarter-inch nylon line to the first section and tied the free end of the line to the six-pound window sash weight. He twirled the weighted line until it was singing with momentum. Let it go. The weight, with the nylon line trailing after it, sailed high over the marsh and landed on the opposite shore some fifty feet away.

He went around the far end of the marsh to that spot, took up the line and gathered in its slack. He pulled the first plywood section into the water and most of the second. He went back around and stapled together the ends of two more sections and added those to the length of the first two. On the opposite shore again, he tugged all but the very end of those into the water.

It took all eight sections of plywood to complete the span, and even then it didn't quite reach, was a couple of feet short. He had to use rocks, some seventy-pounders, to weigh down each end and keep the span in place, and that, as it turned out, was for the better, because it concealed the ends nicely, caused them to be buried in the silt at the shoreline.

Now the span of plywood sections was below the water line, but barely, an inch or so at most. Just enough to not cause a break on the surface. The ugly green-black that the sections were painted was a good, close match to the murky color of the water.

Mitch, aware that the span was there, could make it out; however it wasn't obvious, would take some study for anyone to detect it.

He tested the span. Walked out a short ways onto its two-foot width. His weight caused it to go under another couple of inches. As he went on he found the coating of vinyl enamel was slippery when wet. He sloshed across to the other side, unsure of his footing. After a few back-and-forth crossings he got used to the feel of it and was able to hurry across. He ended up taking several round-trips running.

He was on his way to the pasture when he heard the first shot coming from the direction of the house. When he heard the next three he was already sprinting full out. The have-arounds had come, he thought. He'd underestimated Riccio.

Several more shots.

The sadistic bastards were peppering Maddie. He pictured her all shot up, bleeding, already dead, and, for their amusement, being disfigured by their bullets.

She wasn't.

When she came into sight he slowed to a walk, a casual walk the rest of the way, allowing him to catch his breath. He wouldn't tell her what he'd feared, how grisly and graphic it had been.

She was in the high grass off to one side of the old equipment barn. At that moment jamming another full clip into the Beretta. For a target she had nailed one of his best shirts to the side of the barn and was positioned about twenty paces from it.

Mitch paused, he noticed how indecisive her aim was before she fired a few rounds. He let her know he was there in case she completely lost her sense of direction.

"Getting in a little practice," she said.

"Who is it you're shooting at?"

"Them," she said toughly. "Be a love and go see how many I hit."

He went to the shirt. The only holes in it were its button holes. He examined the barn siding around it and didn't find where any bullets had struck.

"Four hits," he reported.

"Really?"

"Four right where the heart would be and a couple of just misses."

Maddie didn't react as Mitch expected. No self-delight, no smartass grin. "You're fibbing me," she said calmly. "I know you are, so don't bother to deny it."

Best not to say anything, Mitch thought.

"I'm not blaming you. It's me," she said. "I'm just so damn easy to fib to, aren't I? I'm always letting you get away with it because you have sweet intentions and it helps avoid a lot of the silly little bumps and potholes that would otherwise be in our way . . . "

"Maddie . . . "

" . . . but this time there's too much at stake." She scoffed, a self-berating scoff. "Christ, I'm such a mess."

"What happened?"

"I got the shirt nailed up without any trouble and was walking off ten paces when, on about the fifth pace, I stubbed my toe on something, a tuft of grass or an uneven spot or whatever, and I got all turned around. For some reason I just couldn't get my bearings." She disliked admitting that. "I tried to sense where the barn and the shirt were but each time I thought I had doubt got to me and made me less and less certain and I didn't want to shoot in any old direction. Who knows what or who I might have hit."

Mitch discerned the increasing change in her voice, a tightening. She was coming closer to crying with every syllable. As a rule she wasn't a crier. Anyway, not the usual sort. Plights and misfortunes, the hardest-luck and unfairest-unfair stories seldom brought forth a tear. Little patience for those. However, she was very susceptible to all forms of happiness. Merely hearing about happiness happening and various beautiful accomplishments coming about could cause her throat to lump up.

"I'm not going to be any help at all," she said. "Without you, without your helping me to get aimed in the right direction I can't hit the broad side of a fucking barn."

Mitch took her into his arms, held her. He felt her sag and let go. Her tears on his neck. The butt of the Beretta pressing his shoulder blade. "It'll be all right," he told her.

"No fibbing?"

"We'll come out the other side of this and look back on it for shivers and laughs," he said. His actual thought was she should have flown away. He should have insisted on it. There was still time. He could phone Billy and have him come get her, take her to Kennedy and the Concorde to Paris.

He suggested it.

She let it go right around her.

"Is my nose running?" she asked.

"No."

"Feels like it is. What about my eyes?"

"A little red around the edges."

"I'm famished."

"Just do what I tell you and everything will be all right," he reassured.

"How about some pancakes? I'll let you make them."

After pancakes, Maddie sat on the rear porch steps and cleaned her Beretta while listening to an Elmore Leonard. Mitch drove into town with a grocery shopping list.

He was at the supermarket, had nearly everything in his cart and was waiting to be waited on at the deli counter when he spotted the have-around. The fat guy who was usually stationed on the landing halfway up to Riccio's offices; the one Mitch had twice pushed down the stairs. Their eyes caught upon one another simultaneously, caught and held. The have-around had a paper bag in one hand and a glazed donut, like a helpless victim, in the other. Mitch did a contemptible up and down and decided he might as well go over to him.

"What's your name?" he asked aggressively.

"Angelo," the have-around replied.

"What do they call you around?"

"Fat Angelo."

"I never would have guessed."

"My real name is Anthony."

"Fat Tony was taken."

"Yeah."

"A hundred times."

"This is Little Mike. You know Little Mike?"

Little Mike stepped out from behind Fat Angelo. He was appropriately named. About five feet tall at most, a muscle-layered chunk with a bilious complexion. He looked like he'd have no trouble getting in under the axle of a car and holding it up while someone changed a tire. "I seen you around," he said to Mitch. "On the street."

"What are you doing up here?" Mitch asked Fat Angelo.

"Nothing. Just looking around."

"Sightseeing," Mitch said.

"Yeah, that's it. We already saw the sights, didn't we?"

"Enough," Little Mike replied.

"So now you're headed back to the city," Mitch said.

"They got good donuts here but the coffee tastes like shit," Fat Angelo said.

"You should know," Mitch said but Fat Angelo wasn't fazed, maybe didn't get it.

Little Mike was eating potato salad out of a half-pound plastic container. He appeared as conspicuously out of place as Fat Angelo. A pair of midtown lowlifes in white short-sleeve polo shirts that displayed their respective fat and muscles. Unbuttoned to exhibit swag gold chains and crosses that were nearly lost among their chest hairs.

"How about me and you having a private word?" Fat Angelo said.

Mitch moved with him beyond the hearing range of Little Mike, who understood and paid more attention to the potato salad.

"We can do a little business," Fat Angelo said confidentially. "You interested?"

"Maybe."

"You got those two emeralds?"

"Another maybe."

"What we do is you give them to me and I go back to Riccio and tell him you weren't up here like he figured."

"You'd do that?"

"Sure, what the fuck."

Mitch did a considering expression, some blinks. "What if I was to let Riccio know you tried to get between on him?"

"No problem. I just tell him I saw you but nothing else, just saw. Who's he going to believe, me or some guy he wants taken out?"

Mitch turned and pushed his cart towards the checkout.

Fat Angelo flung six Sicilian obscenities at his back.

That he had run into two of Riccio's have-arounds at the supermarket was yet another thing Mitch decided was best left unmentioned to Maddie. No use making her edgier. He imagined how unstrung he would be if he was in the black, dependent upon someone else's eyes under such threatening circumstances.

All along he had believed Riccio would catch on and show up.

Now that was not only imminent but soon. Perhaps tomorrow, possibly before, Mitch thought. He couldn't put anything off.

On the way home there was a short section of road where construction was under way. Marked off by striped orange and white barriers, battery-powered blinking amber lights on them. Mitch didn't care who saw him stop and toss a couple of the barriers into the back of the pickup.

It was early dusk when he went to the bramble patch. After completing things there he went all the way out to the bluff. The river motionless as a deserted road. The hills to the west black and humped like resting beasts. The going sun skulking behind them.

Chapter 31

W_{ait}.

Never had Mitch disliked it more, having to sit there in the recess of a dormer, watching for them. Too much time to think, to not be able to put out of mind that everything had come down to this, all he'd ever done or been, hoped to do or be, compacted to grim wait in this niche above the roof line of Straw's three-story house.

A few hours ago, when there'd still been daylight, this high vantage had provided Mitch with a fairly clear view far down the gravel drive, beyond its twists, nearly to the point where the orchard began. What he'd kept watch for then was any interruption their car would cause on the pale, motionless drive. However, now that night had taken over, the first sign of their arrival would be headlights.

Might they park outside the grounds and approach unseen and quietly? No, that wasn't them. Probably it wouldn't even be suggested. Why should they be unnecessarily inconvenienced? They'd drive in like expected guests, turn off the loud car radio at the last moment, slam the car doors shut.

Maddie had tried to make the dormer niche comfortable. She'd layered it with two down comforters and piles of pillows. Plump European squares and tiny silk-covered rounds. She had also laundered the camouflaged combat fatigues Mitch had bought. To remove the scratchy stiffness from them. She'd washed hers separately in hottest water, given them a long hot cycle and double hot rinse, hoping to accomplish a three- or four-size shrink. But they hadn't shrunk an inch and she was having to make the best of what she thought of as their monstrous fighting man size. She turned the legs and sleeves up several folds.

"Does nothing for me," she complained.

"Put on something else, some jeans or something."

She pretended not to hear. She was wearing the Beretta in its shoulder rig. Extra clips in her most reachable upper pockets. Mitch had on the Glock. The shotgun was propped close at hand. Mitch had discovered a sling for it in the back of a drawer of Straw's gun cabinet.

So, there they sat. Low light coming from the third-floor hallway. The dormer window entirely open. Mitch close to the sill of it, Maddie across from him.

To vary and temper and help pass the wait, she played the guitar. Started out with some Wes Montgomery and without missing a pick or strum, went to the third movement, *Recitativo*, of Mompou's *Compostelana Suite*, and, from that, some vigorous Van Halen. Then on to Mitch's favorite favorite, *Spanish Romances*. She gave him a lengthy dose of the latter, repeated its melodic theme numerous times.

Normally the piece evoked within Mitch a sort of sensuous sway, but this time it hollowed his upper chest and lumped his throat and Maddie, with her finely honed sentience, stopped playing abruptly, laid the guitar aside and told him: "Look at it this way, precious, not everyone gets a chance to accumulate such exciting recollections for their recliner chair years."

She went down to the kitchen and returned with a silver tablespoon and a pint carton of ice cream. Ben and Jerry's Chunky Monkey. She resumed her place opposite Mitch on the comforter and dug into it. She extended the first generous spoonful. Mitch brought his mouth to it. The rich, frivolous treat hitched him up a couple of minor notches.

"Two for you, one for me," she said, as though it should apply to

all things, then thought to add: "Except, of course, when it comes
to comes." She held out another helping. Within ten minutes she
was noisily scraping the sides and bottom of the cardboard carton,
licking the spoon.

She saw to Mitch's pillows. Plumped and re-situated them behind
his back and shoulders. That done, she stretched out face up, per-
pendicular to him with her head resting on his thigh. The house a
silent container of possessions. Squirrel claws scuttling the rain gutter. The night laying siege beyond the sill.

"Tell me one," Maddie said.

"You've heard them all."

"Surely not all."

"I'd have to make one up."

"Have you ever?"

"No."

"Probably have, a fibber like you."

"I could rehash an old one, if you'd settle for that," he told her.
"A real old one that you may have forgotten by now."

"Save me."

"Okay then, you'll just have to accept that as of now I'm all out."

"Don't give me that, you with your extravagant repertoire. Are
you going to deprive me of your riches?"

My riches, Mitch thought. Well, yes, perhaps that was what they
were, all those mainly nefarious West 47 incidents and special little
melodramas accumulated firsthand over the years, along with the
headful of others of the same ilk he'd acquired second- or third-
hand or more. She was demanding a fresh one and he doubted he
could come up with it, his frame of mind being what it was. Her
motive was obviously well-intentioned. She was trying to normal-
ize things. He should cooperate. However, he felt in need of some
good quiet, to just be, be there with her, to observe her and, again,
as he had so often, marvel that she existed. And that she loved him.
And he loved her. And they were attached. Not attached in the ordinary sense, not merely together for convenience or distraction or
to bodyfill the chasm of human separateness, but somehow, miraculously, spiritually overlapped, Mitch felt.

The trouble was if he reflected upon such romantic assets they would soon remind him that they were what he stood to lose, and, as immediate as a shift of thought he would be overcome by gloomy prospect, his and Maddie's slim to no chance against the onslaught of Riccio's heartless have-arounds.

Maddie wasn't going to have any such negative wallowing if she could help it. She did a decisive little grunt. "If you put your mind to it you could," she said.

"Could what?"

"Find them. As resourceful as you are. It's one of the zillion things I adore about you, your resourcefulness. Granted it's not foremost. There are any number of more pleasurable aspects ahead of it, but it's right up there."

Mitch did some silence.

Maddie answered it. "Those emeralds."

"Which emeralds?" Mitch joked, going along with her but thinking *those fucking emeralds.* They were entirely to blame. Had it not been for those fucking emeralds he'd now have little more to cope with than his usual problems, like making ends meet and deciding each night how to get out of having dinner at home. As for recovering those emeralds and being the recipient of twenty-five extra large, forget it. Nothing mattered but survival.

"How much do you buy that story the Iranian what's-his-name Djam told us?" Maddie asked.

"What part?"

"The pious poet who gazed through the emeralds and got back his eyesight."

"Things like that are usually bullshit."

"Usually?"

"Maybe not always," Mitch conceded.

"Anyway, if you did recover those emeralds I probably wouldn't give them a try."

Which Mitch knowingly interpreted to mean she might. He imagined her bringing the emeralds up to her eyes. Holding them there. The verdancy of paradise. When she took them away, instantaneous vision! And he would be the very first thing she would see. That old notion.

"Of course," she went on, "I might if you insisted on it. Would you insist?"

Test question, Mitch thought. How not to fail it? It really asked had her handicap become a burden on him? Had he wearied of her dependence?

At times, not frequently, just every now and then, she had brought up the possibility of regaining her sight. What it would mean to them. It always started out as something she desired and ended up as something she'd just as soon would never happen. She was, she declared, quite comfortable with her condition, in fact, she probably preferred it. While it made her vulnerable it also provided protection of a sort, kept her from having to directly witness sleaze and suffering, the apathy and deliberate madnesses of these times.

Would he insist that, given the opportunity, she have a go with those wonder-working emeralds? He decided against a yes or no, told her: "I wouldn't push it."

She yawned genuinely. The yawn turned into an exaggerated grimace. She sat up and drooped her head. "I've a crook in my neck," she said with only slight complaint. She rotated her head twice counterclockwise and twice the other way and that seemed to do the trick. She raised her left shoulder and, as though she had perfect articulate vision, vamped at Mitch over it. "Jimmy Comforti," she said.

"What about him?"

"Tell me one of those."

"You're weird, know that?"

"Not any more so than you."

"You've got a crook in your head."

"Always," she admitted. "You don't I suppose. Come on precious, stop being stingy, give a girl a fix."

"What if I refuse?"

"You won't."

Mitch was hooked and being pulled up to her lighter level. He did a skeptical grunt.

"Refusal," she warned, "would call for retribution. I'd have to get back at you some suitable punitive way."

"Such as?"

She hardly gave it a thought. "Like never again giving you a massage and so forth while wearing a pair of my antelope skin gloves."

"I don't believe never."

"You'd go begging," she vowed, "believe me."

"You really are weird."

"Everything you say is true," she arched.

How fortunate he'd been, he thought. He had other riches. All the sensational, shame-free-loving times he'd shared with her. Maybe, in a way, it was beyond reasonableness to expect a whole, long life span of it. They'd already had far more than most.

Maddie lay back, returned her head to his thigh and waited while Mitch sorted through his mental Comforti file for one he possibly hadn't told her. From the numerous Comforti exploits both Mitch and Hurley had fed her over the years she more or less enjoyed the illusion that, though she'd never met Comforti, he was a personal acquaintance.

Actually, not even those few upscale West 47 dealers who were the favored buyers of Comforti's pricey swag knew the man well. He was seldom seen on the street, never walked it just to walk it, never socialized along it. When, for some unavoidable reason, he showed up on West 47 it was like the sighting of some colorful rare bird and like such a bird he was quickly gone. As a rule, to do business with him a dealer had to venture out of the district to wherever Comforti stipulated, which might be anywhere from the rear seat of a hired limo to a suite at the Ritz-Carlton.

A swift he was, however no one's swift but his own. Early on, some twenty years ago, he had belonged to a crew, but before he was nineteen he'd outclassed it and defected. He didn't need any such protection or direction. He didn't have anyone who'd need caring for while he did time. He also didn't get enough kick out of doing houses. They were too hit or miss. The city, on the other hand, was a surer thing, a veritable treasure trove. All one had to do was learn how to get to it.

Comforti hung around the entrances and lobbies of the better hotels. Watching the high-grade goods come and go on the necks, ears, wrists and fingers of the visiting well-offs. He took particular notice of how many failed to deposit their valuables into the hotel's vault when they came in late at night all high and happy or tired or anxious to get up to their rooms for some improved, away-from-home sex.

Hotels became Comforti's specialty. Within a year he possessed the master passkey of every major hotel in Manhattan. It was so easy. Before long he progressed from hotel rooms to hotel vaults. The first vault he did encouraged such focus. A hotel on upper Park at three in the morning. Comforti and another guy went in, frightened the resistance out of the night clerks and other staff. Got to the strongboxes with a prybar. It was so easy. The first box they forced open contained two hundred thousand in hundreds. The second and third yielded five hundred thousand in jewels. It went like that, so easy. They gathered up ten minutes' worth, the contents of fourteen strongboxes. Went out the front in no hurry.

Got away with it.

He didn't always, of course. He served some three to fives but the way he accounted life and its pleasures his scores had him way ahead. Glamorous scores, headline scores, seemingly impossible, audacious scores. So many that eventually the police had him come in and, as a favor to them, clear away the unsolved jewelry theft cases from their books. In return one hundred percent immunity. While he was at it, as a gesture of professional largesse, he admitted responsibility for a few sizeable scores he'd had nothing to do with, thus absolving some other swifts he probably didn't even know.

The Jimmy Comforti episode Mitch chose to tell Maddie now was one that had taken place about four years back. It began when Comforti was released from Attica state prison. A Thursday. He arrived in the city and went directly to the Hotel Carlyle.

He had paid a porter of that hotel two hundred a month, half in advance, to hold three pieces of very presentable luggage down in the guest's storage room. The luggage was sent up to the suite Comforti had reserved from Attica using his platinum American

Express. One of the Carlyle's high-priced, high-up suites with an ascendant southerly view. Bouquet of Casablanca lilies. Huge black grapes swagged from a silver salver of fresh fruit. Fax machine, five telephones including one on the wall next to the commode.

The liberated Comforti immediately set about to liberate his belongings. He summoned the valet on duty to have some pressing done and within a half hour was approving of his appearance in a full-length mirror. He hadn't gained or lost a pound or inch while in the joint all those months, so his suits and shirts were still perfect fits. Nothing about him gave him away as an ex-convict, nor would anyone guess that his tasteful guise and easy countenance concealed a first-class criminal mind. For all the world he looked like a respectable civilian, in town for a few days to take care of some little legitimate matter, and perhaps to visit his tailor.

He sat slouched in one of the sofa chairs and brought the nearest telephone to rest on his crotch. His first call was to a certain West 47th dealer named Wattenberg who middled upscale swag behind a straight reputation. Wattenberg was more than pleased to hear from Comforti again. He agreed to the meeting Comforti arbitrarily set much later that night.

Comforti's second call was to a certain young woman he'd never been with. He'd met her just before he'd gone inside and had held her in mind all the while, so she'd become somewhat essential. The given name she'd given herself was Laura. The two family names she'd chosen to go with it were hyphenated.

The thing about this young woman Laura that appealed to Comforti was her well-bred looks and mien, and the fact that she had enough imagination to carry off that impression most of the time.

When it came to women Comforti's preference was unusually limited. No bimbos or go-go's for him. To qualify for his ardent attention a woman had to at least convincingly seem as though she might have had some years at Smith, Wellesley or the like, possess a desperate sort of wildness to compensate for being quickly bored with everything, and whose family could possibly have an engraved brass nameplate on a reserved pew at St. James's Episcopal.

Comforti had never bedded the genuine article. However, there was a type of young woman scattered in the social mélange of Manhattan who looked pretty much the part, who had the requisite features, figure and bones, acquired taste and such, as well as the appropriate range of high-strung attitude. Usually these young women were aware of their assets, relied on them, placed hope in them. Believing that because of them there'd come a day, a just reckoning, when they'd no longer need to receptionist or sales clerk.

This was the wellspring from which Comforti drew. What made this young woman Laura so vital to him. There'd be others like her when he got back into circulation; however, at the moment, she was it.

Maddie interrupted with a scoff. "How could you possibly know what went on inside Comforti's head? You're embroidering, aren't you?"

"I'm telling it the way it was told to me," Mitch said.

"You're not embroidering it for my sake?"

"Not much."

"How much is not much?"

"Shall I go on?"

Maddie re-settled. "Please do."

After the Laura phone call Comforti went out and down Madison a short ways to a branch of a major bank where he kept a safety deposit box. He had four boxes at four different branches in which he stored what he called his "sleeping beauties." These were swag goods that he'd chosen to not sell. A reserve of some of the finer pieces. He awakened two, so to speak, put them to pocket and returned to the Carlyle.

Wattenberg showed up at the appointed hour. Three in the morning. Normally he was in bed by eleven but the prospect of huge gain had him high. A stocky sort with a weak, nearly indistinguishable chin and a pate that looked as though it had been buffed. He said the routine opening lines. No mention of prison. Nice to see, looking good, all that. It was like Comforti had been away on a long trip. Wattenberg declined a drink and accepted one of the chairs opposite the sofa but didn't sit back in it.

Comforti took the sofa. He wasn't merely relaxed. His limbs felt softly, delicately attached to his torso, his edges blunted. He was wearing a suit but nothing else. Bare chest, bare feet.

The door to the bedroom was partially open. A bright light on in there. A section of the used bed was visible, a bare part of woman upon it. Wattenberg couldn't help but notice. He got momentarily caught on that view, then self-consciously looked anywhere else. He tried to sit back but couldn't remain back, seemed to not know what to do with his hands.

Comforti noticed Wattenberg's abruptly increased unease, a give-away of erotic envy. That amused him, caused him to put off for a moment his bringing the bracelet out from his jacket pocket. He placed it on the low sofa table.

Wattenberg took up the bracelet and sighted it with his loupe. First, a cursory all-over look, then a longer, thorough examination of its individual stones.

Eight sugarloaf-shaped cabochon sapphires spaced by eight emerald-cut diamonds, mounted in platinum. It was signed *Cartier*.

Wattenberg asked what was the aggregate weight of the sapphires and Comforti told him without hesitation it was seventy-four carats. Comforti anticipated what Wattenberg's next question would be, and said the total carat weight of the diamonds was a few points less than twenty-six.

Wattenberg remarked that the bracelet was a pleasant piece. An obvious understatement. He hopefully complimented the sapphires by saying they were nice number-one Burmas.

Comforti knew the game, stated that the sapphires were Kashmir. Which made them much rarer and five or six times more precious.

Wattenberg took another lengthy look and pretended only now to recognize the sapphires' Kashmir characteristics.

It was at that point the young woman Laura came from the bedroom. In a full-length bias-cut nightgown of gray silk charmeuse. Bare on top. The thinnest possible straps. She was possibly over twenty-five but not thirty, a fine-boned, slender brunette with every good reason to be confident of her body. There was an attractive disorder about her. Without acknowledging Wattenberg or even Comforti she went directly to the room service cart that was off to one side. Helped herself to a leftover toastpoint.

Wattenberg noticed a tiny price tag discreetly attached to the rear hem of her nightgown by a tiny gold safety pin. He had a momentary battle with distraction, particularly the way the silk charmeuse fabric declared her gorgeous buttocks.

Maddie interrupted again. "Now I'd call that overembroidering."

"Would you rather have it plain, a less colorful, more abridged version?"

"Not really," Maddie decided, "just go a little lighter on the gorgeous buttocks stuff, hmmm?"

Amused by that, Mitch went on.

Telling how this lovely pseudo-highbrow Laura came over and occupied the other sofa chair across from Comforti. True to her affectation, she managed to be blasé about the Cartier bracelet. It couldn't dazzle her. Even when Wattenberg laid it back onto the table where it was right before her eyes, the diamonds shooting scintillations, the sapphires glowing their vivid blue, she disregarded it. As though such a thing was commonplace to her. She also appeared completely disinterested in whatever transaction Comforti and Wattenberg were involved in. It meant nothing to her.

Wattenberg was into his own act, containing his enthusiasm for the swag bracelet, concealing his eagerness to buy it. He waited a long beat, scratched his temple and did an ambivalent mouth before asking Comforti how much.

Comforti had the figure ready. Four hundred and fifty thousand. The amount hung in the air.

Wattenberg wasn't fazed. He had a lady client in Milan who would consider eight hundred thousand a bargain. He nearly agreed to four hundred fifty; however, his West 47 nature caused him to ask if four hundred fifty was the asking price.

Comforti just looked at him.

Wattenberg offered four hundred.

Comforti didn't make a big thing of it. Calmly, he picked up the bracelet, held it up at eye level, dangled it for a moment as though bidding it goodbye.

Wattenberg felt certain it was about to become his.

Comforti tossed the bracelet to Laura. Gave it to her, just like that. No big deal.

Within the next minute Wattenberg was out in the hotel corridor awaiting the elevator. Unable to not hate himself. He realized the gaffe he'd committed. How could he have been so stupid? How could he have forgotten that Comforti always considered his stated price for a piece of swag to be more than fair, a price that allowed everyone to make. Comforti's cardinal rule, as proverbial as the man: no haggling, ever.

Perhaps, Wattenberg thought, all wasn't lost. He hung around the lobby of the Carlyle believing sooner or later he'd catch this Laura on her way out. She'd want the money more than the piece.

Came noon he gave up on that.

The following day, just by chance, he spotted her as she came out of the 580 Fifth Avenue building. Bound for a limo at the curb.

She pretended to not recognize Wattenberg at first, which was understandable, considering prior circumstances.

He didn't waste words, offered her three hundred seventy-five for the bracelet.

Her face went weary, but then she managed to modulate her regret. She did a resigned shrug and informed Wattenberg that just minutes ago she'd sold the bracelet to Visconti . . .

. . . for two fifty.

Maddie chuckled. "You tell one hell of a bedtime story," she said, "but, you know, I seem to recall Hurley telling me that one sometime back."

"When?"

"Four, maybe five years ago."

"Why didn't you say so?"

"You were really into it."

"I suppose it was better the first time you heard it."

"To the contrary," she said turning onto her side and snuggling his thigh. "I'll bet years and years down the road from now you'll forget you told it and tell it again and I'll probably enjoy it even more."

Years and years from now, Mitch thought. He'd discerned a degree of sleepiness in Maddie's voice and it was even thicker as she smiled a mainly inward smile and said: "I love you, precious."

She began to sleep. It always amazed Mitch how quickly she could drop off. He believed it might have something to do with her black. Perhaps her black made it less of a fall for her. He heard her breathing change and although her eyelids were partly open he knew she was a goner. He waited, allowed time for her to get surely, really deep, then, disturbing as little as possible, he got up and lifted her. Carried her down to the second floor to their bedroom and gently laid her on the bed. Placed a pillow close next to her, his surrogate for her hugging.

He hurried back up to the dormer, settled down. For some reason, now that Maddie was asleep and he her lone guardian, he was instilled with even greater resolve. They wouldn't get to her. He wouldn't let them get to her. He gazed out at the night. It seemed changed, as though the dark had solidified everything out there into one piece.

He leaned out the dormer window and gazed upwards. Overcast, no stars, no sky. He told himself that didn't mean no heaven. He settled down again.

He couldn't prevent Ralph Lentini from coming to mind. Ralph and the fur-coated hooker. Their bodies shriveled white and bloated with the gas of decay, risen by now, trying to break through that layer of green scum.

Ruder was another matter. Probably the harbor current and undertows had scuttled him along the bottom, and the fish, all sorts and sizes, the blues and snappers and such, had fed on him. For sure the sharks down off Sandy Hook.

Poor Ruder.

Chapter 32

Riccio's have-arounds didn't come that night, nor the next morning.

Since daybreak a fine rain had been falling, so misty a rain that it seemed to be atomizing the land. Every exterior surface looked slick and darker, as though it had been varnished, especially the trunks and leaves of the apple trees down in the orchard.

The rain contributed to the complacency that was now sharing Mitch's outlook. He had begun to think that inasmuch as the have-arounds hadn't come by now they might not come. Possibly Riccio only intended to intimidate. Wasn't it, after all, a ridiculous vengeance, senseless, way out of proportion? At that very moment Riccio was probably in his West 47th lair operating his money-counting machine or popping caraters out of their mountings, while his have-arounds, all of them, were in that room off to the side eating heros and watching reruns. The killing of Mitch Laughton and wife the furthest thing from their minds, or, if they gave that any thought, it was to laugh at the way they had Mitch shitting in his pants.

On the other hand, quite possibly Riccio had dilated this situation and couldn't bring himself to return it to its appropriate size.

Riccio's old-mob mentality. What he said he was going to do he had to do. Such an ugly face to save.

Anyway, Mitch felt that Riccio's one-sided assault was somewhat less inevitable than it had been yesterday. Less enough to leave the dormer at mid-afternoon, go down and make a fresh pot of coffee and a tuna salad sandwich. Less enough so that when Maddie remarked she felt cruddy and was going to take a bath, he told her, only after brief reservation and no second thought, to go ahead.

He heard the tub filling and went to the bathroom to observe her. She was already in. On the floor lay her combat fatigues and sneakers, shoulder rig and Beretta. A container of bath oil was on the edge of the tub; the air redolent with the scent of lilies. Maddie often had difficulty determining measures and evidently she'd given this bathwater a huge overdose. The oil coated Maddie's skin as she shifted about. She scrunched down, submerged all save her head and, a moment later, when she sat up, the oil caused water to scurry into beads on her shoulders, arms and breasts.

Mitch had to escape from the overly fragrant air. He went back up to the dormer to resume his vigil.

He looked out and saw the rain had let up. He looked further out and caught sight of the chrome grille of a Lincoln Town Car, a black Lincoln followed close behind by another identical. They were coming in on the drive, slowly, as though they were part of a funeral procession. They stopped short of the spot Mitch had figured, a good hundred yards from the house. No one got out. For some reason they just sat there with the engines off. For several minutes not a move.

Mitch waited to see how many he would be up against. He'd expected one car.

They got out then. All at once. Fat Angelo, and Little Mike from the lead car. Bechetti and Fratino from the other. They were regularly dressed, in suits and sports jackets. A city entourage.

Car door slams. A hundred blackbirds frightened out of the pines like applause. From the trunk of the lead car weapons taken out and distributed. There was a brief dispute over who would get a machine pistol. Bechetti claimed it and a spare magazine.

One of the rear doors of the second car had been left open. Another person got out.

Riccio.

Mitch thought it a bad sign that Riccio had chosen to be personally involved. But really what difference would it make? He'd probably given in to his craving for firsthand violence. The old-mob maniac in one of his ill-fitting suits, the collar turned up and the lapels folded across. He paced a couple of circles to get the ride from his back and legs. He looked up at the sky as though ordering it to cooperate. He used the stub of the twisted Sicilian cigar he'd been smoking to light another, puffed up a cloud that, in the damp, heavy air, hung around him and instead of rising descended onto his shoulders. He stood apart from his have-arounds. They, waiting in a group with the pistols on the ends of their arms. Riccio called Fratino over, said something to him and then with a disdainful gesture signaled the other have-arounds to get on with it.

They started for the house. Mitch slung on the shotgun and rushed down the stairs shouting to Maddie. She was quickly out of the bath and, without toweling dry, into her combat fatigues. No time for her sneakers. She grabbed up the shoulder rig and the Beretta and, along with Mitch, using him to lead, dashed down to the first floor and out the back way.

On the run across the maintained rear grounds, past the greenhouse, through Straw's vegetable garden. All the way to the edge of the West Meadow.

They paused there. Mitch glanced back to the house. As yet no sign of have-arounds. He looked at Maddie, beheld her intensely, desperately, feeling perhaps this might be his last sight of her. At least in this world.

"Do exactly as we discussed," he told her.

"I will."

"Don't take any chances."

"I won't."

He thought to head her in the direction of the old equipment barn located far out in the meadow; however she had already set out for it.

It was crucial that she reach the barn before the have-arounds could spot her. Mitch stood there and looked back and forth, from the house to her. If they came out and spotted her in the meadow he would change his plan, follow her to the barn and make a stand there, a stand that he'd have no chance of winning.

He mentally hurried her. She was doing as best she could, unable to run, barely able to stride in that thick, unmowed, thigh-high grass. To make matters worse, the grass was wet and heavier for that. No doubt the legs of her fatigues were sopped by now. Tough going, Mitch thought.

The have-arounds surely must have reached the house by now, were somewhere within it.

Maddie still had a ways to go.

Just grant me this, Mitch pleaded to whatever power determined such crises.

He looked back to the house.

He looked ahead to Maddie.

She reached the barn, entered it, was no longer visible.

Not a moment too soon. The have-arounds came out onto the second-floor rear terrace, from where they had an easy view of the meadow.

Mitch made sure they spotted him. Though way out of range, he fired an attention-getting shot and immediately made a dash for the high piled-rock wall about a hundred yards away, the wall that served as a separating boundary between the West Meadow and the adjacent expanse of pastureland.

He stood on the crest of the wall, and took stock of the have-arounds, who by now had come from the house and were hurrying in his direction. Little Mike, Fat Angelo and Bechetti. All intent on him with no interest in the equipment barn. Good.

Mitch took off across the pasture. The herd of cows was still out. About fifty or so. They weren't a tight herd this day, not gathered at one particular area of the pasture, but spread far and wide as though in an antisocial mood. Soon, out of habit of schedule or using cow sense, they would start for the distant dairy farm. Many were already grazing their way towards it. Others appeared to be through for the day, were at rest on the damp, chewed-up, hooved-up ground. They lay motionless, like ideal depictions of their kind, front and rear legs folded just so beneath them to avoid placing too much weight on their distended utters.

Mitch had thought the cows would play in his plan. He would scurry among the herd, use them in a darting now-you-see-me-now-you-don't manner, while he took a roundabout course back to the rock wall. However the herd was too widespread for that, and he was already about a hundred or so yards into the pasture, committed to it, would have to improvise.

He decided on some resting cows off to his right. A loose group of a half dozen. They were only mildly disturbed by his sudden presence, not enough to rise and move off. He used the nearest cow for temporary cover, kneeled out of sight on the far side of it. Cautiously, he peeked over the bony ridge of the cow's back.

Bechetti and Fat Angelo were standing on the piled-rock wall, like spectators. Little Mike was into the pasture and coming on. It appeared that he was the designated hitter. Either that or he was just much faster and more eager than the others, had gotten to the wall and up and over it ahead of them. Malingering and amused in their typical have-around way, they were letting him do the job, waiting to see how he made out.

Little Mike was some kind of runner. Seen at a distance, with his stubby legs scooting him along, he resembled a wind-up mechanical toy, but, as he drew closer Mitch could see his legs working like pistons. He was closing fast.

Mitch changed cows, made a dash to another of those at rest about twenty feet away. There was the chance that this tactic hadn't been noticed and, if so, Little Mike, coming on so fast and headlong, might overrun him.

Mitch hunkered down behind the cow. A big old bossie, intolerant but too comfortable to move. She whipped her switch at him a couple of times and indicted him with a look. Pink lips, yellowed, cracked horns, a runny nose that she licked with her long tongue. The earlier rain had soaked her down to her hide.

Mitch snugged against her. He heard the thumps of her tremendous heart, which at first he thought was the pounding of his own. He heard the digesting gurgle of her stomachs as she reswallowed her cud.

Would Little Mike overrun on the left or right? Mitch had the Glock in hand, ready for either direction. Little Mike would run past. His back would be the target. It didn't matter that Little Mike would be so disadvantaged, Mitch told himself. He'd never shot a living thing. Don't give it a thought, don't think of the Glock being arbitrary death, make it absolute, stopping death. Just aim, shoot and kill the little fucker. Kill him in the back, side, head, chest, didn't matter.

Three rapidly fired bullets struck the old cow. Easily penetrated her tough hide and tore into her. She threw her head up and bellowed and bucked and almost managed to stand for a moment before her front legs gave way. Her hind half, still useful, wanted to run. It struggled with the wounded rest of her, tugged and staggered.

Little Mike fired again. Two more point-blank shots from fifteen feet. That brought all of the innocent animal down, but not out of the way. Rather sacrificially, her bulk still concealed Mitch.

He was spontaneously filled with shame for his kind, the inhumanity, a shame that converted into rage, a rage that overrode his trepidations. Thus, it was not altogether courage that brought him suddenly upright, exposed him to the next two shots Little Mike got off.

Mitch wasn't sure he hadn't been hit. He only knew there was no pain and he wasn't prevented from pointing the Glock in Little Mike's direction. No time but also no need to take careful aim. It was impossible for him to miss simply because Little Mike so deserved to be shot.

He fired twice.

The first .40 caliber hollow point smacked into Little Mike's chest about an inch or two above the sternum, spread upon impact and was close to twice its diameter when it tore through the right atrium of his heart. The slug that followed a split second later was so equally accurate that it had a ready-made entry, didn't spread until it struck and shattered the spine.

Little Mike knew what hit him. He was jolted back and literally lifted off his feet. Like an awkward, unaccomplished tumbler he went heels over head, and failed to complete a somersault. He lay there, a crumpled extinguished thing in a beige suit, having lifeless twitches.

Now look what you've done, Mitch thought, but immediately revised that to look what you had no choice but to do. There were fourteen rounds left in the Glock, including the one in the chamber ready to be spent. His adrenals had given him another spurt. He felt somewhat beyond control but capable of anything. He glanced at the cow. It was belly-up, flailing with all fours as though kicks could stave off death. Mitch had to look away.

The other two have-arounds were coming into it now, scrambling down the distant rock wall to the pasture. They set out for Mitch at a fast walk. No need to go running after him. Little Mike, the stupid runt, had run and look what it had gotten him. As they saw it Mitch was way out there in plain view with nowhere to hide. Not even a rock or tree, just cows. All they had to do was keep him in sight and keep after him to eventually get to him.

What they didn't take into account was how deceptive a vast open space such as this two-hundred-acre cow pasture could be. These city guys hadn't ever had any experience with pastures. It seemed to them their every step was on a straight course. They didn't realize the illusion until they saw that the piled-rock wall which had been behind them at the start was now up ahead and Mitch was approaching it. He, their only reckoning, had been purposely misleading them, taking a wide gradual circling course.

Now the have-arounds ran after him.

He climbed over the rock wall and crossed the West Meadow, keeping well away from the rear side of the equipment barn. When he reached where the meadow bordered the woodlands to the north he paused in plain sight, looked back and saw that the have-arounds were following the swath he had caused in the thick, high meadow grass. He disappeared into the woods.

Moments later the have-arounds entered the woods on the run.

After going only a hundred feet it was as though they were a hundred miles deep into its world, suckered into a domain that was rife with unfamiliar defiance and contraries. Flagellating saplings, loops of exposed roots that tripped, undergrowth that grabbed at their confining suits.

They couldn't have been more out of their element.

Their hard city heels sunk into the spongy rot of the woodland floor. In some places they went in over their ankles and dirt got into their shoes, their two-hundred-dollar, made-in-Italy, fifty-dollar swag shoes.

Bechetti, as usual, was in charge, and it was he who first spotted the pulsating amber light. They hurried ahead to it, approached it warily, weapons ready. It appeared to be only an ordinary orange and white highway construction site barricade. The single upright sort about three feet tall counting the enclosed battery and light on top.

"What do you think?"

"I don't know."

"What the fuck's this thing doing way out here?"

"Some kind of trick, got to be."

"The cocksucker is trying to throw us off, that's all," Bechetti decided.

"Maybe."

"Kick it over," Bechetti told Fat Angelo.

"You want the fucking thing kicked over, you kick it."

Bechetti went to the barrier, kicked it over. It lay there mocking with its amber blink, amber blink, amber blink. Fat Angelo stomped on it to make it stop. "Okay," Bechetti said, "let's find the piece of shit and do him so we can get out of here." The pursuit had become a search.

They tried to stick together, to proceed in a sort of phalanx, two across. But the woods combed them apart the way unpathed woods can. When they encountered a tight stand of hemlocks, for instance, Bechetti chose to go round the right side of it while Fat Angelo avoided by going left. Dense clumps of undergrowth and outcroppings of sizeable boulders called for the same circuitous left or right decisions. Thus, the distance that separated them increased. Eventually they lost sight and sound of one another, and each was on his own; a rare circumstance for any have-around.

Fat Angelo hated how this thing was going down. From the moment he'd come into the woods there'd been a squadron of gnats attacking him. So tiny he could hardly see them. He needed to keep swatting and shooing them or else they landed and fed on him. Why the fuck were they picking on him and not Bechetti? It didn't seem like this place was making Bechetti half as miserable as it was him. The only other time he'd been in a woods something like this was the day about five years back when he'd had to make a trip to Danbury for Riccio. Driving up 684 he had pulled over and gone into the woods a short ways to take an emergency shit. This was like then.

He was sorry now that he'd come along on this thing. He could have said his hemorrhoids were bothering him, or his ulcer. The reason he came was the other have-arounds wanted to and Riccio had made it sound like it was going to be easy, enjoyable work. Riccio had promised a ten large bonus to whoever whacked the guy and the bimbo. Another twenty to anyone who came up with the goods, those two emeralds. Sometimes Riccio kept his word on things like that. Another reason he'd come along was the guy who was going to get whacked was the one who'd shoved him down the stairs twice and also called him a *fagala*, so this thing would be a chance for payback, Fat Angelo had figured.

Now, however, he figured where he'd much rather and ought to be was back on West 47th in his regular spot halfway up the stairs at Riccio's. He could be relaxing on the daybed looking at pussy magazines. He was thirsty. He was pissed. He decided what he'd do is sit someplace and let Bechetti, wherever he was, do the guy. Just wait to hear the shots.

He was trying to find a place to sit that wasn't wet or rotten when the amber light blinked at him from down the incline. Another of those highway barricades. It was, he guessed, about a hundred yards away, blinking at him through the branches. He decided to ignore it. He found that if he moved a little to the right or left the light was obscured and he could pretend it wasn't there; however, curiosity edged with apprehension compelled his eyes to locate it.

Amber blink, amber blink, amber blink.

Fuck it, Fat Angelo thought.

His legs seemed to think otherwise. They took him down the incline in the direction of the light, with difficulty across a couple of mushy runoffs and through a tangle of wild grape. By then he was inspired by the possibility that maybe the light was on his side, leading him to the guy so he could do him and be the one who did him and Riccio would count him off ten large, which would make him a five hundred across-the-board player when he went to Aqueduct come Friday. Or, he might even get luckier. It wasn't too much to ask that after he'd done the guy he'd find those two emeralds on him. In that case Riccio could keep his measly twenty large. Fat Angelo knew the whole lot more he could get for those emeralds. He'd have to hide them somewhere better than a pocket, though. He'd stick them up his ass. Hemorrhoids or no hemorrhoids, up they'd go.

He paused a moment to check his weapons. He had two. A .45 automatic that he'd killed twice with, but not recently, and a snubby .38 caliber backup revolver he'd never had to use. The latter was holstered to his belt behind his left ham, concealed by his suit jacket.

He was surprised to come upon the marsh, nearly tromped right into its southern end where it was thick with cattails and reeds. The blinking amber light was in the clear at the water's edge about a hundred feet away. Same as the first, mounted on an orange and white stupid highway construction barrier. No reason for it to be there.

Then he saw the guy. About a hundred feet beyond the blinking light. Standing at the edge of the water with his back turned, just standing there, the asshole. Be perfect if he'd just stay like he was, Fat Angelo thought.

Mitch had seen Fat Angelo come down the incline, and, although he was turned away, he knew to the moment when Fat Angelo got to the marsh. From the frogs Fat Angelo had startled, their noisy leaps from the bank into the water.

And now, from those same blurping sounds in succession he knew Fat Angelo was sneaking along the bank in order to get into range. He waited until the frogs told him Fat Angelo had covered about halfway. Then he stepped out onto the precisely submerged span of painted plywood.

Fat Angelo froze. From his point of view it appeared as though Mitch was walking on water. He brought his pistol up to take a shot but he was awestruck. How could he shoot a guy who could walk on water? Besides, both of his previous killings had been close in, practically muzzle against the back of the head.

Mitch reached the opposite bank. Fat Angelo was directly across the way, apparently unaware of the submerged span that was right there below him. Perhaps reflections on the surface of the water prevented him from noticing it. Mitch acknowledged him with the universal *fuck you* gesture.

Fat Angelo emphatically returned two of the same. What to do? He set out for the opposite bank by going around the end of the marsh. A stumbling, sloshing trek.

Mitch jogged easily back across the span, so again they were on opposite sides.

In all his inciteful and frustrated life Fat Angelo had never been more incited and frustrated. He glared across at the inaccessible Mitch, who was now taunting him with open arms and beckoning fingers. Come on, come on over.

Fat Angelo couldn't take much of that. He averted his eyes downward.

He saw the trick. His pointed-toe shoes were pointing right at it: the two-foot width of painted plywood weighted down on that end by several large rocks, the way it extended across the marsh.

No way was he going to go across on that board, Fat Angelo told himself. Not even if he was one hundred percent sure the guy had those emeralds on him. He imagined himself doing the guy and finding the emeralds in one of the guy's pockets. He imagined the ride back to West 47th, him sitting on a fortune, knowing they were his secret, tucked up into him. Some wish.

Compelling enough to cause him to take a testing step out onto the plywood span. It was sort of slippery but it hardly gave. He took another cautious step and another slightly less cautious and, after the next, he was thoroughly encouraged.

However, as he went along he had to split his attention between where he was stepping and the guy on the bank ahead. No telling when the guy would make a move. So far all the fuck had done was stand there, like maybe he was waiting for the Lexington Avenue local.

Fat Angelo was nearly halfway across. About forty feet to go. He thought about chancing a shot from there but, being far from a good shooter, he decided to give himself the advantage of another step closer, and still another.

The closer he got the more he had to keep an eye on the guy, which meant he couldn't pay real careful attention to where he placed his feet.

It took only one misstep.

By his right foot, which happened to be more off than on the span. He went into the water front first, a sort of low-level belly flop. There was some thrashing and spewing before, with considerable difficulty, he managed to get himself upright.

The water was up to his waist. Actually only about half that depth was water. The other half was silt. His legs were mired deep in the mucky decomposed stuff of the bottom. He tried to lift his feet but it was as though he was cemented in place. Bubbles like underwater farts rose to the surface around him and silently exploded dreadful-smelling methane gas. He still had his pistol in hand. He used it as an instrument of surrender, held it harmlessly up and out to the side and let it drop into the water.

Because he was no match for the shotgun Mitch now had pointed at him.

"What you going to do?"

Mitch didn't say.

Fat Angelo asked again.

"I'm deciding," Mitch told him.

"Why don't you get a branch or something and help pull me out?"

"I'm deciding whether to shoot you or leave you there to starve and rot."

An unnerved smile from Fat Angelo. "You're just trying to sweat me."

"Yeah," Mitch lied and lowered the shotgun some.

Fat Angelo figured that was a cue for his plea. He went into a self-deprecating rant. About what a low-life, lowest kind of grease-ball he was. A nothing, a *babbo*, a *shmuck*. Everybody treated him like the scumbag he was, including Riccio. Riccio especially. He'd been a garbage collector before. Had been better off. He was no have-around. Only reason he was up there on this thing today was Caselli got sick. He had to take Caselli's place. Caselli got the shits and pukes and couldn't make it.

Throughout this babbling appeal Fat Angelo underscored and punctuated with his hands. Typical of his nationality, a lot of intri-cate and wide gesticulating.

Mitch appeared to be listening attentively to Fat Angelo. Actu-ally, he was only half hearing him. He was thinking about what West 47th would be like if the likes of Fat Angelo weren't working it. Not a tender-conscienced, guileless, untainted West 47th, to be sure, but enormously improved.

Inside of one of Fat Angelo's gesticulations his right hand went to his belt behind his hip for the snubby .38.

Mitch's mind wasn't that much elsewhere. He fired from the hip. A round of buckshot. In bringing the gun up he had overcompen-sated slightly so the hit was a little high. The tight pattern of 12-gauge steel pellets struck Fat Angelo in the collarbone, throat and face. Didn't merely damage, and probably would have been enough; however Mitch rapidly pumped another shell into the chamber and fired. The 12-gauge slug blasted into the center of Fat Angelo's chest, and that was more than enough.

Due to his obesity and because his lower legs were mired Fat

Angelo went down strangely. A fast flop that settled into a contorted sort of backbend.

Uncomfortable to say the least, Mitch thought. It seemed to be true that a second killing was easier. He wasn't feeling a single pang of remorse. It was as though his conscience was having an outage and he was on his own, telling himself no harm, that this guy he'd wasted had been a waste. He raised his eyes a fraction and vowed to the sky and whatever overseer might be in it that if he got through this day he would never kill again. Wouldn't even swat a fly or step on an ant.

After today.

Chapter 33

Bechetti would come, Mitch knew, surely he'd heard those two shots. He couldn't be far off. He'd come.

Mitch placed the shotgun aside. It might be of further use; however he'd found that it restricted his movements in the woods, especially where there was dense brush and branches. He had the Glock. It would do.

There still wasn't any sun. Everything damp. Drops from tips of leaves. A primeval impression influenced by the marsh. A massive reptile might rise from it. Not Fat Angelo.

Bechetti was coming down the incline at the far end of the marsh. Yet out of sight, but the saplings were being disturbed. Mitch waited, watched for the tan suit, the inverted white triangle of shirt front, the contradicting oblong of human head. There would also be the black of the Tech 19 machine pistol.

Bechetti broke into view and paused at the edge of the marsh, warily taking it in.

Mitch couldn't be missed, little more than two hundred feet away. To make sure he was seen he raised and waved his arms.

What was it with this guy? Bechetti wondered. It looked as though he was signaling, wanting to give up. Like he figured then this thing would end in a push or something. Civilians didn't know, they just didn't fucking get it.

Mitch kept on waving.

Bechetti rushed ahead and was close to being close enough to pull off some shots when Mitch bolted into the woods. Bechetti followed and within thirty paces found himself again surrounded by contraries, the branches, roots and vines. Fallen trunks. Sticky webs on his face, nothing substantial underfoot. It would seem that way out here would be a good place to do a guy, but it wasn't, Bechetti thought. There was too much life here. Be different if this was some stairwell, warehouse, any kind of room. He had whacked fourteen guys up to now, eight of those had been in bed.

So, where was this guy? It occurred to Bechetti that maybe the guy had cut back and was coming at him from behind. He stopped, crouched, scanned slowly all the way around. Everything was different and yet the same, green-leaved and damp. No movement. A dangerous silence. Bechetti convinced himself the guy was somewhere ahead. He hurried on.

Past a gang of boulders, across the trickle of a habitual runoff. To the upper edge of a shallow swale. Directly opposite was a stand of pines. And there on its perimeter between two close, competing trunks, stood the guy. Arms folded, as though simply waiting.

He was close enough. Bechetti opened fire, a couple of bursts.

The guy scampered into the pines.

Bechetti went after him and was immediately in the maze of straight trunks, a darker atmosphere. The ground, carpeted with slippery needles, handicapped him because of his leather-soled shoes.

There was, however, an advantage being among the pines. No undergrowth. Only the tree trunks for concealment.

Bechetti caught a glimpse of the guy. Scurrying from behind one trunk to behind the next further on. The camouflaged fatigues didn't help the guy much here. He'd been clearly visible, but only for an instant, not long enough for Bechetti to get off a shot.

Within a minute the guy again darted from trunk to trunk, but again all Bechetti got was the merest glimpse. He figured the guy now realized what a wrong move he'd made in getting into these pines and was now trying to work his way out of them.

Too fucking bad.

Bechetti focused his attention and aim on the space between two of the tree trunks. Just a guess as to where the guy might next show himself. He held on it for what seemed a long while and was about to give up on it when the guy darted into view, was right there.

Bechetti fired two bursts from the Tech 19. A spray of ten or so rounds. Bullets splatted into bark and ground and, as well, into the guy, according to what Bechetti heard—a loud painful gasp.

Bechetti cautioned himself that even a sound so truly agonizing could be a trick. Shouldn't the guy's legs or some other part of him be in view? Bechetti gave it some time and then advanced stealthily. He would finish the guy off if he wasn't already done. There'd been no other sounds so he was probably done.

The guy wasn't there. Just a lot of his blood. Bright, wet red on the base of the tree and on the layer of brown pine needles.

The fuck was hit bad, Bechetti thought. He wouldn't be able to go far.

There was an obvious trail of blood. Drops of various sizes and smears in places. Bechetti had no difficulty following them, anticipating that at any moment he would come upon the guy unconscious or dead or perhaps just weakened and unable to go on. Bechetti hoped for the latter because of the inconvenience this guy and these woods had caused him. A slow finish would be a payback.

The blood led him on. All the way through the stand of pines and out to a clearing where the terrain was more congruent. No sign of the guy or his blood. Bechetti had lost the trail of blood. He didn't, however, have to search much to pick it up. Bright red on the tufts of wild grasses. Even more apparent on the white, wild daisies that were closed for the day due to lack of sun.

Faint groans.

Also gasps and entreaties to God. They seemed to be coming from across the way where there were a lot of bushes of some sort. Now Bechetti had the blood and the suffering of the guy to go by.

As he approached the bushes he saw what they were. Brambles, a large tight patch of them. The situation wasn't hard to figure, Bechetti thought. The guy, seeking any possible refuge, had taken cover somewhere in this bramble patch, had somehow crawled into it, and maybe that was smart and he might even have gotten away with it except he was bleeding too much and had so much pain he couldn't keep it to himself.

Bechetti stood at the edge of the patch listening to the groans and blubbering supplications. They were alternately louder and indistinct. He watched the top of the brambles for any sign of movement but they were perfectly still. A catbird glided in to light upon one of the high arching canes, had hardly perched before it realized there were humans about and flew off.

Bechetti decided precisely where the guy was. Only about twenty-five feet in. He raised the machine pistol and strafed the spot with a couple of bursts. The 9mm bullets tore through the canes and leaves but it didn't stop the guy's groaning. Nor did another couple of bursts. It didn't make sense, Bechetti thought, the guy had to be there, at least some of those bullets had to have hit him.

He noticed then there were drops of blood off to his right. They led to where, along the edge, the guy had crawled into the patch. It was almost like a tunnel, probably made by some animal, was Bechetti's guess. The guy just happened to find it. Bechetti hunched down for a cautious look in. He couldn't see in very far. It didn't go straight in. He fired several shots in but the groaning continued along with some cursing.

Leave the fuck there, Bechetti suggested to himself. The guy was hit bad so just leave him to die in there.

Bechetti's exasperation vetoed that. He took off his suit jacket, folded it just so and placed it down where he wouldn't miss it later. He removed his tie and unbuttoned his shirt collar. Rolled his shirtsleeves up to his elbows. Like there was work to do, to do this guy.

He got down on all fours and crawled into the tunnel. He found it not as large as it had appeared and denser. Even when he kept low the thorns on the brambles got to his back and shoulders, snagged at the hips of his trousers. As he crawled along his trousers were being ruined, especially at the knees, by the soft earth and fallen blackberries. He swore he'd finish this guy slower than any guy he'd ever finished. When he got to him.

And he was about to get to him. The groans and delirious swearing were louder now, real close, coming from around the slight bend in the tunnel that was just ahead. Bechetti crawled on, more cautiously. He didn't want to get whacked by an almost dead guy.

The guy wasn't there. A big spill of blood but no guy. The guy's voice but no guy.

Bechetti dabbed up some of the blood, felt its slick but slightly gritty texture. He smelled it. A distinctive smell that his memory recognized and connected to the innocent paint of a second grade class thirty years ago.

The voice? There in plain view was the tiny speaker attached to the battery-powered audio cassette player. Still groaning and uttering.

But the guy *had* been there, Bechetti reasoned. No other way could he have spilled the paint along the tunnel and here at this dead end. He must have done it in a hurry and backed out. There was no room to turn around. It seemed to Bechetti there hadn't been enough time for the guy to do all that, but he couldn't see any other explanation, which meant he too would have to make his exit in reverse.

That, as it turned out, was more difficult than Bechetti expected. The tunnel seemed narrower and with less headroom now that he was going ass first. He kept backing into brambles on one side or the other, giving the thorns plenty of chances at him. They were like organized, malicious adversaries, the thorns. Some would snag his trousers as though delaying him, so others might stab and lacerate his thighs and buttocks.

Fuck doing this guy, Bechetti thought. It was a piece of shit, not the piece of cake Riccio had said it would be. Fuck this place, fuck Riccio, fuck everything!

At that moment Mitch was also in the brambles. Crawling out by way of the getaway tunnel that ran from the apparent dead end that Bechetti had encountered. Mitch had created the impression that it was a dead end, had concealed the getaway tunnel by stuffing a large tight tangle of blackberry canes and foliage into place. Bechetti had nearly caught him at it.

The getaway tunnel allowed access all the way out to the far side of the patch. It was straight enough but now as Mitch crawled along it he was sorry he hadn't made it larger. The thorns were impartial, meting out as many or even more inflictions on Mitch as on Bechetti. There were places in the getaway tunnel where hugely thorned canes had fallen and crisscrossed, as though resenting and thus intent on prohibiting passage. There were places where Mitch was so thoroughly snagged, front, back and sides, that he could barely move. He still had a ways to go.

Bechetti, meanwhile, unaware that he wasn't alone in the brambles, was struggling along.

On the way in he hadn't noticed the wolf trap. It was situated at about the midway point a little off to the right covered with leaves. On the way in Bechetti had missed springing the trap by a mere inch or two and now, as he was backing out, his right foot and leg avoided it by about that same margin. So did his right forearm and hand.

It was the machine pistol that sprang the trap.

The steel jaws snapped shut.

The teeth that Mitch had honed so sharp chomped together with tremendous force.

They clamped onto the trigger guard of the pistol and, in so doing, impaled Bechetti's trigger finger, sliced deep into the knuckle of its second joint, nearly to the point of amputation.

Bechetti's howl had some tremolo in it. He knew nothing of traps, hadn't ever seen one. His spontaneous reaction was that some animal had him in its bite, but then, through his pain, he realized the thing was made of metal and had a chain attached to it.

He tried to extricate his mutilated finger from the trigger guard. The teeth of the trap had it, flesh and bone, skewered against the trigger, pressed so tightly that all the slack of the trigger was taken up and the merest additional pressure would cause the pistol to fire.

With his free hand he tried to pry open the trap. It couldn't be done one-handed. The effort intensified his pain.

How could he deal with this? Why was he being made to suffer? That guy. Was he ever going to do that fuck. Once he got out of these bushes.

He resumed his backwards crawl. It was even more difficult now. Not only was he having to contend with the thorns but, as well, his every move aggravated the torment of his finger.

He couldn't bear either.

His impatience exploded.

Without giving a second thought to the consequences, he got his feet under him and heaved upward. Full force against the weave of thorn-studded brambles overhead. Some gave, more defied, refused to relent unless Bechetti accepted their punishment.

His fury was anesthetic.

Head first, he burst up out of the green tangle, then tore his shoulders and arms free. Like a grotesque throwback suddenly risen from its breached domain bearing countless wounds. Blood streamed from his scalp and neck, ears and cheeks. Even from his eyelids. A deep slash on his nose ran from bridge to tip and it must have been particularly vicious thorns that had clawed his mouth.

Just seconds earlier Mitch had emerged from the getaway tunnel. He stood at the rear edge of the patch surveying his advantage. It had gone as he'd hoped. Bechetti was in the thick of the brambles where he couldn't see out but could be easily picked off. Mitch would just stand there or anywhere around the patch and blast away at him. In fact, certain uppermost brambles were being disturbed, betraying where Bechetti was at that very moment.

It was then that the bloodied Bechetti heaved up through the top of the brambles little more than twenty feet away, chest and head exposed.

An easy shot for Mitch. He went for his Glock.

His holster was empty.

At some point in the getaway tunnel it must have gotten snagged out.

Bechetti spotted him, leveled the machine pistol and let go with a burst.

Mitch dove for cover, crawled swiftly along the edge of the patch to put some distance between himself and Bechetti.

Bechetti was resolutely forging his way out of the chest-high patch.

Mitch had to make a run for it. The clearing wasn't entirely level. A zigzagging dash and another desperate dive got him safely to a shallow depression and gave him a moment to consider his options:

He would be exposed to Bechetti's fire when he crossed the clearing and got back into the pines. He would rush through the pine grove and over the boulders and runoffs and down the wooded incline to the edge of the marsh, to where he'd left the shotgun.

The shotgun wouldn't be there. It would be in the marsh where Bechetti must have surely thrown it. Maybe not but most likely.

Mitch craned up and saw Bechetti was now pulling free from the last of the brambles, would be coming on. Mitch was quickly up and out of the depression and into a sprint. Down the clearing in the direction of the river. When he reached where the clearing made a transition to woodland he glanced back at Bechetti and saw he'd gained considerable distance.

Bechetti was limited to less than a full-out run but more than a jog. Because of the wolf trap, the clamp its teeth had on the machine pistol and his trigger finger. He was using his left hand to hold and steady his right, pistol, trap and all. Otherwise it felt as though his finger was being ripped off. His having to do that prevented his arms from moving normally in opposing sync. Then, too, there was the trap's anchor chain. Its heavy four-foot length dangled and kept hitting his crotch.

Still, he pressed on, found a path through the woods that made the going easier. All the way to the granite bluff overlooking the Hudson. He hadn't expected a river, didn't know what river it was. He went close as he dared to the edge of the bluff and peered down. It was like looking from the roof of a thirty-story building.

He disliked heights, avoided them. They always caused his insides, from his balls to his throat, to cringe and go hollow, as though giving him a taste of what it would feel like to be falling a long fall.

After that one look down he backed off from the edge, kept well clear of it as he proceeded along the hard granite shoulder of the bluff. Looking for the guy. Where was he? He couldn't have gone any further unless he could fly, Bechetti thought. He wouldn't put anything past this tricky fuck.

Actually, Mitch *had* gone over the edge. He was now crouched on a narrow mantel-like formation that jutted out just below the bluff's rounded shoulder. He was able to estimate Bechetti's whereabouts by listening to the sound of his steps on the granite surface, the clips and grates being caused by the leather soles and heels of Bechetti's shoes. Shoes surely not meant for such terrain, suffering it. To make matters even worse, or for Mitch, better, Bechetti had metal insets in the heels to save sidewalk wear, an old-mob thing.

Bechetti's footsteps receded. He had gone further on along the bluff. He'd be able to go only so far before coming to a vertical sheer rise of granite, like an insurmountable wall. He'd have to return.

Mitch waited, listened for him. What he heard was distant gunfire. The distinct sharp cracks of pistol shots being fired in rapid succession. Coming from the direction of the house, which also meant the equipment barn. The shots ceased but after ten seconds or so resumed, about a dozen shots again rapidly fired.

Mitch thought the worse, just as he had when he'd heard similar shots from there the day before. Now, however, they certainly wouldn't be Maddie target-practicing. They could only mean . . .

Bechetti was coming back along the bluff. His footsteps on the uneven granite surface became more and more distinct.

To hell with taking a peek, Mitch decided. He loomed up suddenly, leaped up over the rounded edge of the bluff and charged at Bechetti.

Bechetti was turned away. Mitch went at him bull-like, head down, and, before Bechetti had a chance to react, rammed into the small of his back.

Bechetti went front down hard upon the hard granite. Momentum carried Mitch down with him. Bechetti recovered quickly, managed to stand.

The machine pistol was firing skyward, as though it could do so at will. Bechetti brought its muzzle down to Mitch's level.

The burst of 9mm bullets and Mitch were headed in convergent directions as Mitch again charged Bechetti, bulled past the extended machine pistol and into Bechetti's midsection.

Bechetti was driven back but managed to keep his feet.

Mitch held on, kept close in, clutched Bechetti with his left fist while his right delivered three hard blows below Bechetti's rib cage.

The machine pistol quit, its magazine spent. Bechetti used it and the trap as a club. They slammed down between Mitch's shoulder and neck. Twice more.

Mitch hung on, kept the struggle in close. He made a defensive grab for the pistol, didn't get it. However, the trap's dangling anchor chain was whipping about and his hands found it. Before its links could run through his grasp he got a grip on it.

Now he backed off. He pulled on the four-foot-long chain and heard and saw the pain that caused Bechetti. The chain was like a tether connected to the trap and its teeth that were connected to the pistol and Bechetti's deeply incised finger.

Mitch yanked the chain sharply.

Bechetti cried out in pain and, needing slack for relief, came with it.

Mitch yanked the chain again spitefully and then, not allowing slack, he began circling Bechetti.

Bechetti circled with him, alternately pleading for mercy and calling Mitch a *stronzolo*, which Mitch didn't know meant *piece of shit*.

Mitch circled faster.

Bechetti was being whirled, round and round. He wanted to let go, would have, but the trap had his trigger finger.

The fibrous ligaments and connective membranes of that finger were nearly severed. It was a wonder they'd held together until now, couldn't any longer. The lacerated soft tissue also gave way.

The finger tore off, second knuckle to tip.

With it came the pistol and the trap.

For Bechetti it was like being thrown from a speeding carousel. The sudden release from the centrifugal force sent him reeling across the width of the bluff. He tried for balance, fought the momentum, and he might have been able to stop himself had he been wearing appropriate shoes rather than the typical have-around city sort with leather soles and heels that slipped on the granite and couldn't for the life of him put on the brakes.

He was reaching wildly, as though the air might offer him anything to grab on to, when he hurtled over the edge.

Chapter 34

Riccio felt the bathwater. It was on the hot side. She couldn't be long out of it. The tile floor was wet where she'd dripped.

The smell in the bathroom made him not want to breathe. It brought to mind embalmed guys laid out and surrounded like they always were with lilies. A couple of months ago up in the Bronx he'd paid respects to an old, onetime capo, and, although he'd only stayed a polite half hour, he'd come away so stunk up by lilies he'd had to hang his best black suit out to air.

This place was worse than four funerals. So bad it had his eyes watering. He pinched his nose shut and jerked open the door that was at one end of the bathroom. She wasn't in there. Just a toilet bowl with blue water, and a bidet. Only rich people have such special little rooms where they piss and shoot water up their cunts, Riccio thought.

He and Fratino went on with their search of the house. They were sure she was hiding somewhere in it. Probably, because she was blind, it would be an obvious place such as beneath one of the beds or in the back corner of a closet, wishing she was invisible.

Riccio had Fratino believing there'd be something extra in it for him if they found her and got what they wanted out of her. Intentional emphasis on the word *extra* so Fratino would take it to imply it meant one of the twenty-five extra large the two emeralds would bring. Riccio had said all along and too often that to him this thing was first and foremost a matter of saving face. If the emeralds came it would just be a nice plus, he didn't expect them, they probably wouldn't come but if they did it would be as he put it, *nice*.

The have-arounds knew Riccio well enough to see through that old-mob shit. The emeralds were what Riccio had first in his head. Not to say that doing the guy and his wife wasn't also there.

The wife, the rich wife, she'd know where the emeralds were, Riccio reasoned. Mitch wouldn't have kept that from her. Civilians usually made the mistake of letting their women in on such things. She'd know, and when Fratino had her bound and bent over and greased and it became evident what he intended to do to her she'd give them up.

Her give-up, however, wouldn't make a difference to Fratino. He'd keep on with it, and there'd be no reason for Riccio to stop him. Fratino had never had his way with a blind man or woman, someone unable to see how repulsive he was. He'd remarked to Riccio that just the idea of it caused him to have half a hard-on.

They gave the house a thorough going over from cellar to roof. For Riccio, not finding her was an insult. He couldn't accept it. About twice a minute he grunted like he was being poked with a stick.

He went from room to room looking for things to take that might appease his disappointment. Nothing he saw was going to make up for twenty-five extra large. What's more he didn't have the understanding or appreciation for the valuables that were there. None of the paintings. He passed up a Jackson Pollock and a Willem de Kooning and an Egon Schiele nude that he believed must have been painted by some whacko with the shakes.

Grudgingly he settled on a Georgian silver service. Placed it near the front door for one of his have-arounds to carry to the car on the way out.

Fratino uncorked a couple of bottles of vintage red. He and Riccio went out onto the second-floor rear terrace. They sat close to the rail. Riccio lighted another of his Sicilian twists. He grunted between swigs and puffs.

"Did you look on the roof?" he asked.

"Yeah."

"Maybe she's up on the roof."

"I tell you I looked."

"How could you see the roof?"

"I went outside and looked up. It's slanted."

An increase in grunts.

"This fucking place," Riccio grumbled. "How'd you like to live up here?"

"Not me, no fucking way."

"I'd go crazy up here. Think how it must be in winter."

Some shots were heard from deep in the woods off to the right.

"They're doing the guy," Fratino commented flatly, as though reading from a program.

"Be perfect if we could only find the fucking wife. Wrap this thing up. I got to be back in town by seven, no later than eight."

"What can I say?"

"Nothing. Keep quiet," Riccio snapped. His bad cigar was spoiling the taste of Straw's good wine, not that he realized that.

His attention was drawn to a mid-air skirmish almost directly above the terrace. A pair of starlings trying to peck and outmaneuver one another like enemy aces. The two birds were really going at it and neither seemed to be getting the best of it until one took flight out to a field beyond where the grounds were kept.

Distance transformed the bird into a black, indefinite creature that dropped from sight out there in the tall, untended grass.

Riccio, with nothing better to distract his aggravated mind, had followed the bird's retreat. In doing so he happened to notice that the uniform texture of that grass was interrupted by a contrasting line that ran straight all the way to a large white structure. It was worth a look, he decided. He and Fratino went down and out to the unmowed meadow.

It was obvious to them that someone had recently cut through the grass, and they had no difficulty following the same trampled course. To the large double doors of the barn. Fratino slid those apart and they went in.

Riccio knew in a breath she was in there. The predominant old barn odor of the interior was laced with the scent of lilies. Now, exactly where in here was she?

He looked around, then walked around clockwise. An insouciant, old-mob smugness about him as he took in the disparate contents of the place: cardboard boxes of canning jars, storm windows, a stack of mildewed and rusted steamer trunks, various pieces of unfortunate furniture, a dresser minus two drawers, chairs without seats.

He paused every few steps to sniff and gauge the strength of the giveaway scent. At the far end of the barn stood the stove, the potbelly that Maddie and Mitch had pocked up with shots from the Beretta. The scent was not entirely undetectable there but much fainter.

He moved on, down the barn's other long side. Past a pileup of tubular outdoor loungers and numerous sections of cast iron grillwork.

The lily scent was more pronounced.

And even more so when he came to the lineup of forsaken farm equipment. Two tractors, a backhoe with all tires flat, a rake and a hay baler.

Only the hay baler offered a hiding place.

Riccio centered his attention upon it. He raised his chin a fraction to indicate it and gestured to have Fratino come over to him. Riccio was positive that she was hidden in the baler. He savored the moment, relighted his cigar, chewed it from the left corner of his mouth to the right. He rotated his pavéd diamond, ruby and emerald Italian flag ring.

The pressing chamber, the oblong, lidded compartment where the hay was compressed and bound, was just barely large enough to contain Maddie. She was doubled up tight and hunched in a kneel and, for the first time in her life, experiencing claustrophobia. She felt crammed, crunched, as though her flesh and bones were now literally the shape of a bale of hay. And what a relief it would be when, if ever again, she was able to take a deep breath.

Her heart was galloping, the roof of her mouth had gone dry. She had the Beretta in her right hand. Off safety.

Riccio was about to order Fratino to open the lid on the baling compartment and pull her out. No need to be concerned about her being armed. She was blind. At most she'd put up a clawing, kicking struggle.

The lid flew open.

Maddie sprung up like a released jack-in-the-box and began firing the Beretta. She relied entirely on her sense of direction, altering her point of aim slightly every couple of rounds. She fired the clip empty, released it, rammed in a full and rapid-fired another fifteen rounds in the same hopeful left to right manner.

The smell of lilies and gunpowder and Sicilian cigar.

It had been over for fifteen minutes by the time Mitch got there.

Riccio and Fratino were down, sprawled in surely dead positions. Blood was pooling beneath and around their heads. There was an entrance wound in each of their temples. Neat little holes in almost precisely the same spot.

A shaft of sunlight permitted through the barn's old roof was striking upon Riccio's hand, causing scintillations from his Italian flag ring.

Maddie was seated off to the side on the edge of a rusted-out cast iron love seat. She looked bedraggled. The Beretta was still in her hand.

Mitch spoke up to keep her from possibly taking a shot at him. He went to her, held her. To have her in his arms again was an unexpected pleasure. She, however, wasn't able to give entirely to the embrace. Some of her body's usual compliance had been appropriated by rigidity.

"Are you all right?" she asked.

"Yeah."

"No wounds or anything?"

"Some scrapes and scratches is all."

"Tell me, if I could what would I be seeing?"

He told her, but didn't elaborate. It was evident to him that she wasn't too happy with herself at the moment.

She did an on and off small smile, trying to demonstrate her pluck.

"Let's go in," she said. "Maybe a little later on I'll feel up to fixing you something special for supper."

Chapter 35

The bodies of five mob guys.

What to do with them had Mitch sitting in the dark on the side of the bed. Waiting for daylight as though it might bring the answer.

Five dead mob guys strewn all over Strawbridge land. What a feeding frenzy the police and the media would have with that, Mitch thought. He could hear himself attempting to explain it: "There were these two emeralds, see . . . "

A mass grave was the most expedient solution he'd been able to come up with. He'd get that forsaken, old backhoe running somehow, fix its flats and all and use it to dig a hole so deep that hungry dogs would walk right past it. Somewhere remote on the land, in the woods maybe where the disturbed ground would cover over quickly with leaves and brush.

It would take a lot of doing, at least all day.

It would also mar the pleasure of this land for him. He'd never be able to see it the same, knowing its grisly, buried secret.

He dressed, went down, microwaved a mug of yesterday's coffee and at first light, went out to the West Meadow. Along the way he reminded himself that he knew nothing about operating a backhoe. He also wondered by what means he'd be able to extract Fat Angelo from the muck of the marsh. That would take a goddamn derrick.

When he arrived at the equipment barn he didn't believe what he saw, or, rather, he disbelieved what he didn't see.

The bodies of Riccio and Fratino weren't there.

Coagulated blood but no bodies.

Was it possible that his wishful thinking was so intense that he'd manufactured an illusion? Had something supernatural occurred? When he'd last seen Riccio and Fratino they'd been dead as dead could be dead and he didn't believe in resurrections, anyway certainly not when it came to mob guys.

No bodies in the barn.

Nor was the body of Little Mike or the carcass of the cow out in the pasture.

Nor was the corpse of Fat Angelo mired in the marsh.

Mitch hurried to the bluff. At the base of it not a sign of Bechetti, who'd plunged the equivalent of thirty stories.

There was, however, a clue on the exterior ramp of the Strawbridge boathouse. Along the length of it, soaked into its dry, weathered wood were numerous streaks of blood. As would be caused by bleeding bodies being dragged.

Within the boathouse Mitch noticed the boat with the outboard motor was tied up in its slip bow first. It had previously been tied up bow out. The motor was cold. Blood had been wiped from the gunwales, seats and floorboards. Dried, remnant smears of it were visible to a close look.

Mitch gazed down the wide Hudson. Like many major rivers, especially in summer, its placid appearance belied its swiftness and currents. The water he was now looking at would be flowing past Manhattan, including West 47th, in practically no time.

Chapter 36

It was the second day that Mitch and Maddie had been back in the city. Four o'clock in the afternoon.

Since early yesterday Mitch had been putting off going to see Visconti and, now, standing on the corner of West 47th outside 580 Fifth he was still procrastinating.

It seemed to Mitch that Visconti was the final person he'd have to contend with regarding this Iranian emerald matter. He'd expressed to Maddie that it was about seventy-five percent his opinion that he shouldn't wait for Visconti to make a move but face up to him with the truth and hope he believed it. Visconti was new mob, Visconti was not as irrational as Riccio had been, Visconti had enough understanding of the abstract to accept unapparent circumstances. Thus were the sort of persuasions Mitch had been offering his judgment. His better judgment insisted on having its say, to remind him that new-mob Visconti and his type of have-arounds were far more efficiently lethal.

Maddie convinced Mitch's other twenty-five percent that it would be best if he took the initiative. Besides, she said, she had important things to tend to in town. Her birds were, no doubt, in need of fresh water and would stop loving her unless she provided some soon, and Casimiro Ramírez was scheduled for a lesson.

Casimiro Ramírez was a ringing name Mitch would have remembered had he heard it.

"He's an eight-year-old who wants to be a great jazz guitarist,"
Maddie had told him.

"Another prodigy."

"He plays like he has webbed fingers. If anything he should take
up cymbals."

"So why the lesson?"

"That'll *be* the lesson," she'd said.

So, now, while she was high up in the Sherry gently dashing the
dreams of Casimiro Ramírez, there was Mitch doing some last-
ditch vacillating. He thought he was thirsty enough to have an iced
tea somewhere; he thought he'd go to Barnes & Noble and see what
new books on tape they had in for Maddie; he thought he'd stroll
down five blocks, like it was some other day, and sit on the New
York Public Library steps.

Not because he was intimidated to the point of weak-knee by
Visconti. He'd just undergone such an ordeal with Riccio that he
felt, in all fairness, life ought to give him a breather. When had any
straight good guy such as himself had to go up against two crooked
bad guys so consecutively?

Not fair but fuck it, he decided.

He entered the 580 building and went up to Visconti's offices. In
the tastefully done reception were the same pair of youthful have-
arounds as the time before. Dressed to kill in Calvin and looking as
though they swam two hundred butterfly laps every day before
breakfast and did Shorin-Ryn Karate during lunch breaks.

They remembered Mitch by name. It was like he was expected.
His arrival was phoned in and without wait he was shown down
the narrow interior hall to Visconti's private office.

Visconti was in shirtsleeves seated at his desk. On the phone. He
raised his chin abruptly as though throwing his smile to Mitch. He
placed his hand over the mouthpiece. "Be right with you," he said
and continued with his phone conversation.

Mitch couldn't help but overhear some of it. Large sums of
money being stipulated and, cryptically, a hundred pieces of white,

two hundred of blue, which Mitch knew meant diamonds and sapphires.

The phone call in progress gave Mitch time to fit into the situation with more ease. Most of his misgivings were being chased. Coming there had definitely been the right decision.

The phone call also allowed him to appraise this day's Visconti: lively blue custom-tailored shirt with long closely separated collar points and monogrammed cuff, dyed blue ostrich skin suspenders, Hermès two-hundred-dollar silk tie. No casual shirt and canvas tennis shoes this day. For some special reason, Mitch presumed.

Finally, Visconti hung up, stood up and came from around his desk for a handshake. A firm grip with his right, four pumps instead of the usual two, while his left clasped Mitch's upper arm. "I was getting concerned about you Mitch."

"No reason to be."

"For days now whenever I happened to look across your office was dark."

"I've been out of town."

"I thought as much." Visconti squinted, examined. "Hey," he frowned, "that's a nasty scratch." Referring to the perforated-looking scratch that ran from the outer corner of Mitch's left eye to below his earlobe. He also had numerous scratches on the back of his hands. Those on him elsewhere were concealed. "Where did you get that?" Visconti asked.

Mitch evaded the inquiry with admiration for Visconti's necktie.

Visconti let him evade and for a moment Mitch thought he was about to take off the tie and give it to him. Be a shame to undo the perfect, tiny knot.

As before they sat in the visitors' chairs.

"How's your uncle-in-law?" Visconti asked.

"Better," Mitch replied, and because Wally came to mind, added: "greatly improved."

"And Maddie?"

"She's fine."

"I bought a town house," Visconti said.

"Where?"

"In the seventies. East, of course. Actually, I bought it about eight months ago and had it renovated to suit. Practically gutted the place."

Mitch thought of Ruder.

"This coming Saturday I'm having people in for the first time. Not a large crowd. Just a few special people like yourself. You'll recognize some of the faces. And some of the figures too." Visconti did a slightly salacious smirk. "Movie people."

"This Saturday."

"Hope you can make it."

"Depends on Maddie."

"She'll want to come. Anyway, come solo if it gets to that. I'm sure Maddie doesn't keep you on too short a leash."

She doesn't *keep me* at all was what Mitch wanted to say. He was becoming increasingly resentful of Maddie being called Maddie by Visconti, who had never met her, and never would if Mitch had his way. How, under the circumstances, could he turn Visconti down on this Saturday night thing?

"Along with my new town house I have a new lady friend," Visconti said. "I want to impress her with you and Maddie. She thinks my only close acquaintances are emaciated models and way overweight gem dealers. How about a drink?"

Mitch nearly automatically declined but decided he could use one. "Any scotch," he said, "straight or on the rocks, doesn't matter."

Visconti ordered the drinks through the intercom on his desk and returned to his chair. "I'm planning on showing a film Saturday night," he said, "one that hasn't yet been released. Not coincidentally I have a sizeable chunk invested in it." Visconti named a couple of stars who were the leads. "Film-making must be in my blood, the way I'm drawn to it." He directed a glance intended to direct Mitch's attention to the Luchino Visconti poster on the wall to the left.

Mitch pretended to be unaware that was expected of him.

Which irked Visconti but only slightly and he was able to smooth it over. "Something you ought to get into, financing films," he said. "That it's such high-risk is only greedy bullshit spread by those making plenty from doing it. Perhaps you and I could do a film venture together. I'd enjoy that. Wouldn't you?"

Mitch did a very small smile and a single, almost imperceptible nod, meanwhile thinking Visconti's surmise that he was so financially well off came from the impression that he could dip into the Strawbridge money pot anytime for any amount. Or else . . .

He got Visconti eyes to eyes and got to the point. "I don't have those Iranian emeralds."

"Of course you do."

"No."

"Perhaps what you mean is you no longer have them."

"I've never had them."

"You either still have them or you've already cashed them in."

"Neither."

Visconti didn't appear upset; however Mitch couldn't trust that.

"You made a nice score. Why deny it?"

Visconti will turn any moment, Mitch predicted.

"Is it because you think it's so fucking important to me, that I'll press you for a piece of your score, or even all of it?"

Don't say, Mitch thought.

"You insult me, Mitch. That was Riccio, not me."

Mitch noted the past tense.

"Think I got no feelings, I don't mean sympathy, I mean feelings, for what a guy with such a rich wife has to put up with, the constant stretch it is for him to keep his *cogliones?*"

When Mitch didn't comment, Visconti did a little conceding shrug and went on. "Sure, twenty-five extra large isn't chicken fat by anybody's count, and if this particular twenty-five had come my way I would have gladly stuffed it away down in the Caymans or put it out to the street. But the way it went down it didn't come to me, it found you, and I'm not going to begrudge you a dime of it. *Capish?*"

Mitch didn't *capish.* There had to be a catch. Say yeah, he told himself. "Yeah."

"That didn't sound like thanks," Visconti said coolly.

A thanks won't kill you, Mitch thought. "Thanks."

Visconti warmed up as instantly as he'd cooled. "Anyway, it's not entirely magnanimity on my part. I owe you."

"For what?"

"For clipping Riccio, what else?"

How it was that Visconti knew of Riccio's death was only momentarily a question, for just then the answer entered carrying the drinks on a silver tray. Mitch recognized him right off, despite his changed appearance, the immaculate white serving jacket, fresh white shirt and neatly executed black bow tie; despite the polished, mannerly way he acquitted himself as he underlaid the drinks with coasters before placing them just so on the marble-topped table and arranged appropriate, small linen napkins folded just so and, before making his exit, inquired just so with a *sir* if anything more was wanted.

Caselli.

Riccio's oversize, old-mob sort of have-around, the one who according to what Fat Angelo related to Mitch, had not gone along on the Kinderhook move ostensibly because he had the shits and pukes. Caselli wasn't Riccio's have-around but Visconti's on the inside. He knew when the move was made and how it turned out.

As though drinking to that, Visconti gestured with his glass. It was superb scotch. The best Mitch had ever tasted. It went down his throat like molten gold. His belly was a crucible.

"We all know what Riccio was," Visconti said, "a crude, outdated psychopath."

As opposed to a slick, contemporary one, Mitch thought.

"Not only me but the whole street owes you for doing him."

What would be Visconti's reaction, Mitch wondered, if he told him that actually his blind wife had done Riccio. "You could have taken Riccio out whenever you wanted," Mitch said.

"So it might seem to a civilian such as yourself. Sure, Riccio could have suffered what would appear to be a fatal accident. That was always in the back of my mind and frequently in the front. I could have arranged it."

"Why didn't you?"

"Such things have a way of getting fucked up. No matter how far I was removed from it I'd ultimately have to answer and then it would get complicated."

"Like how?"

"The guy who did it for me would have to be done, then the guy who did the guy who did it would have to be done. A lot of words get piled up inside people and eventually come spilling out."

A percipient shrug by Mitch.

"A hooked-up guy like Riccio never gets clipped without permission," Visconti recited as though he'd memorized it from a rule book. He paragraphically downed a gulp of scotch and, when the afterscringe of his face subsided, went on:

"Consider," he said, "how much it pissed me to have to share the street with that thieving piece of shit, the humiliation of having to sit here and accept that he was entitled to half."

Mitch did some empathy. Behind it he wondered if there would be any payback forthcoming for his having been responsible for Riccio's death. He asked Visconti.

"No," Visconti assured, "you've got no worries. The people Riccio was answering to know what went down. The way they see it he got whacked in the line of duty. Matter of fact, I'll be with them later today. They're going to take down the no-trespassing sign, if you know what I mean."

Mitch understood. Those people who got answered to were going to decree that all of West 47 from Fifth Avenue to Avenue of the Americas, as well as the spillovers that comprised the district, would henceforth be the franchise of Visconti. His alone.

"The sit will be only a little sit, a formality," Visconti said. "Already some of my crew are over at Riccio's place with an industrial vacuum. What's your guess how much goods they suck up out of Riccio's wall-to-wall shag carpet?"

"Maybe a million worth."

"I say five, at least five. According to Caselli, who witnessed a great many drops and scatters, there's even a first-quality six-carat Burma ruby lost somewhere in that jungle." Visconti chuckled, shook his head. "What an asshole Riccio was. Be a pleasure to forget him."

"Yeah."

"Understand now why I owe you? Why I'm not going to press you for even a cut of that Iranian twenty-five extra large?"

Mitch's pager beeped. Maddie wanted to be called.

"Use my phone," Visconti offered.

Mitch went to Visconti's desk and dialed home. Maddie picked up on the first ring. She sounded hurried.

"Where are you?" she asked.

Mitch told her.

"How's it going?"

"Okay."

"We're not to have another gang war?"

"Evidently."

"Make any excuse and get your ass out of there."

"I was just winding things up."

"We'll pick you up. We're leaving this minute. Be down in front."

"Ask her about Saturday night," Visconti suggested. However she'd already clicked off.

It was at that moment, while still standing close by Visconti's desk, that Mitch noticed it. Lopped over the gold and ebony pen of Visconti's DuPont desk set.

Pavéd rubies, diamonds, emeralds.

Riccio's one-of-a-kind Italian flag ring.

Mitch had last seen it in the equipment barn on dead Riccio's finger. Seeing it here now triggered off a series of realities for Mitch. What had actually occurred three days ago up in Kinderhook.

Starting with the informer, Caselli. He had let Visconti know in advance what Riccio intended to do and when.

Visconti recognized the opportunity.

He dispatched some of his crew.

They followed along, hung back, kept from sight while they observed every move made by Riccio and his have-arounds. They got their chance when Riccio and Fratino went out to the equipment barn in search of Maddie.

It wasn't Maddie who shot Riccio and Fratino. She thought she had. It seemed she had.

Those precisely placed head shots were the work of Visconti's shooters. Fired simultaneously with Maddie's rapid barrage so they hadn't been distinguished.

How accommodating for Visconti. Slick, the way he'd used the circumstances, used Mitch and Maddie.

Then, there was the overnight cleanup.

Visconti's have-arounds had seen to that, gathered up all five bodies and given them to the river. It was essential that the bodies not be found because of the kind of bodies they were. Too much would have been made of it. By all means avoid that. The people who got answered to wouldn't have wanted that.

Mitch was tempted to let Visconti know he wasn't so clever by telling him how clever he was. He could color that single remark with slight implication, not elaborate on it, just let it hang while his eyes said it all.

Visconti would then suspect that Mitch had undone the twist. It would worry Visconti, build up in him. The satisfaction would be short-lived but the apprehension would persist, Mitch warned himself. It wasn't worth it.

Visconti put on his suit jacket, made sure of his tie, shot his cuffs.

Mitch assumed he was getting ready to depart for the sit. He should hurry his own departure or Visconti would be going down with him. Maddie would be waiting at the curb in the Lexus. It would be difficult to avoid an introduction. Saturday night would be mentioned and Maddie, aware of what Visconti was, would likely accept.

Deliverance. A phone call for Visconti. Important business that required his immediate attention. He got right into it, entirely into it. He was finished with Mitch, merely bade him goodbye with a perfunctory gesture.

Out on Fifth Mitch found Maddie and the Lexus weren't waiting as he'd expected. At that hour both the avenue and its sidewalks

were all rush and clog. Maddie was probably up the avenue somewhere caught in it. Mitch disregarded the New York exasperations
he caused as he cut across the pedestrian flow to reach the curb.

While waiting there, protected against jostle by a perilously piled
city waste receptacle, he thought how fortunate it was that he'd
spotted Riccio's ring. Otherwise he might have remained fooled
forever. Anyway, he'd come out ahead. There'd be no violent con-
frontation with Visconti. That was the main thing. And it would
hardly hurt to have people thinking he was now batting twenty-
five extra large in the independent league.

Mitch was right about the Kinderhook episode. Except for one
thing.

Riccio's body hadn't been sent downstream with the others.
Rather, it had been dumped into the trunk of one of the black Lincoln Town Cars and transported to the Scalise Funeral Home on
188th Street in the Bronx.

Even before the body arrived at Scalise's the death certificate had
been filled out and officially signed. The stated cause of death was
cerebral hemorrhage. Sort of true.

And right away a couple of guys showed up on behalf of the
people who got answered to. They checked out the hole in Riccio's
head, stuck their little fingers into it, heard how it had gotten there
and concluded that yes, Riccio had brought it on himself.

Within an hour Riccio was embalmed. The hole in his head was
plugged with putty and cosmetically concealed, and he was in other
ways made to look better than he had alive.

Visconti's generosity was admired. He insisted on choosing and
paying for the casket. It was bronze but not waterproof.

This very night for respects Riccio would be on display from the
waist up.

Surrounded by several hundred white lilies.

Chapter 37

They were in the Holland Tunnel. Possibly halfway through. Perseverant white tiles machine-gunning by. Light after light after light and the dirty ass end of an eighteen-wheel monster directly ahead.

"We're in the tunnel," Maddie said.

"Yeah," Mitch told her, noticing that her fingers were laced, and she couldn't keep from biting the left side of her lower lip. Since her confinement in the hay baler she'd been susceptible to the *clausties,* as she called them.

Fucking tunnel was enough to undo anyone, Mitch thought. He himself was being made to feel uneasy. He couldn't put out of mind that there was all that water of the Hudson above and perhaps Riccio and his have-arounds, their downstream journey delayed for some reason, were at that moment scuttling along the river bottom overhead.

"We should have taken the bridge," Maddie remarked.

"The bridge would have been out of the way, Mrs. Laughton," Billy told her. He was driving, of course. Hurley was up front with him.

"But not so oppressive," she said.

It would seem that only a sighted person could have claustrophobia, Mitch thought. He chalked it up to Maddie's so-called *spatial reckoning,* her sense of where things were, close or far and all that. "Want to get into my hug?" he offered.

"No, I'm okay," she said with a modicum of courage. "How far to go?"

"Pretend you're elsewhere."

"For instance where?"

"Anywhere you like."

"Help me."

"How about somewhere in France?"

"Be more specific."

Several possibilities trekked across his imagination. The one he chose was where he might also like to be, from what he'd read and photographs he'd seen. "On the soft, grassy bank of a canal in Chantilly, north of Paris," he said as though it was a title.

"It's a sunny day," Maddie contributed.

"We're being dappled."

"There are dragonflies."

"Iridescent."

"I've my feet in the water. So do you. Is there anyone else around?"

"Just us."

"You're sure no one is peeking through the bushes."

"No one within a mile."

"So we could be wicked if we wanted."

"Or we could take a nap."

"After being wicked," Maddie preferred.

Hurley laughed. He'd been occasionally privy and amused before by their fanciful exchanges. At times, without their knowing it, he made their flights with them. Almost to the point of getting a hard-on.

Finally, no more tunnel. Billy paid the toll and got onto the New Jersey Turnpike Extension. It was the same route they'd taken the time before, past Newark Airport on 78.

By then Maddie was entirely recovered. Her mood bright and swollen with anticipation. "A little more foot, Billy," she said.

"I'm doing eighty-five Mrs. Laughton."

"Feels like we're snailing. Give it another ten."

"They're your tickets," was Billy's proviso.

"Hurley will fix them," Maddie promised.

"Which reminds me," Hurley said. "While you were away I got greased with box seats at the Stadium. It was a great game, went twelve innings and ended with a bases-loaded strikeout."

Mitch knew of the invitation. It had been one of the messages on the answering machine. He hadn't told Hurley about what had ensued up in Kinderhook. He might someday but for now he was trying to forget it. And as for revealing things, tonight he'd let Maddie know she hadn't killed Riccio and Fratino. Lift that load from her. She hadn't admitted being affected by it but Mitch was sure she was. No matter that they were bad guys and it had been self-defense. As for his own killings, he'd have to live with the change they'd made in him. A facet hardened.

"Dragonflies," Maddie whispered sibilantly, extending it to nearly a whistle.

She was still on that, Mitch thought. He took her in. She had on a white cotton waffle-knit sweatshirt with HARLEY-DAVIDSON lettered large in black on the right sleeve from cuff to shoulder. A very short white wraparound skirt and white suede sandals. He surmised that she'd put on her makeup hurriedly. Her left brow didn't quite match her right and her lipstick had created a slightly lopsided mouth. But beautiful, oh so beautiful, Mitch thought.

After a few silent miles he asked: "You say it just came to you out of the blue?"

"Black," she corrected. "I was at the kitchen table sorting through beans for a cassoulet. You know, culling out the dry, hard ones, when it was suddenly very obvious."

"An angel whispered in your ear."

"Don't poke fun at me."

"I wasn't. I'm serious."

"You don't put credence in anything supernatural and you know it."

"Don't be so sure." He leaned over and blew a tiny dark hair from high on her cheek. No doubt from one of her fluffy sable makeup brushes.

"Anyway," she said, "it occurred to me that the reason no one has been able to come up with those pair of stolen Iranian emeralds was simply because they were never stolen. Had you ever thought that?"

"No," Mitch fibbed to allow her glory.

"Neither had Hurley," she said. "Isn't that right, Hurley?"

"Right," Hurley also fibbed.

"So," she said, "I immediately stopped fucking with the beans and went into the den to dwell on it, and then I was lying on the floor with my feet elevated, gathering my senses, I mean literally bringing them all together and latching them on to my memory and letting my memory tell me what it knew."

"And it came to you out of the black."

"Did it ever! Exactly where those emeralds have been, were, still are."

An indulgent self-exonerating shrug from Hurley. "I just happened to phone at that moment," he explained to Mitch. "Maddie told me about it and I invited myself along. I figured at the very least we could have dinner, maybe at some fish place, on the way back."

Billy raised his eyes a fraction to have Mitch in the rearview mirror. Mitch assumed by now Billy was used to such far-fetches. "You're serious," Mitch said to Maddie.

"Never been more so."

"You're claiming you know where the emeralds are?"

"Sure."

"Well, where are they?"

"I'm not telling."

"Why not?"

"In case they're not there," she said straight-faced.

Billy asked the Lexus for another five and put it on cruise control.

They arrived at the Kalali house in Far Hills shortly before sundown. No police tape now. The house was no longer designated a crime scene. The electronic gate to the drive was closed. It couldn't be opened manually.

Billy drove around the area and located the road that ran parallel with the rear wall of the Kalali grounds. At about the same spot where the swifts and Peaches had gone over, Billy angled the car off the road and brought it close up to the wall.

By standing on the hood the top of the wall was easily within reach. Maddie, short skirt no matter, was first to climb up and over. Mitch and Hurley followed. Billy would wait.

They paused for a moment to get their bearings. It wasn't yet dark. Dusk had another half hour or so. The large, white, contemporary house was clearly visible a hundred yards from there.

A light went on in one of the rooms of its north wing. And another. Was someone inside? Certainly not Mrs. Kalali. She was still unconscious in the hospital. Hurley had been checking on her condition daily.

"Some of the interior lights are probably on automatic timers," Hurley said. That seemed plausible.

They headed for the house.

"I know," Mitch remarked facetiously, "the emeralds are buried somewhere out here in a mayonnaise jar."

Maddie didn't let that faze her. "You just wait and see," she told him smugly.

The landscaped area of the rear grounds had been neglected and so had the swimming pool. The water in the pool appeared somewhat gelatinous and well on its way to a chartreuse shade. The sight of it pulled a grunt out of Mitch. "I sure as hell hope they're not in the pool," he said.

They went to the door that led in from the garage. It was locked but Hurley quickly picked it open. The alarm pad mounted on the interior wall indicated that the security system wasn't on.

Mitch and Hurley stood aside in the kitchen while Maddie opened and felt around in drawers and cupboards, the microwave and the dishwasher. From what she'd said, from her certainty, they'd expected she would go directly to where she believed the emeralds might be. But now here she was, evidently searching for them. It verified their skepticism; however they wouldn't be inconsiderate, remained silent and let her go at it.

From the kitchen to the living room, the reception hall, the library. Maddie appeared to be at a loss.

Actually, she knew exactly what she was doing. Toying with them and, as well, putting off the chance that she was wrong; that she in her black had gotten carried away and this undertaking would prove to be nothing more than an intuitive error.

She, for her own reasons, needed that not to be so. If she was right about the emeralds it would be a confirmation of her sentiency, a measure of how real and reliable it was. Or, were those extra-ordinary senses only what she believed she had, and it was the strength of her belief that helped her expand, stretch the limits of her functioning? A mere illusory aid; could that be all there was to it?

The library.

It had been left much the same since the night of the robbery. The shards of ancient Persian glass, large and small, had been swept into a pile so they wouldn't be constantly underfoot; however that considerable pile remained in the middle of the slick maplewood floor. The two cushions stained by Mr. Kalali's blood were missing from the white couch, taken for evidence. The long, floor-to-ceiling bookshelves were yet vacant, their hundreds of volumes still where they'd been tumbled in an ugly heap, looking seriously injured.

Maddie moved about the library in the same rather aimless manner. She ended up seated at the baby grand piano. She performed a glissando, slid two fingers along the entire length of the keyboard from left to right, low A to high C. And another upscale on all fifty-two of the white keys, this time ending with several playful plinks of the top-most key.

Mitch and Hurley thought she was playfully giving up, using the piano to convey that her notion regarding the whereabouts of the emeralds was no longer to be taken seriously. Surely that was the case when she insistently plinked that highest key and then worked into a sprightly, Erroll Garner–like version of "I Only Have Eyes for You."

Mitch and Hurley were across the spacious room discussing where on the way home they might have dinner.

Maddie stopped playing and concentrated her attention on the key to the far right. She tried to wiggle it. No wiggle. She depressed it and applied downward pressure. No give. She told herself not to be so careful with it. She placed her knuckle under the small protrusion on the forward edge of the key and pried upward. It seemed to yield slightly but so slightly that it could have been her imagination.

She gave the key a sharp upward snap.

That did it.

The entire key seemed to come up and out. But then, it wasn't the entire key, only the exterior ivory facing of it.

When Maddie had previously played this piano her sense of touch had noticed, upon striking that upper key, that it was slow in coming back up into position. It also felt a fraction heavier than the other keys. All in all it seemed in need of some sort of repair. Perhaps there was something wrong with its balance rail, jack spring or whatever.

She'd thought no more than that about it until today when she'd mobilized her senses and dwelled upon where the emeralds might be. Unstolen in the Kalali house, but precisely where?

Her black had chosen to present her with the possibility of the piano and then, like a camera moving in for a close-up to make a point, it had suggested that particular piano key.

The ordinary reasoning that followed provided support. That highest key was the one least likely to be worn or damaged. Because it was the one played the least. At its best it contributed an almost inaudible note. Rarely was it included in compositions for that reason. Shostakovich, for example, had done so only out of caprice.

Now, having removed the ivory covering from the key, Maddie explored what she had exposed. The wood body of the key, which should have been solid, was partially routed out to create a rectangular recess. Within the recess, snugly cushioned by cotton so it would not rattle and in that way be detected, was a small ivory case.

Maddie plucked the case from its hiding place. It measured about two inches by an inch, a half-inch deep. Delicate hinges. Its lid sprang open with slight pressure.

She ran a finger over its contents. A pair of gems nestled in silk velour. She felt their inscriptions.

No doubt about it.

Mitch was going to be in raptures, she thought. How should she break it to him—him over there with Hurley, the two of them running low on patience, their interest on empty? It was one of those very seldom, absolutely justifiable opportunities for comeuppance. It called for a double dose of the good, old superior female what-for.

Instead, for a show of class, she said nothing, walked over to Mitch with her hand extended, the little ivory case on the flat of her upturned palm.

"What's this?" Mitch asked, hoping, of course, what it might be.

"It's some little something, I suppose," she understated. She wished she could see his happiness.

He opened the case.

Even in the waning light the pair of emeralds gave off a rich, green glow. Mitch switched on the overhead lights and held the open case directly beneath a downward beam.

It was as though the emeralds had been dozing and now, suddenly awakened, were demonstrating how bright and lively they were. In fact, it seemed to him that every stone he'd ever touched had been sullied at some time in one way or another. But this emerald . . .

He held it up to the light, brought it to his eye. Paradise, he thought. Had that blind Persian poet really been God-sent twenty-twenty?

At that moment Mitch tended to be a believer. Possibly the prospect of twenty-five extra large had some influence.

He returned the emerald to the case.

"May I?" Hurley asked, wanting to see. His interest seemed natural.

Mitch handed him the open case.

Hurley took a good long look at the emeralds, called upon his many years of experience on West 47th to determine whether or not they were genuine. No need to sacrifice a friend over a couple of fakes, he reasoned.

He closed the case.

He dropped it into his jacket pocket and in practically the same motion drew his pistol from his hip holster.

Everything that had been going Mitch's way stopped. "You're kidding," he said.

Hurley's eyes were cold now. They spoke for him, as did the pistol when he raised it to Mitch's heart level.

Mitch didn't think Hurley would go so far as to shoot him; however like anyone under gunpoint he couldn't be entirely sure of that. "The Iranian got to you too," Mitch said.

"Why not? He had half the street scuffling around for his big numbers."

"What's happening?" Maddie wanted to know.

"I suppose it never occurred to you that I was in the race," Hurley said.

"Never," Mitch said bitterly. "You were my helper. Remember?"

"Will someone for Christ's sake tell me what's going on," Maddie demanded.

Mitch told her how Hurley had a gun on them and the emeralds in his pocket.

"That stinks, Hurley," she said. "That really stinks."

"What doesn't?" was his attitude.

"Mitch, tell him to fuck off," Maddie said, "tell him he can have the emeralds. We don't need the money, right?"

Mitch was trying to decide which of the many voices in him he should heed. He managed to do some nonchalance. "You know, Hurley, this is a chance for you to come out way ahead."

Hurley agreed.

"What I mean is this is a chance for you to do the decent thing."

"Which would be?"

"We split the Iranian's number and forget about now. You come to my place on the Vineyard when the weather's right; I learn to ride down in Maryland."

Rather than quickly reject that idea Hurley did a considering face. "I turned such an arrangement over a few times along the way," he said. "As a matter of fact during the drive over here today I told myself if it came to it be decent, but now . . . " He patted his jacket pocket. " . . . I'm all out of decency."

"You're tiresome," Maddie said. "I don't know why I haven't realized until now how dreadfully tiresome you are. I should have seen right through you. Go away." She dismissed Hurley and the emeralds with a flaccid, backhanded gesture.

Mitch, at that moment, was looking beyond Hurley, taking care not to fix his attention there and give away . . .

. . . Billy.

Hurley was unaware that Billy was noiselessly approaching from behind, the .357 Magnum revolver in hand.

Reliable, loyal Billy, Mitch thought. Billy was going to save everything. He took back every criticism or disapproval of Billy he'd ever expressed or kept to himself. Billy was a gem, a devoted, single-hearted, first-class, stand-up guy. Billy was going to poke the muzzle of the .357 into Hurley's back and order Hurley to drop his pistol and that would be that, Mitch thought. Billy was now close enough.

He brought the revolver down upon Hurley's head. A vicious, cracking blow.

Hurley dropped, was that suddenly transformed into an unconscious heap.

Dead cop, Mitch thought. Nothing would explain a dead cop. Billy shouldn't have hit him, certainly not so hard. Mitch stepped forward to see to Hurley.

Billy pointed the revolver at Mitch and gave notice with a threatful thrust. "Back off," he snarled.

Mitch obeyed. Was there anyone in this world the Iranian hadn't propositioned? It was hard to imagine Billy with twenty-five million. What a waste.

"Now what's going on?" Maddie asked.

"Just stay where you are Mrs. Laughton," Billy told her.

"Why should I? What's gotten into you, Billy?"

Mitch told her.

She did a loud, intolerant sigh. "Let's just leave," she told Mitch.

Billy leaned over the unconscious Hurley, who was sprawled front down. Hurley's suit jacket was twisted beneath him, so it wasn't a matter of Billy simply reaching down into Hurley's pocket for the emeralds. He'd have to dig in under Hurley.

He transferred the revolver to his left hand and worked his right beneath Hurley's deadweight. He felt for the pocket, squeezed into it and got the case containing the emeralds.

He was so intent on that he relaxed his grip and his point of the revolver, and much of his attention was diverted from Mitch.

Mitch noticed.

No time for thinking twice.

He charged at Billy, aimed a kick at Billy's left hand, missed the hand but caught the wrist.

The revolver was jolted free.

Billy dodged Mitch's grab, darted out of its range. Mitch stalked him. Billy evaded, skipped and paced semicircles. He had the case containing the emeralds clutched in his right hand. Had them. Now it was only a matter of getting away. Millions when he got away, Billy thought. However, Mitch stood between him and the way out. He might be able to outrun Mitch but first he had to get around him.

He feinted to the left, then bolted right.

Mitch lunged and just did get enough of Billy's lower legs to stumble him in the direction of the bookcases.

Billy went down among the books. Hundreds upon hundreds of them strewn every which way in irregular layers as many as ten deep. Slippery dust jackets, jutting spines, the sharp hard corners of covers.

He got to his feet and it seemed he'd be able to easily scramble over and out of the books; however they slid and collapsed under his first step, causing him to fall backwards.

Mitch dove on him, intending to pin and subdue him and wrest the ivory case from his hand.

Billy squirmed and bucked. Mitch raised up in order to get off a punch. Billy rolled aside. Mitch held on and rolled with him and they ended up on the fringe of the book pile with the advantage Billy's. Him on top, straddling Mitch and throwing lefts and rights.

Billy wasn't much of a puncher. Mitch fended off most of the blows.

It must have been the counterforce of Mitch's forearm blocking one of those blows that jarred the ivory case out of Billy's fist.

Mitch saw it fly out. From his low-level point of view he saw it land and skitter across the slick, bare hardwood floor. In a fraction of a second it was all the way to the piano, missing the caster of the piano's forward leg by only an inch or so.

It was like the case knew its destination and was hell-bent for it. It didn't stop until it reached the far side of the piano, where it gently collided with the heel-to-heel angle formed by the shoes, the black and white wing-tipped oxfords.

Djam, the Iranian, had also come to the conclusion that perhaps the emeralds were never part of the Kalali swag. So, for the past several days he'd been spending time here at the house, searching through it. He was giving the master bedroom another going over when he heard the arrival of Mr. and Mrs. Laughton and the others.

Now, calmly, as though experiencing an inevitability, he reached down and picked up the case. He verified its contents and then, by way of the nearby sliding glass door, he slipped out into the early darkness and away.

Getting the emeralds back hadn't cost him a penny.

Chapter 38

Ten days went by.

Mid-morning of the eleventh Mitch was at David Baumfeld's place of business on the sixth floor of one of the better-kept-up buildings of West 47th.

There to choose a diamond for Straw.

Straw had phoned from Monaco to say that he and Wally might be returning home in about a week. *Might* and *about*, told Mitch that Straw and Wally were still caught up in romantic vagabonding. He wouldn't be at all surprised if they didn't show up for another two or three weeks, maybe a month. Lucky them, Mitch thought with a smidge of envy.

Straw said they'd gone to an auction of important jewels in Geneva. He'd wanted to bid on several items for Wally but she wouldn't have it. Each time he'd raised his hand to make a bid she'd yanked it down, maintaining that they were *just looking*

Would Mitch do him the favor of locating a diamond? Straw asked. One suitable for an engagement ring. Surely Wally couldn't, wouldn't deny him that pleasure.

Mitch was happy to do it. He needed to know the particulars: what size, how much?

We can handle a little overstatement, Straw had said.

So now there was Mitch considering the four stones that lay in a shallow velour-lined tray on Baumfeld's desk. Baumfeld's assistant, a dark-haired young woman with an obvious nose job and an unfortunate overbite, had just brought them from the vault.

Baumfeld had his suit jacket on. A minor show of respect for Mitch. He was a third-generation dealer living up to the excellent reputation handed down by his father and grandfather. Shrewd but fair. Mitch had known him for going on twenty years.

The four diamonds Baumfeld had chosen to show to Mitch ranged in size from three to eight carats. He sort of tickled each in turn with his tweezers, causing them to perform glints.

"Some of the best of my inventory," he said, merely stating. "From what you said I gathered you wouldn't be interested in anything less."

Two of the stones were round cuts. They appeared to be identical. Each exactly three carats.

Mitch thought the wish that he could afford those two for Maddie. Extravagant studs. He'd come close to being able to, so close.

He put that out of mind, tweezed up and louped the largest of the lot. An emerald-cut of eight carats, ten points. "Russian goods," he thought aloud.

Baumfeld confirmed that.

Mitch had never seen a better diamond. Just as good but not better. He appreciated its make, the definite, sharp edges of its facets and girdle, its perfect proportions. Not a flaw to be found. The stone was colorless, clear as water. He sighted into it longer than he needed to. Its purity was beneficial. After what he'd been through recently, he could use a measure of purity.

He asked the price.

"Forty thousand," Baumfeld told him.

Forty thousand a carat. Which made it three hundred twenty-four thousand.

Mitch waited for that number to settle. It didn't. It stayed way up there. "Can you do better?" Mitch asked, knowing it was expected.

"Is it intended for family?"

"My wife's uncle."

"In that case . . . " Baumfeld's pupils nearly disappeared up in under his eyelids, as though he was consulting the deity of profit. " . . . I could do thirty-seven without pain."

Mitch allowed some silence for Baumfeld to possibly do thirty-five.

"Less would hurt," Baumfeld told him.

A barely perceptible nod from Mitch to acknowledge rock bottom. He pictured the lovely Wally wearing the diamond, her left hand doing aerial acrobatics for emphasis during a dinner party conversation. Eyes following the glints of the stone as though it was a prompter. Sure, she could carry it off.

"Let me give it some thought," he told Baumfeld in a tone that couldn't be construed as a turndown.

"I'll put it aside for you," Baumfeld assured.

Mitch went down and out onto West 47th. It was one of those bright days that put a sharp edge on every shadow. The street was well into its usual commerce, tourists gawking, sellers of gold chains by weight hawking from the doorways of their shops. Mitch wasn't in the mood to hurry. He went along the street, taking it in, stopping at certain windows to contemplate the goods being offered.

He believed he recognized two or three old friends. Particularly an authentic art deco period necklace comprised of various-colored sapphires. He wondered where it had been lately, and what had brought it back to this sordid temple.

He wasn't seeing the street through the same eyes. It was like something in him, his enthusiasm certainly, had been quenched. What had been colorful was now revealed as blighted. Most of the upper windows of the old buildings hadn't been opened or washed for perhaps a decade or two. Pigeon droppings caked thick on the sills and eaves. The curbs fractured, the gutters grimed. How tacky, really, the legions of diamond rings in the store windows, the way they were stuck into slotted squares of cardboard. And so falsely spotlighted.

West 47th should live up to itself, Mitch thought. Its every window should sparkle immaculately. All its edges, curbs, sills, steps and

fronts should be crisp and sharp as the most conscientiously executed facet. And clean, above all, clean rather than sleazy.

Hurley.

Mitch noticed Hurley headed west in his beat-up but souped-up
official Plymouth. He'd suffered only a concussion as a result of
Billy's blow to the head and had spent two days in the hospital on
restricted fluids and Tylenol. Now Mitch looked the other way. So
did Hurley. They might not ever speak again. Might not.

As for Billy, he'd been let go, was begging for a reference.

Mitch came to Fifth Avenue, crossed over and went up to his office. Shirley was slitting the mail open. She'd been back from Paris
for a week. New hairstyle, revised makeup, recharged with self-
worth.

"I was beginning to wonder about you," she said.

"Yeah, I'm to be wondered about," Mitch said dourly.

"You're still in a funk."

He went into his office.

Shirley shouted in to him. "It's not like quicksand, you know. You
can jump right out of it any old time."

A bearish grunt from Mitch.

Shirley came to the doorway. "No calls," she told him. "Did you
have breakfast? You don't look as though you had breakfast."

"I could use a fried egg sandwich."

"On what?"

"Rye," he growled decisively.

Before sitting at his desk he glanced out the window to Visconti's
office across the intersection. Visconti had people there. Two or
three guys. He was pacing around, ranting, gesticulating broadly.
He appeared upset. Evidently in the midst of some sort of serious
crisis. Mitch hoped so. He closed the blinds.

Today was his day for going over the books. Same as yesterday,
but he didn't blame himself for putting it off. He knew what he'd
be facing. The retainer from Columbia Beneficial would no longer
be coming in, and Northland Providential, his Philadelphia client,
had decided to cut back and given notice that his services were included in that slice. What with Shirley's salary and the rent along

with other operating expenses and his personal living costs the water of merely breaking even was practically up to his nose.

Such thoughts brought to mind that Andy and Doris had gone ahead and leased the store on upper Madison. They were commencing renovations next week. They were still urging him to come in with them.

Andy, as a favor to Mitch, was making sure Roudabeth Kalali got a fair price for her jewelry. It wouldn't go to 47th Street. At least not yet. Some of it had already been purchased by one of Andy's dealer friends in Beverly Hills. The pieces that remained would be consigned to the new Laughton store where it would be displayed and sold to best advantage. Roudabeth had come conscious and been discharged from the hospital three days ago. She and her Roger Addison had gone off to Vermont. Roger behind the wheel of a new Infiniti Q45.

Phone call from Maddie.

"Can you come home right now?" she asked.

"Why?"

"I need you to read something."

"Like what?"

"An instant pregnancy test. I just gave myself one and have no way of knowing if the red strip came up."

"Oh."

"I doubt you'd want me to have the elevator operator read it."

"What makes you think you're pregnant?"

"The way we carried on in the country, the intensity and all that. I felt very vulnerable."

"When are you due?"

"Don't you keep track?"

"No," he fibbed.

"Next week," she told him.

"You're jumping the gun."

"I suppose," she relented. "How's your day going?"

"Fine," he fibbed again.

"Same old kind of day? Nothing extraordinary happening?"

"No."

"I was speaking with Elise earlier."

"And?"

"She started off with a lot of sobbing because . . . guess what?"

"She's overdrawn."

"Marian left her high and dry, went back into the closet."

"Really?" Mitch tried to sound concerned more than amused.

"Marian ran off with someone connected to the Paris Ballet. I believe Elise said he's a rehearsal pianist. Imagine. I stoked Elise with consolation and positive thinking. By the time she rang off she was looking forward to some solo cruising in St. Tropez."

"I'll be home early," Mitch promised.

Shirley brought the sandwich, laid it out for him, little packet of ketchup, pickle and all. The bread was sogged and the fries limp.

"This just came," she said.

A registered letter.

No return address on the envelope.

Probably another client bailing out, Mitch thought, and, that being the prospect, it could sure as hell wait. He placed the letter aside.

After he'd eaten he reluctantly opened it.

And it opened his eyes.

It was from a private bank located in Zurich on Bahnhofstrasse. A very courteous letter informing him that a sum of twenty-five million dollars had been placed in deposit on his behalf by a party who expressly wished to remain unmentioned.

A second page contained instructions regarding the formalities necessary for him to activate the numbered account. Along with details of bank terms, charges, minimums, policies and so on.

Mitch read the letter three times, the last two times slowly and aloud, before allowing reaction.

He made a fist and gave fate a short, victorious jab in the belly. "Yes!"

He felt like doing a time step . . . right up the wall and across the ceiling.

He speed-dialed Maddie.

He read the letter to her.

"Are you sure it's not someone playing a sick joke?" she asked.

"Doesn't appear to be. No," he said definitely, "it isn't."

"The Iranian came through!" she exclaimed happily.

That, of course, was also what Mitch had surmised. But now, all at once, he and realization hit head-on. "So it would seem," he said.

"Think so?"

"Who else but Mononchehr Djam?" Mitch pronounced the name correctly for the first time.

"Has to be," Maddie concluded.

Contrivance and motive peeked out from behind her reaction. And, after a bit more back-and-forth praise for Djam, his being a man of his word and all that, after Maddie had clicked off, Mitch sat there for a long while . . .

. . . asking himself whether or not he should let her get away with it.